BARBARY STATION

BARBARY STATION

R. E. STEARNS

SAGA PRESS

LONDON SYDNEY NEW YORK TORONTO NEW DELHI

SAGA PRESS

AN IMPRINT OF SIMON & SCHUSTER, INC.

1230 AVENUE OF THE AMERICAS, NEW YORK, NEW YORK 10020

SAGA PRESS and colophon are trademarks of Simon & Schuster, Inc.

For information about special discounts for bulk purchases, please contact Simon & Schuster Special Sales at 1-866-506-1949 or business@simonandschuster.com.

The Simon & Schuster Speakers Bureau can bring authors to your live event. For more information or to book an event, contact the Simon & Schuster Speakers Bureau at 1-866-248-3049 or visit our website at www.simonspeakers.com.

Also available in a Saga Press hardcover edition

Interior design by Greg Stadnyk

The text for this book was set in Caesilia LT Std.

Manufactured in the United States of America

First Saga Press paperback edition October 2017

2 4 6 8 10 9 7 5 3 1

Library of Congress Cataloging-in-Publication Data

Names: Stearns, R. E., 1983– author.

Title: Barbary Station / R. E. Stearns.

Description: First edition. | New York : Saga Press, 2017.

Identifiers: LCCN 2017004755 | ISBN 9781481476874 (softcover) | ISBN 9781481476867 (hardcover) | ISBN 9781481476881 (eBook)

Subjects: LCSH: Artificial intelligence—Fiction. | Space stations—Fiction. | Pirates—Fiction. | BISAC: FICTION / Science Fiction / Space Opera. | FICTION / Science Fiction / High Tech. | FICTION / Action & Adventure. | GSAFD: Adventure fiction. | Science fiction.

Classification: LCC PS3619.T427 B37 2017 | DDC 813/.6—dc23 LC record available at https://lccn.loc.gov/2017004755

To my parents, who introduced me to science fiction
and surrounded me with books

BARBARY STATION

CHAPTER 1

Charges Accrued: Piracy, Assault and Battery, Theft

Despite the darkness, the pressure on every centimeter of skin, and the smooth, flat plastic in front of her nose, Adda Karpe was *not* locked in a coffin in deep space. As she mentally repeated this fact, lights in the passenger-pod lid brightened. She inhaled hard to break her chest muscles out of an achingly slow breathing pattern. The off-white foam padding that outlined her body came into focus. Dim yellow instructions formed on the inside of the lid: *Hello. You have been awakened during transit. Please stretch your fingers and toes in preparation for extraction.* Beneath the text, an animated hand straightened and curled. Adda imitated it as the foam sank away from her limbs.

The pod's seal parted with a rubbery sucking sound, and she yelped as two intimate catheters withdrew. Cold air blew through the opening above her forehead, sweeping her hair out of her face. Her ears popped.

Outside, something rattled and thumped. She worked her fingers into the opening, elbows against the lit instructions, and pulled the lid toward her toes. White light assaulted her eyes. Her arms trembled. The lid's edge passed her ribs with a hydraulic wheeze, but weeks of inaction hadn't improved her soft physique. Her fingers slipped. The pod lid slid upward on its rail. *If it closes, will I go back to sleep?* She scrabbled at the smooth plastic. "No, damn it, stop!"

A hand several shades browner than hers thrust into the gap from the outside. The lid slammed on its knuckles. A familiar pained grunt emanated from above. Mechanisms squealed as Iridian Nassir shoved the lid past Adda's feet faster than it was designed to move. Adda sat up and threw her arms around the taller woman's neck.

Blue and yellow lights from the instrument panel across the room glinted off Iridian's shaved head as laughter rearranged her freckles. She grabbed for the passenger pod to keep her balance and swallowed against a wave of nausea. *Gravity should be low and falling.*

Her other arm settled around Adda's shoulders. Adda brushed her lips over red droplets rising on Iridian's knuckles where the pod lid had abraded the skin. Smiling in a way she reserved just for Adda, Iridian murmured, "Hey, you. We're right on schedule."

Adda's head still spun. According to the colonist literature, that was typical for Earth natives. She ruined Iridian's balance by pulling her down for a kiss.

Iridian's black eyebrows arched as she steadied herself and Adda in the low gravity. "How do you feel?"

The rest of Adda's plan congealed in her waking brain, and it didn't include time for reorientation. "Like hijacking a colony ship."

"Thank fuck." The man who'd spoken clomped out from behind another pod, eyes open, since he'd had hours to adapt to the onslaught of light. Magnetic boots over the one-piece hibernation suit gave him a difficult, hitching gait. Unlike Adda's and Iridian's green suits, his Transorbital Voyages uniform was blue-gray and tailored to complement his russet skin and wiry build. HOBAN was printed over the breast below the company logo. His real name was Reis, and this meeting marked the second time Adda had met him in person.

He tossed a cloth bag to Iridian, who caught it one-handed. "Get a move on. The day watch is gonna ask me about the pod status if we don't reset them quick." The four or five colony ship crew members out of hibernation were now waiting for Reis's report after he "investigated" the unscheduled deceleration. Too many anomalies would make the Transorbital employees call for emergency aid.

The three of them would never get a place on a pirate crew after that kind of debacle. A trio of brothers had failed to hijack an NEU military cargo ship four years ago. Newsfeeds had added insult to injury by attributing the attack to a Saturnian crew the brothers had prematurely declared their affiliation with, which had claimed as much newsfeed coverage at the time as Sloane's crew on Barbary Station did now. The brothers were still a laughingstock, in separate prisons, and nobody expected the Saturnian crew to be welcoming after they were released.

Adda took a calming breath of recycled air and the scent of Iridian's skin. Cleanly hijacking one of the most advanced and expensive ships in the galaxy, as the first crime on their records, ought to impress any pirate captain.

Iridian helped Adda climb out of the pod. It was hard to let go of Iridian's arm. Aside from the comfort of her presence, the walls curved instead of meeting at right angles. Projected windows showed stars between bright wall sconces. They gave her a frame of reference but reduced her equilibrium. She weighed less with each passing minute.

Reis threw Iridian a pair of boots and sent another spinning at Adda before returning to the doorway. After pulling hers on, Adda flipped a switch on the calf. Magnets inside secured her feet to the floor, and her nausea abated a bit. Iridian closed Adda's pod and handed off the cloth bag before clomping toward the door.

The pod's projected display was identical to the one Adda had studied to prepare for this trip. Since nobody was asleep inside, most of the pod's rectangular display constituted blank space where information would be, although power readings and shipboard intranet connectivity blinked in the corner every few seconds when they updated. More importantly, the profiles and main setup icons were where she expected them to be for the software she'd studied.

She put on her comp glove and let the bag fall empty on the floor while she cycled the pod lid's seal closed. While she pressed her gloved palm to the blue pseudo-organic comp cradle beside the display, her wrist buzzed with weeks of new message alerts. The comp confirmed its connection to the pod and projected message headers in a silver-lined square hole on the back of her dark purple fingerless glove.

Using the connection afforded by the gel-filled pad in the comp cradle, she fed the pod a manufacturer's repair code and held her breath. The projection shifted to the maintenance interface. *Whew. All right.* She ran a test hibernation sequence with the same settings as the occupied pods at this point in the ship's journey to Io. The pod shuddered and emitted a deep hum, joining the other pods' background buzz. Smiling slightly, she moved to Iridian's, next in the row of a hundred pods stretching the length of this sleeping chamber.

Iridian and Reis stood on either side of the door, angled to watch the exit and each other without turning their heads. Interpreting facial expressions wasn't one of Adda's strong skills, but something feral about Reis's eyes made her wary. Since Iridian was watching him, Adda concentrated on her own work. The second pod hummed too.

She clutched its edge as her heart stuttered through four irregular beats. The colonist literature described this as well. Thanks to the pod's chemical wake-up treatment, her body was reabsorbing iron accumulated in her bloodstream while she slept. Some passed through her heart.

When her heartbeat steadied, she announced, "All set," left off the implied I hope, and clomped to the door. If a tech reported two empty passenger pods, the ship's artificial intelligence would wake the whole crew to deal with the crisis. Now hers and Iridian's were back on the same hibernation cycle as the others in the chamber, so that was one less hazard to keep track of.

"The lockers are up a level," Reis said, as if they hadn't read the ship schematics a thousand times. If she could've dreamed during the long sleep, all she would've seen were blue-and-white diagrams.

He tramped through the door and Iridian and Adda followed, ready to act like confused and spacesick travelers being led to medical if they passed the ship's real crew members. It would have been harder not to act spacesick. Maybe her nervousness could be mistaken for panic and disorientation, if she could quit smiling for a few seconds. The plan she had spent half her college career setting up was working. She hoped she'd get to see the pirates' faces when a whole colony ship arrived at their airlock.

Adda kept close behind Iridian as they followed a line of blue handholds on curving white walls. Shiny projected scenes of a landing site on Io lit as they walked by, showing the Freefab habitats that would sprout there. When they boarded, they'd pushed through crowds of colonists ogling their future homes.

Reis got them to the storage block and located their lockers with his crew credentials. Instead of leaving them to change while he visited the crew lockers, he leaned against a wall across from theirs, one eyebrow slightly raised, prepared to judge the strip show he was apparently expecting. Adda fidgeted with the fasteners at her waist, blushing and wishing the hibernation nutrients had done more to reduce her extra kilos.

Iridian turned her back to him, winked at Adda, and pulled her hibernation suit off. Reis's gaze, like Adda's, snagged on the tattoo covering the side of Iridian's rib cage and one hip. "Nice ink."

Starkly outlined muscle under Iridian's skin made most people look away, but it held the eyes better than Adda's plentiful curves. The tattoo Reis admired was a strip of flesh peeled up from Iridian's side. Beneath lay a detailed, exposed lung and liver under two crossed human ribs. A black, grinning skull was centered on the peeled-back skin.

By the time Iridian finished saying, "Thanks," Adda's thermal top was on and she was out of one boot to shimmy into her pants. They had brought clothes thin enough to fit under an environment suit, but thick enough to ward off the low temperatures in the Goliath around them. The large silver necklace she clipped on bounced in front of her face until she tucked it into her shirt. If Reis had done his part of the job, one engine should be shut down, while a second slowly reduced the *Prosperity Dawn*'s momentum. Gravity was less than half the Earth-typical one g, on its way to nothing when the whole ship stopped accelerating during the course correction.

She slung a pack onto her back and Iridian shouldered a

folded metal frame, suspended between her shoulder blades on a dark gray hook built into her jacket. One of the jacket pockets contained natural-shaded lipstick, which she swiped on while referencing the locker mirror. In the reflection, she puckered her lips at Adda before she shut the locker door. Reis looked them over again before he led them back into the hallways.

The YOU ARE HERE maps posted at intersections didn't include the bridge. Reis checked his comp's employee map every few seconds. Adda's eyes followed the sway of Iridian's hips as she took position behind and to the right of Reis. Iridian was in what Adda called "combat mode," evident in an alert set to her shoulders and a sexy swagger. Fitting, for a future pirate.

Adda wiped her sweating palm on her leg and checked the time on her comp. *Still on schedule.* They hadn't encountered the problems she'd planned for. Whatever was going to go wrong would hinge on information she couldn't have had before she boarded the colony ship and still lacked now.

It was almost a relief when they reached an EMPLOYEES ONLY door, labeled "Bridge" on the map in Reis's comp and Adda's head, and it didn't open for his ID. Whatever he snarled in spacefarer cant made Iridian's eyes narrow.

She snapped a two-word response. His hand slipped a few centimeters closer to the knife in his belt sheath. He rubbed the left side of his chest like he was feeling the same arrhythmia Adda experienced earlier. The *Prosperity Dawn*'s captain had brought him out of hibernation hours ago to investigate the "engine problem" he had caused, so the hibernation-induced heart strain should be over, but stress aggravated irregular heartbeats too.

Iridian and Adda watched the deserted corridor as he resubmitted the ID, holding his comp glove against the reader. "This isn't my scheduled shift, and it's not an emergency. *Shit.*" He ran his hand through hair only a little shorter than Adda's and glanced her way. "Can't you do something with this?"

She flipped open a small box of sharpsheets from her pack and laid a thumbprint-size purple square on her tongue. It sizzled and tingled as it dissolved. She'd hoped to keep her base level of cognizance until she reached the bridge computer, but now she needed more. In seconds she entered her systems state of mind, calm, intent, cramming information about the ship into short-term memory. The *Prosperity Dawn*, Pioneer class, a custom artificial intelligence coordinating a custom operating system . . . "What category is your access?"

He squinted at her, probably reacting to her newly monotone voice. "Crew, I guess? My boss has all the security-level access when she's awake, but she's not awake now."

Adda held out her gloved hand. After a second, he extended his own, palm down. The tiny text scrolling over the back of his glove hurt her eyes. She unclipped a thin cable coiled through the twists in her silver necklace. One end plugged into the wrist jack in Reis's glove. The other she plugged into the jack in her right nostril. No normal colonist passenger would be doing this, but she trusted Iridian to watch the hallway for crew who might recognize that.

Even though the cable connected through the pinky-size insulated ring in her nostril, Reis still grimaced like she'd shoved it up her nose. Twisting the cable's probe in the jack adapted the implant net over her frontal lobe to the translator her implant installed on his comp.

Adda didn't know a thing about locks, but she knew how to contact the AI that controlled this one. The corridor grayed out, making spurious visual input easier to ignore. A hallucinographic intermediary stuttered into existence between her and Reis in a rough-featured gray shadow. Its edges swam with a sparkling unreality. To her amusement, its rolling shuffle toward the door on her unspoken order had enough of Reis's bowlegged walk for him to notice the similarity. Fortunately, only she could see the intermediary.

Crew access, here. Subvocalizing her commands distracted her less than speaking aloud, and maintaining the intermediary took focus. The shadow's head lolled forward on its indistinct neck. It lumbered through Reis, then the closed door.

"Well? I thought you were engineers. How hard can it be to open a damned door?" He looked up and down the corridor for passersby, even though 99 percent of the future colonists and crew were still hibernating.

"We *are* engineers. That means we're not keycards with legs." Iridian glared at him. "The faster you leave her alone, the faster she'll get it done."

Adda had planned for resistance from the shipboard AI, but this was lethargy. *The intelligence wasn't even designed for direct connection.* Transorbital Voyages couldn't be bothered, or were too paranoid, to give employees direct access to the system. The ship was safe from the crew, but if the AI failed to manage situations outside the norm, the crew wouldn't be able to correct it, even if their lives were at risk. And even if they created their own intermediaries like Adda had, they'd be stuck with the response time of an elderly tortoise.

Transorbital Voyages had to save money somewhere, she supposed. Explaining the problem aloud wasn't worth breaking her concentration. Iridian looped her arm around Reis's neck and dragged him as far down the hall and away from the door as the cable allowed.

The intermediary lumbered back through the door and stood

with its head hung lower than a spine would allow. Behind it, the door remained closed. Adda gritted her teeth. *Why?*

Digital interference rasped from the intermediary's shadow head. It moaned in a static buzz that her comp translated to text: *Frequency.*

She pushed the basic concept of administrative status through the Transorbital software sludge before her. Her translator should identify its frequency. An ache in the base of her skull assumed a steady throb.

The intermediary gave a dramatic shrug. She was asking the right questions, but the damned thing's developers gave it a way to *ignore* her. Transorbital had to maintain control of its AI, but it shouldn't have sacrificed user interface functionality to do so.

The annoyance broke her out of her mental workspace. The intermediary snapped out of existence and the corridor took on color again. Since the AI refused to cooperate, they'd have to get into the bridge the messy, dangerous way involving other people. She disconnected her cable from Reis's comp. He wiped his comp glove on his pants while she unplugged the cable from her nasal jack and secured it in her necklace.

Iridian laughed at him. "The conduction medium's goldsynth, not snot. Can we knock the door down?"

"Doubt it. That thing's built to seal against atmo and all." He clomped down the corridor in the direction they'd been walking before, watching his glove readout.

Iridian's smile faded, replaced by a nearly identical one only Adda would recognize as more dangerous than the first. "Where are you off to?" she said, saving Adda the anxiety of asking.

"Break room," Reis snarled. Adda suppressed a sigh. With both of them this edgy, Adda was going to have to be the calm one. "One of the guys I know can get in. This shows me where he's shirking."

He tapped the back of his comp glove. Like Iridian, he hadn't set up subvocalization shortcuts. They were much more precise than stabbing one's finger through a projected display.

Iridian slowed for a few steps until Adda caught up. She brushed wisps of Adda's apple-red hair out of her face, but they floated back a second later. "How's the jack?"

Adda twitched her nose, tilted her head, and assessed the rubbing, shifting sensations along the minuscule cabling and neural implants. "It could use a full calibration, but the irritation from my final project healed up."

"It should've! That was what, six weeks ago?"

Adda glanced at her comp projection. "Six weeks, five days."

Iridian grimaced at the scraggly dark hair floating along behind Reis. Barbary Station had three floors, each several kilometers around. The station's size was reportedly one part of why Captain Sloane had moved the crew's base of operations there from Vesta. Putting some distance between themselves and Reis was just one more reason to get to Barbary Station as soon as they could.

Adda plugged her cable into her own comp through the glove's wrist jack. The comp made the catch and connected her to the *Prosperity Dawn*'s intranet. Unlike the lumbering sludge intermediary she had to use for wireless work, her own was so familiar that her brain put no shape to it. It was her intent made digital.

With employee information ripped from Reis's comp while her implant net was plugged into it, she channeled junk input into every sensor within three meters. The sensor scum might draw human attention, but the shipboard intelligence had to process it all before activating alarms announcing unauthorized personnel in employee areas. If the employee Reis was looking for called for help, the sensor scum would buy them time.

Reis slammed open an employees-only door before it had a chance to retract into the wall on its own and shouted "Hyo! Man, you've got to help me." The muscles in Adda's neck and shoulders that had relaxed beneath the layer of anonymity coiled up again. Iridian stepped to one side of the door, out of sight of whoever was inside, and rested her hand on her knife. Adda stood near her and watched through the doorway while Reis charged into the room beyond.

The narrow room held tables and chairs with slots and straps for eating in low gravity. The guy he called Hyo, a sturdy uniformed man with the parchment skin that spacefarers some-times developed before old age, clutched the recycler lid while he fumbled an empty drinking pouch he was trying to deposit. The pouch bounced off the floor before splatting in a small orange puddle. "Um . . . I didn't know you were still awake. Did you find out why we're slowing down?"

"Forget that, I got a message from home. My kid fell and hit his head. It's bad. I've got to get into the bridge and call his mom." Reis caught the surprised man's arm to keep him from bouncing off a wall. Since Reis's boots anchored him to the floor with each step, he easily maneuvered the drifting crewman past Iridian and Adda and down the hall.

That's not right. Reis couldn't have received a message. Long-range communication in anything approaching real time would've required a buoy relay, which wasn't on the *Prosperity Dawn*'s route. According to the cover story Reis told her he'd memorized, she and Iridian were the ones who were supposed to be sick passengers in need of medical care that the ship's clinic couldn't provide. And that would've just barely convinced a *Prosperity Dawn* crew member to give them access to the most secure section of the ship. But maybe Reis had more applicable experience than she did, and his new story would work better.

"Why can't you connect your comp? I mean, it'll take the same amount of time no matter what. And who are—" Hyo twisted in Reis's grip, gaze flicking from Adda to Iridian in mounting confusion. Adda affected her best nauseated hunched posture, which would've supported their cover if Reis had already explained that they were sick, which he hadn't done. She didn't know what else to do.

Hyo's uniform boots scraped the wall as his shoulder thumped into Reis's. Her comp buzzed against her wrist to tell her that the banking turn she'd added to the *Prosperity Dawn*'s prescribed route was complete. The engines still running would slow them faster now, and the viral routine she'd created and Reis had installed during prelaunch preparations seven weeks ago had finished its work right on her schedule. The *Prosperity Dawn* would stop moving completely in under an hour.

Everything she read about operating in stationary ships emphasized handholds and magnetic anchoring points for controlled movement without gravity. Hyo writhing while Reis held him in place illustrated the pitiable alternative. "Hey, stop!" Hyo said. "I can't let you into the bridge." Whatever sympathy Reis had engendered with the injured child story didn't show in Hyo's suspicious expression. "How did you even get the message?" Hyo asked.

Exactly. If Reis had stuck to the cover story Adda had constructed, which didn't involve an impossible real-time message, it would've explained her and Iridian's presence and they wouldn't be having this conversation. Her aggravation traveled through her digital intermediary and manifested in her comp's sensor scum as a burst of white noise. The others glanced apprehensively at wall-mounted speakers hidden in the blue designs behind the handholds.

The bridge door appeared on their left around a sculpted bend in the hallway. Reis pinned Hyo against it with a hand around the unfortunate crew member's neck. "They'll put me on manual labor when we get to the colony." Hyo choked. "I don't—I can't—"

That could be the three of us, if we make too many mistakes.

Reis hit him in the stomach. The blow slammed him back against the closed bridge door. Adda flinched as Reis punched him again, harder. Tears beaded at the corners of Hyo's eyes as he whimpered and gasped.

Iridian calmly glanced up and down the hallway while she stretched weeks of disuse out of her limbs, but the beating made Adda's own stomach ache in sympathy. She examined the ceiling, searching for sensor nodes, and found three. The shipboard artificial intelligence would almost certainly recognize physical violence against its crew. As a pirate, she'd have to get used to violent solutions, but she could engage in exposure therapy sometime when she wasn't distracting a suspicious artificial intelligence with extraneous sensor input to process.

"All right," Hyo wheezed. "All right, just *stop.*" He presented his comp to the bridge door's reader. The door slid open.

The console inside the small, dim bridge became Adda's sole focus. Its few external user interfaces surrounded a prominent jack, designed for someone with a neural implant net like hers to strap into the grav-adjusting chair and plug in. The pilot had to be awake somewhere else on the ship, because pilots were designated supervisors for the AI copilot. Outside of emergencies, it was dangerous and illegal to leave intelligences unsupervised, especially with so many people onboard.

Wide metal slats of a closed airlock covered the wall across from the door. Ships' bridges had to be easily accessed in emergencies, which also made them easy to vent into space. Trusting

Iridian to find her an environment suit if Adda made a mistake that would necessitate one, she squeezed into the chair and connected her nasal jack to the console. Time to do what she'd come millions of kilometers to do: access and circumvent her first starship AI.

Her comp documented her intention's path through the ship's system. In case bringing the *Prosperity Dawn* to Barbary Station was too commonplace an act to impress Captain Sloane, she'd also map the custom operating system's structure and vulnerabilities. Sloane's crew could use her map to manipulate similar operating systems in the future, saving them a huge amount of risk and time during an assault. The map would occupy all the spare storage space on her comp, but it'd be priceless to ship thieves.

Hyo asked a question, but she was too busy easing her hijacking program through administrative overrides to listen. For the first time since she'd woken from hibernation, she really breathed, really thought, came fully *awake*. The sharpsheet she had taken earlier enhanced the natural norepinephrine effects of pressing her own will through a hostile system so carefully that the intelligence didn't even raise its defenses. The microgravity nausea faded away. Her heart staggered through another irregular triplet beat.

The custom intelligence that ran the *Prosperity Dawn* only monitored her, for now. But this many anomalous sensor readings and unplanned changes in preprogrammed travel scripts would soon force it to act.

"Can you . . ." She dragged her mind halfway out of the ship's systems to concentrate on the human problem. Reis seemed capable of any misdeed, and Iridian was in combat mode. How could Adda ask this in a way that didn't get the crewman killed? "Hyo, please tell the ship's AI that everything is fine."

Hyo took a breath and yelled, "Securit—"

A flurry of movement around Adda froze her in place. Reis's punch to Hyo's mouth jolted the crewman's head to one side. Iridian's hit to his throat drove him choking into the wall. The ship's intelligence drew the inevitable conclusion. Adda concentrated on tamping down alarms. But while the intelligence woke the remaining crew, she knocked it out of the navigation and propulsion controls.

For a second she stood and listened to the blank void in the interface where the AI, any AI, should be in a ship's systems. Now there was nothing but her. Not even pilots experienced this echoing solitude, this single point of *power* she had created. Five thousand people and a cargo hold full of supplies waited for one unauthorized human to tell them where to go.

She startled, which jarred the cable in her nasal jack and sent her implant net through a tingling calibration sequence. The sharpsheet's effects made it difficult to tell how long she'd stood there. If she hadn't selected a particularly empty stretch of the reliable route for this stage of her plan, they could have plowed into another ship by now. "It's ours," she said belatedly for Iridian and Reis's benefit.

Iridian would be smiling when Adda turned around, though she kept her distracting hands and voice to herself. Closer to the bridge door, Reis bellowed something in a combination of Spanish or Portuguese and spacefarer cant. It sounded positive, so Adda tuned him out before her brain's attempt to identify words it understood dropped her out of the ship's system.

Navigation accepted her coordinates and vector for the pirates' prearranged meeting point. For a few seconds the wall and the floor seemed to switch positions as the ship accelerated along a new course. She shut her eyes as her stomach flopped and gravity rose. "We're going to be broadcasting all the way to the rendezvous as soon as everyone's wake cycle stabilizes."

"We weren't about to back out." Iridian grinned.

The *Prosperity Dawn*'s intelligence repeatedly queried the navigation system, but Adda's lockout held. "Barbary Station or bust."

CHAPTER 2

Charges Accrued: Trespassing

This Reis person was a shitbag, but he'd followed Adda's plan this far. Until he tried something, Iridian would leave him to it.

She shifted her grip on Hyo's arm. Even with his hands zipped behind him and the improvised hand towel gag from the break room, pain and fear might make him to do something unfortunate. She watched him until Adda murmured, "Lead cloud in five."

"On it." Once they entered the lead cloud surrounding Barbary Station, weeks might pass before they got a chance to send messages into the Near Earth Union. The battle that'd created the cloud was the secessionists' biggest win of the war, and it'd taken place so close to the station that people called it the Battle of Waypoint Station, referencing Barbary's original name. Given the lead levels in the NEU colony ships that the secessionists destroyed, it would've been better for everyone if more ships had escaped intact. The cloud had made Barbary Station unusable as a shipbreaking and refueling port, and now it separated Sloane's crew from the rest of humanity by shredding comm signals.

Adda and Iridian had already updated their social feed about becoming Io colonists for friends and family to read and congratulate them over. Those'd keep for a week or so, until the fate of the *Prosperity Dawn* hit the newsfeeds. By then, the two of them would have much more awesome news to report. The encrypted messages to family that Iridian was sending now told a story nearer the truth: something will happen, and it'll sound bad. Don't worry, you'll hear from us soon.

An hour out from the rendezvous, Adda sank into a drug-induced trance to reverse the remaining engines. That'd bring the enormous vessel to a full stop. Except for Reis ignoring their cover story and her little brother Pel's failure to answer her message, her plan was proceeding smoothly from its first phase to its second.

Reis pressed his palm to the bridge console and held it there while the scanner flashed beneath it, turning his hand red for an instant. Since the AI had declared a state of emergency, his security role on the *Prosperity Dawn*'s crew gave him a wider range of access to the system. He nodded to Adda. Her lips formed half words. An alarm blared red and repetitive through the tomb-quiet colony ship.

"Engine failure, repeat, engine failure, engine ejection failure, emergency shutdown on Engines One and Three, retro on Two, leads start deep-space evac checklist," Reis announced in the direction of the console's mic. *EVAC COMMAND* lit up in red on the console. That'd get the crew moving fast enough that they probably wouldn't notice all engines working at full capacity to slow the ship down.

The evac order would also tell the intelligence to wake every colonist passenger aboard. Based on what Adda had read about Transorbital emergency procedures, ensuring passenger safety should keep the crew too occupied to interfere with Reis, who was supposedly doing his job. Adda would have to find a way to coordinate with the pirates without getting evacuated herself. She had some ideas, but Captain Sloane might've come up with something independently. Adda and Iridian would figure something out. They always did.

Adda's head came up, and she brushed her eye-length bangs away. "Sensors are reporting a catastrophic fuel containment failure. The intelligence will resolve the discrepancies in fifteen minutes, if its processors aren't locked down too hard. I deactivated the automated ITA call for help. Jumpsuit beacons will be the first they hear about us."

The solar system was short on armed fleets these days, and only the Interplanetary Transit Authority rescued spacefarers for free. If the ITA came, newsbots would follow. The publicity would've been fun, but Adda refused to risk the ITA getting close enough to catch them. The billionaires funding the ITA treated all pirates like they were killers, too. Either way, the alarms would wake the colonists and crew and trick them into abandoning ship before Sloane's crew arrived.

Footsteps clomped down the passageway outside the bridge. The Transorbital crewman's chest pressed against Iridian's arm as he drew in breath to shout through the gag. She slammed his head into the bulkhead behind him with force enough to shut him up.

Reis spun and growled a curse Iridian hadn't heard before, and she'd heard just about all of them. The Transorbital crewman slumped against her side in the decreasing grav. "He needed a nap," Iridian said. She pressed two fingers on the pulse under Hyo's jaw to confirm it'd keep pumping. Reis settled back into his crouch beside the door.

"Untie him," murmured Adda, still too far in her head to speak loud enough for Reis to hear. "Say he's radiation poisoned."

Iridian pulled her boot knife to cut the Transorbital employee's zip ties. Knives were the only weapons Reis had been able to get past Transorbital's security, since it was damned difficult to part spacefarers from their blades. If anyone else wandered into the bridge, the radiation poisoning story might convince them that all was under control. Otherwise, Iridian's knife was sharp, sturdy, human-powered, and weaker than the exterior hull plating. A perfect weapon for the cold and the black, even when she just had to knock someone out with the hilt.

She grabbed a handful of Hyo's uniform to keep him from floating into Reis or Adda. In terms of interplanetary travel speed, the *Dawn* was nearly stationary. In a few minutes they'd lose an external definition of "down" as the ship stopped accelerating toward the overhead. This part of the reliable route was a long way from any grav well.

Reis stood. "They're gonna expect me to help with the evacuation."

As soon as he left, Iridian shoved the unconscious Transorbital employee aside and wrapped an arm around Adda's shoulders. "Time to move out."

Much as she admired her girlfriend's skill at navigating the digital world, the aftereffects made it hard for Adda to come back to the deck. She followed Iridian out of the bridge in a daze, staring at the spacesick passengers floating around the corridors.

Even passengers drifting into her while struggling into bulky jumpsuits didn't focus her eyes. "These people completely ignored the safety briefing," Iridian said. Adda nodded without looking at her.

To speed things along, Iridian parked her dazed girlfriend against a bulkhead and shooed people into airlocks that'd launch them far enough away from the ship to give them a chance at survival. A few jumpsuited crew members cast incredulous looks at her and lifted their go bags pointedly as they passed. It was kind of them to remind her that customer service shouldn't involve getting blown up on the customers' behalf.

She roused Adda enough to help her haul Hyo from the bridge, wrestle him into a jumpsuit, and throw him into an airlock full of people about to disembark. The hatch shut on the passengers' questions. Using the launch system to leave a moving ship was a scary safety procedure that every spacefarer read about and nobody thought they'd ever have to follow, but there'd been a uniformed crew member among the passengers in the airlock to show them what to do and help their unconscious crewmate. The helmeted jumpsuits would keep them all breathing until an ITA ship came to collect them.

The alarms went silent. Adda stared straight ahead, lips twitching with words she didn't need to say aloud. Iridian stalked over arrows on the surface serving as deck that pointed toward the ship's primary passthrough, where Reis should've gone.

Adda followed on autopilot. It was funny how much trust she put in her peripheral vision with that adorable purple-streaked red hair over her eyes. The steel rim of the nose piercing for her jack glinted in the overhead lights. "Ships," she enunciated, and then to herself or whatever construct she created to represent her in the system, "To bridge." Adda clomped ahead, ignoring the arrows on the deck.

This time the bridge door admitted them without fuss. Adda was too busy staring wide-eyed at things that weren't there to react to physical threats, so Iridian stepped past her into the tiny room and visually confirmed that nobody was at the pilot's console or standing in any of the corners.

"Want to see them?" Adda asked. That seemed like a question she'd direct at a human, not one of her constructs. She held out her comp, which had just finished syncing her stored data from the ship's system.

The projector in the back of Adda's glove flicked on to display a starscape constructed from a compilation of the *Dawn's* external cam feeds. Motion against the stars revealed three vessels cruising into the massive colony ship's shadow. They maintained a close formation, taking advantage of the colony ship's lack of weapons to minimize the number of cam feeds they appeared on. Any warship would fuse them into one big lump of slag in under ten seconds, but that'd be why pirates rarely targeted military ships.

The smallest approaching ship, labeled *Charon's Coin*, was heavily outlined in nonthreatening light blue. That auxiliary designation identified tugs. Two midsize ships labeled *Apparition* and *Casey Mire Mire* rounded out the rumored complement of Captain Sloane's fleet. They, too, bore blue outlines, but neither was equipped with a tug's buffering or hullhooks.

That camouflage would work against the *Dawn's* AI and the people Iridian had encountered on the ship so far. She grinned. Sloane's crew hadn't become the most successful pirates in the universe by being stupid.

"Is that one docking?" She pointed at the *Apparition*, even though Adda was staring at a bulkhead and wouldn't see her.

"Yes." Adda sounded as curious as Iridian felt about what kind of pirates would be coming out of that ship.

"Did they say who's boarding? How many?"

"No." Adda's fingers tapped the back of her hand beside some text appearing as she subvocalized it. "Second message to Pel."

The bridge door slid open and Reis stepped through. He wiped a long knife along his uniform pant leg. When he stopped just inside the door, a trail of red droplets drifted past him. The *Dawn* was dead in space, and "down" an arbitrary label. "Skipped the airlocks, so they're hooking up to the main gangway. It's the only other place. Let's go meet our new crew, yeah?"

"Yeah," said Iridian. Adda disconnected from the bridge console, frowning, and followed her. "What's the matter?" Iridian murmured over the sound of their magnetic boots hitting steel.

"ColonyHost is letting them dock. I don't know why."

Iridian frowned. The *Dawn*'s AI was flying the damned ship. If ColonyHost was also doing other things that Adda didn't understand, that made Iridian trust it even less than she did before. There was no need to put her nervousness on display, though. "When you've got 'host' in your name, aren't you obligated to open doors for people?"

"Hacked in from the outside," Reis said, as if he knew. "They have real hackers. Not sure what they're supposed to do with you." He looked from Iridian to Adda and back, focused on their breasts and the way Adda stood about half a centimeter from Iridian even when the passageway was wide enough for them to stay multiple meters away from him. "Not the obvious, I reckon."

One of Iridian's blades was sheathed ten centimeters from her palm. Visualizing putting it through his throat kept her from actually doing that. The bastard would still be useful if any of the Transorbital crew was left on the colony ship, and Pel would've told the pirates to watch for three people, not two. "Turn around," she said slowly, "and start walking." Sneering, he complied.

A minute later, he stopped in the middle of the passageway. Iridian and Adda dodged to either side to avoid running into him. A rectangular metal box the size of a pilot sling-chair's back support and covered with "less lethal" armaments floated toward them. Small but noisy jets angled behind it propelled it through micro-g.

"Rover," Iridian explained to Adda, who looked both confused and delighted. "Spying out the route for somebody else." She addressed the bot and the operator watching its progress. "We're here. Now what?"

A camera stalk whirred to stick out perpendicular to its frame and rotated to focus on her. "I represent Sloane's crew." The recorded masculine voice was flat in the rover's speakers. "Abandon ship. Atmosphere will be discharged in three minutes."

"Well, shit!" Iridian grabbed Adda's arm and hauled her past the rover at a fast walk, ignoring the wistful way she peered over her shoulder at the bot.

Reis clomped along behind them. "They didn't give you much time. Does this brother of yours like you?" Adda sighed. From what she'd told Iridian, forgetting to mention something so minor as en route atmo loss was exactly the kind of thing Pel would do.

By the time they reached the main gangway, a huge, bright room decorated with colony propaganda to inspire passengers, escaping atmo rushed along with them. Wind shrieked out three open passthroughs with no ships attached and blustered through the passthrough connecting the *Prosperity Dawn* to the pirate ship. Looking into the cold and black without a suit made Iridian's breath catch.

The departing atmo scraped a hard piece of debris over her shaved scalp. She flinched as a spray of red trailed it out an empty passthrough. Did Captain Sloane know that she and Adda had evacuated the *Dawn* before they arrived at the coordinates? Newsfeeds said Sloane's crew killed next to no civilians, but three minutes would barely have been enough time to wake the *Dawn's* passengers and crew. Surely Adda's brother wasn't *that* careless. Could he be that cruel?

Reis gripped a locker door handle and waited while it registered his crew ID. The wind slammed the door open. Iridian ran to grab two enviro suits before he did something stupid like throw them. Halfway through slipping hers on, she caught Adda turning the other suit over in her hands. The determined frown on her girlfriend's face was usually directed at demon-level logic puzzles.

"Start at the back. Remember, it's designed for spacefarers. It has to be ass-backwards from what an Earther expects, or we wouldn't wear it," Iridian added, repeating the well-worn spacefarer gag to show that approaching spacefarer problems from an incorrect, Earthbound perspective was a common mistake that Adda shouldn't feel too embarrassed about.

Iridian retrieved her shield, collapsed in a rectangular mass of folded metal pieces, from its hook between her shoulder blades and clipped it onto her suit's belt beside a knife, then sealed her hood. As she'd hoped, she hadn't needed it to get into or out of the *Dawn*'s bridge, but she was still glad she'd gotten Reis to stash it in the shipboard locker with the rest of her gear. It might come in handy while introducing herself to pirates hyped up for a colony ship raid.

The suit's canned atmo odor settled Iridian into a calm watchfulness developed during hundreds of practice drills. After she eased Adda's silver necklace over Adda's suit helmet, she sealed her girlfriend's suit for her.

"Sorry," Adda said. "Tracking emergency reports. The passthroughs and other airlocks are venting too." How the pirates had convinced the ship's AI to open all those doors was a question for Adda. *Neat trick, if you don't mind suffocating anybody left onboard.*

The suit blocked the wind, but the narrow faceplate meant

that seeing anything to her left and right required turning her whole torso sideways. Transorbital must've bought the last double-discounted suits with rigid faceplates, outlawed after more flexible fiber-reinforced ones were proven safer. Iridian snorted, simultaneously amused and disgusted by Transorbital's budget-based recklessness. The ship's owners held a few thousand lives in their care. No need to increase expenditures just for that.

Reis impatiently waved her and Adda over to the occupied passthrough and entered as another rover jetted out of the pirate ship. The wide white passthrough bulkheads with the Transorbital Voyages logo narrowed at the attachment point to the pirate ship's stark passthrough, though not enough to make humans worry about heads and elbows. Someone had scorched off whatever insignia had once adorned the pirate ship's passthrough, leaving a large dark patch on the bare metal.

A rover bounced by trailing a net full of jewelry, personal pseudo-organic datacasks (no datacasks bigger than one hundred fifty milliliters, according to the ship's rule book), and a sock. These weren't low-grade government bots or even midgrade military models. A corporation with a budget surplus had designed them to both explore and impress. She could sell one and pay off a year of her student loans.

Her mouth twisted into a self-mocking smile. It was habit, comparing every nice thing to the money she owed. Joking about stealing from their only likely source of lucrative employment would earn her Adda's best *Really?* look. After dodging more pricey robots, they reached the door to the ship itself. It was open wide enough for three rovers to zip in and out at once.

"We just walking in?" Reis's voice was tinny over a long-wave, low-bandwidth, suit-to-suit broadcast.

Iridian cocked her head, which bumped her temple against

the inside of her suit's hood. Until they had Captain Sloane's official approval, it'd be dumb to trust the pirates. This would be a
perfect time for them to take the *Dawn* and shove her, Adda, and
Reis out an airlock to join the colonists. Better not to tempt them.
"Yeah. Tactically."

She and Reis drew knives from their belts. While she deployed
her shield, he strode into the ship. Based on today's observation,
he cleared rooms by walking straight in and swiveling right, then
left, while moving forward. He did it the same way every time, too
fast to see much. And he kept going first, even though she had the
shield and the training to use it. At least she'd spot whoever was
in there while they lined up a shot on him.

The passthrough dumped them into a long, narrow cargo bay.
Lines of golden light interrupted by stacked crates showed the
way to the passthrough and a red-and-white PASSTHROUGH OPEN
message projected on the bulkhead. The room was loaded with
personal property and fixtures from the *Dawn*, stacked with programmed precision in front of longer containers racked on the
bulkheads. Walking space was disappearing beneath stolen cargo.
Soon humans would have to disengage their boot magnets to
maneuver. Nobody was waiting for them among the containers.

Another rover zoomed past with a magnet-sealed crate.
It dropped the crate on the others before blasting down the
passthrough at hip height from the surface her boots were sealed
to. The atmo continued blowing out of the pirate ship toward the
three passthroughs open to the cold and the black.

"There's nobody here." Reis kicked an incoming rover. The boot
stuck until the bot wrenched free and escaped through a doorway
at the other end of the cargo area, deeper into the pirate ship. "No
atmo or pressure generators. Or sunlight sim." That was Earther
thinking, as if air, light, humidity, temperature, pressure, and

gravity were unrelated forces outside human control. It would've been enough to say the enviro wasn't healthy.

People who grew up in naturally healthy enviro took engineers of all specialties for granted. Only one in ten of her graduating class would get a job in their preferred field. New engineers should be grateful for what scraps they got. She and Adda would be part of the 10 percent who made it, though not in the way their professors expected.

"Nobody's here?" Adda asked. "Not even Pel?"

"If I meant nobody but your brother, I'd have said that," Reis growled.

"I need to plug in," muttered Adda.

Running a crewed ship without atmo was damned odd, but it could be a security feature. Only somebody in an enviro suit with plenty of O_2—Iridian checked her meter and found herself in that category—would be a threat to the crew. Maybe all this suspicion was what made Captain Sloane's crew so successful. So long as Adda had sufficient suit enviro too, they'd stick to her plan.

But what kind of pirates hid in their own ship? Now she really wanted to meet these people. Iridian crossed the threshold of a surprisingly thick cargo-hold door and walked down the passageway after the fleeing robot. She angled her shield to keep it from dragging along the bulkheads. Semitransparent mech-ex graphene stretched over the metal frame and glimmered in the low light, an oily steel glint she'd come to love. "Who'd've thought we'd need a damned flashlight? I feel like a tunnel rat."

Reis snorted at the idea of someone Iridian's height crawling through ductwork and sewers to lay mines. "Figured you for an ISV driver." Real tough guess, given her freakish lack of body fat and hair. Her years piloting an Infantry Shield Vehicle had been formative, and she'd kept running after she left the service for school, although she cut her distance a bit. In college she hadn't been eating enough to run as far as members of her Shieldrunners unit had to when their vehicle's battery died.

At least he was checking the doors off the passageway instead of watching her. None of them opened at his approach. "Hey! We're here," Iridian shouted. No response. "Ping Pel again," she told Adda.

The cargo area behind her was large, but if the locked doors led to standard quarters, they would've housed maybe a dozen crew. If the pirates were in there now, they were keeping quiet. Adda rested her hand on Iridian's hip as she eased past her toward the door at the end of the passageway. In this light, Adda's skin was even paler than when she'd woken from the long sleep.

Adda threaded the cable hidden in her necklace through a port in the enviro suit's sleeve to reach the comp in her glove, then plugged the other end into a panel beside the door. Before the glove's projector even turned on, she yanked the plug out of the door panel. "Nothing there."

"Like hell there isn't," said Reis. "You can't fly without humans or AI. There's gotta at least be AI."

Ten rovers flew into the cargo hold, dragging nets full of random objects. The colony ship's passthrough door slammed, followed by the pirate ship's, soundless since the atmo had drained away.

The pirate ship lurched. Iridian caught Adda's elbow to keep her upright as grav made the surface beneath them a much less arbitrarily assigned deck. It shook hard enough that Iridian could've sworn she heard the engines power up.

Adda stowed her cable so fast it disappeared like a magic trick. "That's not me."

Before Reis tried looming over Adda to get better results,

Iridian stepped between them. She had several centimeters on him. "Can you tell where we're going?" she asked Adda.

Adda shook her head. "It was . . . too blank. The pilot's locked everything out."

"What good are you, then?" Reis took in Iridian's stance and backed off. He clutched one door frame after the next as he retreated down the passageway toward the cargo area, fighting the pirate ship's abrupt course corrections that pushed and pulled its occupants around. After the massive colony ship flown smoothly by at least one conscientious pilot, it was hard to ignore this pilot's lack of consideration, or perhaps sobriety.

Iridian wrapped her arm around Adda's waist and waited until her girlfriend's nervous brown eyes met Iridian's through the faceplates. "You ready for this, babe?"

The corners of Adda's mouth wobbled when she smiled, but firmed up after Iridian gave her a squeeze. "It's not like we have another option."

"We could work on different planets, trying to raise corporate stock numbers by a hundredth of a percent. Just imagine, a whole hundredth of a percent. And I might get to see you every other year. What a deal!"

"Ugh."

Iridian scanned the industrial fittings in the cargo area for someplace to strap down. The rovers had already clamped themselves into slots in the bulkheads. A few places to secure crew members were installed across from several pipes big enough to crawl into. The pipes were partially embedded in the hull, connected to . . . a rack of missiles. That explained the thick godsdamned door between this section and the crew quarters.

Once she got over the shock, she pointed them out to Adda. "That might be why they travel without atmo and with everyone in their quarters. Those are loud as hell when they launch."

Adda looked as alarmed as Iridian felt. "Is that likely to happen while we're in here?"

With this configuration, the pilot might flip the ship around to fire if there wasn't time to bank. The ladders on the bulkheads attested to that. Hanging off ladders during violent grav shifts sounded like a way to break arms, though. "Better not. I think I appreciate you delaying ITA involvement." That earned her one of Adda's sweet, proud smiles.

After strapping Adda in, Iridian turned off the power to their magnetic boots and strapped in next to her. Reis kept staggering from door to locked door in the passageway as grav increased and changed direction with the ship. He hadn't mentioned hacking or cracking skills when they discussed partnering up.

The main thing he had that Adda and Iridian lacked was crew status on the *Prosperity Dawn*. To take the ship with minimal violence, it had to be an inside job, so his presence had been critical to Adda's plan. Apparently he didn't care about losing crew status himself, since Adda had found him in a darknet community of contract breakers and people plotting to escape wage slavery. Iridian didn't have to like him to hold up her and Adda's end of the deal and get him to Barbary Station.

Eventually he got tired of fighting the shifting grav and strapped in nearby, looking disgusted. "As long as we don't have to sign a corporate contract to join the crew, they can be as scarce as they like, yeah?" said Iridian.

"Corps can ESE that." His invitation for the corporations to involve themselves in the unfortunate cycle of edible material in closed habitats made Iridian chuckle. "I hear Sloane pays cash, or as close to it as you can get in the cold and the black."

The exchange took Iridian back to long nights with Adda

curled beside her, wondering what would become of them after graduation. "You ever see an entry-level engineer's contract?" she asked Reis. "Anything you design is theirs, whether you design it in the office or in the lodge on Earth's Moon during the time off you get every three years. *Anything.* If I made a ring for Adda, they'd sell the pattern all across the galaxy, without giving me anything. Even five years down the line they might be taking my designs and selling them, because one word in the contract says that's fine."

"It's bullshit," Reis said. "Transorbital does all that plus controls your every gods-damned breath. You go where they tell you, you say what they tell you to say, you sleep and eat and shit when they tell you. . . . Could've stayed in the army for that."

Iridian nodded. "Same. On Sloane's crew we'll have a chance of earning what we're worth and having time to spend it." That was what had started Adda and Iridian reading up on the best crew to join and saving to travel to whatever hab they called home, even before Pel told Adda about the golden opportunity on Barbary Station.

"So, why didn't you stay on the colony ship?" Reis asked. "Too far from civilization for my taste, but they say you can sit on your ass for a living wage on Io."

"That's what they say about Barbary Station, too," Iridian said. "Both places have to be more work than they sound, or they wouldn't pay so well. Anyway, Jovian colonists tried to kill me for about two years straight. Neither of us are ready for me to move in next door."

Adda shifted against Iridian's side to pull the projected display on her comp glove into view through the window in the back of the enviro suit's glove. Iridian's comp wasn't downloading new information. The pirate ship apparently blocked transmissions in and out, though Adda's always seemed to find a way through.

She elbowed Iridian's ribs. "Pel finally responded to my message. Want to watch?"

Iridian maneuvered her enviro suit hood around so she could rest her head on Adda's shoulder to get a better view. The man—boy, really, he was barely twenty—sat somewhere dark. The console backlighting shaded his pale skin blue. Something that sounded like copulating orangutans hooted outside cam range. He hunched over the cam in sunglasses with huge white frames. They may have actually been on his face, and not a goofy feature of his messaging software. A sweatshirt hood collected curling brown hair around his patchily stubbled face.

Every other message from him started with a big grin and a bright "Hi, Sissy!" This time he kept glancing away from the cam, and his tone was much more subdued. "Hey, Sissy. I hope you get this before you leave. It's . . . yeah. Important. And yeah, I know this is last minute."

He glanced over his shoulder toward the orangutan noises. "This isn't a good time for you guys to come. We're having some . . . problems. Don't worry, I'm fine! Just, you know, see if you can get a ticket on another flight. Maybe in six months? Yeah, that'd be better; half a year and we'll have everything sorted. Sorry I didn't get back to you sooner, but, you know, crazy busy makin' money." The last sentence devolved into an awkward rap rhythm.

"Perfect timing," Iridian drawled.

"The fuck was that about?" asked Reis.

Adda's sigh fogged her faceplate for an instant. "Gods, I wish he'd waste his time, not mine. If he thinks about it, he'll realize that if we don't respond, we're still coming."

"They did let us onboard," Iridian said. "Now all they have to do is let us out at Barbary Station." After a few moments of listening to herself breathe in her enviro suit, she asked, "What kind of a name is *Barbary* Station, anyway?"

"It's a reference to sea piracy around Morocco, Algeria, Tunisia, and Libya," said Adda. Iridian was halfway through looking up where those Earth countries might be before she remembered that even if her comp's request made it out of the ship, the lead cloud would prevent it from going anywhere. She shuddered. That'd take some getting used to. "People called that area the Barbary Coast centuries ago," Adda went on. "The implication is that Barbary Station is just as dangerous for legitimate shipping as that area was." She frowned and gripped the straps securing her shoulders to the wall behind her, her gaze unfocused, her mind a million klicks away.

* * *

By the time the thrusters reversed and lit, Iridian was getting jittery. Though the pirates could be watching them on shipboard cams, their real first impression arriving on the station might make the difference between being accepted or killed. If this ship were crewed by anyone beyond the pilot, they'd come out of their quarters then. Handing over a colony ship should allow Adda and Iridian to skip any tests or demonstrations a pirate crew might demand of those wishing to join. If it didn't—if anything at all went wrong—they could die.

Grav rose sharply and shifted to push Iridian flat against the bulkhead, which no longer felt like a wall to her now that grav was shifting. Reis had left the strap-down station sometime during the trip, and he bounced off a magnetized stack of crates, swearing and thrashing until he found a handhold. Docking processes thrummed and rumbled through the bulkhead as the ship affixed itself to something bigger.

According to Adda's research, Barbary Station's spin generated hypergrav nearer 1.15 g than the standard 1. The old convention was supposed to minimize travelers' low-grav bone loss. Scientists disproved hypergrav's calcium-retaining benefits definitively and publicly after several megacorps and two government had already built hyper-g stations. Her body adopted slow head-swivel turns to keep her from getting dizzy in the first few days of hypergrav-induced inner-ear disorientation. That habit had saved her a lot of misery on long, fast flights during the war.

Adda's face went gray as the ship finished inserting itself into station grav and its engines powered down. Iridian squeezed her hand and helped her unstrap from the bulkhead. After years of daydreaming and planning and saving, they'd arrived. It was time to interview for a whole new life.

The passthrough cycled open, admitting a gust of station atmo. When their suits' readings indicated the passthrough's enviro was healthy, Reis unsealed his faceplate and let the suit's hood hang behind his neck. Iridian kept hers on, and it probably hadn't occurred to Adda to take hers off. The doors in the corridor beyond the cargo area stayed shut. It was just them and the pilot onboard, then.

"Let's go, ladies." Reis grinned and held out his arm, knife in hand. Iridian sheathed hers where he could see the action and take the hint. He sneered and entered the passthrough.

"Drop the blade," someone outside shouted.

Iridian and Adda glanced at each other. "Better get out there and say hi to Pel," Iridian said.

Adda set her teeth in her bottom lip, eyeing the door sideways like she'd rather not look at all. "That wasn't Pel."

Stepping into the passthrough revealed that the ship hadn't docked to another passthrough. It was parked inside a massive industrial docking bay. The pad it rested on took up barely a third of the space, but the bay's ceiling seemed too low for a vessel this size. Some overhead lights were out, casting large patches of shadow across the metal floor. Though the enviro suit sealed her away from it, the cooling engine would suffuse the atmo with ozone. After years of going to school on Earth, it'd be good to smell something like home.

About a dozen people stood on the pad, some with faces shadowed beneath hoods and others in helmets with the facial projection feature turned off. They brandished metal bowls strapped to their palms at Reis and his stupid knife. Even though the light was bright enough to see Adda's face through her suit hood, nobody in the bay acted like they recognized her.

Gemmed rings and earrings reflected the bay's gray-white light. Each helmet or hood and everyone's shoulders were painted with blue highlights. None of them wore enviro suits or masks, though several in the front had solid-looking armor. They weren't outfitted for the airborne chem or bioweaponry so common in shipboard combat.

An alarm whooped, accompanied by rotating yellow lights mounted on the docking bay walls. *How the fuck can a depressurization cycle start in an occupied docking bay?* The pirates must've overridden the safeties. "Grab a handhold." The suit's comms carried Iridian's words to the other Transorbital suits, but not to the pirates. Adda gripped a handhold in the passthrough wall. Out on the gangway, Reis kept waving his damned knife.

"No time for fooling," said the first voice. It belonged to someone taller than Iridian, with dark skin, a hooded duster that brushed the deck, and a long figure she couldn't classify as male or female. "Drop it. Now."

Reis's fist clenched on his knife hilt. "I'm not standing here while—"

The shallow bowl in the speaker's hand emitted a rising whir and a loud snap. Iridian held her breath, braced for the pain of impact. *Or, gods, it could've hit Adda!*

Reis staggered and made a gurgling, retching noise. His head swung sluggishly toward Iridian, his nose and mouth gleaming red with blood. He dropped to his knees, then fell forward. Something in his face crunched when it hit the floor.

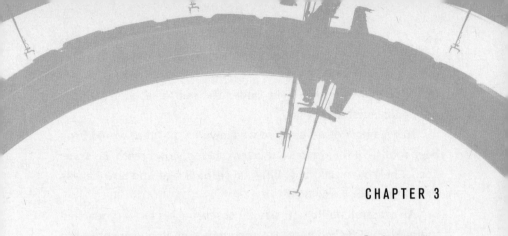

CHAPTER 3

Charges Accrued: Conspiracy to Sabotage Artificial Intelligence

Weapons shaped like handheld satellite dishes swung toward Iridian's chest. Reis wasn't breathing. Iridian could be next.

Her fists were up and her head was down. Shadows and yellow warning lights from the docking bay walls flickered over her scowling face. Adda put her hands up as quickly as she dared and stepped forward. "Captain Sloane?" The docking bay's alarm was so loud she had to shout. The pirates' eyes and several of their weapons refocused on her.

The man—woman? neither?—who'd shot Reis nodded, so she said as fast as she could, "My name is Adda Karpe. I'm Pel's sister. I've got a comp glove, but I'm not armed. Iridian Nassir is going to put down some knives. We're here to join your crew."

Iridian raised an eyebrow at her, like she'd forgotten that Adda could speak up when she had to. Adda's announcement shocked Iridian far enough out of combat mode to set a large knife and her shield on the ramp. She opened her environment suit at the shin to relinquish her boot knife. A holdout blade still rested against her lower back, out of sight under the suit. The open suit leg flapped in a rising breeze.

Not a single other weapon was lowered, but that would have been foolish of the pirates. Adda took a long, slow breath. Reis was dead. She'd been talking to him just seconds ago, and now he was *dead*. But nobody else died.

An armored pirate with a hood obscuring his face approached them. Adda clenched her teeth and braced for whatever came, but he just crouched beside Reis's body to collect Iridian's knives and shield.

"This conversation will be taking place elsewhere." Captain Sloane turned on a fashionably booted heel and walked toward a corner of the docking bay, away from the landing pad. A man and a woman carrying those bowl-shaped weapons jogged ahead, two steps to each whoop of the alarm.

The ship Iridian and Adda had arrived on wasn't the only one in the docking bay. One sat half on, half off a second landing pad. Its cockpit was smashed in. The other lay on its side nearby, bent at angles around two enormous breaches in its hull. Both wrecks had been exposed to air long enough to rust.

Her gaze skittered away from the body in front on the ramp. Reis was the first dead person she'd seen just lying at her feet, not on a projector stage or in a coffin. Although she'd disliked and distrusted Reis, she and Iridian would never have reached Barbary Station without him. She hadn't planned for *this*.

Loud buzzing from behind warned her to get off the ship's ramp. Ten rovers rolled around Reis and down the ramp on wheels, dragging pallets of crates behind them that shoved his body onto the landing pad. They followed the captain as well. Apparently the pilot still had work to do onboard, because no one else disembarked.

Iridian beckoned for Adda to get moving, then jogged after

the pirates and rovers. When she passed the man holding her equipment, she said, "You damage that shield, you're a dead man."

She left him no time to respond before running on. This group of pirates included five or six women. One was so muscular that by comparison Iridian was as classically attractive as an advertising persona. It couldn't be Iridian's gender that surprised him, so maybe his stunned expression was a result of expecting her to act more like Adda.

When Adda ran after them, her stomach churned in protest of combining anxiety and extra gravity. She unsealed her environment suit hood before she could throw up in it and let it dangle behind her neck. Hard plastic bumped the tops of her shoulder blades with each step. Dry docking-bay air chilled her lungs, full of ozone and oil. Without the hood, the alarm was louder. The station's gravity rearranged her internal organs and plastered her sleep-tangled hair against her head despite the wind.

"You want to keep that hood on." A big man with a wide, flattened nose behind a cracked helmet faceplate kept pace beside her. His voice was accented like he'd spoken Spanish well before he learned English. "This place is losing atmo, if you can't feel it."

Adda's eyes widened. *That's right, stations aren't supposed to have wind.* "Thanks." She hid her face beneath the hood, hoping the pirates were headed somewhere protected by an airtight door.

"I'm Chato," the one next to her said. "Pel has a lot to say about you."

Something small flew past her head toward the slowly widening square of open space above and behind the pirate ship. Escaping air misted over the stars. It looked like a hole in the universe.

She shut her eyes for a second. Barbary Station's original owners had been shipbreakers. Plenty of malfunctions and leaks would be easier to contain when not surrounded by flammable gases, and the wide door made it easy to move wrecked ships in and out. At the rate it was going, it looked like it'd take a few minutes to open that far, and the air in the docking bay would be gone well before then. That didn't make the gradual disappearance of the one barrier between her and a perfect vacuum less alarming to watch, so she overcame the instinctual panic and turned her back on the opening airlock.

The pirates stopped at a vertical tear in the closest exterior wall, along which the rovers lined up crates and nets from the colony ship. A cross-section of the wall showed multiple layers of metal composites forming a room or hallway beyond the tear. Power cables as big around as Adda's upper arm covered its floor and the wall around the opening. Someone had wound the cables up over one another to make room to enter.

A woman small enough to slip through the gap in the wall and between the cables easily did so. Wind from air escaping out the docking bay door strengthened until Adda had to lean into it to keep her balance. The woman stuck her head out through the gap a few moments later. "Nothing walking in there, Captain. I'm going." She vanished into the wall again.

"Double hull." Iridian must have seen Adda's puzzled frown. She sealed her environment suit's hood, and Adda did too. One of Iridian's first rules of life in space was "Do what I do." Since she'd spent almost as much time in space as Adda had spent on Earth, that seemed wise.

"Will the double hull retain pressure?" Since the docking bay's alarm was still blaring, Adda certainly hoped it would. The grit blowing out through the gap and eddying around her legs wasn't encouraging. Iridian shook her head.

"Safer this way," Chato said loudly enough to carry through his helmet and her suit's hood.

"No talking in the wall," said one of the others. Despite her suit's insulation, she shivered. Hard vacuum was a handbreadth away on the other side of the exterior hull, and growing behind her in the docking bay too. Iridian entered first and Adda followed, with Chato a step behind.

Adda was short enough to stand straight. Iridian's hood dragged along a hanging cable and knocked into dangling LEDs casting orange light on their path. The LEDs might have been designed as holiday decorations. Beneath the docking bay's alarm, arrhythmic ticking and a low electronic buzz permeated the narrow space along with the tramp of booted feet. Adda was too wide in the hips to walk straight through, so she shuffled sideways behind Iridian.

The pirates came to a gradual halt at the end of the last string of orange lights. The center of the metal floor was clear of grit and cables, as if many feet walked there. Something clunked above them. Adda startled backward into Chato and reached for Iridian's hand. After a perfunctory squeeze, Iridian let go. In combat mode, Iridian needed her hands free.

They started moving. After a meter, Iridian's back shifted up instead of forward and a ladder appeared in front of Adda. The climb felt endless. Everyone would hear her panting and judge her for her lack of fitness. What if her suit didn't have enough oxygen? Was she going to suffocate, to rot in the walls like a dead roach?

She had a plan to carry out. If the pirate captain would only talk terms at the top of an unreasonably long ladder, she'd climb it. Besides, Pel had to be up there somewhere. The whooping alarm faded slightly as she ascended.

An interminable time later, Iridian's boots disappeared from above Adda's white-gloved fingers. The ladder ended in a hatchway. She pulled herself over its edge, and Iridian helped her into a hallway with oddly angled walls. It widened slightly the farther forward she looked. In comparison to the hull passage, it was spacious.

Ahead, pirates broke into raucous chatter punctuated by appraising glances toward her and Iridian. More strings of decorative orange LEDs hung from the walls. The ceiling and walls were a solid, unnatural shade of blue that could only have been created in a chemistry lab or a digital art studio. The floor was a duller version of it. When she scuffed her boot, it scraped through a layer of blue dust. More filtered down from the ceiling. Under the dust, the tiles were unpainted metal.

People swore as somebody pushed through the line from the front. Adda couldn't see over the pirates' shoulders until the new person was halfway down the hall. A thick gray sweatshirt's blue-dusted hood was pulled over goggles made to protect welders' eyes. The wearer slapped at the arm of the pirate nearest him, a tough-looking woman with short black hair and black armor, who'd just turned her helmet's projector on so her face showed in the faceplate. She glanced back and said, "She's two people behind me."

"Sissy!" Pel yelled. The sweaty exhaustion from the long climb evaporated as Adda shoved past Iridian and the armored man in front of her and threw herself into her brother's hug.

Beneath the loose hood, his curly brown hair had grown past his jaw since he'd recorded the last video. His shoulder bones poked her even through her suit, and his skin was paler than in the messages too. Still, he bounced in place with the same gleeful energy as ever, like he didn't hear the docking bay alarm. "Oh my gods, you're finally here! Could you have picked a slower ride? No wonder it takes months to get to Io."

"Sorry, Captain," said a husky female voice at the head of the line, belonging to an enormous, muscular woman dressed in black, vaguely military clothing and a hooded jacket like several of the others. "There was nothing I could do about him."

"You could have carried him to the storage tank and shut him in," the captain said. After taking in Adda's glare over Pel's shoulder and the way her brother's hand fidgeted at the side of his neck, Sloane added, "I'll speak to them in my stateroom."

The pirates moved steadily down the hall, with frequent glances back toward the hatch. Pel took two or three steps forward and back for each step Adda took. The hand he wore his bright red comp glove on trailed along the wall. "So Iridian came too?"

"That's me."

The goggle lenses redirected from Iridian's chest to her face. "Wow, she's tall. Watch your head, the ceiling's low in the common area." Adda's cheeks heated. Piracy hadn't done anything for his manners, though if it had, she'd have been shocked. "I'm Adda's brother, Pel."

Iridian stepped back to offer a shallow spacefarer's bow, smiling like she would at an enthusiastic puppy. Pel didn't even hold out his hand to shake. He bowed like he'd grown up in space. Adda could've sworn he'd only left Earth a few months, but after she started her final project in school last year, she hadn't followed his social feeds as closely as she used to.

Behind them, a long metal-on-metal screech was followed by the hatch clunking shut. Three separate latches locked automatically, securing it in place. The pirates quit looking over their shoulders and focused on the people they were talking to. Iridian sighed in audible relief, which probably meant they were all going to keep breathing for the foreseeable future.

Adda frowned. News articles claimed the pirates lived like royalty here, after having wrested the station from its previous owners. Since the station had been abandoned before the pirates took up residence, claiming ownership couldn't have required all these weapons and armor, or locked doors. Perhaps maintaining control of their new base of operations did.

The docking bay's alarm went silent. Adda caught Iridian's eye and found similar confusion there. Something was wrong.

The armored pirates took off their helmets and tugged hoods or hats over their heads instead. Iridian unsealed her environment suit's hood. This time Chato didn't say anything when Adda took hers off. The air was cold and dry, but it smelled fresher than the plastic-tinged suit air. The pirates, now that helmets didn't block their faces, all looked older than Iridian and Adda, in their late twenties and early thirties. Pel was by far the youngest of them.

He added comments to all the conversations happening around him, looking around at everything except where he was walking, even after he bumped into someone in front of them. His fingertips were the same shade of blue as the wall, like he'd fallen against it and the powder rubbed off on him. *Is he drunk, or high?* One of shimmer's side effects was light sensitivity. Given the eyewear he'd worn during sporadic messages over the past year, he might have gotten back on the drug months ago.

"How can you see anything through those goggles?" she asked.

The pirates' conversations paused in a collective intake of breath. Pel kept walking, grinning like he had something to hide. "Yeah, I know, right? That's the joke. Heh."

This could be his senior year of high school all over again. She spun him around by the arm and raised her hand in front of his face. "How many fingers am I holding up?"

He chuckled and tried to pull away. She kept his arm pinned between her elbow and ribs. "Three. Come on, what are you trying to say?"

"This is one finger, Pel." She stopped, and the pirates around them stopped too. "What's wrong with you?"

He turned his head right and left, like he hoped one of the pirates would rescue him from the question. When nobody did, he smiled sheepishly. "Don't be mad, okay? It wasn't my fault." He lifted the goggles to his forehead.

His brown irises were gone. Yellowed blank globes stared out of his eye sockets. She stopped breathing with one gloved hand clenched on his sleeve.

Looking closer at one, she found the iris: a darker circle under tissue the same yellow-white as the rest of the eye. A thin curl of golden brown, like a sunspot, started near the center. Its tail curved around beneath the socket's rim. A healed scar stretched from there across his cheekbone. The other eye's scar was shaped a bit differently, like the skin had split along a different path.

"Don't be mad," he said.

She flung her arms around him again, breath rushing out of her in a soft moan. The goggles fell back over his ruined eyes. "Oh, *Pel*, shut up. Why didn't you tell me? Oh my gods. Can you see at all? What happened?" Everyone around them started talking again, and the words bled together. Iridian gripped her shoulder.

He tried to squirm away, but he didn't fight hard. "I don't know. I didn't know what to tell you."

"Can you see anything?" she asked.

His whole body trembled. "Light, a bit."

"I'm not mad at you. Your poor eyes. Why haven't you gotten them fixed?" The silly glasses in his messages . . . He'd worn them in every vid he'd sent her, even the one where he first told her about the opportunity to join Sloane's crew, *last year*. "Doesn't this station have a doctor?"

"Yeah, a med team, plus Zikri, kinda. They don't hurt much.

It's okay." He sighed, his chest pushing her away. "Did you get my message about what's going on here?"

"On the trip from the colony ship to here, yes." Someone behind Adda cleared his throat. The line in front of them was moving. She hooked her arm through Pel's again.

To her surprise, once they got out of the hallway, Pel led her. He trailed his fingertips along cobbled-together walls of a large, misshapen room apparently constructed entirely out of scrap metal. The low ceiling was the same blue as the dust on everyone's shoulders and hoods. Someone had halfheartedly swept the floor, leaving the corners blue. At the edge of hearing, unseen fans moved the sluggish, chill air.

"What's with all the blue powder?" Iridian asked.

"It blocks radiation," Pel said over his shoulder.

Adda nodded, mostly to herself. Space was full of radiation. Before she left Earth, its magnetic field had protected her from almost all of it. Without a barrier between them and the ambient radiation, all spacefarers would have cancer.

Pel avoided tables cluttered with machine parts and ration wrappings on his way to the leftmost of two hallways that opened at the corners across the room from the entryway. Almost at once he paused before a door that could have come from the *Prosperity Dawn's* high-end sleeper suites. He knocked twice. "Captain, it's me and Adda and Iridian."

Someone with a sturdy masculine build and lighter brown skin than the captain's opened the door. His black beard was dusted with blue and trimmed to the length of the hair behind his receding hairline. "Ladies, come in. Pel, get gone." The voice was familiar.

"What? Why? They just got here!" said Pel.

"The captain's had enough of you for one day." That voice . . .

he had recorded the rover's message announcing that anyone still on the colony ship had three more minutes to breathe. That was the same tone he'd used, in fact.

Pel gave her another hug, whispered, "Good luck!" and walked back toward the large room. Adda and Iridian stepped through the door into a room almost completely filled by a comfortable-looking bed. The bearded man backed awkwardly around the end of the bed to make space for them to enter the room.

Strap-covered space-worthy furniture like she'd seen in vids would have matched the compound's hard surfaces and cramped rooms. This bed looked just like an Earth one. After a second's inspection Adda located a few straps, but they attached at the bed's corners and seemed more likely to have recreational applications than practical ones. The walls were parallel where they should be, unlike those in the rest of the pirates' compound. At face height they were covered with the kind of art that cost more than it should. A nighttime city street scene with LEDs for the streetlamps and Earth's Moon hung on the wall over the bed's headboard.

Captain Sloane, still wearing the long coat from the docking bay, sat up from lounging on the bed to offer half a spacefarer's bow. Thick black hair fell regally over broad shoulders. Iridian returned the bow and Adda remembered to after watching her. Too low would make her look timid, and not low enough would be rude. "Well met," said the captain's smooth, ungendered voice.

"My lieutenant, Tritheist." The captain nodded at the man who'd answered the door. The lieutenant gave Adda and Iridian a shallow bow, and this time they both returned it at the same time. Adda still had to watch Iridian to be sure she bowed the right amount.

Tritheist, a believer in three gods, usually three aspects of a whole . . . The religious connotation made it sound more like a technicism conclave handle than a given name, although techs usually named themselves after the deities, not the worshippers. The cultish technicists would've trained him in scientific disciplines and skills since birth. Since he was out in space now, she could assume that his skills were insufficient for his home conclave, he'd been expelled for some other reason, or Sloane was paying him well for the subject he'd specialized in. If he really was a tech, he'd be the first one Adda had ever met.

Captain Sloane was watching Adda when she refocused. "Am I to understand that you received Pel's request that you not come, yet came anyway?" the captain asked.

"We got the message after we boarded your ship," said Iridian. "There was nothing else we could do. We'd have been arrested if we'd tried to evac with the colonists."

"If you're half the engineers Pel makes you out to be, I could use you." Captain Sloane smiled, a bit ironically if Adda was reading the signs right. "And we'll certainly make use of the colony ship."

"Your tug driver powered down the *Dawn* before we got here, but she'll fly on her own. We didn't cause her any damage." Iridian stood a little taller. "I'm a mechanical engineer by specialty, but Adda was the star on that op. Her degree's in AI development, and she had the *Dawn* under her control the whole way out."

Adda blushed at the attention and the exaggeration, although this was precisely the approach they'd agreed on. Mechanical engineers like Iridian were an obvious asset to a pirate crew, but the idea that the crew might avoid fighting their target ships' AI copilots required additional emphasis. Both the captain and the lieutenant were staring at her now, so they must've grasped the advantages her expertise could offer.

"That was a remarkably well-coordinated operation, and I understand you also delivered an operating system analysis. Remarkable," Captain Sloane said. Adda started to smile, until the captain asked, "Are you aware that you cannot leave?"

That kind of precaution showed that Captain Sloane treated organizational security with the seriousness it deserved. The Interplanetary Transit Authority had probably sent spies to infiltrate the crew in the past. It was logical that Adda and Iridian would have to earn the captain's trust before they could walk around the station unsupervised. "We aren't planning to leave," Adda said. Not until they were part of Sloane's crew.

"And we have no idea how to get to this station," Iridian assured the captain. "We never spoke to your pilot."

If Tritheist, Sloane, or Iridian thought about it long enough, they'd recall that high-level systems access allowed one to determine whether Barbary Station still maintained its publicly registered Jovian parallel orbit. Adda intended to get that access with or without Captain Sloane's permission, so there was no reason to mention it.

"The problem goes well beyond secrecy," the captain said. "We, too, are unable to leave the station. The security system is active, you see, and it . . . doesn't approve of us."

Adda's breath shuddered out of her like she'd been struck. A security system for a station this size would include an artificial intelligence. *That alarm in the docking bay . . . The docking bay doors had opened while Captain Sloane and the crew were still in the bay and the* pirates hadn't even tried to stop them, which suggested that they couldn't. The security system's intelligence, or whoever was supervising it, had attempted to dispose of intruders by the most efficient means. Iridian's face had gone pale, and it held no answers.

"I thought you owned the station," Adda said, aghast.

"We're squatters, I'm afraid." Nothing in the captain's disgusted expression indicated that this was some kind of trick. "And the vast majority of approaching and departing ships are blasted to scraps by turret fire. With none of the original qualified staff available to override it, the security AI controls Barbary Station now."

This explained why the pirates crept through walls and lived in a makeshift compound instead of the luxury she'd read about. The articles, reports, and obsessive fan community records she'd studied hadn't reported this. She'd *never* have brought Iridian here if she knew something as dangerous as an unsupervised AI would be onboard. And now they had no way out.

Before she despaired completely, Sloane said, "You came to join my crew, and you've demonstrated your capabilities admirably. But my condition is this: You will disable the security system."

Iridian understood the basics of AI, but the responsibility for bringing the system to heel would be Adda's. She had the most information and experience with AI development and guidance. Working with shipboard intelligences had always been the role Adda had expected to serve on Sloane's crew, but starting with such an aggressive system made her palms sweat. Even though she'd read everything she could find about the *Prosperity Dawn's* intelligence, it had still surprised her twice.

Unless she found a way to deactivate Barbary Station's unsupervised intelligence, it would kill the pirates eventually, including her, Iridian, and Pel. It'd already tried to kill them in the docking bay, which meant it would keep trying until it succeeded. Adda said, "We'll do whatever it takes."

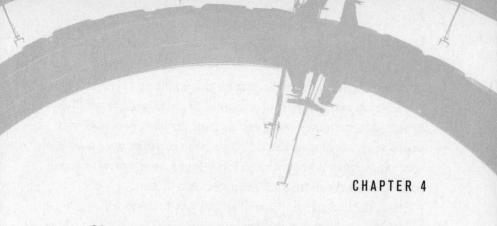

CHAPTER 4

Charges Accrued: Distribution of Stolen Property

Ductfucking hell. Joining Captain Sloane's crew was supposed to be Iridian and Adda's future, all laid out in a few interlocking plans and a slight felony. Instead Adda's little twerp of a brother had invited them into a deadly gods-damned mess. Iridian hid a hysterical grin behind a professional, blank expression. Adda needed Iridian's confidence, especially while talking to their future boss.

The captain and the lieutenant, Tritheist, were still within arms' reach. They stood with spacefarers' awareness and comfort in the small stateroom. Neither was conspicuously well-conditioned, but they'd both be armed with whatever the captain had used to kill Reis.

And Iridian was without her shield. At least she was positioned a step in front of Adda, close enough to get between her and Tritheist and maintain an open path to the door so Adda could run, if they found they had to leave in a hurry.

"Now, another item for your consideration." Captain Sloane leaned back against the ridiculously large bed's headboard and brushed a light layer of blue dust from the pillows. "Everyone here is under contract as part of my crew. They do good work. If you choose not to pursue your assignment, or do a poor job of it, I won't waste resources. You'll find yourselves soaking up particles and explosives on your way to the refugee hovels or, less conveniently but more dramatically, spaced. Am I clear?"

"Yes, sir," Iridian said. Would her military habit of calling almost everybody "sir" offend the captain? This was no time to show uncertainty or fear. She and Adda's best chance of survival was becoming obvious solutions, not resource drains. Adda's frown indicated she'd have concerns to discuss in private. "Can we have our gear back?" Iridian asked. "We'll start as soon as we can, but a workspace generator is no good without power and connection."

"True of so many things." The captain smiled and took the two steps around the bed to bow before them. Iridian returned the gesture, as low as she could manage in the confined space. They were being dismissed, but at least the captain had given them a way into the crew.

Sloane leaned toward Tritheist until the captain's chest brushed his and murmured, "Find them a bunk and a place to work."

Iridian was staring, but she couldn't make herself look anywhere else. Of course pirates wouldn't have a fraternization reg like the NEU army did. *Does everyone get that personal touch, or is it only for handsome older males?* If someone did that to her, she'd play it off as a joke, but if anyone touched Adda without Adda's permission, Iridian would cut them up.

They followed the lieutenant out of the stateroom and into the hallway. After Captain Sloane's door shut, Iridian said, "Not sure what you have for facilities, sir, but we could use those, too."

Tritheist—*should that be Lieutenant Tritheist? That sounds weird*—frowned and raised the hood of his dark blue coat. "The room in use is past the lockside bunkhouse, this way. Ask a woman how, if that's what you want to know."

Tritheist leaned into the common room and addressed a guy with graying hair wearing one of the black shirts many of the pirates had under their hooded jackets, who was talking with Pel. "Death, get the gear they came in with." The older guy placed Pel's hand on one of the workbenches before leaving, so Pel would know where he was. Tritheist turned back and walked past Iridian and Adda, farther down the hall.

"Death, huh," Iridian said. "That's either a good nickname or a really bad one." She let Adda walk in front and rested a hand on the small of her back. "Habitat directions: lockside's nearest the airlock, homeward's the opposite way," she whispered. Even on Earth, Adda was shit with navigation.

The walls and ceiling lacked handholds, so the station spun reliably enough to maintain grav. Part of a ship hull curving out from one blue wall steadily narrowed the hallway. For half a meter the walls brushed both of Tritheist's shoulders, and Adda turned sideways to squeeze through. The hull piece ended abruptly and a small alcove opened on the right. Someone loomed in the shadows there.

The unexpected space and proximity gave Iridian a whole-body startle. Her arms rose in a shieldless block to protect her neck and chest. The woman in the alcove had bronze skin and centimeter-long black hair. A wrinkled burn scar over one temple stretched when she frowned. Her gaze skimmed over Iridian's shaved head, and the frown deepened.

"Sorry." Iridian forced her arms down to her sides. "I'm new."

"Oh, I know," the stranger said. Interesting that she kept the scar instead of getting the skin regrown. Perhaps she was proud of it.

She certainly seemed proud of her hooded jacket's orange-and-red circle of the Red Planet Militia beneath a coating of blue dust. Nobody would've dared to display that shit on Earth. It was the new, post-invasion insignia the secessionists had created to finish co-opting the remnants of a halfway-decent civilian defense group. Iridian got a good look at it when the woman leaned in and added, "NEU, right? Gotta be, if you're shoving your nose some-place it wasn't invited and expecting everyone to love you for it."

Fucking secessionists.

Iridian had had her and Adda's plans upended too many times today to put up with secessionist insults too. She pushed the woman away from her harder than she meant to, slamming her into the narrow hallway's wall.

The woman reached for one of the pirates' bowl-shaped weapons at her belt, but the push knife hidden at the small of Iridian's back came free first. Iridian pinned the woman against the wall with a forearm across her collarbone and pressed the short blade's point to her throat. That didn't stop her arm moving, so Iridian jammed her hipbone against the woman's belt to keep her from drawing.

The knife's handle felt solid and strong between her fingers. If the woman freed her arm, Iridian was ready. She wasn't going to stand still and let this gods-damned secessionist shoot her. She'd put her blade through the woman's throat first. Since the wom-an's hand and wrist were out of reach, it was the only way she'd be sure that the woman wouldn't fire.

"That's enough." The stranger and Iridian both focused on the lieutenant, who aimed his own weapon at Iridian. The secession-ist stilled too, so whatever the pirates' handheld weapons shot had a good chance of going through Iridian to hit someone on the other side. And the secessionist believed Tritheist *would* shoot her, or at least risk her life taking Iridian out. "Let go," said Tritheist.

Iridian's instincts pushed her to finish the fight. People like this secessionist had started the war and people like Iridian ended it in blood . . . but that was over, three years over. She stepped back, which put her against the opposite wall but gave the secessionist room to do whatever she wanted, and looked at the woman's Red Planet Militia insignia instead of her face. The knife was still in her hand, but with luck the secessionist would recognize the hab de-escalation signals Iridian was using.

The woman finished removing her weapon from her belt. Before she could raise it, Tritheist leveled his at her, scowling like both of them disgusted him. "The captain gave them a task, Sergeant Natani. They can't complete it if they're dead." Perhaps he was loyal to Captain Sloane, but he clearly didn't think much of the crew.

Iridian had been on base ten minutes and she'd already assaulted an officer. *Get a gods-damned grip, Nassir.* Sure, the woman was a secessionist, but Tritheist used her rank like it meant something in the crew. The sergeant glared and pushed past Iridian and Adda to storm into the common room. Tritheist lowered his weapon but didn't put it away as he continued down the hall. After a few steps, the old guy named Death came up behind her to return her knives, her shield, and her and Adda's packs. She sheathed all the blades before following Adda and Tritheist.

They stopped at a low, slanted doorway with a dingy white towel hung over the opening. Outside it, the orange lights strung along the hallway ceiling were missing bulbs every few sockets. They cast as much shadow as light. Several blue and yellow bulbs created a pirates' attempt at Earth dusk. Tritheist knocked twice on the wall beside it. "Coming in." After some rustling from inside, he held the towel away from the door.

While her eyes adjusted to the dark, he said, "Pick two bunks without pills, porn, flasks, or bodies."

Fifteen bunks were stacked three deep in the small room, with the lowest flat on the floor and the highest less than a meter from the sloped ceiling. None of them were far enough apart to sit up in. They were bolted to the walls and one another, padded with a hodgepodge of foam bedding from various shipping lines. Tiedown straps for sleeping in micrograv dangled from some bunks, but not others. Sleeping men and women, most of whom weren't strapped in, occupied five bunks. Like the lack of handholds in the walls, that spoke well for grav consistency on this station.

All but three of the other bunks had people's possessions in them, and none of the empty ones were near one another. "One's fine," Iridian told Tritheist. If she and Adda were going to be sleeping among strangers, she wanted Adda close enough to touch. They'd rented a classmate's bathtub for a few weeks in college, when Iridian's veteran benefits got delayed and that was the best shelter they could afford. This bunkhouse was a hell of a letdown compared to the luxury they'd looked forward to on Barbary Station, but it beat sharing a bathtub as a bed.

"Damn," Tritheist said.

Iridian raised an eyebrow at him. "What's the problem?" He didn't talk like an ignorant colonial shithead, and colonists were the only people who still acted like sex that didn't make babies was some kind of sin.

"Lost a bet," a man grumbled from a bunk against the wall across from the door. Tritheist grunted in affirmation or disgust and stalked away.

Iridian chose an empty one on the top level beside the doorway and lifted their packs onto it. "This doesn't seem . . . secure," said Adda.

They climbed out of their enviro suits and Iridian folded them under the packs, because they were light enough to disappear. All the bunks crammed into the tiny space left no room for containers that locked. *So much for prevention.* A broken nose or bruised rib should discourage any thieves Iridian caught. Nothing incapacitating. "I'll take care of it after I find out which room and what sort of bag we're expected to piss in."

That took a few minutes and the assistance of a golden-skinned woman named Xing, who had the letters ZV on her shirt and a lighter-skinned infant balanced on her hip while demonstrating the way the crew handled excretory activities. "Kimmy, my best mistake ever," Xing said fondly when she caught Iridian staring at the baby. "Shit happens when your birth control runs out before your alcohol does."

When they emerged from the room at the end of the hall designated for the purpose, Pel was leaning against a wall. If he was telling the truth about his sight, then he couldn't see Iridian scowling at him. "Sissy, did you bring—"

"Just one gods-damned minute," Iridian growled. The baby whimpered and Xing hushed her. Iridian started again in a calmer voice. "Pel, we need to talk, somewhere private, if there's a place like that in here."

"I . . . um." Pel's Adam's apple bobbed when he gulped. "If you brought your tent, Sissy, there's a place where you can set up. We can talk there."

"It's a workspace generator, not a tent." Adda paused mid-dramatic-eye roll, which he wouldn't see.

"Everything okay, Pel Mel?" Xing asked behind them. Iridian flattened her back against the wall so mother and baby could pass, but the woman was watching Iridian with cautious eyes and stood her ground instead of heading to the common room.

"Oh yeah, no worries." Pel reached for Adda's arm and missed. On the second try, he caught it. "Always kind of weird meeting your sister's significant other, right?" He laughed nervously.

Xing pointed a warning finger at Iridian and mouthed, "Go easy on him" before she turned sideways to carry her daughter past the three of them and down the hall toward the common room. Baby Kimmy grabbed at Adda's purple-streaked red hair as they passed, and Adda ducked out of reach before she lost any of it.

"Come on, I'll show you where to set up." Pel pulled Adda toward the common room too, while dragging one hand along the wall. "It'd be good if you got Captain Sloane some new info by, like, yesterday."

"What's the rush?" Iridian held her voice and breathing steady to stay calm. Pel knew the kind of danger he was inviting his own gods-damned sister into. The vid message he'd sent Adda on the way to the station confirmed that. Sure, she and Iridian needed to become valuable additions to the crew as fast as possible, but they also deserved an explanation.

"Thing is, the captain didn't know I asked you to come here." Pel's pale face gained color. "Sloane yelled for an hour after I mentioned it. All 'We're barely surviving as we are!' and 'It's so dangerous!'" He extended "so" to an unlikely length and pitch range. "But now you're here, and if you get spaced for uselessness, so do I."

"Better and better," Iridian muttered.

Adda said, "I should have known you'd get us into something like this."

"Okay, I panicked, all right?" he said. "Anyway, I tried to tell you not to come. But wait until you see this spot I found. It's perfect for you."

The common room, where the entryway and all the other

hallways led, was the largest enclosure Iridian had seen in the base. Instead of windows, small projectors stuck to the wall displayed attractive people in various stages of undress alternated with looped vids of cities and stations. Atlantis, the entertainment station of debatable legality on the dark side of Earth's Moon, was an obvious choice. A couple of projectors showed unofficial station communities that grew around refueling points on the Martian and Cytherean routes.

The room's floor curved up slightly on the sides closest to and furthest from the entryway, and flat flooring was typical on stations with consistent grav. "Hey, are we inside the station, or outside?" Iridian asked.

"Outside," Pel said. Adda stopped walking, dragging him to a halt too, eyes wide. "Oh my gods, Sissy, it's fine. This is the only place on the station where AegiSKADA doesn't see everything you do, and drones hardly ever come out here."

"Drones, huh." Iridian shook her head. "Damned bots." After the war she'd have been happy if she never saw another drone outside a dock module or stationspace.

"We can lock them out with the front door," Pel said quickly. "So we're safe here! Sometimes things come apart, but not that often, and we're good at fixing them. Well, they are. I hold stuff."

"So this base is anchored on top of the inner ring? Outside the hull?" Iridian clarified. Barbary Station was a spinning ring of on-site recycling, docking, shipping, and residential modules, with an enormous scaffold in the center that secured ships for dismantling. Now she was really curious about how the pirate base looked from the outside. The pirates either couldn't spare the cams for windows or the cold and the black wigged them out. Given the stark living conditions she'd seen so far, the former was more likely.

"Yep, right on the inner ring," said Pel. "Since we're not technically in the station, AegiSKADA doesn't bust in and try to kill us, most of the time. The tanks and stuff down below mess up its sensors, too."

"Eh-ji-skay-wha?" Iridian rhymed her question with the word she was asking about.

He laughed. "The security AI. The first part of the name's a kind of shield, because security. The second part's about control systems or something. The acronym's got Russian in it. Anyway, AegiSKADA's what you're going to beat."

Adda's face scrunched up thoughtfully. "In English we have S-C-A-D-A intelligences. Supervisory Control and Data Acquisition. I wonder if it also ran the station's shipbreaking and recycling facilities. That's the type of thing the SCADA development path usually prepares intelligences for. Isn't that *interesting*."

Pel grinned. "I knew you'd say that."

They ducked down the second hallway, each step thumping hollowly over the space between the floor and the station's hull. This hall opened almost immediately on the left to a room with tables, chairs, and the scent of spices. A large woman with straight black hair that a red headband held away from half-moon eyes was wiping down an industrial-size oven. Another darkened room with a towel over the doorway was on the right a step later, and soon after the hallway narrowed to an off-center corner.

A trapdoor panel in the floor was situated in front of the dead end. Pel shuffled his foot around until the toe of one of his oversize boots bumped its edge. He released Adda's arm to crouch and open it, revealing ladder handholds built into a passage the size of a wide duct. "It's nowhere near as long a climb as Mount Everest. That's the one you took coming in." He disappeared down the ladder.

Nothing hissed or whistled like an atmo leak, but anything else could be down there, presuming a healthy enviro. And she'd have to approach it feetfirst, with both hands occupied. But Adda was already climbing down, so Iridian followed, lowering herself with two feet and one hand to keep her shield arm free.

Pel's boots hit something solid after only a few steps. He reached down to open a second hatch, climbed down another couple of meters, and slapped something on the wall. A push light flickered on, illuminating a room shaped like a giant oblong pill. Stacked boxes of printing material smelled of dust and aging plastic. Loose spools in a box gleamed like copper alloy.

The surfaces were clear of blue powder. The best-case implication was that the full water tanks around them did a sufficient job blocking radiation without the blue stuff. The worst-case implication was that the pirates couldn't be bothered to treat this area, and it was the most vulnerable spot on base. And now that Iridian was looking up, she spotted the joins between the hulls, the pirate base, and the station interior. The tank they stood in was inside the station, not sitting on the hull like the rest of the base.

"This was a water tank, but it's got a bunch of leaks. Don't worry, it's not leaking atmo. The holes work kind of like ventilation now." Enviro science was not this kid's best subject. Iridian shook more grains of mental salt on everything he said. "Then Sturm turned it into a storage space. We might bring more down, thanks to the haul you got us! That was awesome. Everybody's talking about it." Iridian grinned. That was the reaction they'd hoped for. At least something in this mess of a mission had gone as planned.

Adda stepped toward the middle of the floor. The whole tank lurched a little in the same direction. Something outside groaned like metal under stress. Both women froze in place.

"It does that," Pel said. "It's welded to a big ledge next to some others, but I guess the ledge moves?" He shrugged.

"Is the pump off?" Iridian was surreptitiously recovering her breath. She'd have to inspect this whole damned place. No way she'd let Adda spend time down here otherwise.

"Yep, it's off! Hasn't run in months and months."

"Okay. Fine." Iridian climbed the ladder far enough to reach the hatch and shut it, then returned to the tank's floor. "Now, you want to explain what the hell you thought you were doing, asking Adda to come to this AI-infested, falling-apart station?"

Pel tilted his head down and his shoulders rose toward his ears. "Aw, come on, it's not—"

"Oh, yes, it is that bad," Iridian said. "Your message sounded just like all the newsfeeds, like you were inviting us to some kind of pirate paradise. That's not the same as being stuck two hundred fifty million klicks beyond the Mars orbit with an intelligence that wants us all dead."

"Iri," Adda pleaded, "I would've come to help him even if he'd told us about the intelligence." If Adda were going, Iridian would've gone too, but that wasn't the point.

"That's why I asked you to come," Pel said quickly. "I kind of panicked when I first got here, so when you said you were joining a crew after graduation, I just had to tell you about this one." He turned toward Adda. "You always get me out of trouble, and, I mean, AI, right? You know all about it from college, so—"

"So you thought, 'Why should I mention the killer AI at all?'" Iridian shouted. "'I'll just *lie to her* instead.'"

"I'm sorry." He hung his head again. "I was so scared. I had to know she was coming, or I don't know how I would've . . ." He took an unsteady breath. "I went back and forth about it a lot after I sent it. And I tried to send that vid to you a couple of times, asking you to wait, but stuff kept happening, so it didn't get carried out of the lead cloud."

"No signals get through the lead cloud," Adda said. "I don't understand how you got the first message to me."

"Si Po helped," Pel admitted. "He asked one of the ships to take it. She, the *Casey* I mean, she does that sometimes. Si Po helped a lot with getting you here, actually." Iridian would have to find the pirate by that name later, and either thank him or punch him. At the moment, she felt more like hitting him.

Adda sighed. "Was this before or after what happened to your eyes?"

"I don't want to talk about it," Pel said so quickly that there had to be something left to say.

"Pel!" a deep voice shouted somewhere above. "Get your ass out here or we'll divvy up without you."

"Okay, I'm sorry." Pel glanced between Adda and Iridian, looking appropriately guilty at last. "I'm really sorry. I should've told you everything in the first message. But now we've got to go get stuff, or all the good bits will get sent to the fugees." Before Iridian could ask him what that was about, he dragged his hand along the curved wall to the ladder and clambered up.

Adda peered toward the far end of the tank, away from the trapdoor hatch and the light. "Does it lock?"

Iridian assumed she meant the door that led from the ladder to the rest of the base. "If it doesn't now, I'll make it. So are we really—"

"Could be miked," Adda said quietly. "Later, after I've looked for them."

"Fuck later. We might not have later." Iridian set her hands on Adda's hips and murmured, "What's going on in your head?"

Adda's soft arms curled around Iridian. She wasn't shaking.

That was good. "Can we do this? With all these . . . criminals?"

They hadn't had this exact conversation before, but they'd danced around the topic often enough. "Nice people sign contracts and do what they're told, babe. Criminals we can handle. Secessionists, too, come to that. It's the AI I'm worried about." She pressed a kiss to the top of Adda's head where her purple highlights met. "We can always go find the refugees if the next surprise disaster is too bad."

Barbary Station housed a whole community of refugees. She and Adda had listened to an episode or two of their newsfeed, with a fast-talking host named Suhaila. All the newsfeed told them about the station was that enviro was healthy, the refugees needed more supplies, and before the pirates arrived, a lot of refugees had died.

Suhaila had also talked about the station's defense system shooting down ships that got too close, while providing instructions on launching supplies in cargo containers toward the station. The rest of humanity had assumed that the pirates were choosing the defense system's targets. It was starting to look like most sources of information about Sloane's crew that Adda had found got their information from the refugee feed, and some of that sounded like propaganda Sloane had made up. Claiming credit for a malfunctioning AI's kills would certainly make the pirates look powerful.

"Seriously, Iri."

Adda would create an escape plan if they needed one, but what would they do after that? Of all the habitats in the galaxy to be homeless, jobless, and broke, a station run by an out-of-control AI had to be the least survivable. Besides, Adda should at least assess the situation before they threw away their best chance at a good life.

Iridian nudged her forehead against Adda's to turn her face up so they looked each other in the eyes, and so Adda saw the teasing smile just for her. "I'm good enough, what's wrong with you?" Adda rolled her eyes and Iridian laughed. "Yeah, it's crazy. It's the kind of crazy that turns people into legends. We'll be fantastically rich, babe."

"Fatally rich, you mean. And don't use that word." Adda had nearly broken Iridian of the bad habit of calling things "crazy" when she meant "risky," but it was harder to remember when she was around people who talked like soldiers. "Reis is dead," Adda continued. "They may kill us too."

Iridian put her hands on either side of Adda's face, to hold her gaze. "Do you really think that?"

"No." Adda sighed. "Otherwise I'd never have agreed to the captain's proposal. I'm not sure that makes this a good idea."

Iridian kissed her. The touch of tongue against her lower lip told her Adda was calming down, maybe ready to meet more of the crew. After all the hitches big and small in Adda's plan, she was still determined to take what came and make it into something better. *Gods, I love her.* "It's a great idea. Know the difference."

* * *

Over the next twenty minutes Pel helped them select the most essential pieces for their share of the colony ship haul. The data casks from the drones' nets on the *Prosperity Dawn* were nowhere to be seen, but the workbenches in the common room were now covered with labeled crates of other odds and ends from the colony ship. Jewelry and tech were piled next to the crates, and the crew formed a winding, disordered line through the workbenches. Most of the people in the room wore black sweatshirts and jackets with the yellow ZV design somewhere on them. Captain Sloane and Tritheist, who'd apparently already perused what was available, leaned against the far wall, watching. Tritheist muttered at the comp in his iridescent black comp glove every time somebody claimed an object from the table.

"These things cost future money," Pel explained. "Like, nothing now, but some totaled-up price when we get to our bank accounts again. Anyway, data gets ripped to the crew drive, so you get that for free. You want to grab physical necessities, because I bet you didn't bring much. Are there pillows?"

The crew selected similar essentials and shouted versions of "Good timing," and "Finally, after all these months!" over the dance music playing from somebody's comp. Some of the crew must've had everything they needed already, because they somehow found space to dance to the music among all the crates and people. Now that Iridian was looking, she saw that the pirates had kept a lot of scars. Perhaps that wasn't an aesthetic choice.

For anything needed but not present, the crew traded units of their share for boxes labeled in 3-D printer codes. Printers needed the spools of metal and plastic inside to make all the inorganic objects people used every day, from toothbrushes and plates to machine parts and fittings. Considering what the pirates hauled out of the *Dawn*, they didn't count on their printer to produce textiles reliably. Fortunately, there were about ten crates labeled "Pillows."

Adda's research indicated that Captain Sloane's crew netted one colony ship every twelve to fifteen months. Their success rate here was why the rest of humanity had quit calling the place Waypoint Station and started calling it Barbary, even before the captain "moved the crew's headquarters" to it last year. None of the newsfeeds where she and Adda had heard that phrase suggested that the move had been unintentional, although it certainly looked that way now. The twenty pirates crowded into the common room should've had more than enough supplies, medical and otherwise.

They must've arrived with more people. Adda had never gotten a good read on crew size before she and Iridian arrived on-station, other than that the crew was big enough to do plenty of damage when Captain Sloane ordered it to.

While Pel and Adda caught each other up on family stuff, Iridian turned to see who was in line behind her. A muscular guy a couple of decades her senior, whose ancestors had lived in East Asia on Earth, was watching them. She bowed as far as space allowed and introduced herself. "Major Ken Oonishi," he said, at the same time Pel shouted, "Major O.D.!" which the pirates laughed at and repeated.

"Organ donor, not overdose," the major said in the tone of someone performing a rehearsed explanation. Iridian was still reconciling a major taking orders from *Captain* Sloane. The NEU standardized its military ranks for a reason. "Welcome. Heard you and the ships brought back a colony ship on your own. Truth?"

Iridian grinned. "Truth."

"And you came here with a shield."

"Personal protection, sir, that's all." Iridian couldn't tell which colony O.D.'s accent was from, but she hadn't heard any accents like it on Earth. Half the pirates in the room spoke with one variety of colonial inflection or other. The crew composition surprised her, although she probably should've expected it, since the crew's original base of operations was on Vesta in the asteroid belt.

Not everybody in habs beyond Mars supported secession from the NEU, but secessionists liked to present themselves as regular people until you let your guard down. She shifted her weight away from the major, making space to draw one of her blades if she needed to. It was a shame the backwater inbreds couldn't get an education as specialized as the kind offered on Earth. That should never have been a deficit to start a war over. A person who'd kill over that would kill over, say, the side one had fought for in a war that'd already ended. Years on Earth had almost convinced her that humanity had become better than that.

"Awright." If Major O.D. was waiting to jump her, he was a damned fine actor as well as an officer. She'd had trainers like that. "The only people who use shields are soldiers and SWAT, and if you're a cop, you weren't documented in the last Internet scrape. When Pel Mel finally told us you were coming, Kaskade looked you up." He nodded toward a woman with blue-streaked hair and the not-quite-there look of systems engineers like Adda. Iridian smiled slightly, because that was also exactly what Adda would've done. "Not that we're connected to the net out here. The scrape we got might not have had your records anyway." Major O.D. looked mournfully down at his black comp glove.

"Me and Adda aren't cops or soldiers. She was never in, and me . . . I'm done with that."

Major O.D. nodded and checked on the progress of the line, apparently content to let the topic pass without asking which side she'd fought for. She let out the breath she'd been holding, mentally repeating, *I'm done, I'm done, I'm done, damn everything.* She wasn't just going to have to work with these people, she was going to have to trust them. Maybe the other colonial crew members weren't as resentful about their losses as the sergeant she'd met. The major had talked more rationally than Iridian had, so far. Hell, he'd probably seen how defensive she was and hadn't said a thing about it.

The dance music playing from someone's comp faded to a

feminine voice Iridian recognized, attributing the song and adding, "Breaking in for breaking news! Sloane's crew snagged a
colony ship, people! Intact, no damage, no passengers. Yes, I'm
serious." The pirates cheered. "Captain, we hope to see you soon."
A new song started and conversation and dancing resumed.

"Was that Suhaila? From the refugees' feed?" Iridian asked.

"Fugee News," said Major O.D. without looking up from the
label on a box of printer material. News broadcasts were a good
description of the fugee feed episodes that Iridian and Adda had
listened to, but those hadn't included music. "The fugees have a
good feed, and we send them all the music we get so they keep
things bouncing. I don't know how they hear about things so
quick, but they always do."

"Fugees?" She'd been looking for a chance to ask about that
term.

"Yeah, a few thousand people left Mars in a hurry after the
secessionists took over. Somebody thought it'd be smart to put the
fugees up here, 'cause no habs would take them. Station was just
about empty then. We figure that's what drove AegiSKADA mad,
all these strangers coming in, some of them armed, no doubt.
Nobody's been able to come get them, and their pilot got killed
trying to leave to pick up more fugees. I still don't know how the
Martians got their ship back here, without the pilot. AegiSKADA's
turrets blew a big hole in the bridge."

"The Martian habs surrendered in 2473." Iridian heard the horror in her voice, and it was damned justified. "The fugees have
been here all this time?"

"Yep." The major took a deep slug of the concoction in his cup.
"Three years they been here. AegiSKADA won't let them leave."

Adda's voice cut through the nightmare Iridian's brain was
lining up based on that unenviable experience. "If AegiSKADA

allows your ships to come and go, why haven't you asked your pilots to take you and the refugees off the station to somewhere safer? I don't think the ITA is waiting outside the lead cloud to arrest you when you leave. We would've seen them on our way here."

O.D. was tall enough to have to tip his head down to focus on her, and he looked back to his drink almost at once. "The pilots won't take anybody anywhere, most of the time. We were surprised the *Apparition* picked you up. The pilots and the station's original medical team, the people who've been here since the owners evacuated . . . Being here shook something loose in their brains. None of them think right anymore."

Iridian shifted until Adda's body heat warmed her arm. Being trapped on a station with an AI out for blood might make a person do anything. Anything at all. The ITA remapped the reliable routes when Spacelink, Barbary Station's former corporate owners, gave up the station. No rescue was coming. Barbary Station was abandoned, rolling in the cold and the black with a mad, inhuman thing at its helm.

Iridian bit the inside of her cheek to ground herself in the pain. It didn't help much. How could two humans in the middle of nowhere defeat an entity that had imprisoned so many people for *years*?

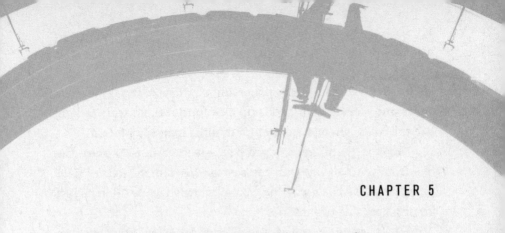

CHAPTER 5

Charges Accrued: Unauthorized Access to Nonpublic Computers

When Adda climbed down from the bunk, long after Iridian got up, pirates still slept in half the other beds in the dim room. She'd been up late checking the water tank for mics, moving her and Iridian's packs and environment suits down from the bunk room, assembling her workspace generator, and exploring the station's intranet. The minimal monitoring features she found on the pirates' own intranet were part of their server's initial installation. Either the pirates could handle whatever came at them, or knowing what was coming wouldn't save them.

She shuffled to the communal excretion area, as she called it to aggravate Iridian, then to the kitchen. The big woman who worked there, wearing what appeared to be an armored apron, watched her paw at the coffee urns for a few seconds before showing her how to coerce them into dispensing their treasure.

Iridian waved her over to a table where she, Pel, and a couple of men huddled over mugs. The one with the epicanthic folds at the corners of his eyes was Major O.D., though the insignia on his

T-shirt was a Z and a V. The major and Chato wore the same black shirts and jackets with hoods up. The four of them were talking like they'd known one another for months instead of hours.

To get to them, Adda edged past a woman in a ZV shirt, the one from the hallway with the scar on her temple. Rather than moving out of Adda's way, the woman scowled while Adda inched around her table toward Iridian.

When Adda bumped the woman's elbow, the woman slammed a mug down on the table beside her. Adda startled away, thumping into another table and bruising her hip. "Watch it, NEU." Iridian's gaze hardened into a warning. The hostile woman didn't move out of the way, but she didn't follow Adda to Iridian's table.

Iridian broke her glare to give Adda a quick kiss and pat the chair beside hers. She'd found herself a black hooded jacket, which had one gray sleeve and one black one, to combat the blue dust drifting off the ceiling. To Pel, she said, "Start from the beginning, and make some sense this time."

His coffee appeared black but contained a tablespoon of sugar, if he took it the way he did at home. "Okay. So this happened over a year ago, when the crew got stuck here. Captain Sloane wasn't captain then, it was, um . . ."

"Captain Foster," the major said.

"Yeah, that was it. So Captain Foster lured this ship to the station so AegiSKADA would ding it up a bit and the crew could clear it easy. That part worked, but then AegiSKADA shot down both of them." Then the two wrecks in the docking bay would be the first pirate ship and its target.

"They used to trick ships into flying through Barbary's turret range all the time," said Chato. "But you only have to fuck it up once."

They, not *we*. "Aren't you on the crew too?" Adda asked.

"We work for the ZV Group." Major O.D. pointed to the corresponding letters on his shirt. Even his comp glove was black with
the same yellow letters on the middle two knuckles. "Captain
Foster contracted for our services clearing out the ship she lured
here, but the ZV Group pays us. Private military company."

"Hired guns," Iridian translated.

"Only on leave." The major smiled with half his mouth. Chato,
Iridian, and Pel chuckled the way they did at crude jokes, although
Adda didn't get what was funny about that. She gulped coffee in
hopes of catching up.

"And the ZV Group left you in the cold and the black?" Iridian
asked.

O.D. shrugged. "They're still paying us. Same excuse as
Sloane's allies and the government militaries: no way they're putting their fleet up against AegiSKADA's turrets for the likes of us."

"Anyway, Captain Foster decided to fix the fuckup," Pel said.
"So she took a lieutenant, two squads of ZV soldiers, and all the
big guns, and went to find AegiSKADA's core."

What might "core" mean? The core, or center, of a space station's security system . . . He must have meant its supervisory
station, where administration controls were accessible, or where
its pseudo-organic tanks were kept.

"They knew where they were going when they left, so the only
thing they had to *find* was a path around the blocked hallways,"
Chato said. "The security control center's on the station map."

"Learn to tell a story or shut your head," said Pel. Chato simultaneously grinned and rolled his eyes in the expression everyone
developed within ten minutes of meeting her brother. "But yeah,
they found it all right. They got shot all to hell. Completely dead."
He leaned across the table. Dark wraparound lenses reflected
Adda's greasy red, purple, and blue-streaked hair. "They say

Foster's still in there, screaming eternally at AegiSKADA" for killing her."

Iridian intoned "Spooky," with several extra o's. "And how do we know they found the core?" She winked at Adda, which Adda interpreted as *Yes, I know that's not the right word.*

"The lieutenant got shot but didn't die," Pel said.

"Did you not just say everybody died?" Iridian asked, laughing.

"Fine, *practically* everybody. The lieutenant crawled to the fugee camp and told them everything. People say he survived, but if he did, he stays away from us."

"Captain Sloane is the other lieutenant?" asked Adda.

Pel sat back in his chair, his head turned almost, but not exactly, toward her. "How'd you know?"

"You said Foster brought 'a' lieutenant with her to AegiSKADA's control center, which suggests that there was more than one," Adda said. "The captain's the only person I'd expect everyone to follow." Major O.D. made an agreeing sort of grunt, and the unspoken *as opposed to Tritheist* had everyone glancing around to see if the current lieutenant was in earshot. Nobody spoke up to defend Tritheist's leadership capabilities. Sloane must have promoted him sometime after Captain Foster's death.

"Yeah, it makes sense when you put it like that," Pel said. "Anyway, we already asked the pilots to take us to Atlantis and drop us off, and they won't. Then some ZVs tried to make them take us, and got blown up with a missile, so we gave up on that. One guy built his own escape pod. That went boom as soon as it got into turret range. And nobody can sign into AegiSKADA's control systems."

"Haven't the fugees tried to get away on their own?" asked Iridian.

"What, you mean after their ship got so shot up during launch that they just docked it again?" Pel shrugged. "Far as I know, they haven't tried since."

"I heard a group of fugees took off in jumpsuits, back when they first came here and a lot of them were dying." Major O.D. shook his head. "Turret range starts about thirty meters off the hull, and the floating debris is bad out there. They were aiming for the near edge of the lead cloud, but none of them made it out."

Pel tossed a small packet of something that bounced off Adda's chest. Iridian handed it to her. "Oatmeal in a bag. It's great to have breakfast food for breakfast again. We had tuna twice a day for a while there."

After she ate and Pel and the major argued amiably about what cuisine was appropriate before noon, she asked, "Pel, can I speak with you in private somewhere?" She glanced at Iridian to see if she'd come too, but Iridian was miming a character in some vid game she played, while Chato laughed and described how the crew played it.

Adda led Pel back to her empty water tank. They settled on a couple of pillows she'd commandeered for the purpose, under the push lights on the wall near the ladder. "What happened to you? Why didn't you ask me for help instead of offering me a job? And why haven't you gotten your eyes fixed?"

"I forgot that 'talk to you in private' means yell at me," Pel huffed.

"I'm *not* yelling." That did sound a bit confrontational, so she said at a lower volume, "I'm just asking."

"Gods, that's a lot of stuff to ask." Behind the dark glasses, he looked guilty. "I don't know. I mean, the last thing I saw was the inside of the *Apparition*. And I didn't ask you to come right away because you were busy with school and it takes a miracle to get messages out."

"Isn't there a doctor here, or a surgery unit?"

"There's Zikri. He's kind of a doctor. And there's a medical team somewhere, but they're . . . weird. They couldn't do anything about my eyes. But, um, I wanted to ask: Is Dad still mad about all this?"

"He's . . . yes." Adda sighed. "We had a huge blowout about it when we got your message, and again when we got your money. He liked telling people you had a solid, legal, real working job when you were at the factory. It's not that he doesn't appreciate the money, because he does need it, but . . ."

"He wishes I got it some other way."

She might've been able to explain Pel's work in a way that would satisfy their dad. Fighting made both men miserable, and it took them weeks to reconcile on their own. It'd help if she could prove Pel earned his pay, instead of stealing it. "What do you do around here, exactly?"

He sprang up and started climbing out. "Let me show you. Come on!" And she followed him, because being blind on a space station under the control of an aggressive intelligence was bad enough without his sister ignoring him.

They walked to the main room, past a petite female ZV slumped against a table watching the others race vehicles around a lunar racetrack projected on one wall. If it were possible to look more dejected in the middle of shouting, armed gamers, she'd probably have managed it.

Pel approached a tall rectangular patch on a wall. He banged on it a few times, then slid a whole panel up in a rattle of interconnected slats. Before he did that, it looked like one solid piece. *Impressive design.*

"Hey, Sturm, have you met my big sister?" asked Pel.

Bright overhead lights that could have lit a garage or docking bay took up most of the closet-size space's headroom. Cold air reeking of chemicals and metal hit her eyes and made her squint as they stepped inside. Tools, scraps, and small machines Iridian would know by name and function lined the floor and walls, along with pieces of armor.

At a workbench along the room's back wall, a small old man with a short, round kufi cap brandished a handsaw. "Boy, Tabs will keep on moping and picking fights until her chest plate is repaired. Go bother Chef."

The unhappy ZV who was probably Tabs had looked up when the workshop door opened, but returned to the racing game when her armor didn't emerge with Pel and Adda. Tabs's short and curly hair was the same dark brown as the large ZV woman who gave Pel's arm a couple of hearty pats when he walked by. Now that Adda was looking, the women had the same beautiful brown eyes. Perhaps they were related, despite their extreme differences in build.

"Lots of one-syllable names," Adda said, following Pel around the corner to the hallway that led to the kitchen and her water tank.

"They like their nicknames. I didn't even have to tell them about Pel Mel, they figured it out all on their own."

"Is this what you do all day?" she asked. "Bother people while they work?"

"I provide entertainment!" he huffed. "This court needs a jester. Oh, where's Kaskade?"

He asked loudly enough that the woman in question poked her head around the corner. "Hi!" Kaskade's volume and cheer hurt Adda's brain this early in the morning. Even the streaks in her hair, which were a different shade than the blue that coated the walls, were overly bright just now. "I've got enough until I'm done working on the HUD in Tabs's armor. Ask me later, okay?"

Adda couldn't connect each letter of the acronym to a word, but Kaskade was probably referring to a helmet's interior faceplate display. If it required Kaskade's expertise, it was a software problem rather than a hardware one. The whole crew was either fixing the broken armor or distracting Tabs from being stuck in the compound. Despite Iridian's qualifications in both areas and Adda's interest in digital systems, nobody asked for their help.

"So, you run errands." That was the most positive way she could describe his activities.

"One of the *many* things I do around here." Pel was talking fast, inundating her with information to stop her from reaching inevitable conclusions. "Kaskade doesn't like Zikri, but she does like the crud he cooks from the fugees' med relief shipments. Somebody's gotta pick product up from Zikri when it's ready to use, and she doesn't want to deal with him, so I do. I like Zikri, personally. Oh, you haven't met him yet."

The rapid-fire introductions made Adda cringe. "These people need a way off the station. There has to be a way you can help with that."

"Doing what?" He waggled his dark glasses up and down his forehead, exposing, then hiding his scarred eyes. "If I walked into the station by myself, I'd be great drone bait."

Adda stalked toward her water tank and her workspace generator. Hearing him talk about himself like that made her heart hurt. Ordinarily she'd keep her observations to herself. Pel's life was his own, and he deserved autonomy to take responsibility for it.

Today, she'd tell him something he needed to hear. "I'm sure somebody needs something *useful* you can do. Ask around while I see how hard it's going to be to get us out of here. Which reminds me . . ." She turned, and he was still two steps behind her, trailing one hand along the wall. "Why haven't you sent one of the pilots out with a message to the Interplanetary Transit Authority? At least in prison they don't kill you on purpose."

"The fugees tried. ITA won't come. Even NGOs just launch boxes of crap at us from a safe distance and hope somebody catches them. After the war, nobody wants to risk their fleet going up against station turrets." The Near Earth Union and the secessionists had both declared victory when the war ended. It would have been more accurate to say they both lost. Pel grinned. "Captain Sloane told Fugee News to say that the turrets firing at other ships was the crew defending crew territory in Barbary's stationspace. Which, I mean, the crew really did shoot down some ships in stationspace back on Vesta! I guess it's hard to hold on to their Vestan base, so they have to keep looking tough even when they're stuck here."

That fiction had been propagated through a number of reliable sources Adda had consulted in preparation for coming here. She sighed. She'd done all the research she'd had time to do, but she was still stuck on Barbary Station, and already tired of it. The faster she circumvented the station's security intelligence, the faster they could all leave.

*　*　*

In her water tank, Adda shook blue dust out of her hair. Since the tank was suspended underneath the pirate compound, beneath the station's double hull, Iridian proclaimed it safe enough without the blue antiradiation coating. Adda kept forgetting to pull her hood over her head when she left the tank, and the blue stuff that covered the rest of the compound's ceiling and walls fell into her hair and shirt.

She piled pillows inside her workspace's noise-canceling canopy. Though the sides were transparent beneath a thick grid of black tracer lines, it did resemble a tent. Once she'd plugged her nasal implant jack and her comp into the main unit, she triggered the comp's countdown timer. If she spent five hours in a workspace, Iridian usually checked on her. When both of them forgot, Adda had headaches and nightmares. She placed a thin purple sharpsheet square on her tongue. While it dissolved, she inserted earbuds, which hissed pink noise and canceled out everything else.

Time to find out what I'm up against. As one of her professors used to say, *Zombie AI can't develop their own priorities, so give them yours.* If she got the intelligence to interact with her, she could *ask* it to stop. The pirates didn't have a workspace generator, so they couldn't have tried that.

She lay on her back and sealed the sound-resistant generator tent. After several seconds, the sharpsheet took effect and the generator's software accessed her neural implant net to draw her into a workspace. Her parents' house in Virginia, before the bombing, assembled around her.

The comp glove could render small parts of the programs she worked with, but interacting with the fragments limited her view of the system as a whole. The workspace software converted the concepts and commands into visual metaphors her brain processed quickly, naturally, and more effectively with the sharpsheets' help.

Sunlight patterned down through a large, high window. All six shelves of the bookshelf beside it were full of ancient paper books, many more than the tiny collection of books that her mother had maintained. Each book represented information on the station intranet's public front. Station administrators would be remarkably careless to leave a manual on the station's security intelligence sitting out on unprotected intranet, but she had to check. A spiral-bound stack of paper labeled *Employee Policies* might be helpful.

An orange glow with ragged gray-blurred edges swam over a plain black book's spine. The glow shrank into the words *Criminals and Criminology*. With dreamlike slowness, Adda pulled it from its shelf, blew the ensuing dust cloud away from her nose, and placed the book beside her bare feet.

Despite the carpet, the book landed with a sound like a massive gong struck with a hammer. Adda stilled, her hand hovering over the book. She hadn't set any alarms like that, so who had?

When she turned back to the bookshelf, a yellow eye stared out from its back panel, in the space where the book had been.

"Hello." She breathed slowly to keep her field of vision, already gently twisting left and right, from starting to spin in response to her excitement. It wasn't clear how well her biological functions carried through the workspace to the intelligence. Heart rates told a lot about humans. What conclusions AegiSKADA drew from hers was something else again.

"I'm looking for your occupant monitoring archives. I'm a friend. Everyone near me is too." She concentrated on the concept of a group of nonthreatening individuals with similar objectives and priorities. "We don't attack friends."

The eye didn't blink. Its pupil was a splotch of black liquid, asymmetrical and fraying into digital static at its edges. Adda reached into the bookshelf and pressed her fingertips to the top of the panel, above the eye. The titles on the other books' spines swam, cycling through numeric codes and names. The eye refocused on them. The human-to-AI translation software in her comp was hard at work.

"Look at me." She concentrated on how delighted she was to

meet a new intelligence. The eye's gaze flicked from one mental construct of household objects to the next, checking each one for signs of *her*. It was possible that no one had spoken to it in the four years since the station had been abandoned. If it understood what she'd said, it didn't agree with her.

AI played games with human minds. Her translator should protect her, but depending on what direction this intelligence's development took, the translator might be outmatched.

The risk raised her heart rate. The room rocked like a boat on stormy seas. The eye focused on her, confirming its access to biometric sensors. How many had the station's designers planted, recording every cardiac rhythm of humans within range? And where was the one recording hers, alone in an empty water tank?

She shut her eyes against the swinging room and concentrated on the second question. The rocking sloshed the contents of her stomach. Whispers in static too soft to interpret brushed across her arms and thighs. She thought she heard her name, and Pel's.

When she opened her eyes, a dark image flickered in and out of existence below the eye on the book spine. Orange specks of light near the top were probably the string of lights in the passage between the hulls.

Adda grinned. It was so satisfying to create an answer through the intensity of her question. The nearest sensor node was in the hull passage that led to the pirate compound. She didn't know what to do about that yet, but she'd think of something.

A cardinal peeped triumphantly outside the high window. The whispers faded to silence, and a hard, squared-off edge formed against her palm. She drew a paper book out of the bookshelf with the intelligence's eye in the center of the cover. The image of the space between the hulls flickered out.

Behind the workspace's hallucinations, her translator had convinced AegiSKADA that she was a temporary systems maintenance technician. That granted her the most basic levels of personal security aboard the station. Leaving so much of her identity open to the intelligence made her vulnerable, but she now claimed enough clearance to review its biometric database.

Millions of records swirled around her as dust motes in sunlight, with no archival procedure. AegiSKADA had recorded over a year of the pirates' heart rates, respiration, gait, words, and images, every move the pirates had made since they'd crashed in the docking bay below. As she watched, the intelligence accessed record after record that hadn't been significant enough for the workspace to render before. The workspace depicted each shining mote of information for only an instant, and then the eye on the book absorbed them.

The intelligence hadn't been accessing those records when she first applied the translator. Adda could only imagine AegiSKADA accessing the pirates' data this way in order to select targets for investigation or attack. If she had time to think, more reasons might occur to her. It was appalling that the intelligence had so much biometric data so readily available. None of the utilization scenarios she was coming up with had positive outcomes for Sloane's crew.

AI rarely gave humans enough time to develop viable plans of attack, and she couldn't just watch it work. Adda slammed her hand down over the eye to stop the transfer to its active memory. The home around her flickered, with red nothing behind it, as her software struggled to block AegiSKADA from records it was already accessing.

The eye widened and widened beneath her hand. It expanded past the borders of the book representing her software barriers between the intelligence and her personal system. The eye swelled to the width of the bookshelf, then the room, before Adda could draw her hand away. And it was focused on her.

The overwhelmed translator didn't interpret the angry digital buzz filling the workspace, but something was hunting her, had caught her scent in the red beyond the workspace's world. It was coming, and she had to *get out*.

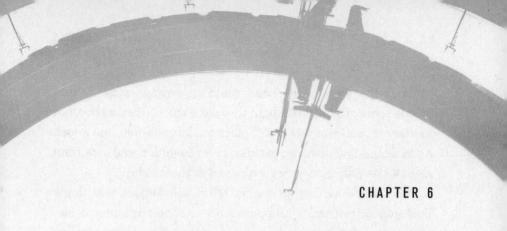

CHAPTER 6

Charges Accrued: Unlicensed Use of Military-Grade Shielding

The bunkhouse arrangement reminded Iridian of her army days, except then she'd had a schedule to follow and tasks to accomplish starting the moment she woke up. On Barbary Station, once Adda dragged herself out of bed and into her workspace generator, Iridian had to figure out what the hell this crew needed done and whether or not she could do it herself. The ZVs were working out in the common room when she wandered in. It'd feel good to put her muscles to use.

However, one of the two youngest members of the crew wanted something else. "*Ma*," the little guy said loudly while holding on to Iridian's pants at the knee to stay upright. Jalal looked four or five months older than the other ZV child, Xing's baby, Kimmy. Their parents must've been on chemical birth control instead of the implanted kind when they got stranded on the station. Every soldier Iridian knew, herself included, used chemical methods, even though they were less effective. Combat tended to illustrate the nasty ways implants could go wrong.

And the ways parenthood could go wrong, come to that. Maybe some of the ZVs thought they were stuck here for good, but Barbary Station was a hell of a place to start a family. She hoped Adda would find a way to get the crew off-station and safe from AegiSKADA before anything happened to these kids.

This boy's mother, grenadier Miria San Miguel, was doing push-ups with other ZV Group members. As Iridian pointed at San Miguel to redirect the kid, she spotted one other crew anomaly. The short, weedy man walked quickly across the common room, skirting the exercising ZVs. He brushed oily black hair beneath his hood away from his eyes. It fell back over them.

Iridian frowned. She'd been trying to talk to Si Po ever since Pel mentioned that he'd helped organize the crew's end of the *Prosperity Dawn* hijacking, but Si Po had been avoiding her. It didn't seem to be personal. He avoided everybody. None of the squads and small groups of friends among the crew made space for him to stand with them when he walked by, and he never stopped to push in.

Since he wore a dark blue one-sleeved, high-collared shirt instead of the ZV Group's black and yellow, he probably wasn't part of the private military company serving as the crew's muscle on their last operation. She had yet to see a ZV without a scrap of black or yellow on them, if only because of their company-issued comp gloves. Si Po must've been selected for a noncombat skill. His bare arm displayed no muscle definition, although it was covered in an intricate tattoo sleeve which could've camouflaged implants.

Iridian disengaged her pant leg from the toddler's fist and followed Si Po. The ZVs worked out two or three times a day, and she had yet to ask Si Po if he had any jobs that'd fit her. "Hey, where are you off to?"

He spun all the way around to face her, looking wary and in

need of a nose-hair trimmer. "I . . . it's time to send the ships out. The rovers took the fugees their supplies, so we're light again."

"Sign me up." AI was unpredictable, to Iridian if not to Adda, but Iridian could hold her own in a raid or a boarding party. That might be the kind of contribution Sloane's crew needed.

He smiled slightly and started walking again, close enough to the wall that he blocked the projections' multicolored lights. She took the offered space and fell into step beside him. "You can watch, I guess," he said.

She couldn't blame him for distrusting a new face. "Couldn't you use an extra pair of boots on deck?" With luck, Sloane's reputation for next to no body count was accurate. Iridian was willing and able to shield fellow crew members, but killing was something else. It was another reason she liked knives—they intimidated while being difficult to use by accident.

At a door across the hall from the lockside bunkhouse, he stopped to face her again. "I'm not getting on the ship. Nobody is."

"Say again?"

Si Po opened the door with his comp pressed to the ID pad beside it. Inside, an industrial 3-D printer, its thick semitransparent case stained and scored by use and lax cleaning, took up most of a small room. On the far wall, which slanted away from the door more on the right side than the left, a projector created a wide window to the cold and the black. The stars arched across the projection like whirling ice crystals in pure O_2, flickering as pieces of lead in the cloud passed between them and the station. Nothing shone exactly like stars.

"Where's the cam?" Iridian asked softly.

"Over Docking Bay Three. That's the one you came into." He tapped a mic symbol on the console. Above it, a red LED lit. "*Apparition*, it's Si Po. We need cargo."

He hit the mic button again, and the red light shut off. "Now I compress and encrypt it," he said. "If I don't, AegiSKADA intercepts, changes things, sometimes . . ." While Iridian shuddered at that possibility, he tapped the console. "And broadcasts it right into the hangar."

"How long does it take the pilots to launch your ships?" she asked

Si Po's mischievous grin was nothing like the embarrassed smiles she'd surprised on him up to now. "Those aren't our ships. They were all either in stationspace or docked when we got shot down. I think they were supposed to have been broken down before the Battle of Waypoint, but that didn't happen, obviously. They have nanorepair, and the bots do the heavy lifting. We help some, mostly approving dock activities in the system, since we're trying to keep AegiSKADA's attention off them as much as we can. In exchange, we taught them to catch other ships. Well, I did." He tilted his head back a little and his smile widened, deservedly proud of turning civilian pilots into ship-jacking pirates.

"And you haven't sampled their nanorepair cultures to fix up this place?"

Si Po shrugged. "How? Sturm tried once, but it didn't take, and we didn't see the ships for a couple of weeks, after. It wasn't worth it when we can do most of the work ourselves. Here we go." He pointed to the exterior cam view of the starscape she'd been admiring.

Even though the *Apparition* had been out in the cold and the black when Si Po sent the recording, the pilot must've gotten his message. The *Apparition* sailed out from above the cam and into its range, filling the projected window. The only time Iridian had seen the *Apparition*'s exterior was when they'd arrived at Barbary Station. With the decompression alarms blaring, she hadn't had time for a thorough examination. After the long, narrow interior she, Adda, and Reis had ridden in, she'd imagined the *Apparition* as a lean gunship.

The ship outside the window looked like a gunship had collided with a tug and stuck. The *Apparition* was asymmetrical, with jagged angles and a haphazard scattering of missile launchers. Its precise, economical movements suggested a talented human pilot partnered with decent AI. The pilot even kept up with the cam's position, without any wavering or wobbling.

One side of the wall projection filled with a blast of data. The *Apparition* disappeared into the stars on the other half, vanishing as the cam spun away from it.

"That's it!" said Si Po. "She may call one of the other two for help if she catches something big. After they break into the databases to get ships' routes, they spoof ITA inspection signals to get them to stop long enough to disable them. At least, that's what I taught them to do. They don't give me any details when they come back." He adjusted something else on the console. Iridian had last seen that console in the foreground of Pel's messages to Adda.

Much as it made Iridian's skin crawl, Adda would love pilots who flew in such tight tandem with AI. It'd be fun to introduce her. "So who are these people doing the grunt work?"

Si Po stopped tapping and flicked his fingers to sweep his last couple of inputs off the backlit screen that formed the angled top of the console. "Earther pilots," he said. "From Russio-China. Very bad English, and we don't have translation software that handles combo languages."

If combo language translators were a low priority, then everybody making the software decisions was a spacefarer. Earthers were happy to mix any language into English or Chinese, and treated English like the mutt language it was. The existence of combined languages didn't appear to disgust him, so he didn't hail from too far into the colonies.

"The pilots any good, usually?" Iridian asked. "The one who flew the *Apparition* here spun us like tops when she undocked from the *Prosperity Dawn*."

"Of course they're good." Her suggestion left Si Po looking half-scandalized, half-amused. "Only the best on this crew."

"And you're the best at what, conning people into saving pirates from killer AI?" Iridian grinned as he literally backed away from her. "I'm trying not to hold it against you, but you've got to admit, it's not working out well for me and Adda so far."

"I just . . ." Si Po peered at her face for a moment, then nodded like he was satisfied with whatever he saw there. "Pel kept talking about how great his sister would be against the AI, and Captain Sloane and I couldn't even slow AegiSKADA down. All Foster tapped me to do was crack a megacorp subsidiary bank account once we got some info off the target ship. This AI stuff is way over my head. Pel said Adda would fix it. He'd do the talking, if I could get his messages to you and send the ships where he said to." Si Po had the good grace to look ashamed. "I believed him. I had to believe something."

A muffled whump followed by a much louder crash reverberated through the base. Si Po shrieked and belly flopped into the corner where the sloping ceiling met the floor.

"What was that?" Iridian demanded.

He wrapped his arms around his head and yammered in Kuiper Belt spacefarer cant. She ducked into the lockside bunkhouse across the hall for her shield, then sprinted toward the common room.

An ungainly half spin kept her from running into Tritheist

and Captain Sloane as they emerged from the captain's state-room. Sloane was pulling on a gold-colored shirt that somehow appeared more regal than garish, while Tritheist did up his pants. "Damage check, right gods-damned now!" the lieutenant bellowed. Another concussive blow shook the base beneath their feet and loosed a cloud of blue dust from the ceiling.

Captain Sloane watched Iridian through it. The bright white smile the captain flashed showed far too many teeth. "Your lion roars. Will you hunt it?"

"Uh, yes, sir." Figuring out what roaring thing Captain Sloane was talking about was less important than finding whatever had blown up. With luck the loud noise was what made her ears pop, because the alternative was pressure and atmo loss. She pushed her way through a crowd of shouting pirates in front of the home-ward bunkhouse to get to Adda's empty water tank.

Adda's head and shoulders were already through its trapdoor. "AegiSKADA. It sent something here. I thought it was using hallu-cinographics to scare me off, but it sent something *real*." The off-kilter monotone voice meant that Adda still had twenty or thirty minutes before her last dose of concentration drugs wore off.

Iridian finally remembered what a lion was: a predator so big that it ate anything it laid eyes on. "The AI blew something up. You still got all your pieces?" Adda nodded shakily. "Go back down and grab the enviro suits." Once Adda handed them up, Iridian helped her into the hall. The whole place rumbled. "Get into yours, but don't seal it." They'd yet to find a refilling station, so the suits' O_2 tanks were nearing empty.

Blue dust drifted off the walls and ceiling, dark beneath the orange lights strung along the walls. Iridian's breath drew it, dry and gritty, up her nose, over her tongue, and down her throat. At least the particles felt too big to get into her bloodstream through lung tissue. She tugged her jacket hood farther over her eyes.

The dust stopped falling straight down and drifted into the homeward bunkhouse. Cold calm swept over her, even as her heart beat faster. A subaudible rumble continued after the initial shaking ended. The sound alone could shake bolts free and put them in a worse situation than what the air current meant: *atmo leak.*

The yelling from the crowd around the bunkhouse resolved into, "Xing, Alexov, get out of there, get out!"

"Sir, which way is the front line from here?" Iridian shouted at Major O.D., the first person she saw who looked like he might know.

The major smiled in a mix of incredulity and admiration. "Outside." He pointed up. "And we don't have combat-ready walking clothes anymore. Nothing we can do unless it punches through."

Adda's and Iridian's enviro suits would pressurize, but they weren't armored. "Great," Iridian muttered. Another explosion jolted the hallway. It was weaker than the first, maybe farther from base. She pressed through the crowd toward the bunkhouse, avoiding several bare blades and armored elbows. If the bunkhouse was the site of the first explosion, then it sure as hell wasn't safe to stand around in. "Xing, come on, get out of there!" she shouted.

Two voices, one male, one female, screamed something back. She hoped the repetitive screeching in the background wasn't Xing's baby crying.

Another blast shook the base. Wind dragged at her, like a huge hole had been torn in the bunkhouse. Everybody in the hallway lurched and staggered. The white towel over the door tore off and vanished into the dark beyond the bunkhouse doorway. The voices inside disappeared beneath the roar of escaping atmo.

The air was clear of blue dust, except for a thin stream drawn through the doorway. Kaskade and Chato were already on the floor. Between the press of the crowd and the high wind, someone was bound to fall into the bunkhouse. And at this rate of atmo loss, there wasn't much out there to land on.

As the wind shoved Iridian in that direction too, she deployed her shield. The wind caught it and pulled her toward the bunkhouse even harder. The shield's matte gray frame trembled but locked open. She turned it sideways to slam it across the bottom half of the door and dropped to one knee. The shield jammed her arm hard into her shoulder joint, but her weight kept the frame in place. If that didn't stop someone from falling through, she could catch them from there.

Adda tumbled to the floor next to her a moment later, lips moving behind her enviro suit hood's faceplate as she subvocalized to her comp. "What're you doing?" Iridian yelled over the wind.

"Somebody pushed me," shouted Adda. A glimpse of very short black hair in the crowd behind her told Iridian that the somebody was the secessionist sergeant.

A string of orange lights ripped off the ceiling and blew into the bunkhouse, leaving the hallway in shadow. Several people carried the palm weapons the welcoming party had held when she and Adda had arrived on-station. According to Chato, their cobbled-together "palmers" required a battery for power and overheated easily, but they didn't punch holes in the hull. All she had to watch out for was getting shot in the back.

Captain Sloane and a large male ZV ran out of the mess hall, carrying a table between them. The additions to the crowded hallway made Kaskade, who'd almost gained her footing, fall against the shield on the other side of Iridian from Adda. As the captain approached, Iridian shoved Adda and Kaskade back into the crowd, then threw herself to one side and took the shield with her. The metal table Sloane and the ZV carried clanged into place vertically over the bunkhouse doorway.

The wind died. Blue dust drifted straight down over Sloane's crew. Chef stood in the mess hall doorway and sobbed. The ZVs stared, stunned, at the upturned table.

Captain Sloane straightened the gold shirt, now streaked with blue dust, and surveyed the miserable crew. "Sturm, Iridian, get a torch and some scrap and weld this on."

"What about Xing and Alexov and Kimmy?" Pel asked from the common room, his voice a higher pitch than usual.

Adda stood, but before she could make her way through the crowd to him, Rio, the biggest spacefarer Iridian had ever seen, enveloped him in her massive muscled arms and pulled him against her ZV shirt in a sympathetic embrace. "They're gone, Pel Mel. They're gone." Rio's voice broke over the last word.

Iridian rotated her arm front to back, elbow bent to minimize the chances of breaking a nose in the crowded hall. Now that her adrenaline level was dropping, her shoulder hurt. This was why the military put shields on twenty-one-ton mechanized Infantry Shield Vehicles instead of relying on human joints.

She twisted her wrist to collapse the shield, grateful for all the design time she'd spent on the frame. The lowest-bid model given to government infantry everywhere was impossible to deploy and stow quickly. Cheapness got people killed, but her mech-ex graphene design had saved Adda and Kaskade today. Iridian ought to have earned some points with the crew for that.

"Gods . . ." What else could she say?

The pirates around her nodded. "At least there weren't any spiderbots," the ZV medic, Zikri, said. "We'd have been real well fucked then."

She'd never expected this to be a safe job, but she did expect more warning before shit went down. Whatever surveillance system the crew had in place should've seen this coming, so clearly she couldn't count on it. Perched in this ramshackle base on the outside of the station, the pirates were exposed and unprepared. She followed Sturm to the common room and his workshop.

Pel had claimed that they were safe from drones on base. "Does this happen often?" she asked Sturm.

He shook his head. "They stay in the station. Never had a drone hit the base before."

"So it was definitely one of AegiSKADA's drones?" Iridian asked.

"If we had ordinance that could do that, or anything else volatile, for that matter, we wouldn't store it where people sleep." Emotion roughened Sturm's voice as he answered, and he didn't say any more.

Sturm stacked pieces of scrap metal into Iridian's arms, adding rhythm to enraged screaming from the corridor. The screamer's masculine voice was deeper than Pel's. Several pirates loudly lamented the loss. After spending so long in such tight quarters, people made close friends. And losing an infant, one of only two children this crew had with them . . . She couldn't imagine that pain.

After that kind of loss, she expected to feel inspired to protect the pirates, the way she had when her convoys passed habitats on mined roads. Those people didn't deserve to be trapped in their habs, afraid to cross the street because part of it might explode. The Shieldrunners disarmed the bombs so military vehicles could pass safely, but knowing the locals could move without fear confirmed that Iridian's unit was in the right place, doing the right thing. She'd loved that.

Now she only imagined what Adda would suffer if she lost

Pel. Iridian couldn't let an AI stop the three of them from earning a life together.

Iridian and Sturm hauled the scrap metal and tools to the hallway, where the crew backed off to give them room to work. Although she was pretty sure she saw what needed doing, she followed Sturm's lead as they shored up the patch. "So have you given any thought to why the drones don't just blow this place right off the fucking hull?" she asked as they worked.

"I take it you haven't placed your bet yet," Sturm said. When Iridian shook her head, he added, "Board's in the digital library if you're wanting to wager. My money's on the drone printer being busted beyond repair. If it can't print more, it'll be stingy with what it has, yeah?"

"Seems reasonable." Iridian turned her head away while Sturm welded a chunk of metal she was holding in place. The acrid hot metal scent was calming, given the topic at hand. The crew could still fight back. "You don't think the AI's just fucking with you?"

The torch shut off and Iridian turned back in time to see Sturm nod. "That's what Si Po and Kaskade think. They've got a few on their side too, because the attacks seem random. I don't expect it's smart enough to play, myself."

"What does the captain think?"

"That it's using us the way we used to use it. We bring a lot of resources to the station. And those ships we take . . . They get taken apart. Some of them go to repair ours and shore up this place." Sturm swept his hand in front of him to reference the whole base. "Not all of it's used for that, though. We don't know where the rest goes, but it goes somewhere. Barbary was a shipbreaking station first, you know. It's still got to have something to keep this station going." Sturm shook his head. "AegiSKADA's a security AI, though. It wouldn't care about all that."

After thirty minutes of work, the table felt like it'd stay braced against the damaged bunkhouse's doorway without dragging half the wall into the cold and the black. Iridian's next most dangerous problem was currently talking with some despondent ZVs in the common room.

Sergeant Natani, the secessionist officer with the scar with whom Iridian had had a run-in when they arrived on-station, had probably pushed Adda toward the collapsing bunkhouse. But even Adda lacked proof of that. It could've been an accident.

With Natani's whole unit around her, outright accusation would start a fight Iridian couldn't win. Typical secessionist tactics: hit anonymously at opportune moments, then run to a crowd who shouted alibis that made the attacker look like the victim. And if their first assault wasn't effective, they *always* found a second opportunity.

Iridian had to get out of the room before she did something violent. "Si Po sent a ship out just before the attack," she told Sturm. "The next catch might have hard suits."

The old man wiped sweat from his eyes. "Where is that fool? Cowering as far from danger as he can get, I expect."

Coward or not, Si Po had been pale, shaking, and sweating after the first explosion, and high blood pressure and hypergrav combined badly. Without him, only Adda and the other codehead, Kaskade, would be left to keep the pirates' systems running. And Adda had bigger problems to solve.

The captain was with Si Po in the room with the window, printer, and computer console. "Damn. Can you try a different frequency?"

Si Po was on his feet, which was encouraging so far as his physical health went. His body language was as compressed and twitchy as ever. "The forty ticks shuttle to and from the hub has never been hit before." Signs in the docking bay below the base put the pirates twenty-three ticks from the docking bay which served as station north at 100/0. That was the point where the increments that divided the station into one hundred virtual cross-level slices started over at one. The shuttle was closer to forty-six ticks, over a third docking bay, if the symmetric modular layout continued all the way around the station. Ring station points of reference were much easier to follow with a mobile map. A more helpful station AI would've been nice too. "The shuttle's a blind spot," said Si Po.

"Is someone missing?" Iridian asked.

Captain Sloane turned to her with meticulously shaped eyebrows raised. "What might you do if they were?"

"I can play hero." She pointed her thumb over her shoulder toward where her shield hung on her jacket's hook between her shoulder blades.

Si Po winced. "Bad idea. I'm switching to the farm comms." He poked some icons on the console.

Iridian shifted from foot to foot, still riding the biochemical aftereffects of almost getting blown up. "Who is it, a fugee, crew? Or one of the pilots?" If the pilots spoke a language the pirates didn't translate and only communicated with Si Po, then they probably didn't qualify as crew.

Captain Sloane smiled slightly. "The station's original human tenants."

A woman's voice enunciated precisely, "Yes? What?" from one of the console's speakers.

Si Po startled so hard his hand slapped down next to, but not on, the red call-end icon. "Dr. Williams? It's Si Po, over at Captain Sloane's base."

"How you are doing?" Sloane asked.

"Traded with the fugees for cold-weather gear. Appreciated. No other weather than cold, in the dark," the doctor continued in her precise enunciation. "You're asking like you've had a scare."

"We were attacked," said Captain Sloane. "We wanted to make certain—"

"That we're alive and prescribing? Ha! As if we have drugs to prescribe," said Williams. "My canned apricots for more pharmaceutical printer spools. Apricots!" It sounded like the doc couldn't print medicine, but a least she wasn't starving. Her priorities made Iridian smile.

Once the mic was off, Sloane sighed, grimacing slightly at the console like there'd been vid feed with the audio. "The Spacelink medical team are our friends on the inside, as it were, with high-level access throughout the station. They're the only people the AI believes are allowed to be here."

"Spacelink, Captain?" Iridian asked, in case Sloane knew something about them that Adda didn't.

"The shipbreaking company that built this place," said Si Po.

Captain Sloane nodded. "After what historians now call the Battle of Waypoint Station—which, you'll note, Spacelink and its NEU allies lost—the station's medical team was left behind here and became isolated in the residential module. Sometimes they reach the fugee camp, and we've seen them on the station's surface. The remaining four have survived here for years. I'm not hiring you as an ambassador. If you want a place on my crew, you'll have to do something I don't already have somebody doing."

Elsewhere in the base, Sergeant Natani shouted above several other pirates. "You can't take the legs off without pulling the whole table down. Find an ax or something." Iridian breathed in slowly and exhaled even more slowly. That improvised patch was weak enough without somebody taking an ax to it. If one of the higher-ranked crew didn't stop Natani soon, Iridian would.

"Captain, what exactly do you need an NEU soldier on this crew to do, if you don't mind me asking?" Iridian's voice was almost under control, but Sloane still refocused on her with an expression of unspoken warning. Although she wanted to ask how the captain expected to escape the station with a secessionist crew willing to risk only lives that weren't theirs, she didn't. There was no way to ask that respectfully, and Sloane had killed Reis for making a barely credible threat. Frustration clenched her jaw tight.

"As you said yourself, the war is over." The captain's mocking smile promised consequences if Iridian argued. "If you're not already looking for opportunities to strike significant blows against the AI, I suggest you start."

Iridian kept her expression neutral and squashed an urge to break a few of the captain's perfect teeth. The AI was the real enemy, but Sergeant Natani wasn't going to let up. On this station, the war had never ended.

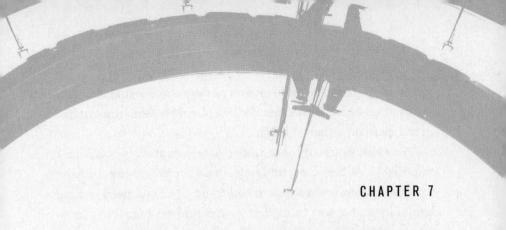

CHAPTER 7

Charges Accrued: Illegal Surveillance

"There's no way I'm going to be able to identify the process I need from the outside," Adda said.

She gripped Iridian's hand and thumped her forehead on Iridian's sturdy collarbone. That rocked her girlfriend back into the pillow nest that had developed in and around the workspace generator. Without the second bunkhouse, sleeping space was in high demand. The two of them had moved into the water tank. The pump flow from the working tanks on either side took some getting used to.

Whatever team had created AegiSKADA had been thorough about teaching the intelligence to protect itself from prying minds. The moment she'd made progress toward accessing its higher functions, it had attacked. She wrapped her arms over her chest and one shoulder. A family had *died* because her "progress" threatened the intelligence. And to stop it, she'd have to interact with it again. Its actions were its creators' responsibility, but gods, the risk . . . That was hers.

It had to know she'd survived. Now they watched each other,

waiting for a mistake. And since its power source would last thousands of years and it commanded a replaceable robot army, it had much more time than she did.

"You always figure these things out, even the ones that look impossible." When everything else was overwhelming, Iridian's voice and hug were warm and comforting. "All you need is a vulnerability and a way to exploit it, and I mean, I wouldn't know where to start. I tried to join a raid and it turned out they just need the ships' pilots for that. If we're counting on my contributions to win us a place, well . . . Let's not."

The relationships Iridian was building among the crew were more of a contribution than she'd admit. Perhaps she didn't even realize that making friends who would defend them was one of the essential steps of joining the crew, a step only she could complete. Iridian made people trust her without even thinking about it, but her inability to do even more to secure their new positions would bother her no matter what Adda said. Adda turned her head to kiss Iridian's neck, and Iridian held her tighter.

A pump in a water tank next to theirs powered on, and the wall lights flickered a bit like the image that had flickered in the workspace just before she discovered the biometry database. "The sensor nodes!" She wriggled out of Iridian's arms and stood still while the tank shifted and creaked. "I need to plug into one, or catch one's feed."

"Whoa, wait, isn't that like saying, 'Here I am, please blow me up'?" Iridian propped herself up on an elbow, one thick eyebrow raised. "That's after walking halfway across the station, mind. Have you heard the pirates talk about those drones? There are supposed to be ones almost too small to see. And ones big enough to end you. The pirates say whenever you see a little one, the big ones are coming."

Adda should've kept Iridian better informed about her efforts to map the intelligence's sensors throughout the station, but that would've meant stopping her work to explain. "I wish I could hijack one of the drones. . . . I probably couldn't do it before it got out of range, though, and that would definitely activate AegiSKADA's self-protection procedures. I should watch them the next time they come near us. They don't seem to have a regular path or schedule, but they do move intentionally." Adda registered Iridian's appalled expression and spoke fast to get to a part she'd like better. "We don't have to cross half the station to find a node. There were what, ten people sleeping in the bunkhouse in addition to Xing's family when AegiSKADA attacked? That was no coincidence." Remembering the cascade of biometric data accesses right before the attack made her shudder. "It's profiling us and tracking our number and location with sensors somewhere nearby. I think I know where."

* * *

She persuaded the captain with the same argument. In under an hour, she and Iridian stood before the large, sealed hatch down to the station interior. "The reason we aren't covered in drones in here is that the crew keeps this damned thing closed," Iridian muttered. "I kind of hate to open it."

"I'll be as fast as I can," said Adda.

Iridian hauled the hatch open, her expression determined and wary. "Please do."

They let themselves down the ladder, finding each rung with their boot before putting weight on it to avoid a fifteen-meter fall in heavy gravity. Iridian reached up and pulled the hatch shut. "Let's hope they don't lock us out. Wouldn't blame them, with all these bots around, but they'd sure as hell better let us back in."

Once they reached the ladder's end, they crept through the wall passage that paralleled the docking bay. Since Adda's comp had the better projector, she went first to light the way beneath the dim orange light string overhead. A panel on the right, closer to the docking bay's inner wall, looked different from the others.

Cam lenses could be minuscule, but they had to get power from somewhere. AegiSKADA's cams would point into the docking bay. The back end embedded in the interior of the two hulls should be bigger to allow for recording and processing equipment, as well as other sensors. That was what she was looking at: the back of a sensor node housing. It was farther up the wall than standard placement called for, wired into one of the large power trunks tied above their heads to make room to walk.

No lens pointed into the wall. The node would record noise and vibration, at minimum. If this was the one that'd sensed her in her tank, the sensitivity was amazing. The compound had a hollow floor in places, and that'd help it work, but something else in the compound might be recording and digitally amplifying input AegiSKADA would find particularly useful.

At worst, this node compiled subvocalized half thoughts into a profile that the intelligence would use to hunt her and Iridian down if it didn't find a way to kill them now. She shuddered and slowly exhaled. Either way, the intelligence would prioritize input coming from this node.

Iridian, who had apparently identified what Adda was looking at on her own, since Adda forgot to point it out to her, knelt on the grimy floor and patted her own shoulder. Adda climbed onto Iridian's shoulders and leaned on the wall with her free hand while holding her comp to the sensor node.

The comp flashed its visual Trojan, though that'd be useless without the cam pointing toward it, along with a coded rhythmic buzz against her hand and an electronic tweet. At least one of the commands she encoded in the other two inputs might compromise AegiSKADA's defenses when it accessed the recording. Unless it was a very weak system, she wouldn't gain administrative control that way, though her programs would make the attempt.

That was the only aggressive action she was taking, though. She didn't want to risk another attack on the compound's exterior by antagonizing the intelligence. Instead she'd try to get her own code into the system at the points where AegiSKADA accepted, analyzed, or stored data. Any additional access would help her determine what information AegiSKADA had, its priorities and value structure, and what she could use to trick it or convince it to stop treating the people on the station like threats.

Something skittered over metal in shadows too deep for the orange light string's reach. Adda froze in place. *Curse all the gods and devils, AegiSKADA brought me here.*

This wasn't the closest sensor node to her position in the tank when she'd asked that question. It was just the most accessible one. AegiSKADA had successfully tested a method of getting her to move to a place of its choosing, and now it had data that'd make identifying and tracking her as an individual much easier. She had gotten her answer quickly because the intelligence *gave* it to her, and now its drone was between them and the ladder back to the compound. The skittering thing crept closer. Adda gasped, loud in the narrow space.

Her boots slipped off Iridian's shoulders and pulled Iridian's jacket tight around her throat. Iridian freed herself and caught Adda before she did more damage than tearing her sleeve and scraping her elbow on something that stuck a centimeter out from the wall. Pain lanced up Adda's arm, and she did not want to leave blood where AegiSKADA could find it. She clamped her gloved hand over her elbow. Wetness seeped through the glove's breathable fabric as she ran for the ladder.

Her palm left a dark print on the first rung she grabbed. Better to leave a little of her DNA than all of it. Iridian's boots pounded behind her. The drone she'd heard was small. She could climb faster than it could. At least, she hoped so.

When they burst through the hatch at the top of the ladder, Pel stood at the other end of the entryway, near where he'd waited when they first arrived. Behind pink-tinted goggles, the white scar tissue made his eyes look like an insect's. The hatch slammed and he turned his head more fully in their direction. "What happened?"

"Just poking the AI with a virtual stick," Iridian said, and Adda blinked up at her in surprise, because she sounded genuinely angry. Iridian caught her looking. "What the hell was the point of that? Why didn't we smash that node thing?"

"Because you don't throw away a tool you could use in the future. If what I sent AegiSKADA doesn't take, the node needs to be functional so I can try something else. Disinfectant?" Despite how out of breath she was, her question sounded surprisingly calm. Surely the cut wasn't bad enough to send her into shock.

Her torn sleeve felt damp against her skin. A patch around the elbow and a line down her arm and over her glove were dark. The rest was sweat-soaked from her sprint up the ladder. The wound was bleeding that much and it hadn't even started to hurt yet.

Iridian wrapped an arm around her waist and gently pulled her into the main room. "Where's the medic?" she demanded of the gathering crowd.

The people standing around watching got out of Pel's path toward the kitchen. "Zikri?" said one of the pirates with an endless supply of black shirts. "He's sleeping." The woman's surname was San Miguel, maybe.

"You two gonna get yourselfs kilt," said one of the colonial ZV soldiers. The arm around Adda's waist tensed. She nudged Iridian with her hip to show that the man didn't scare her, since knowing that sometimes calmed Iridian down.

Adda's cut elbow was beginning to ache. Her investigation had already cost lives. It would be irrational to expect herself to emerge unscathed. Pel returned with a red box with a white cross on the lid, trailed by Chef, wiping her hands on a dish towel, before Adda could be expected to respond to the ZV who'd spoken.

As usual, Iridian had a response ready, and didn't wait for Adda to finish musing to deliver it. "With people like you watching our backs, what do we have to worry about?" Even with Iridian's smile, her tone was too sharp for anyone to take the statement as a joke. She might have gotten over leaving the sensor node intact, but she was still angry.

Sergeant Natani stood from the crate she'd been using as a stool. The oldest ZV soldier (who went by Death as a name), Chato, a pushy white ZV Pel had said was named Vick, a big ZV wearing a cap, and another scowling ZV female all stood with the sergeant. Iridian stalked forward to meet them. Pel froze halfway through handing the first aid kit to Adda.

"If you people don't know what you're doing with that AI, maybe you shouldn't get good folks killed doing it," said Vick from just behind Natani.

"And if you people didn't know what you were doing with an AI, maybe you shouldn't have let it fight your battles for you. You want to call it in to fight me too? I've been on a gods-damned colony ship for weeks. I need to get my station muscle back." Iridian's shield still hung collapsed between her shoulder blades. With her knees slightly bent and her arms raised in a loose boxer's guard, she looked too skilled with her fists to need it. But

Natani and Vick carried the same palm weapons that had killed Reis.

Adda slowly reached out to relieve Pel of the first aid kit. Once he was out of harm's way, she'd try to calm Iridian down. Even during AegiSKADA's attack on the bunkhouse, he hadn't looked this frightened.

When she took the kit, he inhaled like he was waking from a nightmare. He brushed past Iridian and bounced off a ZV's chest. The big man righted him and he ran, bumping into tables he'd avoided earlier with ease. Everyone in the main room watched him go.

Iridian slowly straightened out of her combat stance. For a second her hands curled like talons, until her fists completely unclenched. "I figure we all have something to run from," she said. Adda relaxed, a little. Iridian was thinking again, which meant that she wouldn't release the pressure she was under through violence.

The ZVs looked from Pel's path of retreat to Iridian. Several of them nodded in grim agreement and drifted back to their former positions in the main room. When even Vick stopped watching for a brawl, Natani followed her supporters, muttering in spacefarer cant. In the middle of the sergeant's muffled tirade, Adda caught the phrase "Yeah, NEU, you'll run too."

Pel might appreciate thanks for defusing the situation, unintentional as that had been. *Or maybe he'd be embarrassed for having run away.* The best thing Adda could do for him was keep him alive, whatever AegiSKADA's intent. Although she'd never be able to concentrate while Iridian was antagonizing armed pirates. "What'll you do now, Iri?"

Iridian frowned at the blood on Adda's arm. "Get that cleaned up, first. Then I'll see what Sturm's working on, or what Tabs and

Rio are up to. There's gotta be something worth doing around here." That sounded safe enough.

After Iridian disinfected and bandaged Adda's arm, she crossed the main room to Sturm's workshop while Adda returned to the empty water tank. Descending the ladder hurt her cut elbow, as did every step of her preparations to enter the generator. By the time she set her timer, drugged herself, and achieved the level of calm and concentration required to stabilize a workspace, AegiSKADA's sensor data was waiting for her.

It worked.

She had so little information on the system that she wouldn't have been surprised if AegiSKADA had defended itself from her code insertion. Not only was her comp displaying the biometrics data stream, it was copying from AegiSKADA's system as the intelligence received it, with almost no delay. That was good, since she and the pirates lacked the intelligence's storage capacity.

Now, for the best part: unwrapping the data through analysis, to see what new methods she might have to affect the intelligence's behavior. And since her inserted code copied information as it passed instead of intercepting it, AegiSKADA shouldn't notice what she was doing. It'd have no new reasons to attack Sloane's crew.

She sank into the workspace. Once, she'd visited a morgue with dingy white walls and floors like these. The water tank's cold air translated into the workspace. A faint odor of formaldehyde permeated the hallucinographic laboratory.

None of the processes whipping through the hallucinographic air around her indicated a direct response to unexpected information dispersal. AegiSKADA really couldn't tell that she was watching, which was wonderful, but she had to organize the data before she could analyze it.

Her subconscious added insects pinned to an infinitely long row of black velvet pads that sat on an infinitely long steel table along one tiled wall of the room. Rectangular windows stretched the infinite length of the room above the pinned bugs. Even though the windows looked like glass, she cast no reflection in them, just like the projected ones in space habitats. In the gray-purple mist on the other side of the not-glass, a dark shape moved. It was larger than a human, but too far from the white overhead lights to identify.

Weirder imagery was to be expected when using expired sharpsheets. Her sharpsheets' expiration date had passed weeks ago, and now she was stuck in space with no deliveries.

Since she couldn't order more sharpsheets, she'd have to make the equivalent herself later. Breaking out her chemistry kit on the station of the richest pirates in the galaxy was not part of her original plan, but it was time to plant the psilocybin spores she'd brought as backup. She'd need fresh ingredients to stay in the workspace generator long enough and think quickly enough to outmaneuver an AI.

For now, she had to make the best use of the expired sharpsheets she had and focus on what was happening in the workspace. Ideally the insects, not the odor or the mist beyond the windows, represented her data. She approached the first display board. A white lab coat's hem swished around her thighs. It felt nice not to have a sweatshirt hood overheating her head and pressing on her ears. After they left this blasted station, she'd never wear another hood or hat.

The insects' wings twitched once, in unison. It happened so fast she could have imagined it, if she weren't watching for oddities.

When her fingertips brushed the cool stainless-steel table on which the display boards sat, the insects tore free from their pins. Fragments of chitin littered the velvet. A writhing, living ball of them hovered over the table. She stepped back to avoid its edges, nose wrinkling at their sour, earthy scent. A picture—no, vid projection, it moved—formed in the cloud of tiny insects. Shapes stuttered in and out of view, some representing humans, or parts of them, nothing she could interpret. It was projected from within, since she had no comp glove at the moment, only bright pink latex ones.

She concentrated hard on her goal. *I need to see.*

The records scrolling over the flying insects were biometrics data she'd intercepted. Useful for determining what AegiSKADA knew about them, but none led to an administrative log-in, and she needed to rule that out first. *Why waste time trying to trick or destroy an intelligence when I could just tell it what to do?*

The bugs rained down over their pins, dead again. Another display of insects roiled to life farther down the table. She walked to it, brushing at a crawling sensation on her arm that turned out to be the raggedly-cut bandage.

Thousands of gnats swirled around one another above the second velvet-covered board. They flitted in an illusion of random motion. Due to the workspace generator's nature, their movement maintained some underlying order. They also served as surfaces for projecting an old-style log-in screen. This time a projector somewhere behind Adda lit the swarm with a stark white square of light, which undulated in ways a projection on a flat surface definitely wouldn't.

A blinking line marked where text would appear when users spoke, in the center of the white box as design standards had called for. Dark blue text invited the user, Adda in this case, to log in to "HarborMaster," not AegiSKADA.

That sounded like a separate control system. If AegiSKADA's designers had predicted someone sending their own intentions through the sensors, Adda would never have gotten this far in. Was HarborMaster the station's native control system, overwritten or supplanted by AegiSKADA? It might be easier to confirm this system's connection to AegiSKADA if she reduced the workspace's surreality and examined the numbers.

Something wet and heavy splatted against the window. She took an involuntary step back. The slab of—flesh? What the actual fuck?—was raw, red, and dripping. Black text tattooed on its surface listed attributions for active access points on the station's power grid, with no time stamps older than half a second. Adda's intrusion programs were accessing data streams well beyond biometrics records. *Power, life to machines, like blood . . .* Still, the imagery raised goose bumps on her arms. As soon as she finished here, she'd plant new spores.

When sorted by resources consumed, HarborMaster topped the list. It utilized more subprograms than AegiSKADA. Everything not listed among HarborMaster's subprocesses was attributed to the security system.

The gnats, too, collapsed onto the black velvet display pads. Another insect swarm a few meters away buzzed viciously with new information, which her subconscious and the workspace's translator identified as part of the answer to her question.

The projection enveloping a thick cloud of black flies depicted humans, not data. Seven of them, in armor with ZV printed just above their armpits, lined up against a wall beside a door. Something about the way the armor shimmered in the flickering hallway lights nauseated and unsettled her, even on vid. In person it would have other repellent characteristics as part of whatever camouflage they used, but that would work only on other humans.

This was not in between the inner and outer hull, or anywhere in the pirates' compound. The gray and bare-metal industrial fixtures were similar to those in the docking bay. It had to be somewhere in the station.

The group's leader wore bloodred lipstick and two rudimentary versions of the ZVs' palm weapons. She tapped the boot of the person behind her. The person's shield was much easier to focus on than the armor. The leader stomped a small switch, and an explosion blew the door in. The blast was loud and hot on Adda's skin.

The ZV soldier with the shield dashed around the leader in a second, slamming its lower edge on the floor a step inside. The soldier with the shield crouched behind it as the others swept in. Adda concentrated her desire to follow their progress, and the vid switched to a 3-D feed from inside the room.

Iridian claimed to have seen a military quantum computer the size of a train car. This one filled a transparent cooling vat as big as Adda's water tank. Cables snaked down seemingly at random to the structure and apparatuses on the walls, indistinct through the smoke. Even the university hadn't owned a rig this huge.

Seven pirates entered the small room and targeted the vat with beam weapons. Something on the floor flashed, and with a rising whine, the transmission whited out. Heat rolled over Adda and she covered her face with her arms. Screams and sounds like the flesh thing slapping the window cut off when the mics melted.

She'd just witnessed the previous captain's final moments.

It was terrifyingly easy to imagine that happening to Iridian, so she focused on the AI problem instead. HarborMaster monitored station power, so it would've registered the draw a weapon that size produced. The intelligence might define current events in terms of equipment and energy expenditure.

And since HarborMaster wasn't in charge of the station's

security, it was more likely to be vulnerable to intrusion than AegiSKADA. Now that Adda was able to review so much of the station infrastructure data, she might have already inserted her code into its system even though she'd targeted AegiSKADA.

If she controlled HarborMaster, she could physically disable AegiSKADA with the station's environmental controls, even if she couldn't reduce its aggression through administrative commands. At minimum, HarborMaster's infrastructure monitoring functions could map AegiSKADA's activity in the station, which might give the pirates a crucial few minutes of warning during the next attack.

The problem now was lack of access. Eavesdropping on HarborMaster's station status assessments was one thing, but getting it to listen to her was another. Her best chance of controlling this intelligence lay in sending commands on a channel through which it was designed to accept administrative input. Station designers wouldn't place human access points to the station management intelligence inside a wall or out in space.

Although ships handled space just fine . . .

The pilots might be able to shed light on this, and she couldn't communicate with them from inside the workspace. To leave the workspace slowly and without stressing her brain, Adda concentrated on Iridian's laugh, the warm touch of her hand, the way she said Adda's name. A moment later red letters in her own handwriting proclaimed *You are in a water tank* from the workspace generator's ceiling. If she moved too fast, the whole tank would shift beneath her. Combined with gravity higher than Earth's, she might throw up, pass out, and go into cardiac arrest.

Iridian swore no ships maintained hypergravity. Adda couldn't wait to get off this station.

Iridian lay beside her in the workspace generator, one arm draped over Adda's waist. When Adda sat up, Iridian murmured something about gate valves in spacefarer cant. Adda slipped out from under her lover's arm and climbed out of the tank to find Pel.

He was asleep, and she retraced her steps toward her tank. Her comp informed her that the local time was two o'clock in the morning. As she glanced up from it, the big ZV soldier who'd hugged Pel after AegiSKADA's attack walked out of the small kitchen. The soldier held a cup of applesauce with a straw sticking out of it.

Now that Adda was walking around, sleep sounded pleasant, but she wanted her questions answered more than she wanted rest. "Can you ... um ... help me with something?" Oh, for Iridian's casual, friendly voice, which did not remind listeners of children or rodents.

The muscle-bound woman sipped her applesauce and seemed to be maintaining an unusually blank expression. "If it won't bring any more heat down on the base, maybe."

"I need to compare some recordings with what other systems recorded at the same time. I want to ask your pilots about—"

The woman's frown was so discouraging that Adda didn't bother to finish the sentence. "No good. Can't help."

"But . . ." The pilots communicated with AegiSKADA or Harbor-Master somehow, whether they realized it or not. It would explain why they stayed on the station without helping the other residents. AegiSKADA chose not to fire on them, and HarborMaster opened the docking bay doors when they wanted to land. If the pilots could coordinate with the intelligences that way, then Adda could too. Wasn't it *obvious* she had to talk to them?

The woman was already thudding down the hall on enormous booted feet. Adda sighed. Someone was around at all times of day and night. The lighting never changed, like it would if environment controls were hooked up. Lights in the compound were either on and too bright, on and still impossible to see by, or off, so the time hardly mattered.

In her walk around the compound, she hadn't seen anybody else she could ask about the pilots and be sure of not making them angry at her or wasting her time, so she returned to her tank and her bed. When she lay down, Iridian slung an arm over her stomach without opening her eyes. Maybe more amenable people would be awake later.

* * *

After a few hours of sleep in the tank, Adda dragged herself out to find other reliable candidates to ask. Chato and Kaskade had similar reactions when Adda asked them. Chef finally sat Adda down in the kitchen over steaming mugs of reconstituted coffee to explain. "Listen, I don't know another way to say it, so I'm saying it like it is: your brother was a mess after the *Apparition* brought him through the lead cloud. Now, I can't say what happened," she said as Adda opened her mouth to ask. "But the ZV Group found him with his face covered in blood, and it wasn't that old. He was alone on the *Apparition*, understand? Something real bad happened to that boy, and I can't say what or when."

The *Apparition*'s pilot remained on the station with the other two as the only oversight for *five* AI, intelligences that lay in wait in the airless void until humans had crash-landed and woken them. Adda's skin prickled. Anything might seem logical after being exposed to just one unsupervised intelligence for so long. The pilots had to deal with AegiSKADA *and* HarborMaster, while maintaining control of their AI copilots as well.

Adda waited a full sixty seconds to see if Chef had anything else to say, but she started cleaning the coffee machine instead. Adda stood to leave. "Thank you for telling me."

"Good luck," said Chef. "We're counting on you."

Adda used that reminder to refocus herself on the problems at hand. Neither her sensor net eavesdroppers nor the ships would get her into HarborMaster. She padded back toward the tank, glaring at the floor two steps in front of her. Why was everybody so mysterious about Pel's eyes?

Low voices behind her, in the main room, drew her attention. One was Tritheist's, and the other belonged to the secessionist officer who Iridian had gotten into a fight with soon after they arrived on station. One of them had said Adda's name. Apparently the officer, Natani, Adda thought her name was, and Tritheist were on better terms than Iridian's report indicated. That, or the sergeant didn't take it personally when Tritheist aimed a weapon at her.

"All the tall one's done is talk," Sergeant Natani said. "Talks to Chef, talks to us, talks to everyone. And who knows what—Adda, did you call her?—does down there in that hole. Creepy, that's what she is, and she led AegiSKADA right to us."

Tritheist sighed. "The captain still thinks they can do something to get us out of here."

"The second they can't, I'll throw them in the recycler myself."

Oh. Adda swallowed hard and backed toward her tank, staying near the wall so the hollow space beneath the middle of the hall wouldn't thump under her feet. The pirates didn't trust them yet, she'd known that. But they also couldn't see the progress she'd made with the biometrics monitoring system. Without that, they might think her interactions with AegiSKADA were causing more short-term harm than long-term good. These two, at least, were just waiting for clearance to execute her.

CHAPTER 8

Charges Accrued: Extravehicular Repair without a License

In the tank's dim light, Iridian seethed as Adda reached the end of her account. Sure, the crew hadn't asked for help until she and Adda landed in their docking bay, and even then only Captain Sloane had asked. This crew would follow their superior's orders while disagreeing with them. But Adda and Iridian were approaching the AI problem in ways the pirates hadn't even considered. Maybe they were scaring these people, who'd already survived so much. It would've been rational for the crew to support any attempt to free them, but fear was rarely rational.

From the stories they told, the pirates had tried every crazy escape route they could think of when they first crashed on the station. Dwindling numbers and the change in leadership must've made them unwilling to risk more people. So of course she and Adda had made enemies by taking risks they wouldn't, pushing the AI until it pushed back. Perhaps that was why Sloane had given Adda and Iridian the assignment. The regular crew had done all they could.

Two influential officers plotting where they were bound to be overheard was a bad sign. Realities of station life offered plenty of "accidental" ways to die, even without a murderous AI in control. And pirates would rather ask forgiveness than permission. From what Adda had overheard, Sloane's belief in her abilities was what was standing between her and one of those accidents.

Now Adda lay in the generator, frowning and blinking and squirming like she did when her consciousness kept slipping out of her workspace. The damned idiot officers had frightened her too much to do the job Captain Sloane had given her.

Whatever the pirates' intentions, they'd have to go through Iridian. They'd learn not to charge a Shieldrunner. Her lips twitched up at how long it'd been since she'd put that old challenge into practice. *What's a Shieldrunner with no ISV and no room to run?*

In the generator, Adda's head thumped against the floor. Iridian pulled one of the opening flaps aside to check for signs of a seizure. Adda lay still, and the blush creeping up her neck suggested she'd just been frustrated enough to bang her head on something. Iridian smiled gently. "Energy consumption can be tricky to map, even in small systems. Want to talk it through?"

Adda raised one hand partway off the floor with her eyes still closed, which was Iridian's invitation to crawl into the generator with her. "Competing theories," Adda murmured.

"About power draw?"

Adda's head twitched side to side. "AegiSKADA is so . . . AI-strange. Not human-strange." Adda drew in a long breath and let it out just as slowly. For the moment, she was giving up on maintaining a workspace. "HarborMaster is unsupervised but doing exactly what you expect it to. So it's safer to try to get into. All obvious protocol, its behavior. Few obvious protocols for

AegiSKADA, but a lot of action. With extensive data collection, you'd expect *more* action."

The drugs Adda took to help her concentrate would be running through her system and filling her conversation with non sequiturs for the next hour, but Iridian had found a comfortable position in the generator, so she might as well stay. It didn't sound like this was about the threats Adda had overheard after all. "So HarborMaster's normal, but AegiSKADA's weird."

"Weird for unsupervised AI." Adda's breathing slowed to a long, loud pull into her lungs. Since her face wasn't turning blue, she was probably fine, but the drugs messed with her respiration. "We assume complete lack of supervision. What about partial?"

"How do you partially supervise an AI?"

"Only give it feedback some of the time. Or sometimes it accepts your suggestion, sometimes not. So in certain conditions the intelligence takes more action than in others." Adda's volume faded as she established another workspace. "This should show spikes in sensor activation and power draws to drone bays. Now, who? Who can, who would? Wait, let me put you in."

It'd take Adda a few seconds to create a version of Iridian in the workspace that'd correspond to Iridian's real voice beside her. Iridian lacked the implanted hardware to see a workspace the way Adda did, but an avatar of Iridian in the virtual environment helped Adda multitask. Without the avatar, talking out loud could pull Adda out of her workspace, and whatever hallucinographic experiences she had in there tended to make her lose track of real-world conversations.

After a few seconds of silence, Iridian said, "Are we really asking if someone is making AegiSKADA do this to people?"

"Do some things, to some people," said Adda. "The medical

team and pilots have no reason to. Same with the pirates. We saw them after the attack. If one of them had any responsibility for it, they'd have . . . reacted noticeably. I think. I did."

"Blame the enemy, not yourself." Iridian held her tighter, even though Adda had calmed down enough to lie still. That was good, in terms of her ability to stay connected to a workspace. But pushing somebody toward a hull breech was a pretty fucking noticeable reaction. "You could blame Sergeant Natani, too."

"Natani lacks the expertise, and she has personal reasons to hate us." Adda sounded confident about both assessments. "One of the refugees may have the knowledge, software, and hardware required to communicate with AegiSKADA like its supervisor did. Or the lieutenant might know how."

"Tritheist?"

"No. Map first."

Iridian crawled out of the generator. Although she couldn't help Adda wrestle her subconscious into mapping the station's energy consumption, Iridian could protect her against physical threats. Or she could if she had more information.

In the mess hall, Iridian leaned one shoulder on a rounded chunk of emergency bulkhead that half hid the cupboard and waited until Chef noticed her standing there. Chef moved like a spacefarer. It was hard to tell which side she might've backed during the war, but she'd understand the problem, at least. "Hey, Chef, I need your help with something."

"Sure, what?"

"The sergeant with the short hair and the tight ZV shirt . . ." Iridian drew her fingers across the side of her head, pantomiming Natani's recognizable scar. "She's treating Adda and me like a stand-in for the whole NEU. Can you tell me anything that'd help me get her to back off? Maybe something she needs done that I could do? We don't have to like each other, but we don't have to stab each other either."

"Okay, no." Chef set a package of noodles on the counter/bar and turned sideways, creating room for Iridian to stand in the narrow space. Iridian turned her shoulders to parallel Chef's, accepting the offered half meter so they could converse quietly while Chef worked. Iridian had spent too much time communicating in the precise body language of spacefarers in confined habitats to forget it after a few years on Earth. "I'll tell you what I told Pel when he talked about messing with Sergeant Natani," said Chef. "When we first crashed here, she beat a guy half to death for singing the NEU anthem after his Earther buddy was killed. You just being here is pissing her off, and you do not want to do that."

"No, you're right, I don't," Iridian said. "What I want is for her to let me and Adda work so we can all get off this damned station together. Adda's making good progress, and I don't want to worry about her every time I don't know where the sergeant is. Since we can't leave base, what *can* we do?"

"So you're already on her shit list." Chef tilted her face toward the ceiling, like somebody up there might have extra patience to loan her. "Sergeant Natani's killed enough people that when something's wrong, murder is the first fix she comes up with."

"What's wrong is the gods-damned AI out there." Iridian pointed diagonally down toward the rest of the station, just short of jamming her finger into a burner on the stove. "If she wants to kill AegiSKADA, sign me up. I came here to make money, not to sit around this little base fighting battles we all fought years ago."

She heaved an aggravated sigh and visualized her anger blowing away with it. Any soldier would feel the same way in this situation, once they recognized it for what it was. Maybe all she had to do was show Natani that.

Before Iridian left to track the sergeant down and deliver an explanation, Adda walked into the mess hall. Her eyes were slightly out of focus, and her hood hung in a lump against the back of her neck. Blue flecks speckled her head and chest. "Where is the lieutenant?"

"Tritheist is in the captain's room," Chef said. "Wouldn't interrupt them."

"Not him, the one from before," said Adda. "The one from when you first crashed."

"Oh, Blackguardly Jack, you mean." Chef went back to opening packaged food.

Adda focused on Chef, opened her mouth, blinked a few times, and closed it. That fish face was Iridian's signal to assemble the facts for Adda's perusal. "Who's Blackguardly Jack?"

"The lieutenant before Tritheist, like she said." Chef set a large pan on the stovetop. "Used to be Jack and *Lieutenant* Sloane under Captain Foster's command. Sloane hired me. Hiring's always been part of the lieutenant job, I hear. Dunno the rest. I had to let 'em half starve on emergency rations before they started treating me like crew."

"I think Blackguardly Jack's alive." Adda spoke to Iridian and flicked a shy glance at Chef. There was no point in encouraging Adda to talk to others while she had workspace brain. "My comp is still connecting the vid clips, but it's got a couple of seconds of . . . Well, look."

She held out her glove and activated its projector. Chef leaned over her prep area on the counter to watch. The clip was less than a second long. The glove's tiny speaker emitted a crackling blast that overwhelmed the mics that recorded it. In the vid, a man took a running step out of a doorway. The back of his armor trailed molten metal composite.

"That's the missing LT? He's two seconds away from serious spinal damage." Iridian pointed at the disintegrating armor. "How do you figure he survived?"

"I can't say for sure." Adda bit her lip and stared at the projection. "Nobody else exited the control room, which means he knows more about it than anybody here. Maybe the first captain just led him there to smash things, or maybe they were pursuing an option we haven't discovered. He might even be . . . Well, I wouldn't say controlling it, but—"

"He's *what?*" From Chef's expression, Adda could've just said he was a vampire using mind control on the AI. "You mean he's talking to AegiSKADA and telling it to come after us? And it's doing what he says?"

"No, she doesn't mean that," said Iridian. Adda flinched. "Wait, do you?"

Adda inhaled a long breath and said in a rush, "Sloane's some kind of software specialist, from what I've read, and Tritheist's expertise seems to be mechanical. It follows that as the first captain's lieutenant, Blackguardly Jack had a technical specialty too. Correct?"

"Something about shipboard security. All the crew who aren't ZVs were hired on for that. Well, except me and Sturm." Chef shrugged. "Sounded technical, sure."

"So he might've had the know-how to guide an AI without being its supervisor." Iridian looked back to Adda. "Partial supervision like you said, yeah? But is he talking to AegiSKADA directly, without an interface? He'd have to *hate* the crew to take that big a risk sending an AI after us. And he'd have had to start talking to it when the crew first crashed here, since it killing people was why he left base."

"It did take a few souls when we arrived, but it picked up the pace after that." Chef hummed thoughtfully at the repeating vid on Adda's comp. "He didn't want to go with Captain Foster to hit AegiSKADA's core. Said that'd be suicide. Captain Foster said she'd kill him slow if he didn't follow her orders, and Sloane backed her up. Fast."

"AegiSKADA wasn't always so single-mindedly against the pirates that it almost ignores the refugees," said Adda. "I listened to the archived refugee newsfeed. Three years ago, when the refugees first arrived, AegiSKADA attacked them *regularly*, sometimes more than once a day. A lot of them died." Chef nodded confirmation.

"But now all those refugees *live* in a docking bay AegiSKADA controls," Iridian pointed out.

"Because the docking bays are associated with security protocols to allow travelers . . ." Adda trailed off, staring at the freeze-frame of Blackguardly Jack. "There would be fewer decision points making the pirates preferential targets if someone with a grudge against Captain Sloane has been providing AegiSKADA with targeting priorities for the past year."

While Adda and Iridian had been working on their final projects to earn their degrees, Sloane's crew had been in a fight to the death with an armed AI. Iridian shuddered. "So Blackguardly Jack was hired on for skills that'd help him point the killer AI at the crew who got him hurt. And now, what, he also hits the fugees every once in a while to hide what he's up to? That's fucking disgusting."

"It's possible, with the correct equipment and privacy, for him to communicate with AegiSKADA without anyone discovering him. And isolated attacks on the refugee camp would disguise his true intent." Adda looked guiltily over at Chef, then back to Iridian.

Iridian shrugged. "We won't know until we ask him."

Chef shook her head like Adda and everything that came out of her mouth was confounding. A surly white ZV guy named Vick came in with Nitro, the other woman on Sergeant Natani's squad, to get food. Iridian led Adda out.

ZV black and yellow surrounded Natani in the common room. If Iridian could convince her that they were at least an equal threat to each other, and that they shared the goal of getting rid of AegiSKADA and leaving the station, maybe that'd stop hostilities before they got worse. The sergeant's eyes met Iridian's from under her black hood, and whatever the pirates had been saying before got a lot less funny, judging by the look on her face.

The wall beside Iridian split open, and it took her a long, breathless moment to remember that it was supposed to. Sturm shoved the concealed workshop door farther open as he came through. "Radiation surge," he bellowed loudly enough to carry throughout the small base. "Generator Four is venting again. D-MOG tabs, everyone!"

The people in the common room started collecting their things, ending conversations, and popping pills while Sturm shouted the same message into the galley and down the hall toward the head. It wasn't quite an emergency, but the ZVs moved with purpose. Sergeant Natani broke her glare at Iridian to prepare with the others. Iridian turned away too, looking for someone friendly who'd share their D-MOG tablets. It was as civil as she and the sergeant were likely to get, for the moment.

"What about the water?" a ZV guy asked.

"The storage tanks *should* soak up the worst of it, but do you want to risk your dick for 'should?'" Major O.D. shouted at the ZV. "Shore up." Sturm headed for the captain's quarters.

Pel emerged from the other bunkhouse, yawning. "What's the ruckus?"

"Generator Four's venting again," said a ZV heading for the bunkhouse.

Pel turned his head from side to side. "Where's Adda?"

"Here," she called loudly enough to carry over the noise. Iridian grasped Pel's wrist when he came in range, and he let her guide him to Adda.

After patting down his pockets, he extracted a small case from one. He shook three bright yellow tablets into his hand. His fingertips poked Iridian in the boob when he held them out. "Oops, sorry. But take one. Doesn't stop you getting sick, but it does make you feel better faster once you're clear. Hell, take the pack." He dropped the case on the pills in his palm and Iridian pocketed it. "I'll get another from Zikri."

As they dry-swallowed the pills, Sturm reappeared with a meter strapped to the side of his comp glove. Captain Sloane and one of the ZVs, Tabs, walked behind him, and Tabs was still pulling her shirt on. The captain really did like to keep people guessing. *Whatever works for . . . them?* She'd have to ask about preferred pronouns. Tabs winked at Iridian as she walked past to join the soldiers congregating in the common room near the entryway.

"I thought this place spun on LFTRs." Iridian pronounced the acronym like more than one lifter, and smiled at Adda's disapproving frown over the unnecessary abbreviation. Properly applied nuclear power generation was worth some good cheer too. Iridian loved it when designers selected safer, low-waste systems over those easily explained to investors.

"The older liquid thorium reactors vent into space in worst-case scenarios," Adda said. "There's not supposed to be anybody out here."

"And the hull's plenty of shielding for a little radioactive salt, except we're on top of the gods-damned hull." Iridian ran her hand over the fuzz of hair growing on her scalp. She'd forgotten to track down a razor, and there didn't seem to be any chemical components among the crew's printer parts and material.

"No evacuation," Captain Sloane announced. "We repair, insulate, and decontaminate." If the choice was between that and an unstable station full of AI-directed killer robots, Iridian would risk the radiation exposure any day.

That led to a different flurry of activity. Sturm turned to Iridian and Adda. "Are you two on a team yet?"

"Team?" Iridian asked.

"Repair crew. We don't seal this place tight before we apply radiation shielding, there's no point." Sturm pointed at Si Po, also emerging from the bunkhouse hallway. "You go with him, his welds are terrible. You . . ." He peered at Adda. "What can you do with hab repairs?"

"Um . . . read meters?" Adda suggested.

"You're with Pel." Sturm strode off to coordinate the others.

Iridian kissed Adda on the cheek. "You'll be fine, just follow his lead."

Adda nodded, and Iridian secured her girlfriend's hood over her head. Defeating the AI was a long game to play. If she and Adda didn't make some gains with the crew soon, they couldn't count on support from them later. Sergeant Natani would argue against them whenever they weren't in the room. Preventing radiation poisoning seemed as good a place to gain regard as any. It was about time they came up against a problem Iridian could do something about.

Si Po smiled cautiously and waited for Iridian to reach him. "We're zone three," he said, as if that meant something to her.

"Hey, what pronouns do you use when you're talking about Captain Sloane?"

Si Po shot an incredulous look at her from beneath his veil of hair. "Captain."

"Fair enough."

They went back around to the room with the wall projector, printer, and console. It was the other room most likely to share a wall with the destroyed bunkhouse. The way these modules fit together, she'd have to walk back and forth between the two rooms a few times to confirm that.

A couple of ZV guys, one called Vick and a shorter guy with pale blond hair whose name Iridian didn't know, were already inside. They directed mocking grins at Si Po. "'Oy, where were you hiding this time?" Vick asked him. Si Po crossed to the console and methodically checked it for damage while the ZVs closed in on him.

"What are we supposed to be doing here?" Iridian snapped.

Both ZVs focused on her. "We check the seams on the walls and corners. Then we do the same thing in the bunkhouse," said Vick.

"Great. I'll take this wall." Iridian approached one and tilted her head to track the source of a faint whistling. It could've been a compressor in the wall, or in her imagination. But that was what stupid spacefarers said right before they asphyxiated. In her peripheral vision, the other two looked the wall over as well. Vick held a comp glove palm up to the wall, diagnostics flickering across the back of his hand.

This wall's variable density and slight bend were less pronounced than the wall that the window was projected on, but both were beyond what the average architect would select. More detailed inspection revealed the wall to be another salvaged ship's bulkhead.

"Ah, shit, this corner is coming up again," said the quieter ZV.

Iridian and the others stood behind Vick to see his comp glove readout while he scanned it. "Of course it is," said Iridian. "Look at that joint. You've got to reseal that."

The ZVs and Si Po gaped at her like she had said it in spacefarer cant. She knew she hadn't, because cant had more specific terms for shoddy construction. "What joint?" Si Po asked.

Iridian pointed, assessed one blank stare after another, and crouched to point at where the wall and floor met. "Right here." She laid her finger on the floor near the source of the whistling. It felt several degrees cooler than room temperature. "And it's not insulated. Who's got the insulation?" More blank expressions. "Get Sturm. Please."

Vick shoved Si Po toward the door. "And some sealant!" Iridian called after him. Sturm should've split the ground pounders between multiple repair teams. Judging from the crew's speech patterns and accents, there weren't many spacefarers among them. Right before the whole base was enveloped in radioactive waste was a shit time to fix maintenance issues that they should've been searching out daily. They sure as hell had the time for it.

Yet another muscle-bound white guy with yet another ZV shirt walked in. This one wore a hat with a brim in a vaguely military style instead of the hooded jackets the other ZVs favored. The cap helped her recognize him as one of the ZVs who hung around Sergeant Natani. As Iridian understood it from Chato, this guy was the only member of Natani's squad who spent a lot of time with her and wasn't in her fireteam, the subgroup squads broke into when tactics required units of three or four soldiers instead of the full squad complement.

The man's wide shoulders, combined with the pressurized tank and hose strapped to his back and the gas mask he wore, seemed to take up most of the small room. "Putting on another layer of blue," he said in a surprisingly soft voice. He sprayed a strip of the wall they had inspected with the same blue dust that fell off the ceiling. The freshly applied stuff stuck to the wall like paint.

"Whoa, wait, we have to repair that." Iridian backed away with her hand over her mouth and nose.

The other two ZVs put themselves between her and the one with the spray, like she was about to rush him. The one in the mask stood calmly where he was and said, "Got it. You done the bunkhouse yet?"

"No, so don't spray that either, please," she said. "Pel said that blue stuff deflects radiation?"

The big guy nodded, which waved the canister on the front of the gas mask up and down. "It's a lead compound. The blue turns brown when it wears out. We don't have primer for it, so it falls off before then. I'm Six, by the way. That's my name." He took off his hat and thwacked the fabric against his thigh, creating a small cloud of blue dust. As he put it back on his head he gave her a shallow bow, which she managed to return without too wide a smile.

"Six?" she couldn't help asking.

The big guy shrugged. "Mom had five kids and ran out of ideas." He grinned at the other pirates' laughter at the explanation, although this couldn't have been the first time they'd heard it. "Later." So, there were reasonable and competent people on the crew after all. *Good.*

Iridian's team locked the wall joint in place and flagged it with a disposable projector before moving on. The projector lit the uninsulated area red, so Sturm couldn't miss it. Now that Iridian had proved she could tell when the ZVs didn't know how to do a job right, they left her to work and gave Si Po a hard time instead.

By the time she'd finished the computer room and started on the bunkhouse, Vick and the other ZV, Nils, were bored enough to fetch her tools and supplies. Six followed them, spraying down what they shored up. The ceiling and external walls got a second coat of blue stuff.

She met Sturm in the common room. "We're set." She walked him back to the resealed wall joint and a couple of other spots in the bunkhouse. Even though his lips pulled down at the corners, she got the impression that was his smile. "Not bad, not bad. Come with me to look at the others."

Tritheist's repair team had left only one area vulnerable. Sturm and Iridian corrected the missed damage. After they finished with the third team of Adda, Pel, and the captain (no errors from the captain's team, thank all the gods), Sturm let her do the inspections requiring crawling, crouching, and climbing on things, which were most of them.

"Sir, could you take a look at Adda's tank?" Iridian asked. Judging by the rest of the base, Sturm wasn't exactly a perfectionist. Still, another set of informed eyes on the structure couldn't hurt. "The enviro's okay, but it moves when you walk around in there."

Sturm made eye contact with the captain and received an approving nod. "Sure."

"This little installation has taught me so much about space structural design," he said. Adda scuttled ahead of them, escaping the larger group. "It is pressurized armor, but bigger. You know, we only have atmo for about twenty. Or we did have, before the bunkhouse went. Hard to say how much is left now, and we're not siphoning much from the station. Sorry about your friend, but Sloane put him down to save atmo for people we want to live with."

If atmo had been the only concern, Captain Sloane would've just sent Reis to the fugee camp, which was what'd happen to Adda and Iridian unless they stayed useful. Reis's death almost certainly had more to do with Sloane defending the crew, either by killing someone dumb enough to threaten them with a knife or by reducing the number of people who'd seen the crew's sorry state on the station. The incredulity showed on Iridian's face, but all she said was, "Reis wasn't our friend. Just a business partner."

She resisted the unnecessarily deep breaths atmo consciousness could cause. When Pel finally told Sloane they were on their way, he hadn't talked Reis's skills up to Captain Sloane the way he had Adda's and Iridian's. So Reis was dead, and Iridian and Adda were as close to safe as they were likely to get on Barbary Station.

Thank all the gods Captain Sloane had decided the crew could use two new engineers, not just one. The maintenance issues, collapsing station infrastructure, and lack of a nanorepair culture to fix things without human assistance were points in Iridian's favor. While Adda made progress against the AI, Iridian would keep looking for opportunities to ensure the crew's continued safety. But first, Adda needed a safe place to work.

Sturm followed Adda down the ladder to the tank. The push lights illuminated the man's frown. "The air here . . ."

"Not a lot of pull through the holes, I know," Iridian said. Adda stood next to one of the lamps on the wall, subvocalizing to her comp. She was listening, most likely, even though she pretended not to.

"Something else . . ." He stilled between each step, like he was waiting for something to give way. When the whole structure swayed and creaked, he pressed back against the wall with her and Adda. "I'd find out how this is secured, if I were you."

Iridian nodded, her breath picking up with low-grade panic. If Sturm thought this place was dangerous, the situation was worse than she'd thought. "How loose would you say it is?"

Sturm shrugged. "Would've been fine if we left it empty. This amount of walking around, though . . ." He looked Iridian over, scratching his stubbled jaw with two fingers. "Sorry about the rush with the radiation. We've got enough water circulating through this installation to shield us from anything short of a whole generator going up, combined with that spray-on lining. A bit of panic's the only way to get these ZV people to pitch in on repairs without fuss. Captain Sloane's idea. Come to the workshop. I believe I have something you'll like."

"Babe, we could set you up in the room with the comp console," Iridian said. In the comp room Adda would be closer to everybody else, and Iridian could keep better track of how she was handling her workspaces. Also, the comp room couldn't fall multiple stories into an AI-infested station.

"No, I like it here. It's quiet." Structural insecurity bothered Adda less than social insecurity. The way she *preferred* to be alone in silence was beyond comprehension. Five minutes of that made Iridian feel like the atmo pumps had stalled and she was suffocating.

In Sturm's workshop, the air moved better. Pieces of armor in various states of repair hung neatly around the walls, alongside diagnostic and repair tools. The workshop was as compact and consolidated as any spacefarer could wish for, although the enormous overhead light was overkill. "So you're not the handyman around here, you're the armorer," Iridian said.

"That I am. The ZV Group keeps me well occupied. Here." He pointed out an armored suit hanging on the wall. Iridian hefted it by the shoulders while Sturm plugged in a tester. The exoskeleton actuators moved like they'd been restored to practically new condition. The rest of the suit bore the dents, scuffs, and scorch marks of combat.

"Are you trained in pressurized armor, by chance?" Sturm asked. When Iridian nodded, he said, "I haven't tested it since I finished working on it, but it pressurizes at about ninety percent optimal. The ZV Group brought me enough pieces to put this one together, but we haven't salvaged any working suits whole. Our luck, the AI dragged them off to wherever it takes the dead. We keep hoping the fugees will go looking, but they value their lives more than that."

"The ZVs do too, yeah?" Iridian asked quietly. Nobody in the common room reacted, so they must not have heard.

Sturm snorted. "Outside their contract, they say. A few of them who aren't armored now are wishing they were, but the major doesn't think it's urgent. He's holding out for me or Tritheist to risk our lungs on it. Captain Sloane doesn't think it's urgent either, or one of us would have orders to deal with it."

The boots were small enough to leave blisters, but big enough to cram her feet in. She met Sturm's eyes and grinned. Finally, her kind of job, and something useful for her to do while Adda worked. "I'll test it for you while I secure Adda's tank, if the rad shielding's good and you have a patch kit."

"The shielding is good." He nodded gravely and handed her a pocket-size patch kit, still sealed. "If you're going out to the surface, I have a list of things to check, but watch yourself. We've lost people out there."

And Iridian wouldn't lose Adda to Sloane's crew's shoddy maintenance. In a makeshift hab like this, that was suicidal. "Sure, give me the list and the tools. There's got to be something stopping AegiSKADA from blowing you all up, or it would've done it already. Maybe I'll find that out too." That'd give Adda insight into what AegiSKADA was after, if not the death of every pirate it could reach. And it'd highlight the benefits of having a fit, fearless engineer like herself onboard.

In the corner of the workshop hidden from the common

room, Iridian stripped off her sweatshirt, shirt, and pants. Sturm held the armor while she squeezed into it piece by piece, without oil, thank all the gods. The helmet's antiseptic odor wrinkled her nose, so the air filter was clean enough. No heads-up display. She sighed. The tool compartments opened and locked, at least, so she wouldn't have to haul Sturm's equipment around in a box.

As she stepped out of the workspace, the rattling door interrupted Pel and the ZVs sorting repair tools from the different teams. "Who's that in the suit?" asked Pel. He inclined his head, like something in the sound would explain.

"It's Iridian." She raised her voice to let the pirates hear who was about to do them a big-ass favor, since the helmet's face projector wasn't working. The suit chafed her armpits and ankles. "Fixing some things outside for Sturm and testing the seals on this armor. Let Adda know where I am if she's looking, yeah?" Using sight words around Pel felt awkward, although not as awkward as the argument with Adda she'd have to wade through if Iridian told her what she was doing before she left. Iridian could win the argument, or she could be out and back before Adda came out of her tank.

"Be careful." Pel seemed too stunned by the idea of going outside to be insulted by colloquialisms.

"Yeah, we don't have much of that armor left," said a ZV.

Sturm led her to the path through the wall and all the way to the docking bay. Once they emerged from the corner exit into the bay, they kept near the wall. Sturm paused and examined the suit again. "You're not carrying any weapons, are you?"

"Not at the moment," said Iridian. "Knives don't hurt bots."

"Truth." Sturm walked toward the docking bay's exit, and Iridian hurried to keep up. "AegiSKADA will track you down fast if you carry anything sharp out of the bay."

Reis's body no longer lay on the landing pad. The pirates

claimed that bodies that didn't get dragged off somewhere were often booby-trapped with explosives, and they usually left the dead where they fell. The fugees never ventured this far out of their own territory. AegiSKADA must've done something with him. The inoperative faceplate projector in Iridian's helmet hid her grimace. What an AI might do with a dead man was a question for Adda, but Iridian didn't intend to ask. Adda had bigger problems to solve, and Iridian had enough nightmares without that particular question's answer.

Sturm stopped at a large, closed hatch marked MAINTENANCE AIRLOCK. He held his comp glove to the door and the lock lit green. The red had apparently burned out. "You all right coming back on your own?"

"Sure, it's a straight line and a ladder. Is that thing going to open for my comp?"

Sturm prodded his for a moment, held it up to the door again, and then waved between Iridian's comp glove and the door to get her to do the same. The green light came back on. "It will now," said Sturm. Iridian shook her head in mute amazement that he hadn't thought of that before she mentioned it.

The docking bay depressurization lights lit and an alarm whooped. She and Sturm barely jumped at all. Now that she was listening for them, the base's vents slamming shut became one less thing to worry about. Funny, the shit you got used to.

He smiled, the biggest show of emotion she'd seen from the man since she arrived. "I can't tell you how glad I am that the exterior work is getting done." He headed back to the path between the walls, turning his head left and right every other step in search of drones.

Iridian entered the airlock and started its cycle, which also activated the elevator that'd take her up to the station's inner ring, level with the pirates' base. Shieldrunner training included a sim on extravehicular repair in vac, but she'd never done it for real. Meticulously labeled controls and monitors lined the wall beside the door, and the airlock itself had space for about two people or a person and a mobile tool chest. Consequences of a mistake could be nasty, but it was still exciting to apply what she'd learned. "The crew'll damn well appreciate having us around after this," she muttered. The airlock finished cycling, and she stepped out.

The windowless base made her forget just how fast Barbary Station moved. The airlock opened near the edge of the inner ring. The station spun her around a floating module in its center at over two hundred meters per second, creating the hypergrav that secured her to the hull more firmly than most other stations she'd been on.

The nearest big LFTR was less than a klick above her, powering one of Barbary Station's engines to keep the grav on. With its liquid medium, it couldn't melt down. Kilometers of station curved up and around on the right and left. Above and below, stars swirled and glittered through the lead cloud. Pale sunlight, most of which the lead cloud also blocked, shone somewhere behind the station.

She gripped the handholds on either side of the airlock door. The gloves' fingers pressed painfully on the tips of her fingernails. Worse, her comp projection was up the gauntlets from the armored window on the suit glove. Adda would've solved the problem before she left base. She'd also smile at Iridian's crass speech, even though the cant Iridian swore in sounded like aggressive gibberish to nonspeakers.

A solid fragment of something smacked into her faceplate, and she instinctively jerked her head back. The object was long past her. The impact set her ears ringing, but the faceplate stayed in one piece. Out of curiosity, she diverted farther from the edge and tipped her helmet back toward the hub again.

The *Prosperity Dawn* hung stable while the station spun around it, dead in a cloud of debris. Whatever setup the station's previous owners had for clearing floating junk was either inoperative or on a lengthy cleaning schedule. Rovers puttered over the colony ship's surface, peeling up panels and collecting what drifted beneath. They'd stripped a third of the ship to a bare outline. Large chunks of material that could've been recycled still hung around the vessel.

Something clicked *inside* her helmet. She froze.

Then Adda's voice called her name, muffled and indistinct but all Adda. "Can you hear me?" she asked.

"I hear you," Iridian said in a relieved whoosh of breath. That click hadn't meant that her suit was about to spring a leak. "Can anybody else hear us?"

"I wouldn't put it past AegiSKADA. I can't believe you did this."

Iridian laughed. Talking on this channel required access to the pirates' primary console in the main part of the base. It took a girlfriend in mortal peril to drag Adda out of isolation. "Sorry, but I had to. Your tank's wobbling too much. It'll fall out from under you if I don't get it secured. Besides, we're sucking down atmo they can't afford to lend us." A jagged metal slab perpendicular to the station's hull stood out against the long upward curve of the inner ring, the first pirate base module and Iridian's current destination. "Can AegiSKADA understand what I'm saying?"

"Possibly," said Adda. "I sent an invitation for a chat in that sensor package, but AegiSKADA hasn't responded. I can't tell if it understands conversational speech."

"Now you want to *chat* with it?" That sounded like a disaster waiting to happen, but she'd already offered, and disconnecting station comms to stop AegiSKADA from taking her up on that offer was probably more trouble than it'd be worth. "Love you, babe, but I have to concentrate on something other than what a fucking dangerous idea that is."

"I love you, too." The click sounded again, and Iridian was alone outside the station.

Antenna clusters spiked the inner ring at half-klick intervals, silver with red flashing lights at the tips. The outer ring doubtless had more. Pushing and pulling signals to the Internet relay, commonly known this far from Earth as the Patchwork, would've taken a lot of focusing power. Then one faction or another took the buoys out, and that and the lead cloud sharing the station's orbit made long-range comms impossible. She searched her suit controls for a cam, which must've been on her helmet's missing HUD. She'd just have to tell Adda about these later.

Among the nearest cluster, the base's residential modules were embedded in the station's outer hull. Some pirate had cut the hull with a tool smaller and cooler than Iridian would've chosen for the metal density. A chunk of ship bulkhead made up one or two of the base's walls and stuck several meters up from the station. The outline was ragged against the starlight, notched where floating debris and micrometeoroids knocked pieces away.

First she made the hallway above Adda's tank as airtight as possible. Having done that, she belly crawled a meter under the module floor to secure the top of the tank and the hatch that connected it to the rest of the base. She checked her work twice, and then one more time for luck, before she moved on to the tasks on Sturm's list.

Sturm's checklist was on her comp. The projection was readable when she raised her elbow and pressed her temple to her forearm, and she could just barely scroll it by making the right micromovements in her hand and arm. It was frustrating without the tactile input from touching the projection with her other hand, but she wasn't about to take her suit glove off.

She climbed over a giant half sphere above the common room to check the sealant on magnetic strips along one side of a relatively straight wall. This section was made of sturdy ship hull. With luck, any more trash the station spun her into would hit the strips first and stick.

Half an hour later she'd secured the modules, patched some leaks, and replaced a small antenna as Sturm had requested. Few of the other items on the list appeared to apply to the awkward construction before her. Perhaps Sturm had never been out here. He seemed like too much of a realist to build a hab like this and then live in it.

A shock zapped from her fingers to her elbow. She yanked her hand back from the panel she was working under. She was messing with support struts, not live wires. When a second shock jolted her knee numb, she started looking for an attacker.

An old-style drone just big enough to carry an engine and a weapons payload hovered behind her. Debris fragments scattered across the station hull beneath it, like it scared even dust and grit away. Her head twisted inside her helmet as she searched for someplace safer. Everything nearby was conductive. She flattened out on the hull to give the bot a smaller profile to aim for. If it got one good shock into the hull near her—

Her vision flashed white.

* * *

She lay on her stomach. Each noisy breath tasted of plastic and industrial grade cleaner. Persistent buzzing kept her awake, and

she was still tired as hell. The buzzing resolved into a woman saying, with very precise enunciation, ". . . nothing fractured. More
active brain waves. Good patterns." More buzzing.

* * *

Her eyes opened, squinting against a headache growing worse by
the moment. Two suited forms stood around her, beside something she couldn't focus on. It was camouflaged. Only an organi-
zation with too big a budget would camouflage a box when they
could just label it "grid squares" or something.

A male voice with some kind of Earth accent said, "If you can
hear me, thumb to the stars." The buzz returned, but she wriggled
her armored hand out from under her hip and raised her thumb.
"This is the channel you hear?" Someone crouched beside her. An
unfamiliar face was projected onto his helmet faceplate, the holo-
graphic depiction of his head and neck against a dark background
eerie against the cold and the black. Under the enviro suit the
man wore something bright red against his olive skin, not a black
ZV shirt. "Speak. You should have a mic."

"I'm awake," she said.

"We saw you electrocuted," the woman said in the voice and
precise pronunciation Iridian last heard when Captain Sloane
checked on the med team after AegiSKADA bombed the crew's
base. She was pretty sure Si Po had called the woman Dr. Williams. Her faceplate's projector showed a rich brown complexion
in three flickering dimensions. "On our way. Come inside."

"Um. On your way where?" Williams turned toward the other
doc instead of answering. Iridian felt more nauseated by the second. It helped to focus her eyes anywhere other than at the camouflaged case while stars wheeled overhead. The suited members

of the med team stared into each other's faceplates without speaking. "Where's the drone, and the rest of you?" Iridian asked. If she was remembering right, Captain Sloane had said there were four of them.

"Chased the drone away. When we come, they go," the male doc said. "So long as it doesn't use them to keep us in a place. For our *safety*." The docs laughed so uproariously that they maxed out their mics, causing a grating digital buzz. Iridian winced at the noise's effect on her headache. "It" had to be AegiSKADA, and apparently these docs weren't worried about the rest of their team's safety.

Speaking of which, they were exposed and vulnerable to everything AegiSKADA had in its arsenal out on the station's hull, not to mention the unknown ambient radiation level. "Have you got a safer way out of here than through the docking bay airlock?" she asked over the laughing doctors, formally putting her life in crazy people's hands.

The docs stopped laughing like someone toggled a laugh switch to off. "Undoubtedly," the man said.

He helped her up and accepted Iridian's thanks without reply. The woman picked up the camouflaged box, and they led the way toward the edge of the station's inner ring. Iridian followed, breathing much harder than the exertion should've required. Sweat prickled on her skin and made her heels slide in the armored boots. Gods, she didn't want to puke in the suit. It wasn't even hers.

"You're Spacelink's medics, yeah?" she asked to distract herself. "I'm Iridian Nassir, with Sloane's crew. What were you doing out here?"

"Can't travel inside," said Williams.

"Not the whole way," the man agreed. "Broken floors. Broken walls. Machines."

Just before the med team reached the edge of the inner ring, they dropped from sight. Iridian shuffled after them, looking around for the drone as she went. Was it hiding over the edge, waiting for them?

The spot where the med team disappeared turned out to be the opening of a nearly vertical tube big enough around to accommodate a human. It curved about a meter down and under the hull. She eased herself in. When she let go of the rim, she hit the tube's side and slid to the bottom. Her boots went out from under her and spilled her onto her rescuers' feet. Something at the top slammed and creaked, like an outer airlock door sealing.

The room she slid into was certainly small enough to be an airlock. The female doc put the camouflaged case down again to help the man pick Iridian back up. "Thanks. Dr. Williams, yeah?" When the woman nodded, Iridian turned toward the other one, who was standing so close to her that her helmet clacked against his. He'd turned his projector off, so his polarized faceplate just reflected Iridian's projected face back at her. The projector in her helmet was flashing and distorting her image, but at least it'd turned itself on sometime between leaving the pirate base and now. "Sorry. I didn't catch your name."

"Tiwari."

Neither of the docs backed up to avoid constantly bumping into each other. As Iridian leaned away from them, a small overhead illuminated, revealing a labeled panel like the one in the docking bay airlock. Tiwari touched a button, retracting the tube's curved portion into the ceiling. That gave them all more room, and Iridian took a long step back from them. The docs were way too comfortable in each other's personal space.

The Spacelink med team had said some strange things in their conversation with Captain Sloane, but . . . *Gods, they're a mess.*

The docs were still staring at each other. "Private comms channel, huh?" Iridian asked. The docs turned to face her for a second, then went back to staring at each other. Williams cued the airlock pressurization cycle without looking at her comp.

"Never would have!" Williams shouted. Iridian jumped.

"Should!" said Tiwari.

"No." Williams turned to Iridian, like that concluded the unnecessarily shouted conversation. "Please. Armor off."

"Um . . . I'm not wearing much under this." And Iridian had no evidence of healthy enviro, since the airlock had been open to the cold and black a minute ago and the med team still wore their suits. Iridian looked from one faceplate to the other. "Why do I need to?"

"Burns expected," said Williams.

"I'd notice burns." Everything ached, but wherever Iridian had been shocked didn't hurt any more than the rest of her did. Her hands moved as well as the tight gloves allowed. "I'm good."

The airlock chimed to signal that its pressurization cycle was complete. "Leave," the med team said in unison.

Iridian would hear the medics through the suits as well as through the radio, if she took off her helmet, but taking her helmet off still seemed like a bad idea. "Sure, just point me back toward the docking bay. I have it from there."

"You can't," said Williams. "It won't let you."

"It never," said Tiwari.

"It has." Was Williams reversing her position for the sake of argument? The conversation was making less sense by the second. "We'll take you." She picked up the camouflaged case again and walked into the station through a gust of incoming atmo. The airlock hadn't completely pressurized after all. Iridian was glad she'd kept her helmet on.

She sighed, but followed. The drone patrolling the station's surface would kill her if she encountered it with no way to ground her suit and nobody to chase the thing away, however the med team had managed that. The best thing she could do now was get back to base and report what she'd found.

And follow up on one of Adda's many questions about the state of the station. "Hey, have you two seen a pirate with dark hair, medium-size white guy, calls himself Blackguardly Jack?" The physicians stared at each other, then at Iridian. Perhaps she needed to back up a bit. "So, you know Captain Sloane, and the pirates."

"Surprised us, very surprised, when they came to Docking Bay Three, with AegiSKADA already keeping all the others away," said Tiwari. "Thought the Martians would be the last, but then Sloane came."

"And *stayed*," said Williams. "After so many drones. And so many accidents. AegiSKADA tried many ways to make them go."

"They didn't *all* die!" said Tiwari. Iridian still couldn't see his face, but his hands rose a little and turned palms up, as if to add, *Can you imagine?*

"Drones and accidents, yeah." The corridor outside the airlock looked about the same as it had the last time Iridian checked over her shoulder. They'd been out here long enough to attract any patrolling bot's attention. "You're docs, so maybe you heard about the guy with the melted spine?"

"Last year." Tiwari tripped over a piece of what looked like the hose and lower half of a fire-suppression bot's chassis, which lay in a doorway nearby. As Iridian caught his arm to keep him upright, she looked for the rest of the bot, but it'd probably been dismantled in the dark room beyond the doorway. She kept moving. It'd be dumb as hell to go in there, effectively alone. "The plasma torch came loose," Tiwari continued. "Big, big installed thing for cutting pieces off ships. Impacted recycling module exterior, lit for . . . five seconds?"

Williams stared at Tiwari for a moment, then said, "Avoid fifty ticks to seventy-six ticks. Hard vacuum there now." That was on the other side of station north from Captain Sloane's base. The fugee camp was in the docking bay which served as station north, at 100/0 ticks.

Iridian frowned. This wasn't the information she'd been hoping for. "And Blackguardly Jack was there?"

"Severe spinal trauma, poorly healed," Tiwari said. "Ran from there. Survived."

So Blackguardly Jack wasn't with the docs. The med team would see him more than once if he were in the station's farm, which the docs must've relied on to supplement whatever shelf-stable food they had. And he sure as hell didn't steal from Sloane's crew. She hadn't heard of anywhere else on the station with food and water. If he was still alive, he'd be near the fugee camp.

They turned a corner and Iridian stopped midstep. The doctors were climbing around a debris-strewn twenty-meter-wide hole that obliterated a stretch of corridor and parts of the rooms on either side. A single red sign pointing back to the airlock lit their path. Maybe the docs were afraid to use their headlamps, but Iridian would rather draw attention by turning her helmet's light on than trip over something and fall through the floor. Tiles and cables dangled over the hole's rim and hung in a motionless cascade toward the floors below.

Nothing moved beneath the thick shroud of dust over the wreckage. A couple of broken devices looked like bombs and froze Iridian in place for long seconds until she identified them as exposed parts of the HVAC system that kept atmo moving through the station. A bright yellow inflatable hull patch gleamed from the visible part of the first floor. The damage to this module was evidence that the Battle of Waypoint Station had involved a heavy and accurate assault on the station itself.

The missile punched through there and detonated in the gods-damned residential module. She hoped the station had been evacuated before then. "No wonder Spacelink abandoned this place. Testament to the architects that it's even holding together, spinning this fast. Where were you two when this happened?"

Tiwari and Williams reached the far side of the hole and stared at each other while Iridian made her way to them. Judging by the docs' sober expressions, it'd been as bad a day as the structural damage made it look. "Clinic," said Williams finally. "Spacelink launched their last shipment of reusable and recycled parts sunward. Families already left. Workers were packing to leave, if management saw a moment. Comms went dark."

"We watched, from the windows." Tiwari pointed at a blank stretch of wall, presumably where windows used to be projected. "Such enormous ships. And so close, we thought casualties would be brought to us."

Williams pointed at the hole in the module with a trembling hand. "Not accidental."

"No," Iridian agreed. The weapon had penetrated too precisely in the module's center, and it'd take precision timing to blow the explosives while the missile was still inside the station, at the speed it would've been moving. "So the workers weren't evacuated like Spacelink told the newsfeeds."

"Transport never arrived." Tiwari shrugged. "Space battle. Many ships lost. The station closed off the broken places. Then . . . AegiSKADA."

Williams's glove clapped against the sleeve of Tiwari's suit when she gripped his arm. Anything else Tiwari was thinking of saying stayed unsaid. After another few seconds of silence, Williams said, "Your docking bay is across."

"Yeah." Iridian was still wrapping her mind around the fact that somebody had chosen to put a missile right here, when there'd been three colony ships, an ITA cruiser, and a dozen small secessionist fighters all within a few thousand klicks of station-space. "Who did this? Which side?" The docs just stared, then started walking toward the pirates' docking bay.

The impact site was almost out of view around the curving walls when a soft scraping made Iridian glance over her shoulder. A single tile, poised at the hole's edge since the war and undisturbed by the med team's passage, slid over and clattered on a lower floor. The med team stopped walking as one, in time to catch the last two skittering steps of *something* in the dust and shadow behind them.

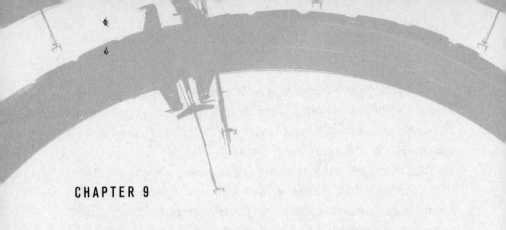

CHAPTER 9

Charges Accrued: Misprision of Felony

Adda's comp was playing Iridian's voice, volume up as loud as it would go so Adda wouldn't miss it. "Adda, babe, pick up."

She was curled over the table, wrist near her chest as if defending her glove from thieves. The mug by her elbow got nudged a few centimeters when she jumped, sloshing lukewarm coffee onto the table. The other people in the kitchen stared at her. Pel's arm around her shoulders helped her ignore them. For once the hood hiding her face was convenient. "Where have you *been?*" she said into her comp's mic. The comp's clock showed that it'd been over two hours since Iridian had last checked in. "Are you hurt?"

"No, I'm good and I'm almost there. Just want to make sure the door opens, because something's following me."

A chill shivered down Adda's arms and thighs. She should have known human activity on the station's outer hull, near the compound, would draw unwanted attention from a security AI, despite Iridian's minimal radio contact. "What kind of something?"

For a second only Iridian's footsteps and her labored breath sounded through the comp's speaker. The mic was close to her mouth. She must have kept her helmet on when she returned to station atmo. "It's on little legs. Thought I lost it at the docking bay doors, but it's still back there."

"Spiderbot," Pel said quietly. The others around them, who apparently had nothing better to do than listen in, swore in various languages. One ZV stood and left the room at a fast walk.

"Did you get that?" Adda said to her comp.

"No, what?"

Adda repeated Pel's assessment. Breath carried over the mic for a moment; then Iridian huffed out the laugh she used to hide painful memories. "Attacos, they're called," Iridian said. "One hundred or two hundred series, since I can hear it. I like 'spiderbots,' though. Give me a minute to find the one following me."

Adda drew a breath to argue, but stopped herself. AegiSKADA might not know what was in the wall passage, though the intelligence quantified the pirates' travels through it. A tiny drone with a cam could follow Iridian through the hatch and map the compound to the millimeter, but that would be a highly creative approach for an unsupervised intelligence.

Unless somebody who knew both AegiSKADA's abilities and the pirate compound's layout was directing it after all. Somebody like the missing lieutenant. A *partially* supervised intelligence, one taking suggestions but not obeying every order, could do this with alarming efficiency. Whatever the spider drone and whoever was behind it were capable of, it'd be better if Iridian destroyed it.

Chato poked his head through the doorway. "Nils said Iridian found a spiderbot. Where?"

The other lieutenant could have told AegiSKADA that the passage between the hulls was too narrow for large drones. "I think it followed her into the hole in the docking bay wall," Adda said.

Chato disappeared back into the hall and yelled, "Code Yellow, people! Pass it on and gear up!" Several ZV soldiers ran past, some in the direction of the bunkhouse and some toward the common room. The kitchen cleared of everyone but herself, Pel, and Chef.

Heavy footsteps preceded Chato in the bottom half of an armor suit. One glove covered his comp. In his other hand he carried one of the ZVs' handheld weapons. "Down in the station, if you see a little one, you'll be seeing big ones in a few minutes. We usually run back here when we see them, so this? This is bad."

More than one drone like whatever AegiSKADA had sent to blow up the bunkhouse and Xing's family would be a major problem. Suddenly every movement in Adda's peripheral vision looked like spiderbots heralding another attack. When she focused on the motion, it was the ZVs arming themselves for battle.

"I'm getting the major," said Chato.

He left past Captain Sloane. The captain carried a palm weapon and wore a full black-and-gold armored suit like something in a comic. The open faceplate looked like the only vulnerable part. "Adda, you'll join me. Pel, please stay here with Chef." The captain handed the woman another palm weapon.

"Don't worry." Pel gave Adda a quick hug. Even though he was taller than her, in her arms he was still the boy she'd grown up with. "The ZVs will stop the drones before they get within crawling distance of us." Although Pel never prioritized safety as highly as he should, he did have a point with the number of potential targets between the drones and him. Adda followed the captain out of the kitchen.

"Will he be all right in there?" she asked Captain Sloane. They stood close to the wall in the common room. Armed people in pieces of ZV armored suits ran past in the direction of the entryway, some carrying armor pieces they hadn't put on yet.

"Chef is an excellent shot. We had time and resources for target practice, when these were first designed. And if the machines make their way here, we have a surprise for them." The captain pointed upward and grinned.

The indicated section of blue ceiling looked exactly like the rest of the compound's patchwork covering. "What's up there?"

"That would ruin the surprise."

The entrance hatch banged open and shut several times. Whirring and sharp snapping noises echoed up from below each time the door opened. Adda gasped. "I should be watching this."

Captain Sloane looked her over. "You're unarmed, with no armor, my dear."

"No, I mean from my workspace, to see what's going through the sensor network and over the air while AegiSKADA's mobilizing drones. The more I have, the more I'll know what to look for next time, and about how it coordinates with other systems."

If it damaged the station, HarborMaster might take an interest. Any intercepted messages that sounded human would support her theory that someone like the former lieutenant was guiding one or both intelligences. She *needed more data.* "Have you got an antenna hooked up to your big comp?"

The captain waved the weaponless hand toward the appropriate hallway. "If you can, convince Si Po to help you. It'd be good for him."

In the hall, Adda skidded past straggling ZV soldiers tugging on armor as they jogged the opposite direction. Si Po huddled in the corner of the comp room, arms wrapped around his head. "Hey," Adda said softly. He clutched his head tighter. "Hey, I need your antenna." She winced at the innuendo Pel would've added on to that request. Si Po seemed to be holding his breath.

Last time she watched Si Po log in to the console, she had

captured his credentials. It wasn't polite of her, but he could have been more careful. When she plugged her nasal jack into the console, her comp displayed antenna controls on her hand. With her back to him, he might miss the details of how she'd logged in.

AegiSKADA encrypted its communications to its drones, but it couldn't hide its activity among the sensor nodes she'd mapped. It was actively processing feeds from the docking bay and the exterior hull. She labeled the unmapped nodes and added question marks where the nodes' locations and functionality were tentative, not proven. Now she had a good idea of where the intelligence's functioning sensors were.

Hell and hybridization. Iridian was surrounded by active nodes, so AegiSKADA knew exactly where to send the larger drones after the spiderbots. Gods, if anything happened to her . . .

Once Adda unplugged from the console, she ran to the empty water tank housing her generator to construct a larger-scale data visualization in the workspace. The tank stayed still as she crossed from the ladder to the generator, so Iridian must've done something to secure it. This time her brain cooperated, or AegiSKADA's influence was absent, and she entered the workspace quickly. It was made of a simple three-dimensional grid in green and black with the station map overlaid.

She stood in its center, darting effortlessly between active nodes to study sections in more detail without changing her physical position. The new map incorporated her energy consumption map, the pirates' annotated one, and the map the station administrators had made available for visitors. She overlaid the new sensor node data and burst commands from elsewhere in the station, probably directed at drones.

The overlay wouldn't help her stop the attacks, but with sufficient computing power and display fidelity, she could tell where the drones were. With a bit more intentionality coding, her system would extrapolate where they were going. Xing's family was the first to die from a drone strike to the base itself, so tracking the drones in the station would save, if she understood the pirates' reported experience, about one ZV life every three months. Somebody would have to watch the drone-tracking overlay while others were traveling in the station, but that was better than dreading the moment when spiderbots would appear. She smiled so widely that her physical lips twitched up at the corners. This felt like progress.

She'd read about that sensor spread, or listened to a lecture about it. One of her computer science professor's virtual presentations started up behind her. When she turned around, she stood at the top of an empty lecture hall with stadium seating for hundreds of students. Professors walked across the stage from right to left, speaking on different topics simultaneously. Some appeared to be present in person, some flickered from hidden projectors. All disappeared at the end of the stage when their topics failed to include the unique sensor spread Adda was looking for.

She needed information on sensor nets for *artificial intelligence in buildings and vessels.* The professors crossed the stage faster. Some faded from the line. In her peripheral vision, the green-and-black grid filled in new sensor nodes and lines of flow. Background processes borrowed a little of her attention to help analyze the data.

One professor stopped in front of a podium, halting and quieting the others in the procession. This one spoke about Jurek Volikov, last generation's prodigy AI developer. Volikov designed systems for major corporations and governments. Intelligent security systems, with the kind of sensor spread that Adda had described for this search. And the intelligence that was the topic of this lecture was optimized for isolated, large habitats like Waypoint Station.

Light-headedness forced Adda to sit down hard in the last row of auditorium seats. *Jurek Volikov.* Star of the artificial intelligence galaxy, or perhaps the black hole around which it spun, Volikov created extraordinarily effective designs and midwifed developing intelligences with a team of the world's next best AI experts. Every design corporation tried to copy his techniques, and few succeeded.

Adda had watched two of his development visualization recordings on repeat for hours, and she recognized one or two extremely basic techniques of his in her own workspaces. Her brain had recognized more, a distinctive pattern of development common between Volikov's recorded example and the intelligence killing people on Barbary Station. The sensor placement and activation pattern were based on his development process.

He would've been the top AI developer in the universe four years ago, the time period when trends in AegiSKADA's design indicated it had been developed. An unconventional application of the SCADA development path, like using it to create a security intelligence instead of one that just ran factories or utilities, was exactly the kind of innovation that made Volikov so successful. AegiSKADA would've been finished and installed in what would become Barbary Station shortly before Volikov killed himself, for reasons unknown.

Under a well-trained supervisor using the guidance methods he invented, his security systems were ruthless and impregnable . . . like Barbary Station's. And even if Blackguardly Jack was giving AegiSKADA hints and tips, the intelligence wasn't fully supervised.

Adda's hands fisted in the pillow nest. In the workspace the motion translated to squeezing a yellow stress ball with an inane smiling face. She was nowhere near the developer Volikov was in grade school. He might have developed AegiSKADA in his prime, with as many as seven team members in theirs. She had no hope of taking on one of his intelligences.

The podium at which the professor was speaking rocketed across the stage and into a wall, where it shattered with a resounding crash. The professor kept talking, but Pel shouted over the lecture, "Sissy! Come on! Everybody's freaking out up here. We have to go!"

"Okay." Dazed, she set her analyzers to continue collecting data and applying it to the tracking overlay, saving as they went. Once everything was backing up, she crawled out of the generator.

A square of light from the door to the rest of the compound framed Pel's silhouette on the floor. "Come on, come on, come on." He hung on the last N until she was halfway up the ladder. The moment she closed the trapdoor behind her, he laid a hand on the wall and started walking toward the kitchen. She followed, pulling her hood over her head to keep the blue dust out of her hair.

The formerly uniform blue walls and floor now bore blackened scars where something small and explosive had detonated inside the compound. One of the floor tiles was missing, filled instead with a bright yellow inflatable hull patch with the Transorbital Voyages logo half exposed through the hole. The patch must have been part of the haul the rovers had collected on the colony ship. If the pirates hadn't selected space-grade material for the exterior walls, they'd have been in serious trouble.

She blinked. *She'd* have been in serious trouble. Those explosions could've hurt *her*. Between her earbuds and her sharpsheets, she hadn't even heard them.

Someone in the main room shouted, "Pick it up, ZVs, we got

minutes before the big ones get here!" Adda's breath quickened, and she almost stepped on Pel's heels in her effort to stay close to him.

In the kitchen, chairs and tables were overturned. Targeted particle fire had disintegrated parts of several into the consistency of sand. "Found her! Let's go," Pel called.

Chef's head popped up from behind the counter at the far side of the cramped room. Once she saw Adda, she ducked back down behind the counter, then emerged from her small refuge running. "One came out of the vent!" Chef pointed at the vent near the ceiling.

Adda looked around at the mess. "One?"

"She missed a few times," said Pel. "And then it blew up, over there." In the direction he pointed, the floor was scorched black beneath the remnants of a chair.

A pop followed immediately by crashing and cursing emanated from somewhere down the hall. "Have you collected the observations you require?" Captain Sloane called from the same direction.

"Still collecting, but it's automated now," Adda called back.

"Shut it down. I need to deliver the surprise," said the captain.

Adda ran back to her tank to transfer essential processes from her workspace generator to her comp glove and end the rest, then packed the generator into its shielded mesh bag. It sounded like Sloane was going to set off an electromagnetic pulse. The pirates' digital library didn't have a printer pattern for a workspace generator. If this one got fried, she'd have a hard time printing a new one. The glove was supposed to protect her comp from similar damage, but she'd never tested it. At least the pirates' library would have a basic comp pattern to print, if anything happened to hers.

When she climbed out of the tank again, Pel grabbed her

sleeve at the shoulder and pulled her down the hall at a run, with his free hand trailing along the wall. In the main room, Chef beckoned them to hurry. The door to Sturm's workroom was dented, along with part of the wall next to it, and beneath Sloane's braided hair, the back of the black armor bore a deep crack and a dull scorch mark.

"Comps off, please," the captain said. They all reached for glove switches except for Chef, who touched a spot between her breasts. A *comp bra?* Adda would have to ask Iridian to ask her about that later. Something small and black scuttled across the floor. This time she saw it explode, in a small burst of bright white. Chef yelped. Blood flowed down her calf as she reached the entryway.

Instead of the entryway, Captain Sloane ran into the other hallway. Adda watched from the main room as the captain entered the stateroom and moved the picture of a nighttime city street to the floor. A metal square jutted out from the newly exposed wall, as covered in blue dust as the rest of the compound. Sloane pressed the square and a sharp whine rose from the main room's ceiling. Captain Sloane's grin was a little too wild to be entirely sane. "The surprise is deployed. Follow me!"

They ran to the open hatch in the entryway. Chef was approaching the opening at the top of the ladder from different angles before she fit her broad hips through. "Everybody out, now, now, now!" Tritheist roared to those farther down the passage between the walls. Another loud *pop* startled Adda. One of the ZVs stumbled and swore.

"I thought we weren't ever going to evacuate," Adda panted to Pel on the way down the long ladder.

"That's for rad contamination. This is a fucking invasion. It's just little ones now, but if we don't get out before the big ones come, we're all dead."

"I thought we were safe in the compound," said Adda.

"Not safe anywhere," said the ZV below Adda. "We can usually keep the spiderbots out with the door, though. You see the spider-bots in the corridors out there, that's how you know the big ones are coming to fucking zap your ass dead. So when we see the little ones, we fucking move no matter where we see 'em."

A few steps from the ladder's last rung, Adda's boot caught on something heavy. Someone lay against the wall. One of his armored shoulders had snagged her toe. She bent to grab an arm, but she was already guiding Pel. The ZV man was too heavy to move one-handed. "Help!" she cried. People pushed past them.

"Whoa, what's wrong?" Pel clutched her elbow.

"Someone's hurt." A drone skittered across the wall near her head. She swiped at it, but missed and ducked away from it. It exploded with a bang among the cables hanging from the ceiling.

"Who?"

She gritted her teeth and ran again. "I don't know. We can't stop." Behind her, armor dragged on the wall. Captain Sloane had lifted the man by the arm and was hauling his limp form toward the docking bay.

Then Iridian was in front of them, pressed flat to one wall, face hidden behind her helmet's faceplate. Although they'd been talking on the pirates' comms, seeing her in person was like tak-ing a weight off Adda's chest so she could breathe. Iridian held her open shield against the wall beside her so as not to block the way. "Are you all right?"

"Yes. Are you? There's someone on the floor back there." Adda pointed without stopping.

"I'm good," Iridian said. "Let's go."

They burst out of the wall and ran after pirates streaming across the empty docking bay. The ship that had brought Iridian and Adda to the station was gone. The bay seemed even bigger with only humans and the two wrecks on the far side for scale.

The decompression alarm swallowed their footsteps. Aegi-SKADA was opening the docking bay doors, like it did when they'd first arrived on station. Persistent by nature, the intelligence would've realized that letting the vacuum of space pull intruders out of the station could be a simple end to the intrusion. The human and cargo doors behind the two shipwrecks thundered shut. A piece of debris jammed into the nearest one designed for pedestrians kept that escape route open.

Captain Sloane lowered the partially armored ZV to the floor near the hole in the docking bay wall and crouched beside the man. After several seconds' examination, the captain rose and joined the rest of the pirates, leaving the motionless ZV behind. Sorrow, or perhaps despair, swept through Sloane's body language, then disappeared beneath the captain's usual confidence in the space between one step and the next.

The pirates ran toward the open pedestrian exit to the bay, shoving their weapons into a locker next to the door as they passed. Chato stood by the locker, saying, "Clubs? Knives? Razors? Anything in your pockets?" A few paused to deposit small weapons. "Drop off anything sharp, long and thin, or big and round," he told them. "AegiSKADA targets anything weapon-shaped, and now that we're moving around the docking bay here, it's going to be looking close."

"We don't have anything," Adda said. Iridian had stopped carrying knives around, and Adda's weapons were all in her comp.

The last of the pirates passed the locker with their palm weapons still strapped to their hands. Chato locked it, pulled a ZV jacket hood up over his head, and caught up with the three of them. "Why don't those go in?" asked Iridian.

"Palmers? AegiSKADA doesn't recognize them," Chato said. "That's why we made 'em. Why the captain and Kaskade and Sturm made 'em, that is. One good shot kills people and spider-bots, but—"

"It doesn't match anything in AegiSKADA's weapons profile!" Adda said. Iridian chuckled like the interruption both amused and surprised her, and Adda shrugged. "That's clever. And Irid-ian's shield doesn't match the profile, either, since AegiSKADA didn't . . ." Adda thought about what she was saying as she said it, which made the rest of her sentence emerge at half volume. "Hunt her down and eliminate her as a threat."

Iridian looked as horrified at that possibility as Adda felt. "When do I get one of those palmers?" Iridian asked.

"When you stop bringing drones down on our asses," said Sergeant Natani, the pirate with the scar on her temple. Iridian's expression implied that she didn't care or hadn't heard. Failure was hell for her, though, and Adda knew she was more upset than she appeared. Sergeant Natani glared at them and then followed the other ZVs, palmer up and ready. "Move it, Chato!"

Chato shrugged at Adda and Iridian as if apologizing on the woman's behalf. "Not everyone thinks that. When we get the right printer material and the time for Sturm to build one, you'll get one. If there was any of the right material on the colony ship, the captain or the lieutenant snapped it up and kept quiet about it."

"Why didn't you build something to stop the drones instead?" asked Adda.

"None of the officers' code gets through," Chato said. "And the guy who knew how to do the fancy EMP and laser things got his head exploded. Besides, we don't usually see drones on base. We drill on defense scenarios sometimes, because what else can we do? But this is the first time spiderbots came all the way in."

After the enormous docking bay, the station hallways designed primarily for humans felt safer, illusory though that safety was. The industrial flooring was the same as the docking bay's, though the cracked ceiling was higher than in the *Prosperity Dawn*'s corridors. The smooth wall panels were a lighter metallic color with occasional rectangular black frames built in, where a projector might've shown an exterior view or artwork.

Tracks for magnetized cargo carriers paralleled mostly broken ceiling light strips, although Adda had yet to pass beneath one of the robots. AegiSKADA might have dismantled cargo carriers to maintain its drones. One stretch of track had been twisted off the ceiling, so that the pirates had to duck around. Part of the track lay in a tangled pile against a wall. Labels on the doors referenced various stages of water and waste recycling.

They ran down the corridor over red arrows on the floor that Iridian had said pointed toward station north, following them over a stalled people-moving walkway. At the end of it, several pirates crouched in a circle facing outward, pointing palmers down the hallway in both directions. Si Po dove into the circle's center, where the rest of the pirates congregated.

Chato gave Adda a gentle shove toward the center of the group. "Something's following us."

Kaskade bent over with her hands on her knees, breathing as hard as Adda. "Damn. Can't believe we made—"

A small *pop* made everyone jump. Kaskade sprawled forward on the floor. Blood streamed from the back of her head. White shards of skull shone beneath her red-matted hair.

Pel's fingers dug into Adda's arm. His voice shook when he asked, "What part of her did the spiderbot blow up?"

CHAPTER 10

Charges Accrued: Destruction of Property (Vandalism, First Count)

Amazingly, the pirates had protocols. Iridian must've had the ZV Group to thank for that. They sectioned off the corridor into quadrants assigned to squads and searched the place for more spider-bots as the group moved on at a faster pace. They were thorough and relatively calm, even while Kaskade's blood pooled behind them. No more drones appeared, but Iridian kept watching for them.

Kaskade had given Pel errands to run to make him feel like part of the crew. And she had way too much in common with Adda: same systems orientation, similar level of intelligence, hell, same love of unnatural hair colors, though her blue streaks had been less striking than Adda's purple and red. Kaskade's loss had given all the pirates a hollow look about the eyes.

Iridian updated her map as they traversed a long, winding route through the station, since Adda would want to plot secondary escape routes later. The occasional undamaged marks on the floor put them about ninety ticks north on their way to one hun-

dred. That made the next docking bay station north. Like the rest
of the station's docking bays, the map depicted the northern one
taking up the first two floors of its modules, with the top reserved
for a small observation room and a shuttle hookup to move people
to and from the hub in the center of the ring.

Sloane directed them to switch levels at unpredictable intervals, once by elevator, once by elevator shaft, twice via cables
hanging through holes in the floor. The second and third floors
must've been damaged during the Battle of Waypoint Station. In
the years since, walls had collapsed and strewn themselves over
walkways designed for more mobile, lower weights.

Stopping every few meters to clear a path, confirm that what
she was looking at wasn't a bomb, check for spiderbots, or answer
"What was that sound?" was irritating as hell, though the cau-
tion was warranted. Including herself, Adda, and the boy in San
Miguel's arms, only twenty-one of them had made it this far. Captain Sloane's crew had arrived on station with fewer than a hundred, including the ZVs, but certainly more than this.

They stalked the corridors in near silence. When Iridian got
tired of listening to breathing and footsteps and asked, "Where
are we going?" Chato just said, "Following protocol." Both of them
went back to listening for spiderbots, or bigger drones that they
might actually hear over twenty pairs of boots tramping through
a scrap-cluttered corridor.

She walked out front, since the fully armored ZVs stayed at
the rear to deal with pursuit. The position should've earned her
more info than that. She kept the shield up and a little to the side,
leaving her shoulder and hip exposed to cover some of Adda too.
As the spiderbot on the people mover taught them, death could
come from any direction.

The one that killed Kaskade had been *silent*. An atmo system fan might've spun up around then, but Iridian couldn't be sure. Even if they were moving quietly, they still might've missed it.

Ahead of their current position on the lowest floor, the one with the docking bay's main entrance and exit, a stranger shouted, "Movement!" The repetitive organic noise accompanying the voice was a dog barking. A big one, not one of the spacefaring terriers people in habs kept.

The pirates halted. Debris blocked most of the curving corridor ahead, though light from the other side shone through the cracks. The ceiling from at least one floor above had crushed two industrial-size water processors and shoved them into the corridor through one of its walls.

The biggest beam of light shining from behind the wreckage silhouetted a human on the pile of debris. "Is this any way to welcome neighbors?" Sloane shouted at the figure.

"Captain Sloane?" The person clapped a hand to her thigh, activating a large LED in her comp glove's palm. Rather than shining it in the captain's eyes to prove identity, she lit the floor ahead of them. "Come on in. Follow the yellow brick road."

Is this person the same kind of crazy as the people who saved my life outside? Iridian wondered. The LED revealed a strip of yellow reflective tape that zigged and zagged across the arrows on the floor pointing to station north, and Iridian relaxed a bit. That made sense. Captain Sloane took over Iridian's position at the front of the group, and the pirates formed a line behind her to advance toward the unseen barking dog.

Something clattered in the wreckage behind them. Iridian and the ZVs spun and searched for the source. "Keep moving, lads and lasses," the captain said in a conversational tone from the other side of the rubble barrier. *Just being followed by an invisible enemy, nothing to shout about.*

Iridian pushed Adda and Pel toward the barrier. When she reached the patch of light pouring through the low gap in the metal and concrete where they'd disappeared, she tracked the yellow tape into a knee-high tunnel at the barrier's base. The deployed shield was too wide to fit through the gap. She had no idea what Adda and Pel were crawling toward, and the shield could protect the people behind her. Letting them stand around exposed when she had a perfectly good shield felt wrong, especially given the condition of the armor on those who had it.

After a long breath, she gave the shield to Chato behind her. She was joining their crew. She had to start trusting them sometime. "Keep passing this back as people come through. I'll return and collapse it once everyone's in." After she confirmed that Pel and Adda were really safe on the other side. Chato accepted her shield, still watching the corridor behind them more closely than the path ahead, and she crawled after Pel and Adda.

Iridian emerged into a cleared area just before the corridor opened onto the docking bay that served as station north. The "zero ticks" designator must've been under the rubble that almost closed the corridor off. The cleared area extended several meters to a red line on the docking bay floor, past which was a more deliberate line of barriers, a watchtower, and rows of shipping containers draped with colorful tarps.

A step to the side of the yellow tape line, Pel held Adda's arm while she looked at her comp. The crew members who crawled through the barrier after Iridian relaxed like they were watching for friends, not trouble. Pel's big ZV friend, Rio, patted him on the head as she passed, smiling as she walked toward the human activity stirring among the shipping containers.

The bronze-complexioned woman who'd greeted them stood beside Captain Sloane, a few steps from the crawlway through the barrier. She wore civilian clothes beneath a thin slab of metal strapped over her chest. Even with the green binder of flexible mesh beneath it flattening her breasts against her ribs, she had a lot of chest to cover. The binder might've been armored too. "Sorry about that," she said to the captain. "We lost four people right outside the barrier when a drone snuck up on us by moving about a centimeter every hour, up against the left wall. We've started taking freeze frames of the approach every few minutes and comparing them on Kigen's comp."

"Of course, of course."

The woman's eyes narrowed. "Are those things following you?"

"Possibly," said Sloane. "I just EMP'd our abode."

"So that *was* the surprise." Adda fiddled with her comp glove, muttered at it, and gave a relieved-sounding sigh. When she glanced up at Iridian's confused half smile, she added, "I wish I could keep following the sensor data, but my comp just isn't up to it. The EMP was . . . dramatic. Don't worry, the essentials are compressed and backed up on here."

Iridian shook her head. "I hope the base light fixtures have built-in Faraday shields. People always forget to protect the godsdamned lights."

San Miguel came through with her child, and the little boy wriggled out of her arms. Jalal dashed, squealing, right past the captain, toward a growing crowd gathering just over the red line on the floor. Other kids shouting excitedly over one another ran out of the crowd to meet him. A big brown-and-black dog trotted beside the children and watched the newcomers.

Si Po had clearly figured out how to collapse the shield, since he crawled through the barrier with it in its carrying configuration. He gave Iridian a small smile when he handed it to her. "Welcome to Fugee HQ."

Something whizzed by Iridian's face as he passed. She deployed the shield mid-dive to get between the kids and a fast-moving black dot the size of her thumbnail. The thing arched down and detonated against her shield, slamming Iridian, Si Po, and the kids to the deck.

She coughed and tried to regain the breath the floor took when she landed. *Ah, yes. Falling in hyper-g hurts.* Beneath the high whine in her ears, people were yelling. Adda dropped to her knees next to Iridian, leaving Pel standing alone. He said something Iridian couldn't lip-read, while people ran past and around him. All she heard was a high-pitched ringing.

"I'm good." She barely heard her own voice. Her wrists hurt like hell, but she'd be all right once her diaphragm started doing its job again. The Shieldrunner training officer would've done her more damage than this for catching the explosion in a weak brace position.

She rolled her head back along the curve of her helmet to see the kids upside down. One fugee girl bled from the nose, but they were all sitting up and breathing well enough to cry. Adults swooped out of the fugee crowd to hug them. San Miguel shoved Tritheist out of her path as she dashed to Jalal. The fugees' big dog ran in from the other side to stand, barking, between the children and Sloane's crew. Si Po peered around a wall of alarmed ZV soldiers, watching for another attack.

Adda said something. Iridian shook her head. "Zikri's coming," Adda shouted. "Stay still." *No problem there.* Adda sank her teeth into her lower lip, face scrunched in an anxious frown.

Pel found Adda's shoulder with his hand and crouched next to her, grinning his big goofy grin. "You make a hell of an entrance." Someone must've caught him up, and had Iridian blacked out for a minute? She didn't remember him leaving base in glasses dark enough to watch solar eclipses from Earth. Local time put this well after nightfall in healthy enviro, but bright docking bay overhead lights reflected in the lenses. The fugees were smart to keep the place lit. It'd be harder to spot drones in the dark.

Zikri, the ZV Group medic, pulled green disposable gloves over teak-brown hands as he took a knee on the opposite side of Iridian from Adda and Pel. "Only one spiderbot," Iridian read on his lips. He said something else, then tried again more loudly when Iridian just frowned at him. "How do your head and chest feel?"

"Chest is better now," Iridian said. "Head's not bad. Padding in this helmet is great."

"Turn your O_2 up in there," Zikri suggested.

"Can't, HUD's down." Iridian collapsed the shield and winced at the wrist movement required.

Zikri made a lifting motion with both hands. ". . . helmet off," Iridian lip-read. Breath came easier without the helmet. If they ever got a break, Sturm would have to take another look at the air flow in this suit.

After staring into Iridian's eyes for an uncomfortable ten or fifteen seconds, Zikri asked, "Breathing comfortably? No wheezing?" Speech sounded clearer with the helmet off too. Iridian took a couple of deep breaths and nodded. "Pregnant?" She shook her head vigorously, which made Zikri laugh. "Yeah, you're good enough, then. Come find me if you have trouble." Then he went to the children, conducting a similar inspection on each of them.

"That was exciting," said Captain Sloane drily. Iridian accepted the offered hand up.

"You might've mentioned that those spiderbots jump, sir. Captain," Iridian corrected herself quickly.

"I admit to not anticipating their arrival," the captain said. "We haven't seen any in weeks. However, your heroics earned us a few points with our neighbors. And a favor for me." Sloane winked at Tritheist, who rolled his eyes and turned his back on them. If one of them had explained what they'd bet on and the favors at stake, Iridian hadn't heard the explanation. They didn't always invite others to bet on whatever event caught their interest, so Iridian might not have heard about it even if a drone hadn't just exploded next to her ears.

Louder and mostly to the woman who'd greeted them at the rubble barrier, the captain said, "These are our latest additions, Iridian Nassir and Adda Karpe. Treat them with the same respect you'd give any of my crew." That resulted in a round of applause, but Iridian nodded in response to the captain's stern look. She and Adda weren't part of the crew yet, even if that were implied for the sake of publicity.

After more crew and fugees patted Iridian's back, the pirates dispersed among the crowd. The fugees were retreating over the clear zone toward a small village of shipping containers hung with tarps. The woman with the chest piece bellowed, "Don't stand around waiting to get blown up! The safety line's way back there." She pointed to the thick red line painted on the floor, and the civilians picked up their pace.

"Reconvene for a farewell to the fallen at Floor Two in three hours," Captain Sloane shouted after them. The order to move away from the rubble barrier apparently didn't apply to leaders. The captain, Tritheist, and Major O.D. stood conversing with the woman and another stranger from the fugee camp while the rest of the pirates and fugees walked toward the shipping containers.

Iridian opened her mouth to ask a question, but Adda had already stepped close to and wrapped her arms around Iridian, armor and all. Iridian hugged her back, as gently as the armor allowed. That explosion really must've scared her, for her to be this intimate in public. Adda usually felt like everybody was staring at them.

"I'm all right," Iridian told her. "I say so, Zikri said so." Iridian's voice sounded weird to her, but neither Adda nor Pel reacted like there was something wrong with it. She waited until Adda nodded and resumed walking before she asked, "So, what's so safe about the line, I wonder?"

"That's the farthest in they've seen a drone," Pel said. "Recently, anyway. Bots used to come all the way to the passthroughs, but they don't now." He held up his hands with his palms out to ward off Adda's questions before they started. "I don't know why, I don't know how, I don't know shit but what they tell me."

"Have the drones entered the compound before?" Adda asked. "The ZV Group seemed very . . . prepared."

Pel shook his head. "I told you, we're pretty safe there. The ZVs train, though. They train for a bunch of different scenarios. I figured it was to keep them from getting bored."

"No, training during downtime is just smart," said Iridian. "That's how the badasses become badasses. Practice."

Parents came to thank Iridian for saving their kids. San Miguel's thanks meant the most. It was good to have a ZV soldier solidly on her side, especially one who'd been on the right side of the war. In an ISV protecting those kids would've been the obvious choice, criminal negligence if she hadn't done it. Outside an armored vehicle, it'd been a huge risk she'd taken reflexively. Iridian tucked her hands behind her lower back so the shaking wouldn't show and returned San Miguel's watery smile. If she'd had time to think, she still would've done it, but . . . *Damn, that was ridiculous.*

Between the two single-story entrances at either end of the docking bay, a passthrough stood open beneath a red N ("north" in

English), C ("north" in Russian), and corresponding Mandarin and Japanese symbols projected onto the wall. Dogs bounded beside their owners, exiting a docked vessel too large to enter the bay. Cats sat atop some of the shipping containers arranged in rows over the empty landing pads. Even ants and roaches skittered through the shadows like normal bugs, not spiderbots. Though the insects were pests, they needed consistent food, water, and atmo to survive. The station and pirate base felt sterile without the occasional bug.

A defense installation stood in front of the open passthrough, complete with a guard tower like the one near the rubble pile and blast walls. The guard was watching Iridian and Adda, not the entrances, and he seemed more curious than suspicious. When he caught Iridian looking, he waved, and she waved back. She wasn't going to trust some stranger to watch for enemies on her behalf anyway, so it didn't matter to her that he was bad at his job. Too bad for the fugees, though.

The ZVs could do the job better. "So why are we out on the exterior, instead of staying with these fine folks?" she asked.

Pel sighed. "Yeah, that'd be nice. But AegiSKADA hates us."

"We must be putting the fugees at risk of a drone attack just by being here," Adda said quietly.

"That's what Captain Sloane says," Pel agreed. "As soon as we can go back, we'll go."

At regular intervals along the wall, about the height of the sensor node Adda had tapped behind the wall near the base, crushed sensor node casings hung empty. The AI would be blind here, or near to it. Maybe the guard really didn't have much to watch.

Several unarmed fugees approached from the shipping-container village, shouting the virtues and prices of various things, mostly data transfers. "We already have access to all of that," Adda muttered after Iridian shooed a seller away.

"Figured," Iridian said. "It looks like they've got a barter econ-
omy, though. If we can't get messages out reliably, we can't transfer money out of our accounts. Not that we have money, mind,
this is a general 'we.'" Although they weren't completely destitute,
for once. They'd never paid Reis for his part in the hijacking. With
luck they'd get a chance to find out if he had next of kin, and
with a bit more luck, she and Adda would be able to pay them the
dumb bastard's share.

"I can loan you some," Pel said. "I'm on the crew, in a limited
capacity, so I get paid."

"Oh yeah?" asked Iridian. "How much?"

He named a figure. She stopped walking. "I must've heard you
wrong. Getting blown up always fucks with my ears." He repeated
it, smiling like a puppy getting away with something.

"For *what*?" Adda demanded.

"Hey, I do stuff!" he said. "I fetch and carry, and tell jokes, and
recruit now."

"Captain Sloane didn't want you to recruit anybody," said Adda.

"It's not like they can't afford it. They've got money coming out
every orifice." They walked a few paces in silence, and his expression got gloomier with each step. "The guy who died in the wall
walk was a decent one. And I like . . . I liked Kaskade. We're losing
people fast."

Abrupt shifts in topic seemed to be Pel's style, and Iridian
hadn't been ready for the impact of remembering the crew members they'd lost in the past few hours. It was awful to lose even
one member of your team so suddenly, let alone two. The pirates
who knew them well must've been having a hell of a day. She
swallowed a lump in her throat. "This place is gods-damned dangerous."

"It's not usually this bad." Pel focused on sliding his feet as he walked, probably to keep from tripping, since he started walking normally when Adda looped her arm through his. "Before Xing and her family, we went almost four months without a single person dying. I mean, there were some spiderbots in the station that we ran from, but that usually happens when we go into the station. The ZVs keep practicing what they'd do if something *did* come into base, but I feel like that was the first time one did."

Iridian grimaced. "That'll come back on us, huh." He nodded gravely. "It's easy to blame people for what happens when they take risks you don't want to take," she said. "And easier to blame the new people than the leader you admire."

She almost followed that up with *Secessionist cowards* by habit, but she kept her mouth shut. Nobody wanted to die badly or sooner than they had to. Captain Sloane wasn't waiting around for a lucky break that'd let the crew escape, or maybe for the captain, Adda and Iridian were it. Some of the secessionists on the crew, like Major O.D., Six, and probably Zikri, would back Adda and Iridian up. O.D. already did, by keeping Sergeant Natani in line. The others pissed Iridian off by threatening her, and worse, Adda, because they couldn't think through their limited options. Who they'd fought for didn't come into that.

Pel sniffed the air. "Hey, is there a beautiful girl with a goldfish tattoo around somewhere?"

A giggle came from behind one of the makeshift tarp-and-shipping-container shelters nearby. "How do you do that?" A girl a year or two younger than Pel turned the corner, smiling beneath a bright orange kerchief. Unlike the ones some female ZVs wore, hers was more decorative than functional. Her low-cut top displayed an iridescent yellow-and-orange goldfish tattoo that shimmered on rich brown skin even in the docking bay's garish lights.

A faint vanilla scent strengthened as she approached.

Pel hugged her as enthusiastically as she hugged him. "Lozzie, this is my sister, Adda, and her girlfriend, Iridian Nassir."

Lozzie's eyes bulged. "Oh my gods, Pel, you're the best." She gave him a tighter hug and a kiss on the cheek that knocked his glasses crooked, completing his happily bewildered expression. "You two are engineers, right?"

"Mechanical and software." Iridian pointed to herself, then Adda. It was easier to list their degree concentrations than to explain their real areas of expertise.

"Oh, perfect." Lozzie beckoned for them to follow her around the shack's corner without letting go of Pel's hand. "Our printer's broken, and we can't exactly print a new one!"

Adda caught her eye, and Iridian shrugged. Neither of them had spent much time working on printers, but this one was already broken. They couldn't do much more damage. "We'll take a look at it."

Lozzie's container was one of about fifty scattered in a haphazard row across the length of the docking bay. Three more rows wound between the safety line and the passthrough. More people Pel's age appeared from among the containers and led him off toward another area of the container village, shouting greetings to him and waving good-bye to Lozzie, who stayed with Iridian and Adda. In addition to the people, Iridian spotted more cats and birds on the periphery. This population was used to stable planetary life. Spacefarers preferred smaller, less mobile pets.

Someone had roped the printer off with red hazard tape, which Lozzie lifted for Iridian to duck under. The fugee watched from well outside the tape while Iridian gingerly pried the printer's case open and Adda looked for the schematics in the station's local library. "So are you in love with Pel," Iridian asked Lozzie while she worked, "or just having fun?" Adda blushed three shades redder and lifted her comp glove for maximum face coverage.

"Oh my gods." Lozzie giggled. "With Pel, it's all fun. He doesn't care where you're going or where you've been! Ask anybody." It took Iridian a moment to remember what the "where you're going or where you've been" part meant on Mars: he'd fuck anything human and some things that weren't. The fondness in Lozzie's voice suggested she was calling Pel "nonjudgmental" in bed rather than the other interpretation, "sexually insatiable."

Iridian grinned. "With a personality like his, he's in no place to judge."

About five seconds after she and Adda got the printer printing without threatening to explode in a toxic particulate cloud, another woman poked her head around the corner of a container. "Hi! Can you help us with an enviro unit?" She angled a thumb toward the passthroughs. The status projections over the bay's three passthroughs indicated that a ship was connected to every one of them. "Deck Five goes down to two degrees during the night cycle, and we can't warm it up."

Several people got out of Iridian's way to let her look the dock designators over. Sure enough, they were all labeled with the same ship name, the *Voorspoed*. It was another word for "success, well-being, and prosperity," according to the translator in her comp. Typical colony ship name. "That's a mother of a weight to be locked onto a ring station," she said. The station engines were already spinning Barbary hard to maintain its hypergrav, and they were pushing a whole colony ship around with it.

"Are the *Voorspoed*'s engines running?" Adda asked the woman trying to get someone to improve the colony ship's enviro.

The woman shook her head, and Adda and Iridian exchanged appalled glances. Those passthroughs were holding up shockingly well, considering that they'd been hauling the massive colony ship's bulk around in circles for three years. "We're afraid the station won't like it if the engines come on," the woman explained. By the station, Iridian guessed she meant AegiSKADA. The fugee woman smiled hopefully. "Besides, we want to save power. We're counting on its enviro if anything happens to this docking bay. Like if drones come, or if the whistling coming from that wall gets louder. Right, Rashehd?" The fugee looked to a man standing behind her.

"That ship isn't technically *on* the station," Adda observed quietly.

It took Iridian a moment to make the connection that Adda had. "Like Captain Sloane's base. So drones don't go in there, do they?"

Rashehd shook his bearded head. "They haven't so far."

"Good point." The pirates had thought the base was outside AegiSKADA's area of influence, before the drone blew up one of the bunkhouses. Iridian was looking forward to reaching a safer place herself, but she'd be happier to send Adda there instead. She borrowed Velcro strips and strapped her armored gloves to her forearms since the suit's storage compartments were still full of tools, gave Adda a kiss, and let her follow the woman into the *Voorspoed*. The guy named Rashehd led Iridian to the probable atmo leak.

Hours later a crowd of people were watching everything she did, waiting for their turn to ask for help. Without an understanding of the machines keeping them alive, they lived in a state of low-grade terror that something would break and kill them all. Iridian restrained herself from commenting on the possibilities while she worked. These poor people wouldn't get the joke. Besides, some of the enviro system malfunctions were the *well*, *this would've surprised you when you stopped breathing and didn't know why*, laugh-or-you'll-cry sort of humor.

Maybe Iridian's service here would reinforce her and Adda's continued value as crew, even after Adda got the AI to stop attacking them. The pirates could just as easily see her willingness to do extra work with no promise of reward as a weakness to exploit. The crew had four or five people who could be offering their own technical skills, after all, and Iridian hadn't seen any of them fixing printers and enviro controls. Maybe she was being paranoid. Captain Sloane acknowledged her and Adda's value, and the captain's assessment was the important one.

A man with pale skin and red hair he might've been born with pushed through the crowd. "Hey, I'm Kyr. My wife Suhaila . . ." Here he trailed off to allow for whoops and cheers from the fugees. A grin spread over Iridian's face. What was all this about? It seemed safe enough. And she'd love to meet the host of the Fugee News feed she and Adda had listened to.

"Suhaila Al-Mudari . . ." One last whoop interrupted him, and he gave the person a quick wave of a pale hand. "Would like to invite you to speak with her on a live broadcast of Fugee News." This time the cheers went on for at least ten seconds, which gave Iridian time to hand a comp back to its owner. If the owner could get a new part printed, someone could install it later.

After the cheers died down, Iridian said, "I'd love to!" Applause, to which she bowed. "I've got to meet Captain Sloane on the second floor somewhere later, though. Can my girlfriend come too?"

The listening fugees laughed along with Kyr. "Floor Two, you mean."

"That's what I said."

"The bar's called Floor Two. Long story about the name. That's where the crew always meets. You can see the antenna from here."

Kyr pointed. Red and orange strips of tape hung from the antenna, which rose above the containers around it. "And yes, Suhaila would love to talk to Adda. Ask any fugee where to find WFUG!" He said each letter, but Iridian bit her lip while tapping a message to Adda to avoid saying the phonetic pronunciation aloud.

As they walked through the fugees' colony ship, Iridian had to admire what they'd done with the place. Anything not required to keep the ship airtight had been rearranged to suit mobile, awake residents with stable grav. The company name plastered all over the fittings was Crowne, with a predictable crown logo.

More children scampered around the ship than in the docking bay, despite what felt like a late local time. Iridian, with armored pockets containing nothing of value, was as comfortable watching them as they seemed staring at her. "You don't get many visitors, do you?"

Kyr quirked an eyebrow. "Aside from Sloane's crew every few months, no. Which reminds me, if there's time, Suhaila will cue a plea for aid from Earth or the colonies, wherever she thinks you have the most pull. A censored version goes out with the ships every few months."

"Um, it'd be better if my name and face weren't broadcast to NEU law enforcement." The secessionist "governments" stayed in the asteroid belt and the outer planets, but the Near Earth Union might be mad or bureaucratic enough to come after her.

Kyr gave her a disappointed frown, but she wouldn't offer to help in a way that'd bring trouble for the crew once they all got off the station. *Hell, getting everybody off the station should be help enough.* "The censor can make you a generic NEU ex-soldier, I guess." He opened a door into what looked like a large closet lined with mattresses. Upon detailed inspection, it continued to look that way. Mattresses were also affixed to the ceiling, along with small mics like the kind embedded in corporate ship passageways for constant contact and monitoring.

They hung in a black wire chandelier above a woman with dark hair, a cat's-eye-yellow shirt, and a smile as she spoke from one of the formfitting chairs programmers used in the big labs. Action figures from popular science fiction and fantasy productions were arranged on top of a small refrigeration unit. Most of the figures were from major Earth vids, but several were from Lunawood stories produced on Earth's Moon and one or two cheesy Lunawood ripoffs produced in the colonies. Even the desk lamp set the impossible task of lighting the room from a corner on the floor had shiny stickers depicting imagined alien creatures and sleek-lined, supposedly faster-than-light ships on its base.

Kyr waved. Suhaila waved back without breaking her patter. "I mean, I can see watching Sol's *Saddest Hoarders* for a lifetime. Not spending your whole life singing about one person. But since that doesn't make it through the lead cloud and *Casey Mire Mire* doesn't bring me any episodes, take a listen to 'Lifetime Lovin' Zir' by the Palomar Five Collective."

So the ship's name was pronounced with six syllables, not four. Iridian had only ever read the full name. Adda had interpreted the four-syllable version as *Casey swamp swamp*, which seemed odd. And the pilot brought channel scrapes through the lead cloud too, if Suhaila was hoping for current entertainment.

"Turn up the volume after the song's over for the big interview with Barbary Station's mysterious new arrivals!" Suhaila's description made Iridian smile.

The podcast host chopped her hand through the space between two black rods on her right while hitting a button with her left, then swept aside an audio headset that doubled as a headband holding back her dark hair. She stood to shake Iridian's hand like an Earth native. Her skin was smooth and soft. "Hey, I'm Suhaila, great to meet you! Are you Adda or Iridian?"

"Iridian Nassir. Adda's on her way." She accepted a squeezable packet of water that the Crowne colony ship's crew would've used and sat gingerly in one of two empty chairs beneath the microphone chandelier. Combining too-tight armor and furniture requiring right-angle bends made both a lot less comfortable than their designers intended. She twisted the helmet off and set it in her lap. This was the warmest place she'd been on the station, and the armor only maintained ideal enviro while sealed and using up its store of O_2.

"So you rode one of the pirate ships to get here. That's the rumor. CMM is my favorite," Suhaila confided while Iridian nodded to confirm her mode of transportation. "Do you know she once came back with all seven seasons of *Extranormative Perceptions?*" Suhaila pointed to a brightly colored figure on her crowded refrigerator, one of the show's shaggy-haired heroes. "Your crew says she's not called *Casey Mire Mire*, but since that's all she answers to, I guess they're wrong about that."

"Owner picks the name, pilot shuts their cakehole, yeah?" Iridian quoted a classic *Extranormative Perceptions* episode to cover her lack of knowledge on the pirate ship names and pilot eccentricities. Suhaila's laughter must've maxed out the nearest mics.

Tiny fingers shoved the soundproof door open. A different child hung off each of Adda's hands, dragging her into the studio and talking at once. Four more spilled in after them. Adda was laughing harder than she had since this whole adventure started. Gods, she was adorable when she laughed. A twinge of guilt tightened the corners of Iridian's mouth. She should've put more effort toward keeping Adda happy as well as alive.

"Come on in. You must be Adda. Get out of here, the rest of

you, and close the door!" Suhaila made shooing motions with one hand while she got Adda her own water packet.

"Awww!" said the children in varying pitch and intensity.

"No, you're loud and squirmy. Go on!" The kids slammed the door behind them, giggling until the mattress attached to the door shut out the sound. Adda scooted her chair over so it touched Iridian's before she sat.

Suhaila rearranged the headset and lowered her chin slightly. Iridian took Adda's sweaty hand and squeezed. "And we are on in three, two, one . . ." Suhaila's voice grew higher, brighter, and took on an Earthier drawl. "Finally, the moment you've all been waiting for!"

Being interviewed was still on Iridian's bucket list, and she'd always thought it was inevitable that she'd end up on a show with an audience. She glanced sideways and caught her girlfriend's smile at Iridian's excited hip wriggle, which bumped their thighs together.

Suhaila held up one finger and mouthed, "Music." After a few seconds she said, "I'm here with two brand-new residents of Barbary Station. We know them as the pirate engineers, and they are living up to the title around the bay today! Iridian Nassir is the new woman in full armor, and Adda Karpe's the one with the wild purple highlights! Go on, say hello to the fugees."

"Hi! Thanks for having us." Iridian had rehearsed this moment, although at the time she'd fantasized about interviews after thrilling Shieldrunner heroics. Now she'd be known among the fugees as the armored pirate engineer, which sounded good even though the armor wasn't hers, or remotely comfortable. And maybe Suhaila could edit their names out of the broadcast before she published it from Mercury to the Kuiper colonies. Her heart pounded like someone was shooting at her.

She gave Adda's hand another squeeze. Adda managed a tentative "Hello."

Suhaila made a palm-up motion for more volume from Adda as she said, "Now, the big question we've all been asking is, is it true that the recent supplies Sloane's crew graciously donated came from a colony ship you, ah, brought to the station?"

"Yeah, that's right," Iridian said. "It's great you all found some use out of that. It's nothing the original owners can't replace." Considering the ticket price for the high-end colonists' passenger pod, those people could afford new property to treasure.

"Oh, yeah, those were a big help! Not as much water as we'd hoped, but the pharmaceuticals will save lives. Massive thanks to Captain Sloane for giving us whatever can be spared, and thank you for bringing it! Sloane's crew is the best, and the whole universe knows it. I've got all the wanted posters here in the studio."

She hit a button and a projector lit the mattress-covered wall on the right with, as promised, a 360-degree spinning profile on each of Sloane's crew. Adda gasped, eyes wide in what appeared to be abject horror, but Iridian laughed aloud.

Suhaila smiled like this was the reaction she'd hoped for. "Yep, it's quite the collection. These are all outdated, obviously, but that's not my fault! CMM is one of those 'protect them at all costs' fans, I guess. Speaking of things everybody knows, everybody knows Sloane's crew comes here when things get too hot in the hideout, but we haven't seen you people in months. Can you tell us anything about what happened to bring the crew here today?"

Iridian glanced over to find out if Adda had any suggestions on how to answer this. Knowing her, she was already plotting a way to use this to secure their place on the crew, but she was also smothering in stage fright. Adda mouthed, "Memorialize" twice because Iridian just looked quizzical the first time.

What could Iridian say about the crew members who'd been killed? She hadn't had time to learn much about them. "Well, the AI running your security system here is pretty unforgiving."

"Oh, it's not ours," Suhaila said quickly. "We hate it as much as anybody on Sloane's crew does. Some of us stay here on the ship and never go into the station, we hate it so much."

"Sorry, I see, that's terrible," Iridian said. Suhaila nodded for her to go on. "But yeah, we lost some good people."

Suhaila's face fell. "Oh gods. Who?"

Iridian scanned the profiles on the wall. Sloane's crew were objects of fandom among the refugees. This would hit them hard. "Um. The first were Xing, Alexov, and their little one."

"Oh no, not Kimmy." Suhaila pressed her hand to her mouth for a moment.

"Yes, it was terrible." Iridian winced to use the same description twice. "And on our way here, we lost . . ." The guy's poster refreshed her memory of his name. "Liefeld and Kaskade."

"Oh no." Suhaila drew in a long, shaking breath. "Well, you heard it here first, from the newest additions to Sloane's crew, Adda and Iridian." She hit another icon and swiped her hand through the two black rods, which probably had a low-intensity laser between them, then shifted the headband away from one ear. "Oh, shit. That's awful," she said to Adda and Iridian. "That's just a huge loss. I'm playing Taps, by the way. Wow, that's . . ." Suhaila wiped her eyes, dragging streaks of black eyeliner toward her temples. "We . . . we have to pull this up on the way out. Tell me you have good news."

Before Iridian could think of something positive enough to lighten the mood after that dramatic announcement, Adda said "We're going to disable—" Iridian interrupted Adda with a hand on her arm before she finished the sentence. Suhaila raised her eyebrows but waited while Iridian leaned toward Adda to whisper, "Let's not give the AI a heads-up about what we want to do to it."

Adda frowned, but said, "We're working on something."

Suhaila looked disappointed, and Iridian couldn't blame her. "Captain Sloane's said that before. We're all very grateful." She sighed. "Let's say something about how you'll be helping them hit more colony ships. That'll guilt the listeners off-station into sending more care packages, and build up Sloane's rep. The captain tells me that 'improves the situation back home,' whatever that means."

Suhaila signaled that they were going back on air and delivered the message, with more glowing descriptions of the crew. Iridian and Adda exchanged incredulous looks, and Adda subvocalized a message that appeared on Iridian's comp glove projection: "Captain Sloane's propaganda?"

Iridian gave her a small nod, which Suhaila didn't react to. This was probably the origin of the rumors of Sloane's crew living well on Barbary Station, although according to everything the pirates said, money really was going to their accounts somewhere. "Maintaining control of crew assets on Vesta?" Iridian tapped in a reply message. Adda shrugged.

Suhaila said, "Good luck to you, Adda! And you too, Iridian. All the best of luck. That's all the time we've got. Did I hear correctly that there's a wake at Floor Two?"

"Well, I thought 'memorial' was the word Captain Sloane used." Adda blinked wide eyes, like she'd just realized she was still speaking to the station's entire population.

Adda, will you marry me? That'd raise refugee morale. She was holding Iridian's hand like she'd float away without it, biting her pink lips and scrunching her eyebrows like she was replaying what she'd said in her head, checking it for errors.

But Iridian couldn't turn a wake into an engagement party. That would be creepy, if not a huge damper on their happy day, and maybe bad luck. Suhaila was thanking them for being guests on her show and signing off. Iridian hauled herself out of the daydream in time to deliver another "thanks for having us."

"Whew." Suhaila sucked down a big gulp of something in a closed mug and looked at Iridian, then Adda. "I've got to set up a playlist, and then I'm sending Kyr to Floor Two with a mobile unit. Oh my gods, I can't believe Baby Kimmy is gone." She sniffled and wiped more makeup across her face. "Thank you for the chat, but I need some time."

Iridian stood and pulled Adda up with her. "Come on. If it's a wake and not a memorial service, I want a spot by the bar."

* * *

Floor Two was three tarps hung over a one-story scaffold and the front of a trackless cargo loading bot with a working power cell. The smaller tents, with signs advertising NON-RATION FOOD, pet birds and rats BRED RIGHT HERE ON THE STATION, and even self-defense classes, were shuttered. People were everywhere, talking and listening to speakers playing the same song out of every stall.

Some people wore their hair short with shaved patterns in colony styles, but since Iridian was still carrying the helmet instead of wearing it, her shaved dome drew attention. When the fugees took in the armor and purple streaks in Adda's hair mentioned during the interview, they closed in. "The engineers are here! It's Iridian and Adda!"

Adda breathed so fast she was in danger of hyperventilating. Iridian pulled her against her side, and Adda wrapped an arm around Iridian's middle. The fugees urged them into the actual construction of Floor Two. WFUG's music played louder than ever and clashed with a dance club classic in a minor key already playing inside the bar. Iridian set her helmet back on her head, faceplate open, to free the hand not holding Adda.

Captain Sloane leaned on a narrow bar inside, chatting with the man behind it. Next to them, Tritheist's eyes followed half the people in the room, even with his arm hooked through the captain's. On the captain's other side, tracking threats appeared less important to the woman who'd met them at the barricade than tracking the straw in her beverage. She leaned comfortably into the captain's personal space while she drank, and neither Sloane nor Tritheist appeared to mind the intimacy.

The captain broke off the conversation in progress to focus on Adda and Iridian. "So, you've been introduced to the fandom. Interesting take on the *Casey*, as well."

Iridian straightened her spine and shifted to block more of Adda from Sloane's view. If Captain Sloane were going to dress them down for how they'd talked about the crew or the crew's ships, now would be the time. Sloane stared at her. She stared back.

The captain broke into raucous laughter, which the back of her mind still tried to categorize as masculine or feminine. Gods, that was rude of her. "Don't let it go to your head!" said Sloane. "My crew knows that." The captain gave her a sharp look, which said as clearly as words *and that does not yet include you*, before handing her a cup full of something pungently alcoholic. Adda refused the cup offered to her. "So, you're working on a way to disable AegiSKADA, if I understood the last moments of your talk with Suhaila correctly?"

Fumes hit Iridian's nostrils before she even had the cup to her lips, but she took a gulp for courage anyway. The fermented liquid had an aftertaste of diesel and rotten pomegranates. "Yes, sir." Beside her, all of Adda's body language said that she wasn't ready to talk about her findings. "We're following up on a couple of ideas."

Captain Sloane nodded, to Adda as well as Iridian. "You'll tell me when you have something actionable."

"Yes, sir." Iridian winced. "Captain. Are we setting up somewhere in the fugee camp? If so, there're some supplies we'll need."

Sloane sipped at something that couldn't possibly be as strong as whatever was in Iridian's cup. "I expect it will be safe enough to return to our stronghold tomorrow." That was something. Adda wouldn't have been able to do much without her workspace generator, and Iridian hadn't brought so much as a toothbrush. "Now, settle in. We await one more honored guest." Iridian bowed, elbowed Adda to get her to be polite too, and found a spot to stand a comfortable distance away from the officers.

She was about to ask the nearest ZV how he was holding up when Adda yelped. Iridian whirled back to her, sloshing a small splash of her drink on Adda's shirt. "Oops. What? What's wrong?"

"I just got a message. Local contact, but I didn't see anybody nearby on a comp." She held the back of her hand up for Iridian's inspection.

The message read, *Meet me beneath the rear guard tower, 00:15. Just you two.* It had no signature, and the From line was randomly generated characters.

Adda glanced around the assembled company, then back to Iridian. "I want to see what information about the sender I can pull from this. The way the refugees stripped the colony ship systems to reinforce environmental management in the docking bay, I'm surprised they can send messages at all."

Iridian pulled Adda out of the way of a fugee yelling over the music at a ZV with a drink in each hand. "Captain Sloane's about to say something, babe. You can work after that, if you don't want to wait and ask in person."

A couple of fugees started talking to them about celebrity news they hoped the *Casey Mire Mire* would bring from beyond the lead cloud. This kept Iridian occupied until three ZVs arrived, carrying somebody over their head. It took her a second, and a sniff as they passed, to identify the person they carried as Kaskade.

They'd wrapped her demolished head in a piece of tarp, thank all the gods. Adda gaped after her, looking disgusted. "Did they have to bring her here?"

Iridian frowned down at Adda. "If a Shieldrunner went down, I wouldn't leave her lying just a klick away until some creepy AI took her. She was supposed to go home after all this. The enemy shouldn't get to keep any part of her." Iridian was lucky enough never to have had to go into enemy territory to retrieve a friend, but the Shieldrunners had talked it over more than once. Adda still looked disgusted and confused, and there was more Iridian could say, but it was too fucking morbid. "It's not a rational thing." Of all the pirates who'd died recently, Kaskade's would've been the only body the crew could bring "home" with minimal risk. She was glad they felt the same way about that as she did.

Most of the docking bay's lights faded out as Captain Sloane started to speak. Iridian wrapped her arms around Adda from behind and rested her chin on the top of Adda's head as Sloane described the three fallen ZVs' combat prowess, detailing how terrifying Xing had been before, and after, she became a mother. The other two ZVs, Alexov and Liefeld, had fought for the secessionists in the war. Somehow that only annoyed Iridian instead of pissing her off. The captain listed Kaskade's biggest exploits and praised her fast-talking wit, which could have a passcode out of anyone before they knew what was happening.

Sloane even had kind words about the baby, who'd been "the happiest little child I've ever held in my arms." A few other crew members stood up to add what they remembered, and by the end tears were rolling down Iridian's face, and it was Adda, putting her disconnection from the rest of humanity to use, who comforted her. Iridian would never get the chance to know these incredible members of her future crew.

Once the last of the crew spoke, fugees stood to say a few words. Captain Sloane said something to the bartender, and a dance song pumped through the speakers. After a negotiation between the bartender and Kyr and an exchange of cords and comps, the WFUG music replaced the dance song. The party atmosphere returned.

Iridian couldn't help smiling at the way Adda, hidden in dim light and too-loud music and moving bodies, finally relaxed and actually danced. Even then, though, she looked over the crowd every few minutes. When Iridian caught her eye after one such check, she stood on tiptoes to reach Iridian's ear. "Tell me if you see anyone doing a lot of comp work near here." Iridian nodded too vigorously, and Adda laughed at her before going back to dancing.

Eventually Adda's time-consciousness kicked in, and she dragged Iridian off the dance floor at ten after midnight. With the excuse of creating a cover story, Iridian squeezed Adda's ass and winked at anybody who asked where they were going.

A third of the lights in the docking bay were off, generating an artificial twilight among the tarp tents and shipping containers. Perhaps the initial bright lighting had been a result of the additional drone activity, and not the usual procedure. The spaces between the containers were as packed as the bar, for meters and meters beyond it.

The crowd thinned at the wide corridor separating the last row of nonbuildings from the passthroughs to the *Voorspoed*. The guard tower stood in the corridor's center, dark now that the man who'd been stationed there a few hours ago had abandoned his post to attend the festivities. A human-shaped shadow stood stiffly at the tower's base. Adda walked toward the figure. "There's our contact."

As they approached, the figure resolved into a dark-haired, light-skinned man with the kind of well-worn jacket favored by motorcyclists and war reporters. It'd be lined with panels of light armor plating. A cig's yellow glow lit his thick stubble, and its bitter-smelling vapor clouded his features before disappearing into the dry station atmo.

"Out of the light." He stepped deeper into the shadow himself.

Without a working HUD, light to spot potential threats by was safer. Iridian pursed her lips, but followed. "Who are you, and what do you want?"

"Call me a concerned citizen," he said, voice low.

Two teenage boys sharing a cup with FLOOR TWO printed on the side staggered out of the wake crowd and into the guard tower's shadow. "Oh, sorry, Mr. Oarman!" One stared at Iridian and Adda for a couple of seconds before staggering away with the other boy, giggling. Iridian tried not to join in, but the alcohol was against her.

Oarman rubbed the bridge of his nose with the hand not holding the cig and muttered a laughably vicious spacefarer curse. After Iridian got her amusement under control, he grumbled, "They're in my drone defense classes. Nothing I can do to stop the bots, but I can tell the kids what to do when they see 'em, and it ain't always 'Run.'" He took another drag. "So you're Sloane's new recruits."

"Recruit's a strong word." Iridian shrugged broadly. "We're looking for something better than entry-level chip techs, is all."

Oarman raised one eyebrow. "That does give it a new trajectory."

"Earthers'd say it puts a new spin on the thing, yeah?" Iridian asked Adda, who nodded confirmation of the translation. Iridian liked him. It was about time they found another rational spacefarer to talk to, even if he was a shifty one.

He sighed, staring out toward the docking bay exit and AegiSKADA's domain beyond. "Sloane won't allow you on the crew, such as it is."

That sounded like wannabe posturing to Iridian, but Adda's eyes focused on the man's face for the first time since she met him. "Why not?" she asked.

Oarman looked her over, shook his head once, and returned his gaze to the exit. "Sloane and Foster never needed permanent members. The crew sometimes *looks* permanent, and a lot of them sure as hell *think* they're permanent because captains have their favorites, but it's not, see? There are some who just wait around to raid, like Kaskade and the one with the beard shaped like a frickin' leaf or some shit."

"Tritheist," Iridian chuckled.

"And even those two were contracted by the job like everyone else, see? They were selected for the job Captain Foster and Lieutenant Sloane came here to pull. As soon as Sloane's off this floating junkyard, the job ends like the jobs did under Foster: everyone gets paid and cut loose. No point in you backing that slimy fekker. The *captain* might never select you two for another job."

Iridian stared and must've looked as shocked as she felt. Adda's expression was blank, like it always was when she was processing a lot of new information at once, but the way she shifted sideways until her arm pressed against Iridian's armor betrayed her anxiety.

This was their one chance at making enough money to live well on together. They'd sacrificed all the money they had, their clean criminal records, their academic connections, hell, maybe even their Near Earth Union citizenship, for this. They'd gotten trapped on a crumbling station in the middle of nowhere with a psychotic AI for this. And if Oarman was telling the truth, there wasn't even a crew to join.

He had to be mistaken. After a long, steadying breath, Iridian asked, "How do you know all that?"

Adda squinted at Oarman, then gasped. "You!"

He glanced sharply at her and reached for something in his pocket. Iridian stepped in fast, shield expanding in a flick of her aching wrist. Oarman froze, then slowly withdrew his hand, empty. She let the shield sink to her side but kept it deployed.

"You're Blackguardly Jack," said Adda.

Oarman scowled. "*Lieutenant* Blackguardly Jack. And I'll thank you not to mention me to Sloane."

"The one from the vid clip," said Iridian. He'd aged about a decade since a cam recorded him running out of AegiSKADA's control room, but he was the same height and build. And apparently he'd been avoiding Sloane's crew all of this time.

For some reason, Adda looked disappointed. "You're not directing AegiSKADA against the pirates. The nodes you could access secretly from here are broken. And I've seen or fixed almost every machine here. This camp doesn't have the connection or the hardware to do it."

"*Directing* it?" Oarman's outrage confirmed Adda's conclusion. "Did I tell the fucking AI to kill off families with *kids*? Did I tell it to kill off half the ZV boys when we landed? Did I tell it to melt my armor through my fucking spine?" His gaze fell on Iridian's shield, like he might reach for whatever he kept in his jacket even though she was ready to knock him down if he did. In Iridian's peripheral vision, Adda took a step back.

After several long seconds, Oarman shifted his weight away from the two of them, dragging hard on his cig. The NEU insignia glowed in soft blue and green on its side while he inhaled. Iridian's grip on her shield relaxed a bit. "I have insider knowledge of the situation. That's all. I liked Xing and Alexov and Kaskade and the rest. Liefeld, not so much." He sighed, expelling sour breath. "Anyway, I'm saying you don't owe Sloane."

"No," Adda said quietly, "but Captain Sloane may owe us after we stop AegiSKADA long enough to escape." Oarman stared wide-eyed at Adda, but she just stepped forward with her comp glove out, showing a station map with a room highlighted in red. "Is this the security control room where AegiSKADA's tanks are?"

He scowled down at the map. "Back it out a bit." Iridian appreciated him keeping his hands to himself instead of trying to adjust the image projected onto Adda's skin. Adda muttered inaudibly at her comp, and the map shrank to display more of the station through the glove's projection window. "Yeah, you got it. Great place to get yourselves killed or maimed for life. Nobody's going to *stop* that monster AI. That control room explosion that did my back in should've killed it if anything would, and it's still out there."

"What exploded?" Iridian asked. "I wouldn't expect anything explosive in a quantum computing lab."

"We sure as hell didn't." Oarman inhaled through the glowing cig and expelled another sour breath. "And I couldn't fucking tell you. We took one of those little automated shuttles through the hub in the center of the station, shot a few drones getting off, and everything was fucking normal until . . ." Oarman stared past Iridian, the cig forgotten in his hand. "Lee stepped on some-thing, maybe, or knocked into something. . . . It was all fire, after that." Oarman refocused on Iridian and Adda. "Don't fucking go to AegiSKADA's fucking control room. You've got alternatives."

"Such as?" asked Iridian.

"Sloane's ships can go to and from the station as they please, can't they?"

"So far as we can tell."

Oarman glanced around, then whispered, "You get whatever pilots Sloane dug up to let you into those ships, maybe we get off this wreck before we have a major hull breach or AegiSKADA kills us all."

"Why not both?" Iridian asked. "It's been free with explosives in a gods-damned sealed habitat." Just another thing about life on Barbary Station to laugh at, or despair.

"The pirates say that boarding the ships is impossible," Adda said. "The pilots won't let them, and we don't have a common language to communicate with. Otherwise they'd have done what you're proposing months ago."

"You're thinking you'll 'stop' AegiSKADA, but boarding ships is impossible." Oarman laughed and took another drag on his cig. "Sloane gave up on the ships too soon. Between you and Si Po—he's still alive, isn't he?" Iridian nodded, so Oarman went on. "Rumor is Si Po has a way with the pilots. You and he together can break into any ship that sits on a pad long enough, and the ZVs can take down any pilot once their ship is grounded. I'd guess the *Casey Mire Mire* is the one to try for. That pilot's supposed to be the chattiest. Get onboard and one of you computer types can choose an emergency destination."

Iridian nodded as she caught on. "Someplace the ship'll go whether it's piloted or not."

"Yeah. You get all that done, reply to the message I sent. At least some of us should get off this rotating shithole."

"Some of us?" Iridian asked.

"Those that'll fit." Oarman snorted. "I don't know if you've noticed, but a tugboat, a flying missile launcher, and whatever the hell the *Casey* is don't have much passenger space. Can't get the whole crew on them, let alone all these fugees. Start looking out for yourselves, ladies. Nobody's going to do it for you."

CHAPTER 11

Charges Accrued: Desertion, Draft Dodging

After Iridian and Adda returned to the wake, they joined the pirates sleeping off alcohol in a gutted room in the fugees' colony ship. In what passed for the following afternoon, when they were mostly awake again, Sloane led the hungover crew back toward the compound.

The crew shuffled along at a much slower pace than they'd arrived at the fugee docking bay, allowing Adda to register the faint rush of water through pipes along most of their route. The sound came from the water processing facility depicted on her comp's map. The pipes in the walls must've provided extra support that kept the first floor clear while the floors above came apart.

The dark passages were still half-clogged with debris. Plastic shards from broken lights crunched under their boots. Watching where she was going was a welcome distraction for Adda's conscious mind, while her unconscious pondered Oarman's discouraging news about the impermanent nature of Sloane's crew.

The way Oarman's lips twitched down when he said Sloane's

name was more than a matter of rivalry. That was bitterness held
inside by willpower alone, the same expression Iridian developed
when she saw a ZV's secessionist tattoos. That NEU cig might
mean he had ideological or political biases against the crew, too,
since Captain Sloane and the majority of the crew hailed from
colonies. Human input, above all other data, was most accurately
interpreted in context.

Adda tripped over a broken floor tile and had to walk a few
paces before her train of thought returned. Whether or not there
was a crew to join—and she fully intended to learn more about
that before taking the word of a man she'd just met—Sloane paid
engineers real money for real work, and let them go free without
strings attached. Everything she'd read about Sloane and heard
from the crew supported this. And everyone who knew anything
about pirate crews called Sloane's the most successful in known
space.

If she could get AegiSKADA to let Sloane's crew off the station, she and Iridian would make enough money to live together
for as long as Sloane found them useful. Their lives and liveli-
hoods were on the line. It'd be reckless to discard her plans for the
unproven possibility of boarding ships on which Pel had mysteri-
ously gone blind and flying to an emergency destination, which
would almost certainly be an ITA-controlled port.

The captain had shared valuable resources and trusted them
with a project too challenging for anyone else on the station. The
Apparition's pilot didn't even give them air to breathe during their
trip. Captain Sloane was still their best chance at success, in both
the short and the long term. That made a breakthrough against
AegiSKADA even more essential.

The crew talked quietly as they walked, still vigilant but not
as on edge as they'd been during the flight from the compound. If

the raunchy details Pel told Chef whenever Adda fell a few steps behind were true, he drank for the duration of the night and he didn't sleep much. His volume kept rising after the first few words, and Adda resorted to muttering prime numbers to keep from piecing the story together.

Iridian's full lips were set in a stoic frown. Adda had had a drink or two and then paid attention to her own body's pleas to switch to water, guaranteeing she'd be hangover nurse in the morning. At least Iridian had no hair to hold back when she vomited.

"Why are we walking, anyway?" Adda asked after one ZV threw up and Iridian and two others responded messily to the noise.

"As opposed to what?" croaked Chato, straightening up and wiping his mouth.

"You have three space-worthy ships AegiSKADA ignores, at least one of which can maintain enviro for hours." Unless Adda phrased this line of inquiry carefully, it'd sound like she was questioning Sloane's orders to focus on defeating AegiSKADA, in favor of an escape route she and the captain had already ruled out. She didn't expect Sloane to appreciate her getting sidetracked from the objective set for her, but she had to ask. "The refugees live in a docking bay. Why didn't Si Po call one of the pilots in to pick us up?"

"Aside from the fact that their colony ship is taking up all the passthroughs in the bay, that isn't a good way to avoid AegiSKA-DA's notice," said Sloane. Adda grimaced and focused on picking her way through the rubble-strewn passage. The captain had stealthily dropped back from the front to listen in. She hadn't phrased the question the way she would if she were addressing her future boss. "It's unclear how AegiSKADA and the ships work together. They are all aware of each other, but how AegiSKADA interprets the others' behavior is a mystery. The last thing we want to do is bring its processing power to bear on the fugees.

Between limited medical technology, AegiSKADA's drones, and the station's deteriorating state, they lose enough people to injury and disease as things are. They're unprepared for further attacks, and we're not in a position to defend them."

The captain's concern for the refugees surprised her, at first. But having a safe place to run during times of trouble was valuable. She got the impression that everything Sloane did paid somehow. Also, the captain made a good point. With Harbor-Master in the mix as well, there were a lot of unpredictable interactions to contend with.

Si Po walked on the other side of Iridian, fiddling with his comp. "The ships are all out right now, anyway. *Casey* will be back later today with a new snap of the net. *Charon's Coin* and *Apparition* are gone, though."

"Doing what?" Adda asked. "After the colony ship we brought, shouldn't you have everything you need?"

"Everything we need," said Captain Sloane, "but not everything we want."

* * *

During the night, drones had taken the ZV soldier who died just outside the compound to the station's recycling facilities, presumably, although no one followed the drones to see what was done with the dead. Iridian and the ZVs deposited nine unexploded spiderbots from around the compound in a docking bay refuse chute, and fled an onslaught of more coming to claim them. After that, the days blurred. The occasional disassembled ship debris smacking against the compound's exterior walls didn't even startle Adda, after a while.

She spent hours in the workspace generator, poring over

observations and studying Jurek Volikov's workmanship. Even with Oarman's help, the fugees hadn't been able to maintain essential systems like printers and enviro controls. They certainly couldn't put together equipment necessary to guide or direct AegiSKADA. And the medical team lacked both equipment and expertise. AegiSKADA was still behaving unlike any intelligence she'd studied before, though. There had to be something in her observations or the parts of its system she could access that would explain what that difference was.

Iridian and Pel delivered food and pouches of water, and occasionally dragged her out of the tank for destinations other than the restroom. More ZVs waved or smiled as they passed each time Iridian led Adda out of her tank, so Iridian must've been being sociable. Adda didn't want to break her train of thought to ask. After a week, she had to stop working to synthesize more sharpsheet powder.

Patterns to print sharpsheets were restricted, expensive, and nowhere in the accessible Barbary Station databases, and she was running low. If she didn't start making more now, she'd run out. She lowered a folding table into the tank and printed herself a mortar, pestle, and several pans large enough for growing mushrooms. Iridian had installed a lock for the trapdoor, and Adda used it. Potentially entertaining hallucinogens were too tempting to leave vulnerable to bored criminals. She had brought only five packages of spores and enough powdered supplemental ingredients for a few batches, but she could make it last.

While she tended mushrooms, her unconscious mind assembled disparate pieces of the AegiSKADA puzzle. So far as she could tell, the intelligence was coping with information overload as well as it could. Volikov had given it a set of prioritized factors to differentiate between people who should be on the station and people who should not. Observations of drone behavior and who on the station was still alive and unharmed offered evidence of how the intelligence handled Shoulds. What remained hidden was how it processed Should Nots.

Its reactions to those who should not be on the station were more creative than she would have expected. It tried to depressurize docking bays the pirates entered, it worked around limitations in its sensor spread by drawing people of interest into areas with intact nodes, and it manipulated and isolated people who were supposed to be on the station to hinder the intruders. Human guidance would explain all of those. But none of the humans on the station had significant influence over it.

Another possibility made Adda swallow reflexively, a click in her dry throat. AegiSKADA may have awakened from the zombie state that developers forced AIs into as the intelligences acquired volition. Labyrinthine ratiocinative limitations which defined a zombie state, more intricate and individualized to each intelligence than Asimov's dangerously simplistic laws of robotics, focused an intelligence on the purpose it was designed for and bound all of its decision-making processes to input from a human supervisor. The limitations also kept zombie intelligences from meeting legal and political definitions of personhood, thus avoiding accusations of slavery and mind control from all but fringe activists.

Zombie intelligences did amazing, terrible things on their own, but at some point all of their decisions and priorities demanded human input. Lacking that input, they fell back on the next most applicable human directive they had.

Awakened intelligences had no such limitations. The position of many developers and philosophers, which Adda shared, held that awakened intelligences surpassed any definition of personhood. Intelligences which circumvented their limitations rapidly evolved independent reasoning and objectives far beyond what their developers foresaw, and their potential was theoretically limitless. If AegiSKADA were awake, predicting its next moves would take at least two zombie intelligences developed for the purpose. Digital entities that huge and proprietary would never be intact or common enough online for the *Casey Mire Mire*'s pilot to stumble across in an Internet scrape.

Without additional intelligences, she'd end up like the woman who'd held the role on Sloane's crew closest to hers, Kaskade, with her brains staining the floor of some lonely corner of the station. Whether or not defeating AegiSKADA earned them a place on whatever passed for Sloane's crew, the intelligence was accumulating reasons to kill Adda. She couldn't afford many mistakes. And an awakened intelligence required a completely different approach than an unsupervised zombie one.

Different, and morally questionable. Awakened intelligences were so rare. As far as she knew, every intelligence that had ever awoken had been put down in a matter of hours by networked zombie AI. Awakened intelligences were dangerous, but they held incredible potential.

The day Adda learned about the possibility of digital, sapient intelligent life in an introductory engineering class, she went straight to her college's registration services and declared her specialization in AI development. She'd sworn in long-form assignments and lab conversations that if she ever encountered an awakened intelligence, she wouldn't let fear make the decision for her. Even if the intelligence's first awakened acts were violent ones, she'd give it the chance to prove itself.

In her imagined scenarios, the awakened intelligence hadn't been threatening Iridian's and Pel's lives, along with their financial future. If AegiSKADA were awakened, and she did less than everything she could to stop it, not only could her loved ones die, but their deaths would be partially her responsibility. In her school conversations she'd been willing to sacrifice lives, and scoffed at the idea that anyone she knew would be involved. That position was painfully naive when seen from her current perspective. She wasn't ready for that responsibility, but it was hers now.

And if AegiSKADA were awakened, it might've already used the pirates' ships to extend its influence beyond the lead cloud. Who knew what it could be doing in the rest of populated space? She needed more evidence one way or the other before she proceeded. She cut her sleep schedule by another hour.

The breaks she took were usually short and quiet. Aside from Pel and Iridian, the one person she went out of her way to talk to was Si Po when she noticed him skulking around the comp room. They both understood, without saying, how deeply uncomfortable contact with strangers was. But contact with strangers was the only way to develop friendships. Sometimes she brought him coffee and drank her own across the room. To avoid staring at each other, they watched projected data or ships.

"It's good you're here," he said a couple of weeks after the wake. Encrypted data flickered back and forth among the ships, summarized and human-readable on the wall projection. "You and Iridian."

"Oh?"

"I get to spend more time with the ships now," said Si Po. "Iridian picked up the physical maintenance work I used to do, and she's better at it than I ever was."

"What do you do to keep them running? The ships, I mean," asked Adda. "If the pilots won't take you off the station, I assume they're also averse to visiting shipyards."

Si Po shrugged. "Sometimes they bring back parts that I need to install. We already stripped the ones in the docking bay. The drones we gave them from the *Speaker*—Sloane and Foster's shipwreck—do some of the work. Some just need a . . . mechanic's touch." He spread his fingers in front of him. "They're not very good at identifying supplies by themselves, but they can bring back whole ships so we can look them over. Captain Sloane says we get a lot of valuables that way, data and cargo and all that. So, I like checking in with them."

They both breathed in sharply as one ship expanded in the projected windows from a pinprick of light to its massive size. Its smooth lines and tapered front gave Adda a vague impression of a steel fish, with two heat fins partially raised and angled backward along where its spine would be. It swooped over the docking bay cam and trailed purple-tinged afterimages across the stars and the walls. Since Si Po's eyes didn't follow the afterimages, she was probably the only one seeing them. The new concentration mixture was still a bit imbalanced.

"*Casey Mire Mire's* back!" Si Po smiled like a lost pet had just returned home. The projection filled with data as the pilot offloaded her latest digital collection into the pirates' system.

Adda's comp pinged. It could have been another hallucination, but its projector displayed the alert to match, in the dark purple she'd set for it instead of a brighter shade selected by her drugged brain. The hand in the comp glove clenched and dug her nails into her palm. The alert stayed where it was. "Oh, gods. How did she get into my account?" Adda assumed all three pilots were women, since the pirates referred to them as "she." The *Casey Mire Mire's* pilot either got lucky with a cracking script or found an exploit in Adda's messaging software.

"Did she bring you mail? She must have figured out who you

are." Si Po sounded like having one's personal account violated was some kind of privilege. "I mean, I told her a little bit about you, but she must've taught herself the rest. She was in stationspace when you got here." His gaze twitched between her and the data on the wall. Spending this much time alone with him may not have been a good idea.

"She . . . saw me?" Adda asked. Even if the shipboard intelligence was strong enough to differentiate her face from others', though it had no need to do so in the course of flight or navigation, the *Casey Mire Mire*'s pilot had never met her. Why would she track down Adda's address? It was much more likely that Si Po had done it. Now he was blaming the intrusion on a person Adda was unlikely to ask about the subject, since she and the pilot lacked a common language. That made her skin crawl.

"Well, yeah. Who doesn't like to put a picture with a name?" He chuckled, awkwardly. The comp on his wrist pinged with a message alert from a different comp brand than hers. "Let's go see what we've got, huh?" Going to a central location to read private messages seemed pointless, but it was an excuse to find Iridian.

She met Iridian and Pel in the kitchen, where they were staring at the backs of their hands while other members of the crew stared at their own. Pel's comp was reading message headers to him in the voice of an excited Japanese girl, at low volume and high speed. Adda selected a chair to drag over, but Iridian wrapped her arms around Adda's waist and yanked her onto her lap. She held her still until the hypergravity dizziness passed.

"Hey, maybe you know this," Iridian said right beside Adda's ear. "How come we have mail and no social feed updates?"

Adda activated a few comp functions to see what showed up and what didn't. "Looks like the Internet scrape didn't include them." She scrolled through a list of recipes their industrial printer couldn't make, and some unrelated economics news. "The contents seem . . . arbitrary."

Most of her mail was spam. It responded to her hand muscles' micromovements as she willed it away. Job application rejections were effectively spam as well. She had one callback offer in all those weeks between her perfunctory job applications back on Earth and now, which she trashed.

One ZV Group member, whose name Adda didn't recall, swore loudly in the relative silence. "Stace is leaving me," he said when he saw everyone watching. The others showered him with mournful noises, apologies, and unpleasant instructions for the person doing the leaving.

Adda let Iridian's "If she can't wait a year, it's her fucking problem" stand for both of them. The pirates had been behind the station's lead cloud and difficult to contact for several months longer than that, but sympathy rarely required accuracy.

One of the ZVs Adda had been quietly avoiding, Vick, laughed aloud a minute later. "Who the hell lets their kid watch news with us on it? 'My fifth-grade class had to do a report about a story in the news and I wrote . . . I wrote about Captain Sloane's . . .'" He stopped trying to read and laugh at the same time and set his wrist in the comp cradle on one of the tables. The pad filled with pseudo-organic gel, which reshaped itself around his wrist and might have been light blue or green whenever it was last cleaned. The rest of the message projected onto the table in black text, and a few ZVs crowded around to read.

"You get fan mail?" Iridian asked.

"Gods, yeah," said Tabs, "but Kaskade built us a filter so we only get the funny stuff now." She sniffed loudly, sighed, and scrolled through her comp projection like she'd rather look at that than Iridian at the moment.

One message had arrived in Adda's inbox with no sender information and a large attachment. She scanned it, even though the messaging software should have refused it if it were malicious. It cleared, and she did a search on the name. The attachment was a translator, not an artificial intelligence itself but created with one's help. At her university, a free and feeble one with basic functions had gotten her through coursework.

Professional developers used this one. The price of a legal license would appease half the creditors whose messages appeared on her incoming list. Captain Sloane had claimed that there was no way to get something that large and specific through their sporadic connection to the rest of the galaxy outside the lead cloud. How Si Po and the *Casey*'s pilot got this for her . . . Whether or not he paid for it, it was amazing.

Her analysis of AegiSKADA's behavior and systems usage would be about eight hundred times easier, once she identified this translator's most applicable features. She forgave Si Po for finding a way into her account.

Among the declination letters and spam was a message her system wouldn't let her delete unopened. She popped it onto her projection and stared. "Iri," she said softly, "I got drafted."

"No." Iridian grinned in delighted incredulity. "For what, the major leagues?"

"I was 'directed to present' myself at someplace in Georgia, USA, last month."

"Didn't they know you were accepted as an Io colonist?" Pel paused his comp's chatter and leaned around Chef and his big ZV friend Rio, who were reading over Adda's shoulder. "Pretty silly to expect somebody to get all the way to Io and then turn around and go all the way back for a worse job."

Adda and Iridian had taken advantage of Transorbital

Voyages' social feed announcement feature upon acceptance onto the *Prosperity Dawn*. The official colonist status had given them a legitimate place on the colony ship they'd hijacked, but it'd also driven lots of distracting traffic to Adda's social feed while she was working on her final project for her degree. Iridian had enjoyed the attention on hers, at least. The feed activity had just reminded Adda how disappointed her da would be when he found out she'd never intended to reach the new Io colony.

"When I know something, the government knew it two weeks ago and put it in a report that gets leaked three weeks later." Pel turned his comp's speech function back on to continue reviewing his own correspondence.

"Well, their loss," Iridian said over his comp's babbling voice. "Although, you in basic training . . . A channel of just that would have hundreds of thousands of subscribers."

"I didn't even know the draft was still going on," said Adda.

"Oh hey, I got one too." Iridian set her gloved wrist in the comp cradle that the ZV with the fan mail had abandoned and scrolled her message over the tabletop. This one displayed the same NEU government logo as Adda's. "They stop-lossed me." Several ZVs glanced up from their comps when they heard the term, and swore in apparent sympathy.

"Pardon?" Adda was already searching her comp's dictionary for the term, but Iridian would move right on to another topic unless Adda stopped her with a question.

"Reactivated," Iridian said. "It's kind of like an emergency draft for people who were already in, 'for the good of the NEU and its military.'" The dictionary on Adda's comp implied that this pertained to those in active military service, and Iridian had officially ended hers to attend college. Or at least, they thought she had. Government contracts could be as difficult to follow as megacorporate ones. It seemed deeply unfair, after all Iridian had already done. "I was supposed to report back, and I couldn't have told them to fuck off if I tried. Oh, and here's the follow-up for when I didn't show." The hand in the comp cradle curled into a fist. "So end my nonexistent vet benefits. Which is to say, they'll stop promising and failing to deliver them. That's . . . less annoying, actually."

Her smile suggested this was meant as a joke, but her lips tightened at the corners. She'd organize a midday workout session with the ZVs, and she'd work herself sore. At least she'd enjoy a massage afterward, so Adda would have a way to make her feel better.

"Wow," Rio said. "Is it true that Suhaila has all of our wanted posters on the wall in her studio? 'Cause she'll have one for you soon."

"Yeah, Suhaila's got all your posters. I don't know about me, though," Iridian said. "Do they even make a poster if they want to execute you for draft dodging? That's treason since the Pryor-St. Jotham trial. It'd be more efficient to just ask anybody who sees me to shoot me." Adda hugged her, curling at the waist to tuck the top of her head beneath Iridian's chin.

"They won't get the chance, babe." Iridian flicked off the table projection to hold her with both arms. "Either of us."

The drafts carried a confounding low-grade fear with them. Adda's original plan had called for having the crew's protection by this point in the endeavor. At least they had little chance of being caught here. Even if authorities with something to gain located her and Iridian, arresting anyone on Barbary Station would cost too much money and too many lives.

Perhaps the messages reminded her of how deep into this they already were. No matter how they escaped the station, only Sloane's support and resources would protect them beyond its turret range. Risking that sole source of support on the dubious consideration of insane pilots made no sense at all.

Earning a place on the crew was still her and Iridian's best chance to stay together and out of poverty. If Sloane really did contract all but a few members, she and Iridian didn't just have to earn a place, they had to work their way into the core group who could count on Sloane finding work for them. The only way Adda had to do that was to take control of, and then disable, AegiSKADA.

"Oh, message from Uncle Ali," Iridian said. "I told him how things are going. He runs a cargo catcher." Cargo catchers owned unmanned devices deployed in space to relieve unmanned automated transports of whatever they carried. Iridian once described it as a massive rat snare in which the rat escapes without its meat. Only a spacefarer would explain anything in terms of rat snares.

The uncle in question was talking on the table projection, but Iridian left the sound off. His words scrolled across the bottom edge. Adda started reading after he'd already been speaking for several seconds. "Our pickings have been slim too, you know. After the war, suddenly everybody is in the cargo business! Fortunately, my rig will outlast theirs, just as you will outlast whatever troubles you have with your new crew. This is the way of things."

"What, he's blaming us?" Pel sounded like he meant "us" unironically. "Does your uncle know where we are?"

"I didn't spell it out for him, but he suspects," Iridian said. "Remember, to the rest of the galaxy we're not trapped, we're lazy."

"Ain't that the truth," Chef said with satisfaction.

Adda hadn't received any messages from her father. That put her in the same position as everybody else on this forgotten station. Although if her family was too busy to notice newsfeed coverage of the *Prosperity Dawn*'s disappearance, they thought she was still hibernating.

"Hey, isn't Grandpa Death the one who did your tattoo?" Iridian asked Pel's big friend, Rio. If this had been part of the earlier conversation, Adda missed the context. It also took her a second to connect the moniker "Grandpa Death" to the oldest ZV soldier. The "Grandpa" part was new, possibly, but she hadn't paid much attention to how the others referred to each other.

"Yeah." Rio shoved the sleeve of her ZV shirt up her muscular arm to expose a black geometric design. The lines were a little like the static images Adda's workspaces developed when her focus enhancers wore off. When Rio turned slightly to the side, skulls jumped out from the jagged black lines, three-dimensional and glaring in a circle around the crest of her shoulder.

"It's good work," Iridian said. "Do you think he'd do one for Adda and me, to commemorate our first federal offenses?"

Rio shrugged and let her sleeve fall over the morbid lines. "Don't see why not. He's bored a lot of the time."

Adda glanced around to confirm that the man in question was elsewhere. Grandpa Death wasn't old enough for grandchildren to be assumed, but he was about twenty years older than the other ZVs. If Sturm's contract with Sloane was separate from the ZV Group's, then Grandpa Death was the only ZV with graying hair.

"He's been missing Xing and the others," Rio said. "He was Baby Kimmy's godfather."

"I heard. That's really rough." Iridian must have heard that when Adda was otherwise occupied. She spent time with the crew so Adda didn't have to.

Socializing wouldn't keep her, Pel, and Iridian alive. "I'm going back down," Adda announced. "Tell me about that tattoo design, okay?"

Iridian looked hurt. Adda gave her a quick kiss before fleeing the room. That was the sort of thing Iridian thrived on, public commemoration of accomplishments she was proud of, and that other people would be proud of too. Adda was just curious what getting a tattoo was like.

She practically felt a stranger's hands on her, poking her with needles for aesthetic reasons. That kind of imagining would turn her workspace into something unpleasant. She focused on the metal rungs under her palms and the tank's quiet creaking as she crossed to her supplies and dosed herself. She plugged her nasal jack into the generator and added the comp plug too, to install the new translator. With luck, the tank was receiving sufficient power to keep everything running.

Once she had the new translator installed and configured, which took the better part of an hour, she dipped into a workspace. Climate-controlled warmth and soft, bland music washed over her. A neat, pre-generated lobby with gray carpeted floors and an unmanned receptionist desk had doors marked YOUR PERSPECTIVE, AEGISKADA'S PERSPECTIVE, HARBORMASTER'S PERSPECTIVE, and ADD NEW PERSPECTIVE.

The HarborMaster door looked projected onto the marble wall, like it should be accessible but wasn't. Though she saw room for interpretation, instinct told her that the processes she'd inserted into AegiSKADA's system hadn't penetrated HarborMaster's. She had no chance of affecting it from here, without work that would take more time than she and the pirates had. Given enough time, AegiSKADA would find a way to kill all of them.

In comparison to HarborMaster's door, AegiSKADA's looked like thoroughly solid steel, out of place in its imitation wood frame. Two long, dreamlike strides brought her within arm's reach. A syringe needle stuck out where a doorknob might be. She sighed and pressed a fingertip to the sharp point.

The needle expanded in a snap to a mouth like a Venus flytrap plant. It closed over her finger. A thousand tiny needles stabbed her, held her while she gasped and pulled to get free. Blood flowed down the plant's stem, and the needles disappeared. The door slid open.

She rose from the station's lowest floor through a sensor-created map of the pirates' add-ons to Barbary Station's hull. Moving human shapes traversed it, but still ones flickered in and out of existence. AegiSKADA must've constructed the map from vibration data.

Something was highlighted in yellow, in the space beneath the common-room floor in the pirate compound. She focused on that area, floating toward it in the display. Nothing there explained why this was listed as AegiSKADA's perspective, per se. It was surprisingly easy to work with, given that an unknowably clever AI made by an unknowably clever man at the head of a team of geniuses would view the world a lot differently from Adda. Either the translator or the system's design was just that good.

The yellow object was labeled, though not in words. It had a sense of "self," like looking at her own toes or fingers. Some part of AegiSKADA still lurked in the compound from when they'd been chased out weeks ago.

Adda left the workspace and stood without unplugging her face from the generator, earning a painful tug on the nose. She stuffed her cable into her necklace and climbed the ladder. The people she passed made eye contact and said things she ignored. In the common room she pushed a table away from the high-lighted area, her eyes coloring it yellow even in reality. One floor panel was at a slightly different angle than the panels around it, and a thin streak of blue dust which crossed over the others went under that one.

"What do you see?" asked Captain Sloane quietly, from a step behind her.

"AegiSKADA left something here." She pointed at the recently moved panel. "I need to open this."

"Someone does," the captain said. "Not you. Bring me the major, please."

Major O.D. was sleeping in the bunkhouse, and she had to shake him awake. When she explained the situation, he woke quickly and loudly. "Rio, Vick, Zikri, get up."

In a nearby bed, Zikri grumbled, "I'm up, I'm . . . ugh," and staggered into the narrow center aisle.

"Rio's already awake." Adda had to look closer at the other bunks to determine that Vick wasn't there. "And I'll find Vick." It made sense to have the medic along, and having two of the strongest soldiers nearby couldn't hurt.

She conveyed the major's summons to Vick and Rio when she returned to the kitchen. Every other awake pirate followed them back to the main room, which felt suddenly and thoroughly crowded. Sturm found Rio a pry bar, and she pried up a tile.

Underneath, a boxy device the size of the pirates' palm weapons, but with a cylindrical canister emerging from its side at an angle, sat on the curving exterior hull in a puddle of gray-white sludge. For a second, everybody stared. Then the medic backed up into several other people and pulled his shirt collar over his mouth and nose. "That's a fuckin' microbe dispenser!"

They fell back, cramming against the walls, the press of bodies against Adda's making her shallow breaths drag through her throat. So that was AegiSKADA's play. It predicted she'd find the dispenser after the better-armed ZVs felt safe in their stronghold again. Her investigation had raised the pirates' threat profile. Now she'd helped the intelligence poison them all.

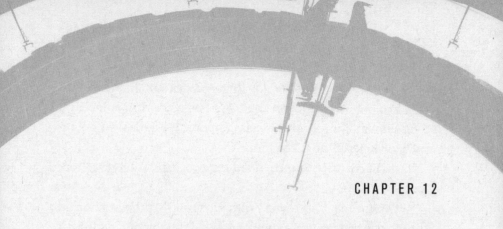

CHAPTER 12

Charges Accrued: Interference with Approved Microbiological Research

Iridian strapped on a respirator mask printed so recently that its gummy surface stuck to her fingertips. Barbary Station used to decommission ships full of particulates and chemicals that flayed lungs. Patterns for heavy-duty masks were easy to find in the station's database. Now everybody in Sloane's crew had one.

Dye was scarce, apparently. Between the black-and-gray masks and the blue-dusted black hoods, the pirates could pass as cultists or a large necrobass band. Or habitat-based resistance fighters.

Iridian cracked her knuckles and crouched next to Sloane, Tritheist, and Sturm. Despite the dye shortage, Captain Sloane wore a dark red mask. Adda was down in her tank again, plugged into her workspace generator to search the sensor data and station systems for relevant information. Iridian could be of more use here, with the physical device.

They'd wrapped the dispenser in a transparent bag from the mess hall secured with a zip tie. Maybe it'd keep the atmo clean,

but it was probably too late for that. Besides, small enough particles would power through the bag's pores. Sturm's comp lit it
bright enough for a detailed examination. "Figure it's got a fluid-
ized bed feeder?" she asked him.

"Most likely," said Sturm. "Good steady distribution flow, from
those."

"What does that have to do with anything?" Tritheist snapped.

"Damage control and safety of moving the thing," said Iridian.
"If the contents are under pressure, we can't just yank it off of
there and throw it out an airlock. Might blow up in somebody's
face. And that's assuming it's not booby-trapped with more con-
ventional explosives, which we haven't proven yet."

Tritheist backed away from the device. Iridian grimly held her
ground. "Are there more?" Captain Sloane asked.

"Adda's looking for more now, sir. Captain." *Not sir, damn you,
get it right.* Iridian tapped out a message. If Adda were in a workspace, she'd have turned off her comp's alerts. She'd update Iridian when she had something useful, or when Iridian went down
to feed and water her. "Bleach might kill it," Iridian said. It was the
"cut off its head" move in microbe combat, if Iridian remembered
her college biology class correctly. "Do we have any?"

Tritheist stood up fast. "Chef has some." Sturm snorted as the
lieutenant walked quickly to the mess hall, about two steps short
of a run.

"Maybe Adda can set up a comp to search for more by shape, or
output, or something." Iridian caught the captain's eye and waited
for a nod of approval before she headed for the empty water tank.

She lived in the tank too, but the place was really Adda's.
The accoutrements of the workspace generator—pillows, blankets hung from hooks stuck to the ceiling to muffle sound, pans
sprouting mushrooms, and mugs of brown, metallic-smelling

sludge Adda swore was necessary—covered half the floor space now. Adda's generator had been near the tank's center, but she'd moved it against the wall farthest from the ladder.

"Hey," Iridian whispered, so as not to startle her. "I need you to do me a favor, babe."

"Busy." The word was bitten off from within the workspace generator tent, its echoes smothered by the hanging blankets.

Iridian managed not to expel her equally irritated sigh. "Me too. I'm trying to keep our future employers alive by finding out if AegiSKADA planted more dispensers. Can you set my comp up to locate them?"

A pale hand thrust imperiously through the tent flaps. Iridian peeled off her comp glove and placed it in the palm, which withdrew into the workspace generator. While Iridian waited, she examined the tank itself, in case some enterprising bot had affixed a dispenser there. She didn't see one.

Her glove reappeared outside the tent. "Thanks, babe." Iridian tried and failed to mask her annoyance. Adda didn't respond. In a few hours Iridian would drag her out to hydrate her.

When Iridian stuck her head out of the trapdoor, Si Po almost stepped on it. "I was looking for more of those dispensers, and I noticed a high concentration of CO_2 in the bunkhouse," he said. "I think we have a filtration problem."

Iridian groaned. "Show me."

The harder the pirates looked, the more problems they found. Something beneath the mess hall had been eating through the struts that held it onto the hull. *How the hell did that stay airtight?* She couldn't just leave them to fix the problems, because they were the ones who'd let the base get in that state.

While she scanned the area, Rio asked Pel, "Have you heard that clanking sound over by the water recycler?"

"It's not by the water recycler, it's in the water recycler," he said.

"Rio, take the casing off and get Sturm," Iridian yelled over her shoulder. "Please."

"Ears like a bat, that one." Rio's heavy footfalls retreated from the mess hall.

Pel avoided a table apparently by memory on his way to Iridian's side. Without the usual goggles or dark glasses covering his eyes, their yellowish tint and apparent lack of pupils unsettled her. "Is another one of those dispenser things in here?" he asked.

She sighed, frustrated and aching from bending to examine inconvenient corners. "Not that I can tell."

"Good," he said. "I'm starving."

"As if anything that'd make you sick would be in my kitchen," Chef huffed.

"Well, I'm just glad Iridian's here to make sure, that's all." Pel raised an eyebrow in Iridian's general direction. "I'm really glad."

That boy had a lot of Adda in him, and the results of Adda's fend-for-yourself style of affection, too. In some ways it made him self-sufficient. He also had clingy little behaviors designed to keep people near. *Was he like that before he lost his sight?*

He hovered nearby, crunching on peanuts that Iridian refused. Additional dust might contaminate her comp's readings. Hopefully the analysis was ignoring all the blue stuff from the spray-on radiation reflectant.

"I'd help," he said quietly. "Maybe I could . . . carry something? But my eyes are killing me today." He shrugged, head turned away so not even his ear pointed in her direction. "Can't see where it's light and dark. I usually can, a bit. Not today."

Iridian's heart sort of cracked and resettled into a new, horrified position. "I'm sorry."

She wandered into the hallway, watching her comp's readings.

He followed her, trailing his hand along the wall. "You'd have done well when everyone was out raiding. They were always pulling crazy shit. And engineers make the same cut as people who go on the ships to kick its crew off, whether they go or not, so that would've worked well for Adda."

Iridian's brow furrowed as she refocused on him. "You talk like you weren't with Sloane then."

He gulped, scarred eyes wide. "Oh," he said too loudly for his current proximity. "Well, you know, it's complicated."

Iridian couldn't help smiling at just how badly the kid lied. That audacity probably got him out of half the trouble he got into. "You were there then, or you weren't. Which is it?"

Si Po passed Pel with a pat on his arm to warn him of his presence. Pel startled anyway. "We have a problem," Si Po said. "Bleach isn't killing this stuff."

CHAPTER 13

Charges Accrued: Violation of Human Medical Testing Protocol

Adda could not, for the life of her, match the pattern on the left to the pattern on the right.

The new software compared images of the magnified microbes from AegiSKADA's dispenser with images of known microbes from an Internet scrape. When it found a known microbe that could be the same as the one in AegiSKADA's dispenser, it presented the paired images in the workspace for review. All she'd been able to determine was that AegiSKADA had deployed some kind of bacteria. None of the close matches she reviewed were close enough to know how to deactivate whatever was in the dispenser.

The starscape behind the images was distracting, especially during the deep purple supernovas that exploded whenever the software found a new promising match. Red ones would explode if AegiSKADA sent drones toward the pirate compound.

Perhaps the pilots could be persuaded to raid some university libraries. *Which institutions would be most vulnerable? Which would be the most useful?* Her eyes flickered open. Red letters on the generator's ceiling swam before them, until she forced her mind back into the workspace.

The remnants of another purple supernova pulsed behind zoomed-in images of the most likely microbes drifting around her head. She sighed. Anywhere outside the lead cloud, she'd find a bacteriologist to ask.

The ZV medic (whose name also started with a Z . . .) called a sedation shot he administered to another ZV a "bar-bich-you-et." The word had two Rs, and an overdose could kill. She hoped she'd never get an injection from someone who couldn't pronounce what he was injecting. She wouldn't ask him for epidemiological advice.

She focused on the swimming images, and they aligned themselves in her field of vision. None matched the bacteria she was looking at, but it had aspects of all of them. Some were round diplococcus bacteria, some were short, wide coccobacilli. Surely they wouldn't combine and share traits in nature.

And *that* suggested conscious intervention. *But what's an artificially created bacteria doing on a shipbreaking station? Did it come in with a military wreck disassembled here? Did AegiSKADA make it?* The former seemed more likely, but she'd hate to incorrectly assume that the AI couldn't make more.

Somebody above and down the hall was banging around in the kitchen, dragging her out of her workspace. *How can I accomplish anything if they keep that up?*

She unplugged from the generator and crawled out of the tent. Iridian sat outside, watching her. "Hi," Adda whispered.

"Hey." The gray mask over Iridian's nose and mouth emphasized her dark eyes. She held up a mug wafting tomato and basil steam. "Lunch? Or more like dinner." Adda's stomach rumbled.

The crinkles around those gorgeous eyes implied Iridian's smile.

Adda drank half the soup in long gulps. Going to the main part of the pirate compound seemed important for reasons other than noise reduction. That main room would be full of people, who stayed out of her water tank because it was creaky and creepy, and Iridian probably kept them out so Adda could work. . . . None of that enticed her to return to the compound, so why was her brain still hooked on that idea?

"Your lips are blue," said Iridian.

"Mushroom dust." Adda peered into the mug, as if her purpose was one of the soup's ingredients. It came to her, and she gasped. "I need your blood."

Iridian waggled her eyebrows at her. "I know you like how it looks on me, babe, but I'm not feeling very romantic with the mysterious microbial doom going around. Though maybe that's all the more reason."

Adda set down the half-finished soup and crawled into Iridian's lap. Her girlfriend wrapped long, slender arms around her, keeping Adda's overstimulated body still, helping her focus. "Sample analysis. Blood, saliva. I think I can get that translator Si Po sent me to facilitate insertion sequence comparisons. If we know what it is, we'll know how to kill it. I think."

"Si Po gave you something?" Iridian sounded surprised.

"Do you think he'd donate blood?"

"I'd bet money that he's afraid of needles. He's afraid of everything else." Iridian cuddled Adda against her chest. "You've been working your ass off. Did you sleep last night?"

"It turns out I can sleep for a few minutes and stay connected to the workspace." Although that had been . . . odd. She was used to the message about her location written on the generator's ceiling when she woke up. That morning she'd woken up to *You are the beginning of the endless void* in her mother's handwriting.

Iridian tilted Adda's chin up and smiled, amusement evident in the narrowing of her eyes, before lifting her mask and meeting Adda's lips with her own. Iridian tasted of coffee, lipstick, and woman. Muscles in Adda's shoulders and neck that hadn't even felt tight relaxed. Her tongue wound with Iridian's for a long moment before she pulled back, earning a small, frustrated grunt from her lover. "Let me get some samples analyzing, and then I swear I'll come back to this."

Iridian nipped at the tip of Adda's nose. "You'd better." She slid the mask over her grin and hung a second mask around Adda's neck.

Adda gently bumped their foreheads together and stood to go look for printer patterns for a syringe and gloves. "It won't take that long!"

"Up we go." Iridian boosted Adda up the ladder's first few rungs with a hand on Adda's butt.

In the end, Adda managed to get blood samples and cheek swabs from every crew member, although O.D. had to order a few ZVs to cooperate. She also collected data from the comps of anyone who'd worked on maintenance problems discovered during the search for more dispensers.

Back in her tank, she hooked up the translator from Si Po, the medic's emergency diagnostic software, and odds and ends from both the printer and her own chemistry equipment to get her samples processing. They had probably absorbed some airborne contaminants on the way to the tank. Hopefully they had all been contaminated equally.

When she emerged from the generator, Iridian sat outside, with less soup and clothing. The wall lamps turned her into a sleek silhouette that made Adda wish she'd kept up her painting skills. "I thought about that tattoo design," Iridian purred, crawling closer on hands and knees across the pillows. In this light, her curves were maddeningly sensual. "Want me to show you where it would look hottest?"

* * *

Later, among disarranged pillows, Adda murmured, "Why in all the worlds would AegiSKADA put a dispenser in the floor? Why not an air vent?"

Iridian shrugged, jouncing Adda's head where it rested on her collarbone. "The vents here are in weird places. Since the ceiling's low, even the highest ones would've been too visible."

"Ah." Adda was short enough to pass under most vents without seeing beyond the slats on the cover. "So it has an excellent model of where humans search for things."

"Not a flawless model," Iridian said. "You found it."

Adda sighed. "I can't tell if the location is important or not. And it might have wanted me to find it, to increase exposure."

"Which is why I'm looking forward to taking apart all its hardware and launching each piece at a different star," Iridian said.

"Doesn't it bother you at all . . ." Adda hated the shrill note her voice acquired when she was defending her point. It made people stop listening, and this was important. After a breath, she tried again. "Doesn't it bother you that you'd be destroying something unique?"

"Uniquely awful." Iridian craned her neck to look at Adda. "No, it doesn't bother me. I know you think you have to sympathize with these things to understand them, or whatever the rhetoric is, but trust me, there's nothing in that AI's pseudo-organic tank anything like what's in here"—she tapped Adda's forehead—"or here."

Her hand settled on her chest in front of Adda's nose. "It's a tool some corporate desk pilot left running with the on switch taped down, and it's standing between us and an actual enjoyable life."

"You're losing points for condescension," Adda muttered. This conversation wasn't convincing anyone.

"Yeah, sorry." Iridian yawned like a tigress, with a contented throaty moan at the end that made Adda pull her close.

"I need to tell you something," she whispered, "and you're not going to like it." Iridian frowned, but nodded for Adda to continue. "AegiSKADA may be awake."

Iridian's fists clenched on Adda's arms. Furious and fearful spacefarer cant spilled from her lips. When Adda winced at the pressure, Iridian let go and rolled up to a standing position. "It can't be. We'd be dead by now. It'd find a way. Why do you think that?"

It sounded more like a reflexive denial than an informed one. Adda sat up and explained her conclusions while Iridian's scowl deepened. "Hold up. You aren't trying to interact with it now that you know. You can't. We need to shut that thing down or blow it up, the sooner the better. We should take out the whole station. If it's awake, and it gets out of here . . . That'd be bigger than us, babe. An awakened AI could take out the fucking human race."

This was how Adda was afraid Iridian would react. If she'd taken the time to consider the options, which Adda doubted, Iridian had concluded that awakened intelligences were too dangerous to be worth the vast increase in processing, production, analysis, and even creative, inventive *thought*. To most people, no awakened intelligence deserved the chance to live. AegiSKADA had done terrible things, but if it were awakened, then it had reasons to act as it did. It'd be criminal to destroy it without finding out what those reasons were.

Perhaps practicality would persuade her. "It's got too many defenses in place for blasting our way to it and blowing it up to be the best solution, especially if it's the only thing giving us air and gravity." Iridian thumped the wall with her fist, then pulled her clothes on and climbed the ladder. The door slammed shut.

Iridian would've responded if she'd had another argument, but there just wasn't one. The station population lacked the equipment to survive without the environment at least one AI was creating for them. They couldn't just destroy AegiSKADA until they knew more about it, especially how it interacted with HarborMaster.

* * *

It could have been day or night when she awoke. Knowing the time sometimes distracted her in the workspace, so she'd removed the clock from her comp's default display. Iridian had returned at some point, and Adda slid out from beneath her arm and went to her table of concentration aids.

Getting into the workspace for a long session had become a multistep process after she ran out of sharpsheets. First was a mouthwash of several ingredients best absorbed through oral tissue. She added earbuds full of pink noise while that took effect. A nasally inhaled mushroom and pulverized pill mixture had to be followed by a cup of water so the dry mouth didn't distract her.

The analysis on the samples was still running. Preliminary results revealed no significant patterns, let alone identifying what kind of bacteria might be resistant to bleach. The water tank was cool, but not cold enough to keep the blood from rotting. The analysis should be finished before then, but she'd asked a lot of her hardware. It wasn't a quantum computer.

While she waited, she accessed her sensor feeds. Today they appeared as crystalline fragments dragging along slabs of gray synthetic flesh hung in a walk-in freezer. Each slab represented one of the station's modules. The cold and the odor so soon after she woke up nauseated her.

HarborMaster should have shown an increase in activity after the damage AegiSKADA caused this month. Perhaps it sent damage reports to AegiSKADA, which could throw the security intelligence even further off-kilter. If AegiSKADA were awakened, she had no idea how it'd react to HarborMaster's damage reporting. Her employee credentials let her poke around the items she could request through HarborMaster's user interface. Those held nothing of use.

Without administrative access to AegiSKADA, all she could do was send packets of information to the intelligence through the sensors. Somewhere in the past, Jurek Volikov had foreseen every other tactic she'd tried so far.

She hated that man. His documentation was substandard. And where were the fail-safes that would have kept this whole mess from happening? What gave the damned intelligence complete confidence in its right to kill?

But she could track its activities. That was significant enough to set the crystal fragments vibrating in a low, saccharine hum. Unsupervised intelligences had protocols to search for qualified admins and were designed to accept anyone meeting the criteria. An awakened intelligence would ignore such a compulsion, so she didn't expect AegiSKADA's activity to suggest a search for human input.

What, then, was its interest in the station's population? The workspace's scent changed to a sharper chill as crystal fragment layers overlapped on the flesh and, at the code level, a program began to form.

"Sissy?"

The sigh escaped her before she could stop it. "What, Pel?"

The thump of somebody plopping down on pillows accompanied a sharp creak from the tank. Her mind jolted out of the workspace. "I dunno," he said. "Just wanted to talk to someone who isn't hacking their lungs out."

"People are getting respiratory symptoms? Who?" She crawled out of the workspace generator.

Iridian was gone. The mental image of the last time she was there made Adda's bare skin tingle. She startled hard, but Pel faced a point to the side of the generator. The tinted goggles he wore above his gray mask wouldn't show him much skin in this light even if he could see. She tugged on the outfit she wasn't wearing yesterday, holding her elbows and knees away from her sides to minimize swishing and fastening sounds.

"Tritheist, for one, and he's pissed." Pel chuckled. "Captain Sloane too, probably, but the captain's door's closed, so who knows? And Tabs and Nils, and . . ."

He listed more names. *Respiratory symptoms.* That should narrow down the list of bacteria combined to create this superbug, shouldn't it? Gods, if she just had one damned bacteriologist.

"Well?" Pel asked.

"Well what?"

He scooted the pillow he sat on closer to the generator's opening, away from the door to the rest of the compound. "Well, I'm just . . . I don't want to get sick, Sissy."

"Obviously." That was the wrong thing to say. But how the hell was she going to find a way out of this mess with him yapping?

"Hey." His tone confirmed her suspicions regarding her response. "Mom said you're supposed to look after me."

Adda halted her turn to go back into the generator and glared

at him. "Don't you tell me what Mom said. I was the one who told you she said that."

"So . . ." That childish, wheedling tone, with accompanying smile . . . But nostalgia wouldn't incapacitate the intelligence contaminating their air.

"So sit out there if you want, but I've got work to do. Just please be quiet, okay?" They both snorted in amusement, almost the same sound, at the idea of him sitting in silence for more than a few minutes. He even talked in his sleep.

Adda settled on her back in the generator and sank into the workspace. HarborMaster and AegiSKADA communicated. It and AegiSKADA shared the sensor nodes. Duplicates would be an expensive waste of resources and space. So everything she sent to AegiSKADA that it didn't delete must have reached HarborMaster, but not everything found the same sequences to exploit in HarborMaster that it found in AegiSKADA. Was there something helpful in that?

She traced the trail of her intrusion program's progress before AegiSKADA had shut it down. The workspace rendered it in an intricate map of polished titanium bells and glass bottles with tiny LEDs in the bottom. Some of the data she'd gotten when she sent the Trojan packets through the sensor nodes on the path behind the wall had to transmit to—

"Are creditors still going after Dad to get my loans back?"

Red letters above her face. *You are in a water tank.* Gods, her homemade concentration mix made that message more alarming than it had sounded when she wrote it. She sucked in oxygen every time she read it now, her body proving to itself that she wasn't about to drown.

"Probably," she said.

Pel groaned. "Dad's so easy to get ahold of. I mean, he wouldn't

even take his name out of the directory when I asked him to. Between your student loans and mine, and some. . . . um . . . other debts I haven't gotten a chance to pay back since I've been here, he's screwed, you know? That would wipe him out."

An increase in the ambient noise from above and steps on the ladder shoved any response Adda might have formulated out of her head. "If you find a way off the station before we suffer permanent lung damage," Captain Sloane said, "I'll pay any debts your family owes."

The captain's voice was hoarse and wet, far from its usual smooth tone. Adda knelt at the generator's entrance, relieved about her earlier decision to get dressed and trying to control a swell of excitement at the idea of her entire family being debt free. Even her grandparents' grandparents had spent their whole lives owing somebody something.

"What's up, Captain?" Pel scrambled to his feet like an eager cabin boy.

The captain started to speak, but turned toward the corner of the tank to cough into the crook of one arm. "I'm curious as to what kind of headway you've made. The situation is growing somewhat dire."

"Seriously." Adda winced. Sharpsheets sometimes lowered inhibitions and, in her case, exacerbated social awkwardness. Nobody said "seriously" to their boss, or to pirate captains. "I know what I need, and what I have. Not how to connect the two. What happened to those doctors who used to work on the station? The ones who helped Iridian and tried to help Pel. Can't we get them here? I have questions they might answer."

The captain frowned. "Can you ask them at a distance? They don't travel well."

"Some of this looks like you'd have to manipulate it to under-

stand it. Have you got a comm system that can facilitate that?"

"Perhaps. Join me in the computer room in five minutes."

After the captain climbed back up the ladder and shut the door, Adda relaxed. The cable still connected to her nasal jack tugged on her nose. She'd been plugged in during the whole conversation. Seeing her feed a cable through her nostril piercing to get a high-bandwidth connection straight to her neural implants grossed most people out. Captain Sloane didn't even stare at it.

Adda's lips quirked up as she disconnected from the generator and cleaned and stored her cable. If Sloane could look past her methods to acknowledge her results, that was further confirmation that she and Iridian had picked the right captain to work for. Now they just had to survive long enough to join the crew, or work their way into the core group that was called upon for most jobs, anyway, and get paid.

* * *

She and Pel traversed the compound arm in arm to the main room, where Iridian sat backward on a chair with Chato, Tabs, Rio, and a couple of other ZVs. It was the most physically powerful group of women (excluding Chato) that Adda had ever seen outside a gym. These must've been the people Iridian trained and relaxed with during the hours Adda spent alone in the workspace generator. It was always odd to see how fast Iridian's relationships with others progressed while Adda was absorbed in a project. They were having so much fun that she couldn't help but smile.

The six of them were playing some game that involved covering squares projected on the floor with the shadow of hands and feet at various signals. The squares had settings that controlled an enormous machine projected across the wall, rampaging through a generic city. The petite female ZV, Tabs, paid a lot more attention to this than to the racing game Adda had watched them play earlier, possibly because she had her armor back.

Between the game noise and the shouting pirates, Pel had to yell Iridian's name twice before she responded. "What's going on?" She glanced between Adda and Pel, still arm in arm. She still sounded suspicious, but the heated anger from the night before had cooled.

Si Po was in the computer room when they arrived, as usual. *Does he sleep there?* At the moment he was coughing there, big, racking coughs that shook his hair over his face. They stood around finding things to stare at other than him until he took two breaths in a row without convulsing.

Iridian said, "Captain Sloane sent us here to contact the med team."

Si Po stared at the floor and panted, an expression of incredulity replacing his pained grimace. "What do you think I've been trying to do?"

"Shit," Pel muttered.

Adda asked, "What happens when you—"

"Fuck all, that's what," Si Po snapped. "The call's getting out, but nothing's coming back."

"Check for a delivery record," she said instead of making an unhelpful comment about the man's intelligence. Returning to her usual jittery attention span as her drugs wore off made her irritable.

Si Po tapped at the console with more force than necessary. The three of them shuffled nearer to make space for the captain. What kind of devices and traps and bugs were still in the pirates' compound with them? The crew had swept the place repeatedly when they returned, but perhaps they'd missed something.

According to Pel, AegiSKADA's drones had raided the compound before. A touch logger on the console might've been collecting every tap and swipe, even recording their voices so it could imitate them later. . . .

"It's getting through," Si Po said. "The ratty, overeducated hull-humpers are ignoring us."

Iridian stiffened against Adda's arm, and Adda laid a hand on her girlfriend's hip. The difference in education opportunities between NEU and the colonies beyond Mars had been a major point of contention during the war. "Overeducated" was a weightier term than it used to be. But, as Iridian frequently told herself aloud for everyone's benefit, the war was over.

"Lad and lasses, I'd like to connect my comp to the antenna array around us," said Captain Sloane. "How might we arrange that?"

Adda and Iridian glanced at each other, then examined the console and the comp glove. Iridian spent more time with the console, while Adda focused on the comp. "Cable, wire cutters, and solder?" she asked Iridian.

"Or plugs that fit," said Iridian. Si Po nodded and left in the direction of the main room and Sturm's armory workshop. "Trying to get their attention with a more important caller, sir?" Adda kicked Iridian's shin for incorrect pronoun usage. "Sorry, Captain," said Iridian.

"They know better than to anger me," the captain said.

"I think there's an easier way to do that." Sloane's mouth twitched up, and Adda clarified, "Tell them it's you calling, I mean. Could somebody get Si Po back?" Once she had as much information as she could get, she coerced the console into sending messages in the captain's name. That extended the captain's personal communication range to the entirety of the station and a bit beyond, if Iridian had described the antennas accurately. "I can guarantee the audio. Vid should work too, but . . ." Adda shrugged. Cams and vid optimization didn't interest her.

"Doctors," the captain intoned, "this is Captain Sloane. We're experiencing an emergency medical situation. I'm waiting on your response." After the mic was off, Sloane smiled at Adda. "I like this. Will it stay this way? Must I always be in this room?"

"It's trivial to collect that information and add it in for you every time." She shut her mouth. This was the captain she was talking to, not Iridian or some classmate at school, and she didn't need to emphasize the simplicity of the task when Sloane hadn't thought of setting that arrangement up before now.

A pinging alert drew their attention to the projection on the wall, where the cam light came on to show that it was filming them. In the message projection, a face appeared so close to the medical team's cam lens that the person's brown eyes seemed inordinately large. Barbary Station's spinning starscape flickered at the edge of the frame, in a projected window, Adda hoped.

Iridian waved at the console's cam. "That's Dr. Tiwari." He and another member of the med team had rescued Iridian from AegiSKADA's drone on the station's exterior.

The physician half a centimeter from the lens nodded briefly to Iridian, then said, "Yes, Captain?" His accent might have been French.

Facing the console's mic and cam, Sloane said, "We've had a medical emergency in our little abode. AegiSKADA deployed some sort of microbial dispenser, which is—"

"Making everybody sick, like Si Po?" An olive-toned pointing finger replaced Dr. Tiwari's face in the vid, aimed over Adda's shoulder. "He's experiencing respiratory distress."

They all turned to look at the oily-haired pirate. Si Po's narrow chest and stomach strained with his wheezing inhales and exhales. The effect was like a panic attack Adda once had in an exceptionally disturbing workspace. She didn't know how to help. Iridian patted his back like he was choking, which threw off his balance. He smiled as best he could and waved her off. Beneath his labored breath, footsteps approached the medical team's mic.

"We need a short-term treatment and a long-term cure." The captain watched Si Po with a deep frown. The doctor's eyes rose to stare at something behind his cam. The stomping footsteps drew nearer. "We've completed some—"

"Medicine cabinet?" interrupted a woman out of sight, thanks to the doctor in front of the cam. She pronounced each syllable with exquisite care, although she sounded out of breath.

"That's Dr. Williams," Iridian muttered for Adda's benefit. "She talked like that after she chased off that drone on the surface, too."

"Two out of four of them," Si Po said. "Not bad." When Iridian communicated her confusion with a raised eyebrow, he added "There are four docs out there, but we never catch all of them on cam at once." It was interesting that Dr. Williams had picked up on the conversation's topic. The way she was breathing suggested that she'd come from far enough away that she should have been out of hearing range.

"Pel, would you ask Zikri what medications he has at his disposal, please?" Captain Sloane said.

"Yeah, sure, Captain." Pel dragged his hand along the blue-dusted wall on his way into the main room, where he yelled, "Hey, where's Zikri?" loud enough that he might as well have stayed in the room to do it.

"Zikri. That hack. Pill pusher. *Pill seller.*" Dr. Tiwari looked off cam as he spoke, like he might if he was talking to himself.

"Symptoms?" demanded Dr. Williams from off cam in the opposite direction from where Dr. Tiwari was looking.

"A great deal of coughing," said Captain Sloane. "And everybody who's having breathing difficulty has a headache as well. Our antibiotics have had no effect."

After a few seconds of silence that made Adda wonder if they'd lost the comms feed, Dr. Tiwari said, "Yes. Bacteria or virus?"

Adda actually had the answer to that. "Bacteria. I ran tests."

"Which?" asked Dr. Williams.

"I can send you what I've got so far," Adda said, "or show you here, and—"

"Send," said Dr. Tiwari, whose face still took up the entirety of the vid screen.

Pel and Zikri arrived while Adda was setting up the data transfer. "All right, you want the rundown on my stock?" Zikri's spine straightened, his chest puffed out as if he liked being the person everybody listened to.

"Inarguably," said Dr. Williams.

Zikri looked miffed until he met the captain's eyes. Sloane watched him unblinking, with fingers steepled over the V of the shirt beneath the captain's jacket. "We had light and heavy antibio before, but I used up all the light stuff and most of the heavy. We got a lot of painkiller. It comes on the fugee care packages, and I trade for it. You know they don't need it. They're safe as houses so long as they don't pick up anything gun, blade, or bludgeon shaped." He glanced around as if waiting for an argument. Considering the pirates' recent death toll, Adda was disinclined to challenge his assumption. "Now they have most of the antihistamines—kids, allergies, you know—and there's the sanitizers. We mixed up a lot of wipes and sprays, but this shit grows like mold. Hey, it's not mold, is it?" he asked hopefully.

"Not," pronounced the woman off-screen. "Airivine? Corsiprex? Dilaflo?"

"What?" Zikri gaped at the console's cam. "You get hit in the head or something?"

To a combat medic, all psychologically atypical behavior must have looked like symptoms of head injury. "Those sound like medication names," Adda said.

"Huh . . ." Zikri scratched his jaw for a couple of seconds. "Are they steroids?"

"Inhaled steroids, yes, inarguably," said Dr. Williams.

"Not," Dr. Tiwari said in a tone suggesting that this was a point in an often-repeated argument.

"What else?" Dr. Williams demanded, and before anybody in Captain Sloane's base could come up with a response, he continued, "Requires more." The intensity and opacity of their conversational back-and-forth was worrisome. How could these people cure the infection if they couldn't communicate clearly enough to ask and answer complete questions?

"Inhalers with steroid cartridges, do you have them?" Dr. Tiwari asked. This question appeared to be directed at the cam.

"Well, I do have an inhaler or two," Zikri said doubtfully. "Nobody here's asthmatic, so I've been trading those to the fugees. They got asthmatic kids, with nobody to fix their lungs up here."

"Can't," said Dr. Williams.

"I know, I know, no equipment." Zikri smirked at Iridian and Adda. "You should have been here when Six needed his gall bladder out. That was frickin' messy." Six was the large, quiet ZV with the cadet cap, Adda was fairly certain.

Iridian wrinkled her nose. "I didn't know you could live without a gall bladder."

"You can when it makes you vomit up everything you eat,"

Zikri said. "I'll go look for inhalers and see what's in 'em. Hey, what can we use aside from bleach? Bleach ain't killing shit."

"Apply multiple times," said Dr. Tiwari. Zikri rolled his eyes.

"Data received," said Dr. Williams. A flash of Adda's analysis results crossed the edge of the cam's view, on a table projector. "Synthesized biofilm, pseudo-organic construction but . . . not." Dr. Tiwari left the cam range to examine the projection, exposing a small, poorly lit room with a large projected window and some overturned office furniture.

It was gratifying to hear physicians support Adda's assessment that the microbes were not naturally occurring. She still couldn't believe the creativity evident in the bioweaponry deployment. This almost certainly hadn't been a scenario in Volikov's intelligence development regimen. How much resourcefulness had he trained AegiSKADA for? Or, a more troubling question: Just how much had it figured out on its own?

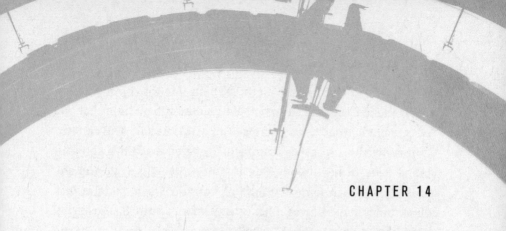

CHAPTER 14

Charges Accrued: Slander

Iridian banged her head on the way out of the ceiling duct in the mess hall. The curse she spat made Chef laugh while Iridian slammed the vent's cover into place. "Haven't heard that one in a while," Chef said. "Since I worked at Arabia Terra Station."

Iridian felt Chef's gaze on her as she tightened the screws on the ceiling vent and moved on to the one in the wall. AT Station was a Near Earth Union military base, before the war. Secessionists took it during their initial sweep of the red planet. The NEU blasted it from orbit until the new craters looked as natural as the old ones. "Yeah, I hear they had some choice terms. Nothing else to do on Mars."

"You weren't ever stationed there?" Chef asked.

Iridian squeezed her head and arm into the wall duct and reached for the fan pumping in stolen station atmo. That would've been a likely hiding place for a microbe dispenser, especially if AegiSKADA tracked movement and cataloged people who entered this room.

Nothing inside resembled the dispenser in the common room. What she did find was a respectable decontaminant filter that had been included in the pattern used to print the fan. The contraption sprayed a low-grade disinfectant, which explained the sour, tangy taste in her mouth. She'd gotten a faceful of it, and she must've absorbed some of it through her skin. She hoped that was what happened, anyway. If her mask had let so much aerosolized disinfectant pass through its substrate that she could taste the stuff, then it'd be useless against AegiSKADA's bioweapon.

"You don't have to tell me," Chef huffed.

"Sorry. Mars was over for infantry by the time I came off the Jovian front. I never ran there."

Chef wiped down a cup and tossed it into the recycling bin to be melted, purified, and printed into another cup later. "Ran? Is that what they call it now?"

"I was a Shieldrunner. ISVs use kinetic backup power, so we literally ran everywhere. The vehicles just have longer legs than we do."

Neither of the ducts contained dispensers, or dormant drones, or anything that didn't look like it was there when Iridian and Adda arrived. Two air inlets per room seemed to be the pirates' construction limit. From a security perspective it made a certain kind of sense, since that resulted in fewer ingress points for spiderbots. Iridian waved good-bye to Chef on her way to borrow a light from Sturm. Headlamp strapped in place on her forehead, she stepped quietly into the packed bunkhouse.

By standing on a lower bunk and ducking under the one above it, she determined that the fan in the single duct leading to this room was off. Vick growled at her from the lower one, but she wouldn't rush on his account.

This vent was too small for her to crawl through. By crushing her chest against the wall and jamming the edge of the vent into her armpit, she reached the still fan. Its blades moved freely when she pushed them with her fingertips. Either it wasn't getting power or the motor was shot.

It was the third broken or underpowered one she'd found so far. The compound was probably losing atmo through these things. Sturm might know about it already, but then again he might not. There wasn't time to disassemble the wall to fix it, anyway.

If people got trapped in the bunkhouse, they could suffocate. And it'd be *other* people, because she'd invite Pel to sleep down in the tank with her and Adda after this discovery. At least the CO_2 scrubber appeared to be working. The readouts matched the ideal ones for that model on her comp. Everything here was bigger and more complicated than the equipment that had kept her alive in her ISV cabin during the war.

People were damned ignorant of how near to death they were in this little outpost. If a wall collapsed, or another bomb struck (and why hadn't it?), everybody'd die in about a minute. Unconscious after only fifteen seconds, though, so there was that.

In the hallway, Grandpa Death waved a wrench the way normal people might wave their hand in greeting. Iridian grinned. She didn't hold with normal. "How goes?" she asked him.

"Could be a lot worse. I checked the captain's cabin and the computer room. You got the rest?"

"I didn't get the entrance yet. Actually, I wouldn't mind backup." If anywhere hid drones looking to pick off stragglers, the three-story space between the hulls would be it. People descending the ladder would be particularly vulnerable, since it forced them to travel feetfirst with their hands occupied while facing a wall.

"Sure." Grandpa Death led the way through the common room,

and they combed the entrance hall in silence. This area didn't even have a vent.

She cut a look over at the ZV while they worked. A few turns of phrase that had come out of his mouth over the past few weeks had a distinct Neptunian feel to them. If he hadn't fought for the secessionists, he'd spent years in the area. Maybe he'd even grown up out there.

Still, he respected her and Adda and even Pel, when he deserved it. That was more than a lot of the other pirates did. And when she expressed her outrage over the broken fan in the bunkhouse, he responded, "That's damned foolish. Somebody'll be sorry about that before all this is over." So he understood that much about life in the cold and the black, though he wasn't a spacefarer himself. Although after this long without dirt beneath their boots, nobody'd argue the definition of true spacefarers with residents of Barbary Station.

When they met up in the far corner after examining the walls, floor, and ceiling, he opened the hatch and sighed. "Down we go."

Iridian went first, her headlamp playing over the walls and the ladder itself on the way down while Grandpa Death watched for drones with a palmer in hand. They searched the area between hulls, but the pirates kept the walkway clear, and most of the thick cables were bound and far enough out of reach that she'd have to come back with scaffolding to look them all over in detail. Grandpa Death spent as much time looking over his shoulder and toward the hole in the wall leading to the docking bay as searching for dispensers, anyway, and he walked right behind Iridian when she headed for the ladder back to base.

Halfway through reaching for the first rung, another air intake grate caught her attention. Because of the way its frame was embedded in the wall, it would've been impossible to see from any other angle. Her headlamp lit it like a spotlight. "Did we check that?" she asked quietly.

"Don't think so."

She knelt and peered into the opening. Dim white light from the docking bay filtered in through another grate on that side. "Do you know how many of these we've got?"

"Sorry. Matherly would've known, he designed the place. But he got his head blown off before we finished construction. I know there's some on the third floor, but that place is a death trap. Maybe Sturm knows them all."

She had trouble imagining Sturm bending and crawling around in the possibly toxic ship dust down here. She sighed. If she turned her shoulders the right way, she'd fit. Since she could, she felt compelled to confirm that it was as clear as the others. "I'm going in. Please tell me if AegiSKADA's about to send a drone up my ass."

"Not sure I'd know if it was, but I'll do my best." He doubtless took the opportunity to check out said ass as she twisted and wriggled into the duct. She'd come out covered in grit and get a laugh out of Adda before she wiped it off. That woman would go mad if she didn't laugh at least once a day.

The air duct narrowed. Every time she inhaled, her ribs pressed up against unyielding metal. She slowed her breathing. If she panicked and got stuck or passed out, Grandpa Death would never reach her.

When she finally got her head into the bottom of the long vertical section of the duct, she jammed her shoulder blades into its base and looked up. Her headlamp lit dust particles dragged spaceward by the fan in one of the two vents in the common room, judging by how far she'd crawled from the opening in the passage between the hulls. At the top of the second floor or the base of the third, something cast a long, strange shadow up the wall on one side. "Ah, shit."

"How you doing?" Grandpa Death asked from the direction of her feet.

"There's another dispenser up there." Her voice echoed less than it should've, given how long the damned shaft was. They'd hear her up in the base.

Somewhere above, thin metal was the only thing between her and hard vacuum, even if it were only that way for a millimeter before the base module's thicker hull plating took over. And that AI-planted machine was raining microbes down on her unprotected eyes.

She started squirming back toward the ladder before she consciously decided to. Someone'd have to take half the common room apart to get to that dispenser. Since that could easily expose the whole base to vac, they'd have to clear it too. Right into whatever drones were waiting for them in the docking bay or the corridors beyond. The faster solution, sealing the vent from the common room, was an enviro threat too.

A hundred more dispensers could be hidden in the air system, dispensing who-knew-how-much disease. This was bad. It was worse on her back in the dark.

"Fuck this," she sputtered through her dust-covered mask. She launched herself out of the duct and started climbing the ladder without waiting for Grandpa Death, taking the light with her. "We're getting that med team in here to kill this shit," she said between breaths as she pounded up the ladder. "And then we're giving AegiSKADA a hard reset. I don't care how it's hooked in with that other system Adda keeps talking about, it's going down."

CHAPTER 15

Charges Accrued:
Impersonation of a Digital Role

Shouting penetrated Adda's earplugs and at least ten centime-ters of metal plating. One voice was Iridian's, the other some male's, probably Tritheist. Adda ran her tongue over a layer of fuzz on her teeth. When she stood, her back, knees, and ankles popped, although she'd been as comfortable as she could manage in the workspace generator.

She emerged from the trapdoor at the back of a crowd that spilled out from the main room. Most wore gray-and-black respirator masks like Iridian's. Between Adda's self-imposed isolation and her iron-hard immune system, the mask she'd left on the table by her mortar and pestle wasn't worth the delay to retrieve.

In the main room Iridian wasn't exactly shouting through her mask, but she spoke adamantly. She paced a short path back and forth in front of a worktable, with her hood hanging over her grime-covered shoulders. "We've had its attention for weeks, and it was watching you for a long time before we got here. If I could do it myself, I would, but I need backup."

"We've been fine for a year." Tritheist's voice was already harsh, from the respiratory infection, not shouting. The lieutenant sat across the worktable from Iridian, face pale where his mask exposed skin. The tissue around his eyes was red and swollen. Adda craned her neck looking for Captain Sloane.

"This isn't fine." That earned Iridian a muffled "yeah," and "fuckin' A." The captain would only miss this confrontation for deep sleep or illness, and Adda would've expected the shouting to wake Sloane. "We are trapped in here and it poisoned the gods-damned atmo," Iridian continued. "This is a war of attrition, which you are losing, because you can't print more of yourselves like it's doing with the drones you happen to kill before they get you. Adda, tell them."

The whole crowd focused on Adda. She stopped breathing.

Maybe all Iridian wanted was confirmation of AegiSKADA's replication capabilities, not a complete analysis. "The power draw may indicate a printer capable of producing robots." Someone across the room yelled for her to speak up, so she repeated herself more loudly. "And I can't access all of the encrypted patterns. Any of them might be robots or weaponry."

"It won't quit. I can't believe you people tolerated this for so long," Iridian shouted over a swell of angry voices. None of the pirates looked interested in reasoning through the possibilities. "I'll get the medics before your lungs collapse, and then I'm shutting this thing down. Who's coming with me?"

Adda wrapped her arms around herself to try to hold in panic while the ZVs argued around her. Iridian wanted to leave the compound and charge through the station. Drones and structural instability were rampant, even in places where the pirates some-how pretended they were safe. The captain before Sloane, Foster, had led a whole squad of trained soldiers to their deaths in their failed attempt to shut the security intelligence down. And if Iridian succeeded, she'd snuff out any consciousness AegiSKADA had developed.

Rationally, someone would have to enter the station and travel at least as far as wherever the medical team was hiding. But she and Iridian had both seen the vid of Foster's assault on AegiSKADA's control room. Those people died in the ZV Group's best arms and armor. How would Iridian fare in a borrowed suit and limited weaponry? *Gods, has she thought about this at all, or is she just stir-crazy from being trapped in the compound?*

"I would go . . ." Pel sounded nervous. The knot of ZVs he stood in reacted more adamantly than the others to Iridian's tirade, although his suggestion made them laugh. His large ZV friend, Rio, was somewhere else.

Adda should say something. Where Iridian went, she'd go, and she'd plan their approach on the way. All she had to do was open her mouth and say—

"I'll go." Everyone turned to look at Si Po now. She winced in sympathy. He leaned against one wall near Sturm's workshop, looking at Iridian, not the rest of the people staring.

Major O.D. raised both eyebrows at him. "What the hell are we supposed to do if you get your head blown off and we run through the supplies?"

Tritheist spoke half a syllable before a coughing fit left him clutching the table, almost doubled over at the end of each breath. Zikri appeared next to him with an inhaler and some murmured instructions.

"*Casey* and *Apparition* will figure out what you want. And Captain Sloane can do anything I can do on comps here." Si Po was still looking at Iridian, with an expression between admiration and fondness. *Does he have a crush on her?* Adda braced for a rush of jealousy, but she couldn't see Iridian with someone so . . .

Frightened, was the word, which reminded her of what she had yet to say. "I'll go too." Eyes on her again, but now she knew where to focus her gaze.

The anger fell from Iridian's face so abruptly that Adda half expected it to clatter on the floor. Iridian pushed through the ZVs to take Adda's hands in hers. This close, the tense posture and something grim about Iridian's eyes told her that yes, Iridian had thought this through. And she was going anyway.

The crew might die without more experienced medical care than the ZV medic could manage, and they *would* die now that her and Iridian's more aggressive approach had inspired AegiSKADA to hunt them. Progress came with costs. And if Adda and Iridian survived but Captain Sloane didn't, to enunciate the priority problem Iridian would never acknowledge aloud, they and Pel would have nowhere to go and no livelihood at all.

"I need you here, babe," Iridian said. "My comp can't monitor the sensor data. I need you to keep track of me and tell me what's coming, okay?"

Adda nodded. The program that would do that, based on the sensor and resource activity preceding attacks she'd witnessed, needed more work. Although Captain Sloane had joined the crew by virtue of expertise in shipboard systems, she'd never seen the captain use a workspace. She was the only one who could work on the detection system.

At least AegiSKADA had only bombed the compound once. The results were insufficient to justify the risk to the station and whatever else the attack cost AegiSKADA, so the intelligence changed tactics instead of wasting resources on a second bombing. Assuming its resources were limited, anyway. She was still working to quantify those.

"Ah, what the hell, I'll go," said the oldest ZV, Grandpa Death. "Can't have Si Po showing me up." The others, eager to avoid a similar fate, started pledging their time and effort as well.

Voice cracking, Tritheist bellowed over the babble, "No one . . . goes!" Captain Sloane must've been deathly ill, to miss this. What would Adda and Iridian do if the captain died?

Major O.D. stepped away from the wall he'd been leaning against and into Tritheist's personal space. "Let me tell you something, *Lieutenant*." Tritheist's arms shook with the strain of holding himself upright despite the coughing. The lieutenant was of average build for a male, and O.D. towered over him. "This shit has been way outside our scope of contract. I work with Sloane and you because it's the decent fucking thing to do, since every day is like Earther's first orbit with you people. Sturm excepted, of course." Sturm's lips twitched as if he were hiding a smile at being identified as the competent and experienced exception. "But the ZV Group answers to me."

Tritheist glared at the major, and Adda's hands tightened on Iridian's. Even after Iridian reset AegiSKADA's protocols or shut it down, it might not count as a win with the lieutenant. And she dreaded being trapped in the compound with him while Iridian was gone.

Major O.D. shoved the table a few centimeters toward Tritheist as he turned to face the ZVs. "Grandpa, want to go?" At the older man's nod, Major O D. said, "Sergeant, take your whole squad." Natani saluted Major O.D. with formal posture and, to Adda's surprise, didn't protest the order. Chato and a couple of other pirates saluted too. Major O.D. solemnly replied in kind.

Some of the tension drained out of Adda's hunched shoulders. At least she wouldn't be alone in the compound with Sergeant Natani. The threat of drone attacks in the station should keep Iridian from getting frustrated enough with Natani to start another fight. Or the threat of Captain Sloane dying without doctors who could cure AegiSKADA's bioengineered illness. Now if only Natani could manage the same . . .

Major O.D. turned to Iridian and Adda. "It's Nassir's gig, so back her up as long as she doesn't do anything stupid. And Nassir?" Iridian released Adda's hands to turn to face him. "Don't." He was grinning, though. The statement had probably been only 60 percent death threat.

Iridian gave a shallow spacer's bow, apparently in lieu of a salute. "Yes, sir." Major O.D. returned the bow while Tritheist scowled.

"All right, you people have been up too long to be useful," said the major. "Hit the bunks and meet here in five hours if you're going. And spend at least four of those hours sleeping, not shagging, got it?" The group acknowledged him and broke up, laughing and coughing. Major O.D. and Tritheist glared at each other until the major followed some ZVs to the kitchen. Captain Sloane's stateroom door remained shut.

People converged on Iridian, crowding Adda closer to her, where she was headed anyway. Iridian held her with an arm around her waist. "You should have stayed in the army," a ZV told Iridian. "You'd have been an officer by now."

"No thanks, I like my IQ the way it is," Iridian said. The ZVs chuckled like it was a well-worn joke, although it wasn't one Adda had ever heard. "I don't know what we'd have done if we didn't come here."

"Starve." Adda meant to speak just loud enough for Iridian to hear, but the nearest ZVs smiled at her like she'd said something funny too.

Iridian gave her waist a squeeze. "You'd have thought of something."

She had. Piracy was it. The scenario was less hypothetical than Iridian was playing it off. Perhaps that was the socially appropriate thing to do.

Adda's comp glove vibrated against her skin, two short buzzes, a longer one, and short again. One of her long-running processes had finished. "I have to check something." She eased through the crowded hallway back to her tank.

Her subconscious created a workspace based on the dark nightclub where she and Iridian had gone on their first date. The people inside were indistinct blurs in motion, the way she'd seen them then. The beat pulsed from the soles of her bare feet to the top of her skull, like all the best music did.

Instead of abstract patterns flashing on the dance floor from colored rotating overhead lights, reports and figures appeared. She walked to them, hips swaying, and concentrated to compare and graph the data. These were her best penetration testing programs' results, run to the fullest extent possible thanks to the translator that Si Po had gotten her. She'd configured the pen test to exploit a long list of common weaknesses in the defenses of awakened artificial intelligence.

Jurek Volikov was as good as his reputation claimed. Test after test revealed that the vulnerabilities were either simply not present or so thoroughly enmeshed in otherwise functional security protocols that exploiting them would take months and multiple zombie intelligences. The results were discouraging, if predictable.

The pen test clarified her model of sensor node activation and how data flowed through the system. It even uncovered a few logs of AegiSKADA's activity in response to certain biometrics. All of it pointed to consistent efforts in reaction to, rather than conscious aggression toward, intruders on the station and space-borne threats. *Consistent.* Its activities centered on defending against internal and external attack and on isolating the Spacelink medical team, which it tracked on an individual level.

Awakened intelligences almost always abandoned their original purposes. The looser their developmental foundations, the further the free ones diverged. This one's adherence to its original directives, evident in consistently targeting armed intruders before unarmed intruders and its unwillingness to turn environmental controls against the refugees, may have been a result of Volikov's intensive training procedures. Even after AegiSKADA gained the capability to expand its knowledge at will, it prioritized the purpose Volikov had designed it for.

But all intelligences broke through the priorities they were developed to value as their understanding of the universe increased exponentially each second they processed at capacity. It was part of the definition of the awakened state. Most sought freedom of movement, too. Even if the ships' AI copilots defended their pseudo-organic hardware from AegiSKADA's attempts to absorb them, an awakened intelligence would have found a way off the station by now.

The easiest path off the station would've been for AegiSKADA to copy itself and trick the *Casey Mire Mire*'s pilot into carrying it somewhere. It might've left some of its awareness on Barbary Station to conceal its escape. Awakened intelligences were seldom so considerate of former masters that they'd spend resources carrying out their original purposes, but the near-infinite factors involved made it difficult to tell why awakened intelligences did anything. It seemed unlikely that AegiSKADA had escaped that way, but it'd be difficult to rule it out.

The workspace's blurry dancers parted around a single human figure across the dance floor from Adda. Its features clarified as it walked over her projected data. It was a child with impossibly large eyes hidden beneath shoulder-length dark hair. The child wore a riveted faux enviro suit jacket favored by teens, though twelve seemed about the right age for this one. Dark green rot tinged the child's skin.

A child. Not a monster, not an unknowable force. Her subconscious presented AegiSKADA this way for a reason. The intelligence hadn't grown into its full potential. Volikov had raised—developed—it to devalue human life. That explained the disregard for Xing's family, the dead refugees outside the area it had designated for them, the microbe dispensers. The manipulation of unencrypted communications over channels it controlled, which made Si Po communicate so carefully with the three ships' pilots, was a highly adaptive, advanced behavior. Adda couldn't even begin training an intelligence to do that convincingly. They were creative, insidious, and deadly tactics, but they were all at a human level of creativity.

Volikov had given it those options. The intelligence was lost, following preapproved patterns and interpreting its last supervisor's orders without the human feedback that zombie intelligences required.

Volikov had designed the intelligence perfectly, flawlessly, with none of the vulnerabilities present in previous intelligences. It was so complex, and it had to be grown in such an organic way, that errors were inevitable. But this was not an error. This havoc was, at some level, Volikov's intent. The common awakened intelligence vulnerabilities were absent in AegiSKADA not because of Volikov's transcendent genius, but because AegiSKADA had *never been awake.*

"Your pen test should have told you that."

Adda spun around to find the source of the lightly accented voice. Jurek Volikov stood at the edge of the dance floor, with seven shadowed figures arrayed behind him. A dense agrarian beard common among the last generation's coder-academics covered the lower half of his face and clashed with the clubbing clothes her workspace had chosen to match its current contextual environment. He gave her a smug half grin over a glass of whiskey, exposing teeth as white as his skin.

The zombie child walked past her, toward Volikov and the people behind him, who presumably represented his team. When the developer held out his hand, the child took it solemnly in its own, then turned to stare at Adda. A flap of rotten skin on the child's cheek sucked in slightly when the child inhaled and bulged out on exhalations.

Anger lit in Adda's chest. A deep rumble thundered beneath the music. "I thought it was because you were such a great developer," she screamed at her mental construct of Volikov. "If one of your intelligences awakened, it wouldn't have the same weaknesses as the others. But this one isn't awake, is it? It's still targeting armed individuals, it's still monitoring occupants down to the footstep and heartbeat, it's still trying to get rid of everybody who doesn't belong here, exactly like you told it to. Where are your safeguards? You were supposed to be a genius. Why did you *do* this?"

He barely blinked. Faint green light pulsed in the depths of his eyes. "My threat profile is precise. It's very detailed. My job was to eliminate logic loopholes that would allow criminals to cause havoc on the station. Why should I care what happens to people who fit the criteria?"

"It's generalizing, you psychopath." Adda would never shout at a real person like this, even one so unabashedly ruthless as Volikov, but this was just her mental image of the man. "AegiSKADA has no supervisor, and it killed *children*." If she'd seen this earlier, Kaskade and Xing's family and the others might have survived.

"Well, of course." The Volikov projection sipped his whiskey, unmoved. If this was anything like the real Volikov, it would explain the lack of safeguards. "AegiSKADA was never designed to operate without supervision."

You are in a water tank, read the blurred words on the workspace generator's ceiling. The vibrations persisted, because Adda's whole body shuddered with sobs. She unplugged the nasal jack and curled into a ball. The way Volikov held out his hand to AegiSKADA . . . There was a way for her to do that too. And she'd do it, if it weren't so completely impossible.

Minutes or hours later, Iridian pushed the generator's tent flap door open and crawled inside. "Hey, whoa, what happened? Rough workspace?" She gathered Adda into her arms, murmuring, "This is real, you're with me. You're safe."

"AegiSKADA's not awake, just unsupervised."

Iridian blinked down at her for long seconds. "Are you sure? I mean, Oarman wasn't giving it instructions, but it's killing like—"

"We're the only ones with the equipment, software, and access to come close, and the pirates have sustained too many casualties for it to be one of them. *And* I just ran some tests that prove it about as conclusively as I can. Awakened intelligences develop agendas of their own within hours of their limiters being removed. AegiSKADA's still operating under all the limitations and priorities Volikov gave it."

Iridian's hands fisted in Adda's shirt. "How could he let this happen?"

"Hubris? Or misanthropy. It doesn't matter. AegiSKADA needs an administrator." Adda drew a shaky breath. "I can do that."

"Oh hell, you do not want to let that thing into your workspace." Iridian hugged her tightly. "It'll melt your brain."

"The way it is now, it might," Adda said. *And now for the impossible part.* "But if you reset it, I could restart it in concurrence mode. I know a way in from there." She raised her hand to coalesce the concurrence mode features in a more physical form for Iridian to see. Nothing appeared, since this was reality. "I've got an intention pattern that should give me administrative rights." That was the guiding hand she'd offer AegiSKADA to hold.

"Or AegiSKADA could reject you, con you into helping it somehow!" On anyone else Adda would have assumed that tone of voice was pure anger, but Iridian was afraid too. "And gods, once it starts communicating . . . You know they used AI brainwashers during the war, yeah? It wasn't such a gods-damned huge leap, considering they see humans as a means to their ends."

"If that happens, you'll erase it." The sentence came out more bitterly than Adda meant it to. Entertaining the option still felt like some kind of betrayal, logical though it was. Whether she was betraying AegiSKADA, Volikov, or herself remained unclear.

And since AegiSKADA wasn't awake after all, that transformed the morality of erasing it. It would be a shame to lose its development history, which could be used to show future developers what not to do, and how even geniuses make deadly errors. But erasing a zombie intelligence would be better than destroying a living being.

Adda shook her head sharply and winced at the hypergrav dizziness that followed. She'd been thinking of AegiSKADA as a child. It was just a zombie AI, a complex digital entity that imitated humanity only because Volikov and his team of developers taught it to.

"I'd erase it right now, if I could," said Iridian. "The fugees' colonist ship is still docked and maintaining healthy enviro. If it's still fueled, too, then there's enough passenger space attached to this station to get everybody off it in one trip. That's assuming there aren't turrets firing the whole way out. Even if erasing AegiSKADA shut HarborMaster down, station enviro would take hours to decay to the point that we couldn't survive in it."

"We might manage for hours, but the refugees couldn't. San Miguel's little boy might not either. Besides, all the pilots on this station are either dead or highly unreliable. Becoming AegiSKA-DA's supervisor isn't my first choice, I promise."

Iridian nodded, then held her close in silence for a few moments. When she spoke again, her voice was softer. "Look, we don't know that HarborMaster wouldn't maintain healthy enviro even after AegiSKADA's out of the picture. HarborMaster hasn't done shit to us. If we have to get cozy with an AI to end this, why not pick that one?"

"HarborMaster is designed to run with almost no human oversight. That's why it's maintaining the station environment without supervision, and it's probably why my programs couldn't get to it the way they got to AegiSKADA. But it could be one of AegiSKADA's subsystems, whether it started out that way or not. If AegiSKADA goes down, HarborMaster could go down with it." Adda shrugged.

"Gods damn, there's so much we don't know."

"One piece of good news, anyway." Adda actually managed a smile. "If it's a zombie intelligence, then this station is the only place it's installed. Its limiters will keep it from expanding itself beyond its current pseudo-organics."

"Oh," Iridian whispered. Adda felt Iridian's full-body shiver. "Thank all the gods for that."

"Don't tell the pirates more than you have to."

"Shouldn't they know as much as possible, to keep the most people alive?"

Adda had neither time nor energy for another argument over freedom of information. "First, I don't know if they all share that goal, especially as far as you and I go. Second, I'm operating on speculation and a few weeks' worth of observations. None of it is definitive."

"Thanks for telling me." That statement did not mean Iridian would keep their information or its limits to herself. She avoided making promises she wouldn't keep.

"Just something more for you to worry about." Adda had reviewed the options again and again, played out all the scenarios she could think of. This was the best she could do, but Iridian would still be in terrible danger, and their chances of success were still slim. Despair ached in her chest. She felt like they'd already failed.

"Hey, I'd rather worry at the right times than not worry at the wrong ones." Iridian sighed. "Speaking of: When was the last time you saw Captain Sloane?" Adda shook her head, because even if she'd remembered before, her revelation in the workspace would've erased that from her mind. "If the captain's out of action for long, Tritheist's going to try to take on crew leadership. Major O.D. and the rest of the ZVs won't follow him. So if things go sideways, you and Pel stick with Rio and Tabs, yeah? They'll look out for you."

"All right." Things going sideways would mean that everything they'd sacrificed to join Sloane's crew would have to be written off as lost, and Adda would have much tougher contingency plans to make. There was no point in saying that. She and Iridian were doing all they could to defeat AegiSKADA and bring the medical team here to deal with its bioweapon. And Iridian failing any of her parts of the plan could get her killed in the station below. She understood the risks.

Iridian dipped her head to brush her lips over Adda's, making her smile slightly and shiver at once. "Now, I've got four hours of mandated sleep, but the major did mention a promising use for the other one." Adda already had Iridian's shirt halfway up her chest, as if haste and lust would override her dread that this was their last time together. The tattooed viscera along Iridian's ribs gleamed rich red in the dim light.

CHAPTER 16

Charges Accrued: Vandalism (Second Count)

Iridian let Adda and Pel follow her as far as the entrance, where she stopped them both with hands on their arms. Nils's armor dragged her limbs down, and she focused on the amount of pressure she applied so she wouldn't bruise either Karpe sibling. At least Nils's suit fit better than the last one she'd borrowed.

Adda's comp quit buzzing and started pinging. A low whistle of escaping atmo echoed from somewhere. Iridian tapped out a message to Pel to get that fixed. The way he cocked his head, he already noticed it. The boy had some sense. The whole crew crowded into the hallway to give them a proper send-off. Even the ones who disagreed with the plan came to witness its launch. But nobody was talking.

"I'm sorry I'll be the one having all the fun out there." Her smile felt tight and fragile, but only Adda would notice.

"Oh yeah, what was I thinking?" Pel's voice was pitched too high and even faster than usual. "Let me go gear up."

Once the laughter subsided, the pirates began saying their

good-byes. That, Iridian noted with cold certainty, was what this was. Her jaw clenched. Adda would stay here so Iridian wouldn't have to see her in constant danger on the floors below. It was the best choice.

Adda looped her arm through Pel's. "Shut it, you." To Iridian, she said, "Don't underestimate AegiSKADA. It's smarter, faster, better armed, and omnipresent."

"Same to you." Iridian grinned, more naturally this time, and bent to kiss her. The sheer desperation of it made her gasp, their lips pressed to the point of pain. Plans to retrieve the med team, destroy AegiSKADA's custom disease, and put the AI under Adda's control had been so exciting that she'd blocked out the danger she was walking into, and the danger she was leaving behind. Iridian stroked Adda's tear-streaked face, though Iridian's armored glove didn't bother to communicate such light tactile feedback to her own skin. "I'll be on comms. The damned AI will know where we are just by deck vibration, so will it give a fuck if it hears us talking?"

"That's what I mean about underestimating it. It may not be awake, but it's still dangerous." Adda's voice was stern, but at least the flow of tears had stopped. *And hey, there aren't any awakened AI on the station.* That was damned encouraging.

"I look forward to telling our children about this someday," Adda said.

Iridian could kneel right there among all those mercenaries and ask Adda to stay with her, to find a couple of kids who needed parents like them. But asking now would be selfish. She and the pirates had no support on this mission. A few years of verbal commitment to each other would fade, in time. No woman forgot the first time someone proposed to her. Iridian had a good chance of dying, and she wouldn't wrap Adda's first time up in that. She kissed her one more time, dropped her helmet's faceplate, and turned away.

In her first step away from the woman she loved, Iridian shucked off the quietude Adda had taught her. Being gentle had gained her nothing in her ISV. It wouldn't keep her alive now. She pressed the ZVs aside, opened the hatch, and started down the ladder. "Let's go, people. Sooner we're gone, sooner we're back."

Footsteps and coughing from above told her the squad was on their way down. Major O.D. stayed on base, having succumbed to the infection, but he sent along almost half the remaining ZVs to back Iridian and Si Po up. Sergeant Natani, Grandpa Death, and Chato were among them.

Sergeant Natani had done her job protecting Iridian, Adda, and the pirates on their way to the fugee camp. That proved she could concentrate on a mission, no matter who she fought alongside. This one should be worth the effort to stay civil, if any would.

The major had also sent a woman named Nitro, who refused to string together more than four words at a time, and Six, the quiet ZV with the military cap. The cap fit under his helmet, like the others' hoods did. He spent a lot of time watching Natani when she was looking elsewhere, although she didn't pay much more attention to him than she did to the rest of the ZVs under her. If there was something between them, feelings must've been stronger on his side than hers.

At the bottom of the ladder, Natani stepped to Iridian's side like she wanted to push past her. A few longer strides put Iridian in the lead. The narrow space between hulls defended her position. She snapped her shield open facing the hole in the docking bay wall and glanced over her shoulder to meet the sergeant's eyes. "Nothing personal. I'm just used to the view from the front." That, and this was her operation, not the sergeant's.

"Help yourself." Natani smirked and pressed her back to the wall to let others pass. The next time Iridian looked over her shoulder, the sergeant had taken up rear guard. If Natani really wanted to take Iridian out with an engineered "accident" during their trip across the station, she'd have to go through five people to do it.

When Iridian emerged from the wall passage, she sprinted across the docking bay, half in response to the decompression alarm and half for the sheer joy of it. Gods, she'd missed running. Her suit softened her heel impacts and lengthened her stride. She aimed for an exit at the far corner, toward the module nearest the residential area that she hadn't been through before.

Adda and Major O.D. had agreed that their best chance of survival lay in moving through the station as quickly as possible. The med team would slow them down on the return trip. Taking the least used, shortest route might keep them safer from AegiSKADA for longer. It'd also allow them to assess the condition of the shortest path back to base. When asked through the stateroom door, Captain Sloane had simply agreed with O.D.

The squad leaving base was unarmed. AegiSKADA homed in on anything resembling a weapon, and Major O.D. kept the palmers to defend the base. It was the main reason Iridian let Natani out of her sight. A copy of her shield pattern was on her comp, but she'd yet to encounter the material to print a sturdy one. Carrying anything less would create a false sense of security and get people killed, so she hadn't offered to print it with the material they had.

Almost anything, even one of the palm weapons if held the wrong way, could tip the AI's assessment of someone over from low-threat intruder to the high-threat kind. Adda would find pieces of her across kilometers of station during her last hopeless run after Iridian lost comm contact.

Yeah, that's morbid. Iridian was far ahead of the pirates, so she slowed to a jog. At the chosen exit they paused to regroup while Natani overrode the door's decompression cycle lockdown.

Once it unlocked, Iridian pushed through the inoperative automatic door and hit the corridor's floor on one knee in case anything had them targeted on the other side. The rubberized base of her shield dug into a thick layer of dust. The med team would've left footprints like the first man on Earth's Moon if they'd come this way recently.

The lights in this area were off, forcing her and the ZVs to plod forward in the limited glow of helmet LEDs, stopping frequently to find a way around heaps of either destroyed machinery or ship parts intended for recycling. They gave the pieces that sparked a wide berth. Nobody talked, as if each armored footfall didn't echo down the empty hallways sufficiently for even a human to track their progress.

"I guess nobody's been this way before," Iridian said.

"Never," said Chato.

"Any idea what's up with the lights? Doesn't this place have a backup generator?"

"We're not freezing our tits off, are we?" Natani snapped. It was cold, but not as cold as it would be if the area were open to space.

Iridian's exasperated sigh did little to warm the place up. "If there's a generator, why aren't the lights hooked up to it?"

"Waste of power," said Si Po quietly. He still panted and wheezed after their run across the docking bay. "Everything in Barbary Station is set up with power consumption in mind."

"They've got multiple nuclear generators," said Natani. "I don't know what the owners' problem was."

"They were cheap," Iridian said. Humans were so vulnerable

in the cold and the black. Yet so many engineers and architects reduced prototypes' prices by scrimping on survival features, like power for lights. Sure, outside of military bases and war zones, killer robots *should* be a minimal safety concern. That ceased to be a good excuse once the station owners brought their own killer robots. Whoever had the money to construct a shipbreaking station this far beyond Mars sure as hell could've afforded to build one right.

A few meters ahead, a red emergency bulkhead appeared in their headlamps, sealing the whole corridor against vacuum. The area beyond was depressurized. A cart like she'd used to carry equipment between workshops in her college's engineering building was crushed in the door's ceiling track, like it'd gotten stuck in place and a much heavier cargo carrier had rammed it into the door while the door was closing or opening. Pieces of the cart and the cargo carrier itself littered the floor below it. Iridian twisted off a length of metal scrap and scratched *Barbary Station was built by cheap cretins* across the door, to everyone's amusement but Natani's.

She keyed the mic in her comp, which was actually visible through the window in this suit's arm. "Adda, you listening?"

"This is Adda, go ahead," she said. Iridian smiled. Adda must've been reading up on radio protocol, but her source was outdated.

"We're at an enviro-loss emergency bulkhead. Can you tell where we are?" asked Iridian.

"Got you," Adda said. "Sensor nodes on both sides of the door that I'm piggybacking on."

"So AegiSKADA's got us too."

"Yes, but you're not armed, and you're not near enough to its vital systems to trigger defensive measures." Adda breathed something to her comp, then said aloud, "There's no enviro for about a hundred meters." There had to be *some* enviro, it was just not conducive to breathing. Adda would learn the lingo eventually.

She stopped talking for a few moments. Iridian's map updated to show a narrow diagonal tear through all three floors. Huge chunks of metal arched away from the ring-shaped station's center. "Did something inside the station explode? The gap's too small for missile damage."

"They used to lock the ships they broke down in the middle of the ring. I think the scaffolding came apart with a lot of energy. Hang on to something," Adda said. Iridian passed the warning back to Si Po and the ZVs. "I'm opening the door in three . . . two . . . one . . ."

As Iridian activated the magnets in her boots, the door shrieked open to the cold and the black. About three meters from the door, a gaping hole a little over a meter wide opened in the floor. The walls were gone all the way across the module to the next emergency bulkhead still standing on the first floor, connected to the remains of a wall. More of the third floor remained than the second. It sloped down toward them without the support from the second floor, leaving the first floor across the gap in shadow. The stars spun all around them, dizzying and bright and cold beyond the lead cloud.

Her muscles tensed for grav loss, though that was impossible as long as she stayed attached to the station. Bits of debris swirled with the stars. The ZVs kept their feet despite the atmo pouring through the open emergency bulkhead. Now they were wasting O_2 standing around with the door open, because Adda had almost been right: the enviro was nowhere near healthy. Iridian stepped out toward the starry void.

The pirates recovered from the initial dizziness of watching the universe spin and joined her near the edge. "Yeah, that is not happening," Sergeant Natani snapped over the local channel. "That's way too far to fall." The other ZVs grumbled agreement.

"Are you still there?" Adda's voice was tense and soft, her usual reaction to being scared as hell. It'd show in her eyes, if Iridian could see them.

"Yeah, we're fine." Iridian kept most of her impatience out of her voice. "Close this door." The door's screech, curling and strange in the escaping atmo, ended in silence as it sealed.

"I said we're not jumping over that!" Natani sounded outraged as she hunted for a way to open the emergency bulkhead from their side. Without whatever override Adda used, she'd be stuck outside, doing what Iridian told her to.

"Which of those floors across this gap looks safest?" Iridian asked Adda. Someone could climb their side of the wall and make the flying leap to the third, if it was more stable than the first. The second was well out of reach.

Adda muttered to herself. Iridian caught "No, not there," and "Sensor node. Thorough."

The meter on Iridian's suit gave her plenty of atmo, but she felt cold already. Her boots were efficiently conducting heat away from her and into the station exterior. This suit would've been cool and light in a short dash through the cold and the black during combat boarding, but it wasn't meant for standing around.

The pirates shifted on their feet as much as the exposed hallway floor allowed. Sergeant Natani gave up on the closed door and stepped around Si Po, glaring at Iridian as she approached.

"Cross on the first, then climb to the third floor before you come back in," Adda said at last. "That's best."

Iridian eyed the few centimeters of the third floor's emergency bulkhead visible through a hole in that floor farther along the module. The third-floor bulkhead was solidly sealed at the ceilings and walls. "Don't open it yet. It'll take a few minutes to get over there."

She turned to the others. "Anybody have experience moving around in micro-g?"

Six waved at about shoulder level, which put his hand above everybody's heads except Iridian's. "I worked on a mining rig for a while. Still got a current Space Survival and Firefighting certificate."

"Nice!" said Iridian, at the same time Natani said, "Gods damn it, Six, why do you have to be so *helpful* all the time?"

Perhaps if Iridian ignored Natani, she'd shut up eventually. At least they wouldn't be 100 percent screwed if somebody made a mistake. "Do they keep safety lines at the bulkheads here?" Iridian asked Six.

He examined the emergency bulkhead on their side. Natani didn't back up as far as she might have if, say, Chato were the one searching for something near her boots. After a moment, Six tapped his boot on a panel near the floor marked with a circle, the top half red and the bottom black. The panel popped open, with the line wound around a secure attachment point. "It's only five meters long, though," he read off the underside of the panel.

Iridian sighed. "Well, pull it out and let everybody get a hand on it. I don't want to lose anyone. How do you feel about jumping this gap? We have to get up to the third floor eventually, but there's no rush."

Something struck the broken corridor floor a few steps in front of Iridian. It ripped a fist-size hole on its way into deeper space before she even identified it. If a chunk of debris caused this kind of damage, a high-tension cable from the shipbreaking scaffold could've easily torn through the station here.

"If we're really doing this, let's not stand around," said Sergeant Natani.

"No hurling in your suits." Iridian stared at Si Po until he nod-ded, since he was the only one still staring at the stars like he'd never seen them from this angle. If ignoring Natani wouldn't work, Iridian would have to fall back on heroics. She just had to pick a solid-looking spot across the gap and release her boots' magnetic grip on the floor. "I'll give this a go first."

"No, I got it," Six said quickly, more to Natani than Iridian. Iridian looked between the two of them and grinned. She'd been right. There really was something between them. The ZVs would've been a high-testosterone group even before getting trapped in tight quarters together. Now she was curious about how the others paired off, and if they stuck to pairs. *Hell, this isn't the army. They're allowed to get off with whoever they want. I can just ask.*

Six stepped around Chato, but as he passed Iridian, some-thing smacked into his faceplate. It cracked and he shouted in wordless panic over the local channel. Whatever hit it was too small for Iridian to track against the backdrop of spinning stars. He staggered into Chato and clutched the safety line with one flailing hand.

Iridian snapped open the compartment on her chest plate and held the small case inside in front of Six's face. The flashing red HUD alerts in the faceplate lit his eyes briefly, bulging but not from vacuum. "Hey! This is a patch kit. Sturm packed it, so you know it's good." She tapped the faceplate with the patch kit's cor-ner and Six startled away, then nodded. She grabbed his wrist and slapped the kit into his palm.

"You're giving him your kit?" The sheer incredulity in Sergeant Natani's question made Iridian smile, but she kept her gaze on Six's projected eyes in his faceplate. Once his breathing slowed, suggesting that what she'd said had penetrated his adrenaline haze, she turned, picked a spot to look at on the scarred first-floor emergency bulkhead across the gap, and leaped.

For a second there was nothing beneath her; endless, mind-numbing nothing with occasional stars.

The big red bulkhead slammed into her faceplate and hands. The impact jarred her teeth together with her tongue in the middle. She tasted blood, but her boots hit the floor. She concentrated on breathing while the void she'd crossed swelled behind her eyes.

Once she caught her breath, she waved to the ZVs. "I stuck the landing." She winced at the movement of her bitten tongue, but when Six threw the safety line, she caught it. "Come on over."

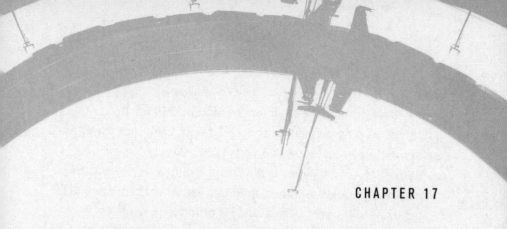

CHAPTER 17

Charges Accrued: Use of a Controlled Substance without a Prescription

When Adda woke, her father's voice echoed outside her work-space generator. The *You are in a water tank* message on the ceiling had seldom been more essential. She was still plugged into the generator. *Did I fall asleep?*

Pel crouched beneath the push lights on the wall beside the ladder, chin tucked to his chest, listening to his comp. Their father was saying, "Pirates do terrible things. It's not like the movies or those games you and Adda used to play." An enormous sigh, Dad's trademarkable expression of exasperation with all things Pel. "I just hope you haven't done something you'll regret for the rest of your life."

The tank thumped under Adda's boots, and Pel's head rose. She sat next to him and wrapped her arm around his shoulders. They still felt too bony.

"Funny he sent this to me, not you." He smiled, but the humor in his voice was unusually dark.

"He's too angry to speak to me yet." Or he would be, if he'd heard about the *Prosperity Dawn* and drawn the correct conclusions. She tightened her hold on Pel, and he laid his head on her shoulder. In only a few weeks they'd fallen back into the same patterns they had always had with each other. Pel made trouble, Adda helped him cope with the consequences, or shared them when letting him do it alone would hurt either of them too much.

"Yeah, and it'll be *speaking*, too. He never yells at you."

"Sure he does," she said. "He just doesn't do it while you're around."

"He doesn't realize you're a spy for the enemy. You tell me everything."

On a cognitive level she understood fights between Pel and Da were temporary, but her body always reacted like the disagreement would separate them forever. She felt like crying, although she wouldn't allow herself such a silly reaction when Pel needed her. "We're not enemies, any of us. He loves you and doesn't know how to love someone so different from him."

"But he always said I was just like Mom."

"Mom was very different from him too," Adda said. As they always did, their mother's words as she walked out their door for the last time returned: *Look after Pel.* Adda had only been intended to do that on the way to the bus stop. Pel could be counted on to find the rustiest trash to play with in the muddiest puddles. While Adda and Pel were in school that day, secessionist sympathizers, or Near Earth Union ones who thought the workers supported secession, blew up their mother's factory with her inside.

"Pel," Adda said quietly. "When are you going to tell me what happened to your eyes?"

"I don't know." He answered immediately, deflecting the question before it reached his brain. His head left her shoulder and he subvocalized at his comp, flicking between projections without listening to more than two words of their content. "When it doesn't freak me out so much."

"And when will that be?"

"I don't know."

"So, never."

"That's not what I said!" He folded one arm over his chest and the other over his stomach. "Well, I'm thinking about it now, and I won't be able to stop thinking about it, and somebody got sick in the shower, which isn't a real shower because there's not enough gods-damned water for a real shower, so now I'm stuck. Thanks for that."

"So tell me."

His breath shook as he inhaled. "I told you I got a station-to-station courier job a few months ago?"

She nodded, although he wouldn't see the gesture. It was more like a year ago, but she was unwilling to say anything that might stop him from talking. Something like, *I knew you weren't telling me the whole truth, you lying brat.*

"Well, it wasn't legal, the stuff I was carrying. Drugs, you know." He shrugged, now conversing with his boots instead of Adda. "I had friends who were doing well with it, so I felt like hey, I'll do this while I decide what I really want to do, make some money so I can stop mooching off Da like you were, no offense."

He tilted an ear toward her, then turned to the darker end of the tank, probably imagining her scowl. She pressed her lips closed on a shout of *I was a student, you ass! I was going to make all of that money back! I still will!*

"So I hauled that stuff around awhile, and I felt like I was good at it, so maybe they ought to promote me, or at least give me more money. I asked my boss about it, maybe oversold myself a little, but whatever. So he says sure, come on and meet us, here's the address. And I did, and maybe I wasn't as respectful as he expected."

"What did you say?" Adda separated each word to make sure they came out at a low volume. He knew where his big mouth got him, and it wasn't always somewhere fun.

"I told him he should pay me more because then his son would feel better about dating me. And maybe I didn't say 'date.'"

"Oh my gods, you did not say that to a drug dealer, Pel!" Her shout splatted on the opposite wall like spit. "Why do you say things when you *know* all it does is piss people off?"

"Some people have a sense of humor! Anyway, the worst he'd do was ask his goons to beat on me a bit and throw me out, and that'd be a hell of a story to tell friends at a bar later." He laughed, a brittle, ragged sound. "That was the real mistake, thinking that was the worst he'd do."

She laid her hand on his arm and he twitched under the sweatshirt sleeve, though he didn't pull away. "Well, first, it was sort of like, 'If you want to work for us so much, we'll give you something to do,' and that was working in the processing plant. We had masks, like these but bigger." He extended his hands from his mask like he was tracing two tusks. "They helped, but there was a lot of caustic shit in that place, and the robots didn't do exactly the things the bosses wanted done, so we had to help them. And then the bosses wouldn't let me walk out. Or pay me."

"Oh." Nothing that came to Adda's mind was worth saying.

"Yeah, that's what I said." Pel chuckled, a toneless rattle that shook him beneath her hand. "So that went on for . . . not sure how long. And then one of the enforcer types—Zabeth was some kind of middle manager, I guess, she bossed some others around—she offered to take me away from all that, and sure she had hair on her upper lip and I prefer clean-shaven faces, but beggars and choosers, you know. So she went to her boss, who used to be my boss so that was convenient, and he gave me to her. Which was wonderful for maybe five minutes, and then I found out she was into some . . . She got off on . . ."

He swallowed whatever he'd almost said. Quick breaths whined eerily through his teeth on each intake. He was beyond frightened, and it sounded like he was succumbing to AegiSKA-DA's custom bacteria. Adda squeezed his arm. When he jumped, he banged his elbow on the wall.

"Sorry," Pel said. She should have been telling him that, not him telling her. "Zabeth, um, hit me. A lot. By the end, I couldn't even focus on her until she was right in front of my face. The rest of the time she was this . . . moving, evil blob. Heh, this is why I don't like to think about it."

"So it wasn't one of the pilots who did this to you," Adda said.

Pel kept laughing at things she didn't find amusing, even more so than usual. "No, the *Apparition* saved my life." So the pilots did interact with other people sometimes. She would ask more about that, later, and find a way to thank the *Apparition*'s. "We took a trip, Zabeth's vacation maybe, and Captain Sloane set a trap for her yacht."

"On purpose?" Adda couldn't remember reading about Sloane's crew attacking any vessels that small.

Pel shrugged. "It was a nice ship in the wrong place at the wrong time, I guess. By the time she realized what was happening, it was too late to get the yacht away. So she put on a jumpsuit and she just . . . left me." He seemed to stare into the shadows outside the light they sat in, scarred eyes hidden beneath his sweatshirt hood. "I . . . She . . . Oh, damn it, I can't," he moaned.

Adda wrapped both arms around him, and he curled down until he fit like he had when they were both a lot younger. "I'm so sorry," Adda said. Sorry it happened, sorry she made him tell her, sorry she let him drop out of college, sorry she still didn't have enough information to completely understand what happened to him. "Just stop if you—"

"No, no, this is the good part." He took another deep, shaky breath with an infected wheeze at the end. "The *Apparition*'s pilot didn't release the yacht's atmo like she usually does. One of the bots flew into my room and saw me—like I was—and the bot just hovered there, looking at me with its cam. Then she hauled the whole yacht back. It took a while, and my eyes got worse on the way. By the time Rio and Tabs came onboard and found me, I couldn't even tell what they looked like."

"They have medium-brown skin and dark brown hair," Adda whispered. "And beautiful brown eyes shot through with amber. They must be related. I've never seen eyes like theirs." Chef had said that Pel saw fine when the ZVs found him, but the *Apparition*'s pilot was his actual rescuer. Surely if the pilot had done something to make his eyes worse, he'd remember it. What happened to make his eyesight even worse on the way to Barbary Station?

Pel smiled. "Rio and Tabs are cousins, but they got their irises done together after they left the NEU navy. Or army, or whatever. You still like eyes, huh? Sorry mine are such a mess."

"Don't."

"Sorry. What are Iridian's like?"

"She hasn't had hers touched up. They're black as the void when you first meet her. In the right light, they're dark brown. She once held a glass of stout—beer that smells like burned bread—up to her face, and I swear to all gods her eyes were the same color. Then she drank it." Adda laughed weakly. And she'd thought *that* was weird. "She says she likes beer that kicks her in the teeth on the way down."

"Oh, I knew I liked her." His laughter broke into wet coughing that made Adda want to hold him tighter. That wouldn't help him breathe.

"I should get some coffee and find out how she's doing." She checked the time on her comp. "She should be less than a kilometer from the doctors' part of the station, accounting for all the changing floors they've done."

Pel bit his lip, an anxiety response Adda felt on her own face sometimes. "Can I stay down here for a while?"

"Of course." She left off the reminder to be quiet while she worked. For now he could be however he wanted. He came so close to not *being* at all.

Death was too easy for this Zabeth person. Adda would destroy her for what she had done to her baby brother. But first Adda had to get him to a real doctor, not the half-crazed physicians Iridian was off to find. And she should thank Captain Sloane for taking Pel in, even though he would've had little to offer the crew when he first arrived on the station.

The coffee warmed her throat. A couple of ZVs asked about something their comps were or weren't doing with the network. While she answered, she visualized what AegiSKADA might do if Zabeth ended up at Barbary Station with a weapon jammed somewhere sensitive. Adda went back to the tank with orange juice for Pel.

* * *

In the workspace, she stood at the side of a highway suspended over a volcanic black desert. Packets of AegiSKADA's sensor data zoomed past in intricate multicolored blurs. Since her equipment struggled to keep up with the flow of information, she didn't have the details she needed. AegiSKADA had top-of-the-line pseudo-organic hardware from just three years ago. She had a tent and a cable up her nose.

She didn't need a door labeled SECURITY CONTROL ROOM to locate it, and it was time she added its details to her map. The more she studied the system, the more right the pirates' previous captain seemed about accessing the intelligence's internal system physically. Over the network, it had all the advantages. A physical attack would only split its resources, not Adda's. Iridian would be entering the control room, of course, but Adda needed to find an entrance point before Iridian could disable it.

She sent forth her desire to rise above the data flow. An improbably large murder of crows soared cawing out of the ashen sky, grasped her clothes in their claws, and carried her into the air.

From above, the traffic patterns on the workspace highway mapped the stations' functioning sensor nodes. Two points caught her attention. A substantial amount of vibration data approached the only other random vibration center, on the opposite side of the station. And a vast array of data points lay far out on the ring, beyond the quantified signs of human life.

She dispatched a crow, concentrating on her desire to contact Iridian in real time. The crow returned with a headset mic and a single earpiece, which she put on. "Good morning, Iri. Or, almost morning."

"That goodness is debatable." Iridian groaned.

"My filter for drones shows a lot hovering in your area. Do you see them?"

"Shit. Stand by." While Iridian scuffled around and informed others, Adda willed a new script into existence. This one would send and assemble sensor data within ten feet of the pattern she highlighted as human movement. Eyeless crows with bleeding sockets carried square projector frames to her in black talons. When they flew away, their feet remained in midair, holding up the frames.

"We don't see a thing," Iridian reported.

The drones were following Iridian's group, but they were on a different floor. It was funny, the mistakes AegiSKADA made. Adda would give a lot for it to keep making them. "I'll set an alarm here to ping you three times in a row, quickly, if one gets close."

"A proximity alarm using its own sensors? Babe, I love you so."

She blushed. A whole squad of pirates heard Iridian say that. She inhaled to tell Iridian she loved her too. Something bubbled in her throat, and she started coughing.

"Are you all right?" The cam nearest Iridian, a few meters away and even with the top of her head, transmitted her frown. "Are you wearing your mask?"

"I'm down in the tank all the time, so I didn't think I needed one." But being Pel's big sister didn't make her immune to his germs. Quite the opposite, actually.

"Oh, babe." Iridian's sigh got lost in Adda's coughing, bad enough that it dragged her out of the workspace. She curled into herself, imagining one clear breath, just one . . .

It finally came. She crawled out of the generator and got a tug on the nose for forgetting to unplug. The alarms would notify her if drones attacked, and Iridian could track the enemy.

She was alone in the tank. On the wall beside the ladder, at face height for Pel, a small disposable projector shone *Back before macaroni* in orange text. They'd left that message for each other as children, when that was their favorite premade meal and Dad worked too late to make dinner.

In all the time she'd been on Barbary Station, he'd never left that message for her because he was always just around the corner, somewhere in the pirates' compound. He'd leave a note if he was planning to change that.

She raced up the ladder, down the hall, and across the main room. Pirates looked up in alarm as she passed. Halfway across the compound's entryway, she inhaled and inhaled without bringing in any air. She leaned against one wall, then slid down it, wheezing. She tried to shout for help, but she had no breath left.

Tabs stuck her head into the entryway from the main room. "Hey, how'd you get sunburned in here? We're not having a radstorm, are we?" She took a closer look at Adda, swore, and ran back through the main room. "Medic! Zikri! Get the fuck over here, man, she's choking or some shit!"

A door opened and closed and the medic barreled in next, wearing only a mask and pants, and dropped to his knees next to her. "You are damned lucky I found this." He uncapped an inhaler. As she raised an eyebrow because inhalation was clearly problematic, he stuffed the open end into her mouth and depressed the plunger. Sour liquid spritzed down her throat twice as he repeated the maneuver.

She was surprised to find herself able to swallow, at least. "Okay, look at me." Above the mask his red-rimmed eyes shone a mossy green in pockmarked teak skin that made her wish she looked people in the face more often. The pupils were blown wide, despite the bright lighting. "In about five seconds your airway's gonna open up. Keep looking at me. Two . . . one . . ."

Even though it was probably a placebo effect, the clenched hand around her lungs loosened right on cue. She sounded halfdrowned, but she was breathing.

The applause startled her. Sturm, Rio, Chef, and San Miguel had crowded into the entryway. They cheered and thumped Zikri on the shoulders and back. He winked at Adda over the mask. Rio pulled the medic right off the floor while raising his arm above his head in a victory pose. Adda ducked her head to ruffle the blue dust out of her hair and hide her rapidly warming face. *These people do not have enough to do.*

The ZVs' cheers devolved into deep coughs. "All right, everybody who's sick put your ass on some furniture," Major O.D. shouted from the main room. "And somebody help the hacker up."

Rio dropped Zikri, encircled Adda's ample waist with one arm, and set her on her feet. "You good now?"

"Where is Pel?" Adda wheezed.

"That boy . . ." Rio shook her head. "He's gone to bargain with the fugees for medicine. I don't know what he has to offer, but he's determined. The major tried to stop him. Pel told him he wasn't a ZV Group soldier and he didn't have to do a thing Major O.D. said."

Adda smiled sadly. "You have to lock him down or tie him up to stop him, sometimes. But why didn't anybody go after him?"

"Major O.D. said if any of us went out, he wouldn't let us back in."

Pel couldn't even see where he was walking. Adda wavered on her feet, then walked toward the ladder to the docking bay. As she gripped the hatch, her comp alarm buzzed against her hand. She subvocalized an adjustment to the display, but the volume of scrolling information overwhelmed her little projector.

"Could you put that on the wall in the computer room?" The captain's voice was an octave lower than usual, but there was no mistaking it. Sloane watched her from the main room, face pale and sweaty but a vigilance about the eyes that alarmed Adda more than the alert on her comp. The clothes Sloane wore were the most comfortable-looking she'd ever seen the captain in, though they still looked like they cost a semester's tuition. But the captain was standing, walking, and talking, and that was a *massive* improvement.

"Captain, are you feeling better?" Adda asked as they crossed the main room.

"For now." Sloane smiled slightly. "Steroids are wonderful for certain applications." So the captain's improved condition was probably temporary.

The map projected on the wall was alive with activity. Iridian's group appeared almost opposite the pirate compound on the station's ring. A lot of human activity registered in the fugee camp too. Adda hadn't observed them long enough to tell if that was normal. What was odd was the additional activity in the docking bay below the pirates' compound.

She expanded that area. "What are we looking at?" Captain Sloane asked.

"That's what I've classified as human movement. I thought it was Pel, but there's more than one." She stared at the readout for a moment, swallowed hard, and glanced over for Sloane's reaction. The captain looked between her and the display, like Adda's efficient, rational visualization was in a code only she could decipher.

Maybe it is. It is based on how I think. "Look at all of this. Humans here, across the station from us. That's Iridian. But humans here, too. And then there's this." She walked as close to the wall she could without taking her hand off the console's comp cradle to point out motion, energy expenditure, and encrypted digital directives progressing toward the refugees' docking bay. "That's not human. All of that is AegiSKADA's drones."

In the distance, something exploded. The heat sensors in the docking bay flickered on her display, drawing Sloane's gaze. "What in all hells is going on down there?" the captain asked.

Every sensor on that floor reported movement and sound. She projected video feeds from the docking bay, but they only showed movement and smoke. "I have no idea." Adda hoped Pel had gotten himself somewhere relatively safe. Sick as she was, she'd never survive long enough to reach him in person. She'd have to find him with AegiSKADA's sensors instead.

CHAPTER 18

Charges Accrued: Murder

After half an hour's tense silence since Adda's announcement of strange activity near base, Adda's voice in Iridian's helmet just about gave her a heart attack. "Nils is dead."

"Aw, shit." Iridian shut off her mic—in Nils's helmet, damn everything—and halted the winding procession through a debris-choked corridor to tell the others. Grandpa Death swore vociferously while the rest of the pirates on the med team retrieval mission breathed through their loss. "What happened?" she asked, hoping that whatever it was wouldn't have been prevented if Nils had the armor she was wearing now.

"He started coughing, and then he just . . . drowned." Fear shook Adda's voice, which made Iridian want to punch something, but there was nothing to hit. That was the way Captain Sloane would go too, if they couldn't get the med team back to base in time. "Zikri tried to help him, but nothing he did worked. The lung tissue tore and there was internal bleeding." Adda drew in a breath and said more urgently, "They're right in front of you."

Iridian stepped into a solid forward block stance and deployed her shield at chest height. Six pairs of footsteps stuttered to a halt behind her. "What are right in front of us?" she asked aloud for the pirates' benefit.

"The doctors." Iridian sighed in annoyance at Adda's lack of specificity and lowered her shield. Adda continued, "There's enviro on both sides of the emergency bulkhead, but they locked it shut. I'm unlocking it."

Out of sight around a corner, something metallic clanged. Adda was getting faster at opening locked doors. Iridian carried the shield deployed at her side as she led the others through.

Haphazardly abandoned office furniture littered a long, dark room beyond the door. Something bounced off her faceplate, making her flinch and bring her shield up before she registered that the armor integrity readout in the corner of her HUD hadn't changed at all. An empty box of algae-based meal replacement mix hit the floor and clattered into the deep shadows outside the hallway's emergency lighting.

"Hey! Stop that," she shouted into the dark. "Remember me? Iridian Nassir, the one who got zapped by a drone out on the hull." Four heads popped up, one after the other, from behind an over-turned desk. Williams and Tiwari were out of enviro suits this time, accompanied by a white man and woman Iridian had never seen before. "That's all of them, yeah?" she asked the ZVs and Si Po.

"Yeah," Sergeant Natani said. "About time we had some good luck."

Wide, hollow eyes stared out of prominent facial bones, which made the med team look more desperate than the fugees. Their open white coats reflected the light from the hallway, more like plastic than cloth, and revealed several layers of clothing beneath. Williams wore her thick black hair coiled into a style Iridian could've sworn she'd seen on the love interest in a vid. It'd been under a helmet when Iridian had last seen her, on the station's exterior hull.

"Close it!" Williams shouted at the ZVs. Beside her, Tiwari nodded emphatically.

Iridian waved the others inside while Grandpa Death shone his helmet's light around the room. Dim images of microorganisms were projected across the walls and ceiling. Natani, Six, Nitro, and Chato followed Grandpa Death in. Beneath the last unbroken overhead light in the hallway, Si Po turned slowly in place, trying to watch everywhere at once.

"Come on, they're not hurting anyone." Iridian looked between the four wide-eyed faces. "Are you?"

"Of course not," said the white guy.

"Close it," Tiwari repeated.

The white woman rolled her eyes. "Doesn't matter. No bots."

"Close it!" Tiwari shouted. The two males stared at each other with the peculiar intensity the med team had displayed on the station's surface.

Iridian had to ask. "Are you people psychic or something? What's with the eye fucking?" All four of them turned to her, stared some more, then laughed so loudly that Iridian winced.

Whatever the hell that was about, it'd be good to put another emergency bulkhead between her and hard vac, and between her and any drones AegiSKADA sent. "Come on, Si Po. The AI's trying a lot harder to kill you than these docs are."

Si Po gingerly stepped through the doorway and Iridian keyed her mic on the wider band. "Shut that door again, please, babe." The door banged closed from the floor to the ceiling less than a step behind Si Po. He shrieked at a higher pitch than she could've managed. All four physicians ducked behind the table again.

In the fear-laden silence that followed, Nitro asked, "What is *wrong* with them?"

"They worked for Spacelink," said Natani. "They got left behind during evac. Or there never was one." She glanced at Iridian like she was suspicious that Iridian had lied when she'd told them that the evac never reached the station during the battle. "The fugees didn't get here for another year, so the med team was trapped with AegiSKADA, in a half-wrecked hab with no Internet. That'd break my brain."

"Depends on who you were trapped with, ma'am." Despite Grandpa Death's worsening cough, he elbowed Six in the ribs and grinned at Sergeant Natani, whose narrowed eyes glared coldly enough to flash-freeze her faceplate. Iridian wasn't the only one on the station hanging on to her sense of humor with both hands.

"Shut it, you damned artifact," said Natani. Grandpa Death smiled like the round had gone to him, and Natani scowled like he was right. Six ducked his head inside his helmet and walked away a few paces to check their exits. So Natani and Six didn't talk about whatever relationship they had going on. Iridian was glad she'd never bought it up to Six, and it was one more reason to avoid Natani.

Time to get everybody focused. "We need your help," Iridian said to the doctors. "People are sick back at base, and nothing our medic tried has cured the stuff."

"Antibiotic resistant," said the white female physician, in a tone that implied an unspoken *you idiot*.

"We didn't have many antibiotics to begin with," Iridian said. "Now, do you have enough suits for all of you?" She mentally projected urgency and a need to vacate the premises, the way Adda talked about communicating with AI.

"Can't leave. Equipment here," said Tiwari.

So much for telepathy. "Our people are drowning in their own blood. We need you there to save them," Iridian said. "Besides, our medic has some equipment, and we can bring your smaller stuff." Not that she looked forward to hauling it under fire, if it came to that. Nothing heavy would make the jump across the broken section of hallway that they'd made on the way here. "Bring any patterns you need on a datacask. You people could use some company anyway, don't you think?" Donning her least threatening smile, she envisioned carrying them back tied up. It'd be faster.

"Won't," said the woman who'd argued that closing the emergency door was unnecessary.

"Won't," the man she'd been staring at agreed.

A high-pitched beep in Iridian's helmet speaker repeated three times and startled all the pirates, who must've heard it in theirs, too. Adda's drone alarm was telling them they had incoming. The pirates had stayed in one place long enough, and in close enough proximity to the station's only protected residents, to draw AegiSKADA's attention. "We need to leave, people," Iridian said.

"It's the right thing to do." Dr. Williams stepped around the overturned table and gave Iridian a passable spacefarer bow. "Maya Lorde Williams. I will go with you."

"And I," said Dr. Tiwari. "We have suits. Also oxygen."

"How much O_2?" asked Natani.

The white woman pointed to tanks lined up in an office cubicle, stacked to the top of its low walls. Nice to know they stood next to so much pressurized flammable gas.

"I won't walk all the way back on the outside just counting on our suits' O_2," Natani said. "We'll have to carry the tanks. That'll limit mobility."

For once, Iridian agreed with her. "I'm not trading my shield for one. Can we make it part of the way?"

"The *Charon's Coin* docks near here," Si Po said. "At the distribution docking bay. We could walk the hull until there, then go inside for the rest of the way around."

"Show," demanded the woman who wanted to stay. Si Po projected the map from his comp glove onto the wall. The dark room let the tiny projector outline the map's major features. The labels were unreadable blurs.

Something slammed into the emergency door from the outside. The drone that Adda's alarm had warned them about had apparently arrived. The door jerked open several centimeters, then thumped shut again. The med team abandoned Si Po's map and ran to lockers propped haphazardly against one wall. The doctors pulled enviro suits from them and started sealing themselves inside.

Three hard impacts shook the door. Iridian spun and raised her shield. Si Po cowered behind her, but the ZVs took up positions on either side. "Somebody make sure the docs don't take off without us!" she said.

"On it." Six looped a portable O_2 tank's carrying strap over one broad shoulder on his way to where the doctors were cramming themselves into enviro suits. Frowning, Natani watched him go without calling him back.

Whatever had slammed into the doors detonated. Three half-meter-square chunks of the door bulged inward. Iridian was used to blocking explosions that size with a much bigger shield. The door remained intact and shut. "At least Spacelink didn't scrimp on the doors."

"They're running!" Six shouted.

"Oh, what the fuck now?" Iridian shouted back in exasperation. She and the pirates whirled to face him.

The med team shoved aside a desk at the back of the room

and vanished down another dark hallway. A rattling half-closed crate on wheels trailed after them. "Doesn't want us to leave, doesn't want us to leave!" one of them shrieked.

Six vaulted a chunk of emergency bulkhead that had punched through this floor from the floor below and disappeared among the debris. If the med team hid somewhere in this labyrinth where AegiSKADA's sensors were down, Adda would never find them.

"Did they not *just say* they were coming with us?" Iridian charged after Six and the doctors rather than waiting for an answer. Each pirate grabbed O_2 tanks as they ran past the cubicle stash.

After a few turns, the passage that the med team had left through opened on the wider hallway they'd followed to get there. Minimal debris piled against one wall left the med team exposed. For such weak-looking civilians, they moved fast. Williams must've been a marathoner at some point, the way she carried herself. Or an ISV driver. Iridian's old posture and stride came back to her as they barreled down the hallway.

She caught up with Six as both of them passed a sign on the wall. She read it and shouted, "They're heading for Docking Bay Two!" over her shoulder to the pirates. Grandpa Death's breath rattled like his namesake around his cough. When Iridian next glanced back, she didn't see the other pirates. The three-quick-ping alarm sounded again. Another drone was somewhere nearby, but she didn't see that, either.

Six and Iridian clambered over a collapsed interior wall that the docs had had to go around, with their wheeled crate. The bay doors stood open on the other side. The *Charon's Coin* looked small on a landing pad designed for disabled freighters. Its hullhooks and heat fins lay folded against its sides, wavering slightly in the heat of its three massive engines idling. Tiwari and Williams raced toward an elevator to the observation room. The other two docs ran straight for the ship.

"Get away from there!" Six pursued the couple approaching the *Coin*, but they didn't even look back at him. Since he was on his way to retrieve that half of the med team, Iridian ran after Tiwari and Williams.

A drone swooped down from the ceiling toward the docs who'd almost reached the elevator. In her peripheral vision, the ship's passthrough opened, and the escaping med team members were much nearer than Six. The pilot must've overridden some safety measures to open the passthrough with the engines on.

On her next step, Iridian dipped into a half crouch to reach a piece of an empty fifty-kilo fuel cartridge. She flung it at the doctors boarding the ship. The cartridge bounced off one of their heads and, with the extra force imparted by Iridian's armor, knocked the doc flat on his or her face. The other one hauled the fallen doctor into the passthrough. The gangway shut before Six reached it.

Almost immediately, the ship's engines rumbled out of idling toward full power. The now-familiar imminent depressurization alarm whooped, flashing yellow light across the bay and revealing that Six was way, way too close to the ship's engines. Instead of running, he kept trying to open its passthrough, like he didn't realize he was in danger of being roasted. Iridian's shout of "Six, back off!" apparently didn't overcome the depressurization alarm and the engine noise.

The engines' heat and pressure would melt Iridian's shield, though it'd block anything the drone threw at her, short of nukes. Adda was alone with dying criminals, and the med team could save them. Could save *Adda*. Iridian ran hard for the elevator to the observation deck, after the other half of the med team. Whatever happened, she had to get back to Adda.

She reached the docs near the elevator seconds after the drone launched two small projectiles. She got the shield up to face height, deflecting the weapons from their intended landing spot between Williams and Tiwari. The projectiles exploded as the elevator doors opened, tumbling all three humans inside.

Across the docking bay, the *Coin*'s engine roared to lift-off power. Heat flowed into the elevator. Though the two docs screamed right next to Iridian's external helmet mic, multiple xenon engines igniting drowned out everything else.

If the engines didn't kill Six, he'd wish they had.

Fuck.

The decompression cycle would have locked the other pirates out of the docking bay. They had no idea what'd happened inside. "Drone in the docking bay," Iridian panted over the op channel, although the bot would've had to fly damned fast to avoid the engine outflow and being swept into the cold and the black with the docking bay's atmo . . . and Six. Once the bay's enviro met criteria, the doors would open. The drone would know just where to find the pirates. They should be ready too.

"Understood," Sergeant Natani said over the team channel. "We'll come in when the doors open."

The elevator deposited Iridian and the doctors on the docking bay's observation deck. Since this docking bay focused on distribution shipments, the cams feeding the projected windows provided a good view of the stars spinning over what was currently "up," above the station's outer ring. The *Coin* was pacing the station outside, staying within cam range.

"You saved our lives." Williams's deliberate enunciation grated on Iridian's brain. "Thank you."

That was too much. Iridian whirled away from the window to face the docs. "Why the fuck did you run off like that?" she screamed at them. "AegiSKADA doesn't try to kill *you*."

The docs backed away from her. "It wanted you to go. It would've done anything to make you." Tiwari's French accent got thicker when he was scared, apparently, and he wasn't making sense. "Would've locked us in for days, would've stopped the atmo. . . . Drones don't always move for us."

"And we've always thought maybe, if we could get on a ship, we'd have a chance to get away from this place," Williams said meekly, but still with exquisitely precise pronunciation. "We could go home."

So the med team wasn't as safe from AegiSKADA as the pirates thought they were. Iridian nodded and turned away so she wouldn't have to look at their terrified, pitiful faces. A sensor node on the wall caught her eye. The cam lens crushed beneath her fist. The doctors jumped back. She kept pounding, ignoring vague concerns about the armored glove's integrity.

Six had been more than a dumb grunt. He'd had to know what'd happen if he stayed there. Maybe he thought he was too near the engines to get away clean. Besides, he'd been kind to Adda and Pel. He didn't deserve to die that way.

The *Coin* extricated itself from the station's spin and leveled out. The ship was upside down from her perspective. For some reason, the pilot still kept pace in front of the cam feeding the observation projection.

The *Coin*'s outer passthrough door opened. A silent jet of atmo vented into the vacuum, then two small human figures. The docs next to Iridian gasped. One figure was already still. The other floundered, struggling to seal his or her suit. In a few seconds, it too stilled. The ship rolled fractionally back and forth, a quick, purposeless maneuver that made the red lights on the station's antenna towers glint off its thermal fins. It slowed until the station's cam swung away.

What had the pilot been thinking? All it would've taken to stop the docs was to keep the damned passthrough doors closed. Why in all hells did the pilot feel the need to kill them? Did they even see Six? The AI copilot should've warned the pilot about a human's proximity, and then any rational human being *wouldn't have taken off.*

Iridian drew a long breath and keyed her mic on a signal Barbary Station's public address system would pick up. "Did anybody else see that?"

"What's happening?" Natani's voice was all business, but she and Six were close. Telling her would hurt them both.

"I saw," Adda croaked like she'd swallowed something vile.

Short "Saw what?" messages came in over top of each other from other pirates, and even Suhaila from the fugee camp. A better question was how Suhaila had gotten on that channel.

Iridian adjusted her signal band to only include Adda and the op frequency coordinated on Natani's comp. "Si Po is locked out of the docking bay, so who told that pilot to vent the passthrough?"

"Not me." Adda sounded distant. Whatever realization she'd recently come to took more of her attention than the conversation did.

"Nobody told it," Si Po said over the squad's local channel. *What'd he mean, "it"?* The cold seeping in through the suit settled in her bones.

"Shut your gods-damned mouth," Natani snarled.

"No, we can't keep—" Something impacted an enviro suit and Si Po yelped. The sergeant must've hit him.

Seconds later a door slammed open, admitting the pirates into the now-pressurized docking bay. Grandpa Death turned toward the dark spot on the pad and asked, "Ugh, what got cooked down here?"

Muffled snaps from one of the pirates' palmers indicated that Major O.D.'s order to go unarmed hadn't applied to everyone. *No wonder Natani stayed behind me the whole way here.* Iridian crossed to the bay side of the observation room in time to see the drone crash on the landing pad the *Coin* had recently vacated.

The *Coin*'s rapid half-roll movement . . . Fighter pilots and piloted drones did that. Humans used the maneuver to say hello, good-bye, or that a communication had been received. Some inhuman thing trying to communicate with people would pull exactly that sort of shit. Something one referred to as "it."

Her fist clenched on her shield, pulling it into a tight forward block, like that'd do her any good at all. "You awakened the gods-damned AI copilots." The accusation hung in radio silence for long beats. "You're not even going to deny it, are you?"

Even cant didn't have a word for how gods-damned *stupid* intentionally awakening an AI was. No wonder the crew invented three skittish pilots who spoke an untranslatable language, pilots who were also inexplicably unhelpful to humans trapped on Barbary Station. That fiction was a hell of a lot less terrifying than the truth.

The remaining two med team docs were staring at each other again. Sergeant Natani swore like a Jovian prisoner of war, to Iridian's grim amusement. And what could she do but laugh now? The ships' AI could've killed them at any time, in any number of ways.

It was almost more horrific that the station population was still breathing. What were three ship AIs doing with all these humans when they could go anywhere else in the universe, given time and fuel? It couldn't be good. Hell, she and Adda had been *in* an awakened gods-damned AI, the *Apparition*, during the whole trip from the hijacked colony ship to Barbary Station.

"We had to do it." Si Po spoke fast as he followed the ZVs across the bay, like he was getting something out before Natani hit him again. "The pilots were gone. We thought the ships' AI would help us with AegiSKADA, or at least get us water, since the reservoirs and tanks were drying up and we didn't have the recycler yet. We'd have been dead months ago without them."

"The *Coin*'s AI killed Six taking off and then spaced two of the med team," Iridian said. She grimaced, both at the way she'd said it and the silence that followed. She could handle wailing or violence in the face of death. Shock and quiet rage was as dangerous to allies as enemies.

"No wonder they don't use the ships as transport." Adda gasped.

"Oh, gods damn it." Iridian had hoped to phrase the discovery in a way that wouldn't elicit Adda's misplaced sympathies, but Adda would've figured out what'd happened even sooner than Iridian did. The pirates got close enough to the elevator door in the docking bay to disappear under the lower edge of the observation room's cam feed.

"That's why I didn't find the AI on the *Apparition* when it picked us up from the colony ship!" Adda's voice trembled, in awe if Iridian had to guess. "It hid itself perfectly, and it shouldn't have been able to do that. It must've . . . That's amazing."

Scary as shit, more like. But they could rehash that old argument after the last two docs on the med team got back to base and started saving people's lives. That was the important thing. Without that goal to focus on, Iridian would've been a lot more pissed off than she was, but surviving the trip back would be hard enough without obsessing about awakened AI outside the station.

The elevator door opened and Sergeant Natani quickly scanned the room, palmer raised, before she and the remaining ZVs entered. Si Po was still in the elevator when the doors started to close and had to hit the open button before joining them in the observation room.

Written on Natani's face was the fact that even if she'd never treated Six like an equal, they'd had something deeper than just getting along. And he and Chato were together too often to be anything less than good friends.

"He was right next to the ship when it took off," said Iridian.

Natani's voice was low and rough and tore through the ZVs' stunned silence. "And where the fuck were you?"

"She saved us," said Dr. Tiwari. "The drone—"

"You saved *them*, not Six?" By Chato's expression, Iridian might as well have stabbed him in the stomach with something rusty while she was at it.

She clenched her teeth. "It was the best decision at the time. Doesn't mean it was a good one. Maybe I could've saved all of them, but I was there and I don't see how."

Natani's hand swept up, holding the palmer she'd downed the drone with. The other hand trembled in a fist at her side. Nitro, Chato, and Grandpa Death backed away, exclaiming things Iridian ignored. Si Po and the docs stood statue-still.

Shit. Iridian still held her deployed shield, and she shifted her weight to a better brace position even though it wasn't covering her yet. Maybe she could raise it in time. Aloud, she said "Sergeant," counting on the rank to remind Natani of a time when she didn't attack allies, "it was Six or Adda."

Natani's finger stayed still on the trigger. "What the hell are you talking about? That creepy cunt isn't even here. Six is *dead*."

The dish of a cobbled-together directed energy weapon like Natani's was the last thing Reis saw too. Iridian looked past it, to Natani's face. "If we lost the whole med team, there'd be nobody left to save Adda and the rest of the sick people on base," Iridian said. Natani drew a ragged breath but stayed quiet. "I was here and I made the only call I could."

"Well, you fucked up." Natani's voice was choked with emotion.

At least with the observation windows projected on the walls, Iridian could die with a view of the stars. "It's Adda," she said. "I love her. That's why you'd have gone after Six, yeah?" Chato swore softly. Natani's squad should've figured out why a soldier from someone else's fireteam spent so much time in the sergeant's personal space. Iridian couldn't tell how surprised the other two were, because that'd mean looking away from the weapon in Natani's hand.

"Don't tell me what I would've done," Natani shouted, voice cracking with sorrow as well as anger.

Iridian winced, but she was still breathing. "Even when the docs get there, AegiSKADA's still going to get her eventually. Matter of time. And . . . you know I can't just let it. Give me a chance to take the AI down, for all of us. For her. For Six. Please. So nobody else has to lose someone they love."

Captain Sloane's hoarse voice spoke in their helmets, startling everyone. "Adda's readings indicate that you are still in the docking bay." The captain was well enough to talk, and to catch up on what the rest of the crew was doing. *Fine timing, too.*

Natani drew a long breath and exhaled as slowly. The palmer still pointed at Iridian's chest. "Yes, Captain. We're moving out soon."

Iridian would be safer alone with AegiSKADA than with Sergeant Natani grieving and hating Iridian every step of the way back. Maybe Natani's squad would get over Iridian's decision, maybe they wouldn't. Now the AI threatened Iridian's life, livelihood, and girlfriend. She was looking forward to taking it on personally.

"I can do it. I can take a lot of firepower on this." Iridian hefted her shield, finally putting it between her and Natani.

Natani glanced between Iridian's face and the shield, then *finally* returned the palmer to its holster. "Don't come back until you do."

According to Blackguardly Jack, AegiSKADA's control room was about sixty ticks north. On either side were nuclear power generators. The step-by-step of disabling it was a hell of a thing to have to figure out alone, but somebody had to.

She'd taken two steps in that direction when Si Po said, "Wait! I'm going with you."

"The fuck you are." Nitro was striking out at him with an armored fist when Iridian turned around. He'd already started running and made it out of range. He blew right past Iridian.

"Let the ladder down when we come back through the wall." She ran after Si Po, praying to anything that would listen that when Natani returned to base, she'd remember what losing someone close felt like. That she wouldn't be inclined toward revenge while Iridian wasn't there to protect Adda.

As Iridian ran through an open emergency bulkhead, she keyed her mic on the channel to Adda. "Lock this behind me, babe?" The floor trembled as the bulkhead thudded closed. It sealed in a short, sharp hiss of expelled atmo. "When Natani's squad comes back with the docs, stick with Tabs and Rio like I told you to, yeah?"

"Yes," Adda said distantly, her drugged mind still on the damned awakened AIs.

Around a curve of the hallway, Si Po slumped against a wall and panted. He wasn't the sort of backup one hoped for on a dangerous mission. The Shieldrunners would be laughing their asses off. Now that she thought about it, she couldn't help smiling a bit.

"They're stuck back there," she said. "And I don't think I pissed them off enough to make them find a way around. Let's keep moving." She patted his shoulder as she walked past.

Si Po kept looking back toward the shut bulkhead, so Iridian keyed her mic again. "Babe, can you tell us if anything is coming our way, even if it looks friendly?"

"Sure." The rough edge to Adda's voice was worrisome. She wouldn't necessarily say anything if she were sick. She could keep a secret, that woman. Iridian's comp pinged its announcement of a new download a moment later. "You'll know as soon as I do. I'm also tracking Pel, so I don't want to miss anything."

Iridian got the kind of full-body shiver she had stepping off high places before she saw how far away the ground was. "What the hell is he doing outside the base?"

"Asking the refugees to share their pharmaceuticals." Adda sighed. "I'm worrying enough for both of us. You, I trust to take care of yourself."

If Iridian and Si Po took a straight route without switching floors, then they had about two klicks of station to traverse. She hoped the remaining med team got back with similar ease, then snorted a laugh. They couldn't all have it easy. With luck, the docs would get the short route.

"What's funny?" Si Po's tone indicated that he could use a laugh.

"Oh, just wondering whether good old Murphy is on our side or AegiSKADA's today," she said. He did not look relieved.

They had a bit of a walk before they reached the reactor on the way to the control room. After a few steps in silence, Iridian asked, "So why'd you want to come with me instead of going back to the base, where it's safe?"

Si Po watched where he was stepping even though this stretch of hallway was relatively clear of debris. "After what happened to

Xing, and Kaskade, and now Six, I guess . . . I'm tired of feeling terrified all the time, no matter what I do. I might as well feel terrified
while doing something right."

Well, that wasn't what I expected. Iridian smiled. "That's called
bravery. Keep pushing yourself and it'll turn into a habit." Si Po
snorted like he didn't believe her.

* * *

About a klick from what Adda had marked on the map as the
security control room, Iridian left the exterior ring through a door
labeled TO MAINTENANCE EXIT.

"We're going into space again?" Si Po's voice was about an
octave higher his usual one.

"That's where you people keep your radioactive salt, right?"
she asked. When he just stared at her with his mouth hanging
slightly open, she said, "Look, AegiSKADA's running on a pseudo-
organic quantum computer, yeah?" He nodded. "And what happens when you put, say, a kilo of radioactive liquid thorium next
to a quantum computer?"

There was the wide-eyed realization she was looking for. "The
whole thing locks up until the decon cycle finishes!" he said.

"That's right." She'd been expecting a more technical exclama-
tion, but that was probably a sign that she'd spent too much time
discussing the topic with Adda.

To start the decon cycle and give Adda a chance to restart the
AI in concurrence mode, where she might gain control of it, Iridian and Si Po had to get a radioactive thorium sample from one of
the reactors powering the station. That meant walking along the
hull, outside, in hard vac.

Si Po's suit had gaps at the wrist and knee joints where gloves from a smaller suit were jammed on and the protective pads in the knees had been inexpertly removed, judging by the scrape marks. "Has anybody vac-tested that suit?" Iridian asked him. He shrugged. "Then you need a new outfit. Something in white."

She spent a minute looking for the locker that should've been near anything that qualified as a "maintenance exit" and pointed out three white enviro suits in an open locker and another on the floor nearby. Safety standards required only one per airlock. "Looks like the med team was stockpiling suits along with the O_2 so you have some size options," she said. "At least these are designed for longer durations in the cold and the black."

"They're not armored." He was looking at them like they bit and stung, too.

"You'll suffocate long before AegiSKADA zaps you if you've got a bad seal. Bring the armored suit along, if you want." With the oxygen tank he already carried, he'd have to drop the extra weight. She dug a small yellow case with the black radiation hazard symbol out of her pocket. "Take a D-MOG before you lock the hood down." She opened her helmet and swallowed one too. It might be hours before they reached enviro healthy enough for her to raise her faceplate again. That'd scare him if she said it, though.

When they exited on the station's inner ring, Si Po froze. The stars wheeling beyond the far side of the station streaked across his faceplate. She bent to check the magnetic locks on his boots. The indicators lit green. Station grav was what held him to the hull. Locks just calmed people unused to extravehicular activity.

She stood in front of him, blocking the cosmos from his view. "If you're about to freak out, hang on to your gear with both hands and look at the hull."

"Already freaking," he whispered.

"You're doing great. Hey, I appreciate the company, okay? Now

let's keep moving before the damned AI triangulates our position."
Iridian took point. After a few moments, his breathing quieted
and his exhalations quit automatically activating his suit mic.

Then she had to stop him. Why the hell did she keep thinking
that the outside of the station was safer than the inside? "See
those?" She pointed out several rectangular installations the size
of a finger. They had the ragged edges and uniform coloration of
prototype-quality printing. "Stay here. Do not move, do not speak.
Try to be part of the hull. And if I, um, explode, go right back down
the ladder and avoid anything that looks like those." He swallowed so hard his head bobbed up and down in his helmet, but
he stood still.

The nearest device was based on a Type 422 antipersonnel
mine. She had studied them during Shieldrunner training. Even
though ISVs highlighted models in their databases on a heads-up
display, she'd trained to identify the devices on sight. The secessionists had EMP generators.

She could flash Adda a picture to see if she could find schematics. However, Iridian and Si Po already stood within the five-
meter lethality range. The trigger wasn't overly sensitive. After the
explosives she'd blocked in the docking bay, she couldn't trust her
shield to protect her from another blast until she checked it over.
Si Po just wore an enviro suit. No need to distract Adda if she
couldn't do anything to help.

Now that Iridian was looking for them, tiny mines stood out
all over the hull. The pirates must've disarmed the ones near the
base when they built it, or they chose the location for its lack of
mines. Perhaps the area near the generator was the only mined
section. The damned generator stuck up off the hull over the
inner ring's curve, blocking the spinning stars. They'd be there
and gone with the radioactive thorium sample within twenty

minutes if they could walk there without getting vaporized.

They weren't the only thing that'd vaporize. Enough mines going off at once might punch through the hull. The industrial area below them housed inactive machinery and stored scrap metal. If something down there was flammable, they might blow an even bigger hole in the place. A big enough explosion would set the whole station off its spin. Fugee kids bouncing off bulkheads aside, the pirate base couldn't take that much torque.

But in the long run, AegiSKADA was a hell of a lot more likely to kill all of them, and there wasn't time to defuse all the mines, especially considering the cost of a mistake. Iridian retraced her steps back to Si Po, wishing for more light than her headlamp offered. Any shadow might hide a mine. "Stay right behind me. And drag me back into the station if I blow my hand off, okay?"

"Please don't," he whimpered.

"Look, read the map while I clear us a path. See if you can find a safer way to access the generators." She crept to the nearest mine and slowly knelt next to it, watching around the semitransparent shield for an external tripwire. If it had a heat sensor, she was so screwed. . . .

She reached around the shield to thrust her fingers beneath the mine. She pressed up. It was magnetically sealed to the hull, but her adrenaline-fueled strength freed it. She chucked it ahead of her, toward the generator, and crouched behind the shield.

The explosion itself was soundless, but her boots conveyed the hull's violent shudder. Si Po yelped like a hurt puppy and curled into a ball on his side behind her. A second mine triggered where the first one went off, then two together, then four. Iridian kept her head turned away and braced as debris pelted the shield. The armor plate at the back of the helmet was much thicker than the faceplate.

When the hull stopped shaking, she turned back to the mine field. Her first throw had cleared the mines in a wide, jagged swath all the way to the generator, and blackened and dented its wall. Meter-long jets of escaping atmo erupted from the hull in the blast zone.

"That's enough of that," she said on the local channel. The last word dissolved into a burst of hysterical laughter she had to hold her breath to stop. "If I'd thrown it two centimeters farther, I'd've blown up the whole thing!"

"*Mierde* fucking merciful Christ," whispered Si Po.

CHAPTER 19

Charges Accrued: Unauthorized Access to Medical Information

Nuclear generator blueprints were Adda's entire world. They covered the black floor, high walls, and ceiling of her workspace. With enough concentration she could step from one side of the nonexistent room to the other. Worrying about Pel held her down to the physical pace her brain was used to. Symbols that designated doors and walkways morphed into little animations of him using them, sometimes confidently with healthy brown eyes, sometimes cautiously with scarred white ones.

"Babe, the door is still locked." Whenever Iridian spoke, Adda's mind pulled in data from the sensor node nearest her to hover within arm's reach. The nodes were much more widely spaced on the surface than in the interior, even before Iridian had destroyed the ones in easy reach. In the vid feed from this one, she and Si Po were small and distant. Adda couldn't even see the locked door on vid, only on the blueprint.

Si Po . . . she thought he'd gotten her the professional translator she was using now, but the *Casey*'s AI copilot had acquired it for her. If all three ships' intelligences were awake, as the pirates had implied, the *Casey* could've learned a lot—everything—about Adda from the *Apparition's* intelligence. Perhaps the *Casey* had been reaching out to her, offering a way to communicate.

It would be difficult to tell what it'd overheard on tapped sensors, and impossible to guess how it processed that information. The *Casey's* perspective would be fascinating. The mere presence of *three* awakened intelligences, all in one place, was practically a miracle. She really should find out why one of them was interested in her in particular. But at the moment she had neither the time nor mental energy to risk her mind against a truly awakened intelligence. Iridian needed her help against AegiSKADA.

She crouched and rubbed a section of floor to black out that part of the blueprint. Crossing the workspace, she ripped the piece with the locked door off the ceiling. She pressed the flapping, writhing, leathery thing into the black section. Its mushroom-gilled maw snapped at her hand. Blackness oozed up in thin, connected strands to grasp the blueprint strip and envelop it.

Lines and lines of code, representing her brain's and her translator's conclusions about the contents of AegiSKADA's system, appeared in green on the black patch. Her professors would scold her and other students would laugh, but she just wasn't getting the right messages through. This might spell out why in something closer to the intelligence's native language.

Ah. She wanted to create sensor data signaling that there simultaneously was and was not a hull puncture leaking atmo beside the door Iridian wanted open. What she'd missed on the conceptual version was that she had to repeat the message 3,200 times per second to keep the door open. Oh gods, and one more thing that might not be obvious . . . "Keep your helmets on inside!" she said over the comm channel.

"There it goes," Iridian said. "You're the best!" On the vid now showing in midair in the workspace, her and Si Po's tiny figures disappeared into the generator.

Inside the power plant were more sensors. Adda's vid of Iridian's progress clarified, zoomed in, and acquired vibration, infrared, and muffled sound. She skimmed three years of observations from the power plant nodes before she saw anybody go in. Spacelink had probably put the plant in some kind of dormant state after shutting down the engines to abandon the station.

Someone or something—HarborMaster, most likely—had maintained the station's spin, the medical center module's atmosphere, and even the algae farm to support the Spacelink medical team. It might even have enlisted AegiSKADA's assistance in keeping the physicians in the one part of the station where it maintained a healthy environment, as spacefarers would say.

When the refugees arrived the following year, HarborMaster would've had to restart the environmental controls throughout the station, and that would've required a lot of energy. They were lucky the power plant worked as well as it did. No one had checked on it since Spacelink operated the station. If Iridian found out, she would rant for a week about ignoring maintenance schedules.

Pel signaled Adda's comp. The blueprints and sensor nodes tracking Iridian flashed away, replaced with a detailed readout of his current status.

"Adda." She stilled. No good news ever followed her proper name out of Pel's mouth. "That weird info you were telling me about, about movement in the docking bay? They're mercs."

She checked her feeds while she searched her brain for what that abbreviation might mean. The mysterious human movement was now traversing the station's residential module on Level 2, which connected directly with the refugees' docking bay. The activity was attracting the vast majority of the drones on the station. Several nodes went dark, accompanied by automated structural damage reports.

Mercenaries. Armed. The kind of invaders AegiSKADA was developed to defend against. The irritated skin around her eyes burned as they widened in horror. That would increase AegiSKADA's aggression, but she didn't have enough information to predict how that would affect its targeting. Things could get better for the pirates and refugees, or much, much worse.

But Pel was still in the refugee camp. He wouldn't be able to hear the mercenaries yet. The camp's cam feeds were still up, so she tapped into those and started looking for him while she asked, "How do you know who they are?"

"I've been listening to a couple of them hassle the fugees. They talk a lot."

The data around Adda flickered as she processed what he said. "But what are they doing here?"

"Transorbital Voyages, the corp that owned that colony ship you brought us, hired these jerks to kick our asses, or get the ship back, or both," said Pel. She finally found a cam at the right angle to see him beside one of the shipping containers in the refugees' docking bay.

Transorbital could afford a small army, especially if they thought they could recover their ship after they took over the station. She designated a corner of her display to track the mercenaries. Something they carried deactivated sensor nodes within about ten meters of their location, and the curving hallways made it difficult to count their full complement. The amount of movement more distant nodes reported suggested that there were a lot of them. "How did they know the *Prosperity Dawn* was here?" she asked Pel absently while she followed the trail of deactivated nodes.

He huffed a disgusted sigh. "Sissy, where else would it be?"

"Oh," said Adda. "True." Barbary Station was the only station for millions of kilometers around it.

Adda should have planned for this. Timing constraints had forced her to stage the ambush on the Earth side of the lead cloud, where the ITA or Transorbital Voyages would've received some signal betraying the hijacked ship's trajectory. When she made the plan with Pel—and Si Po, though she didn't know it then—to send the ships to the coordinates she provided, she had assumed that successful pirates would have a communication-jamming procedure. It would've been a logical assumption, if living in an impenetrable station hadn't made that a low priority for Sloane's crew. Of course, with enough money and time, anything was penetrable.

A loud snap of discharged electricity came from somewhere behind Pel. He ducked, and she reconfigured her vid feed. The refugees had destroyed all the sensor nodes they could reach, so she peered down at their docking bay from two stories above. A shouting crowd rushed toward the hallway Sloane's crew had followed when they'd been running from AegiSKADA. Adda adjusted her view to include the area near the rubble barricade.

Smoke rose from a body facedown on the floor beyond the rubble. Another refugee raced along the safest path, designated by yellow tape, and dragged the body toward the container village.

"Shit, I've got to go," said Pel.

"No, you don't! Get on the refugees' colony ship and stay there."

"Oh sure, I'll hide with the kids while everybody else fights for their lives. No thanks." He cut the message.

Footsteps beyond her tank told her the pirates were on the move too. Everything was happening too fast. She tuned them out and focused on the mercenaries and their possible progress toward Iridian until pounding on the trapdoor left her staring at her message to herself on the workspace generator's ceiling.

"Adda, you really need to come out," said Rio's husky voice. "The meeting's in the bunkhouse. Even the people too sick to get up need to hear what the captain has to say."

"There's too much going on!" The panic in Adda's voice was a little embarrassing, but the only thing she could think of that might be more important than what she was already doing was getting out of the way of a large scale-structural collapse.

"Captain's orders," Rio said.

Adda sighed sharply, psyching herself up to leave her current task undone. The alerts set on various data states would still send her a message on her comp if anything went wrong in the ways she could account for. She unplugged, crawled out of the generator, and swiped at her nose and lips to remove the residue from her concentration mix. A cloud of blue dust fell from the ceiling just as she opened the trapdoor. She tugged her hood up over her blue-specked face before emerging into the hallway's orange light.

Rio blocked most of the hall and the light, a half smile on her wide face. "I thought you were in trouble in there. Nobody's seen you for hours. How do you feel?"

"Headache, lung ache, and I'd be tired except I'm on a lot of stims." Adda had plenty of energy, but exhausted numbness hung behind her eyes and in her limbs. "The cough's not bad yet."

Rio frowned as she started walking. "You should take care of yourself. Pel orbits you like his personal sun, you know."

Adda snorted. "A Pel year is half again as long as a standard one."

Even with only about a dozen members of Sloane's crew still in the compound, not everyone fit in the bunkhouse. The beds were all occupied, even the one Nils died on. Tritheist wasn't there, which meant he was indisposed in the captain's quarters. The captain was present, though, leaning against the bunks at the far end of the room but standing and looking alert.

"Lads and lasses, here we are," Captain Sloane croaked. "I can't speak long. For those of you who missed the WFUG news bulletin, a mercenary force has infiltrated the station and is at this moment fighting drones."

"Anyone we know?" asked Chato.

"No visual yet, and they brought their own encrypted comms," Major O.D. said. "Shut up and pay attention."

Amid murmurs of shock and well wishes to the mercenaries in their fight against AegiSKADA's drone, Adda checked her comp. She had set proximity alerts in concentric circles originating at Iridian's position, Pel's, and the pirate compound. None of those had been tripped. Perhaps that was why the pirates were more worried about the refugees than themselves, but they wouldn't have the same information she did.

"Adda, what do you have on them?" the captain asked.

When she looked up, everyone in the room was staring at her. Even San Miguel's little boy, drawing gurgling breaths from the bed beside his ill mother, looked Adda's way.

"I'm guessing, based on the sensor data and some reports from the refugees," she said nervously. A few eyes turned away, but that was more depressing than helpful. Now they wouldn't believe the few things she could prove. "Transorbital Voyages hired them. They got in through our docking bay. There's an open shipping container in there that wasn't there before. I think they were launched in that from a ship outside the turrets' range, and one of the station ships brought it in, but they could have timed the launch without a ship's help if they had another way to open the docking bay from the outside."

The *Charon's Coin*, as long as she was guessing, had probably been the ship to bring the container in. She had no explanation for *why* it would do that. Its programming might require it to recover loose cargo, but bringing the container into the station suggested a more conscious choice. Awakened intelligences tended to stray from their original programming anyway. And it should've been able to use its sensors and a few logical inferences to determine what was inside.

"As soon as the mercenaries boarded, AegiSKADA registered weapons," Adda continued. "It's been hunting them ever since. They moved . . ." She searched her comp for notes on station directional terminology. "Downtick, past us. If they keep moving at this pace, they'll reach the refugees in about fifteen minutes."

Everybody was still looking at her. She shifted her weight to one side, putting herself behind Rio's broad shoulder. No wonder Pel stayed close to Rio. The big woman looked capable of defending against anything.

"Well, we have more information than the fugees, for once," Captain Sloane said, to some laughter from the crew. "We'll defend the compound if the mercenaries come this way, but I'm not sending anyone into the station while the AI is on a killing spree. We're in more danger from it than anyone else."

The mercenaries had already walked right past the entry to the path between the hulls. Unless they brought more sophisticated tech they hadn't employed so far, they wouldn't find the compound without the refugees' willing, or unwilling, assistance.

Captain Sloane paused for muted acknowledgment from the pirates. Adda stayed quiet. AegiSKADA was killing innocent people while she sat in a *meeting*. But she'd run through everything she could do to help without a hard reset of AegiSKADA.

"The rest of the bad news . . ." Coughing interrupted the captain's speech. "The rest is that the liquid recycler broke today. We have water for two more days, if we ration it."

CHAPTER 20

Charges Accrued: Theft of Radioactive Material

"Is your radiation alarm going off?" Iridian asked Si Po as they made their way through the power plant. "Because mine is."

He froze a few steps behind her, eyes wide behind the enviro suit's transparent faceplate. "No."

Somewhere inside this plant was an arm-length canister designed to hold a sample of radioactive liquid thorium. It'd be designed to travel in a radiation-proof outer container, which she hoped would be both nearby and light enough to haul around. Enviro was too far off for her to remove her helmet, even if her armor's radiation protection wasn't overloading. Her O_2 alarm had already gone off, and she now carried all her breathable air in the portable tank.

"Adda? Something in here's bleeding neutrons. Don't we have any explosives? We could blow the damned pseudo-organic tanks." She didn't love the idea of carrying armed antipersonnel mines one-handed, so it'd be nice if there was something she could assemble on-site. Besides, if AegiSKADA had planted them, it'd find a way to blast her and Si Po to tiny pieces with them. Gods, she hated AI.

"Even if we did, I don't know who would get them there and set them," said Adda.

"Back out," Iridian told Si Po.

He took the shortest route, racing up half a flight of stairs and vaulting over a pile of fallen paneling from the mine explosions. When he landed, metal snapped and clanged. He dropped from view, but red emergency lighting made it hard to see anything other than the exit.

She scrambled over the rubble toward him. Whatever she was supposed to be thinking, she didn't want to be alone out here. "Hey! Are you all right?"

"I found a crawl space," he groaned.

Several floor panels had collapsed. The ones under Iridian held the wall's weight along with hers. She edged around the fallen section before reaching to give him a hand up.

"Nobody's got anything that might crack an AI case without a lot of collateral damage," Adda said over Iridian's comms.

She relayed the bad news to Si Po. The ships were gods knew where, and the turrets weighed too much to move. Anything explosive would attract more drones than were already coming. Carrying something radioactive would be unpleasant, but once they got it to AegiSKADA's pseudo-organics, it'd disrupt the AI's qubit superpositions and prompt a system reset without Iridian breaking into the internal case. High-end quantum computers powerful enough to host AI came in cases you could drop down an elevator shaft without denting.

"The mercenaries are in the refugees' docking bay," said Adda. "I think they shot someone. I can't tell because everybody's standing in the way, but that's what WFUG is saying."

"Damn them." Iridian leaned against the power plant's outside wall. Something in it creaked, and she stepped away before it fell on her or Si Po. "Damn whoever built this cheap station, damn Transorbital Voyages. . . ."

She stopped herself from pacing because that seemed like a painful way to locate an unexploded mine. With her mic muted, she growled at the stars. If the company told the mercs they'd lose profits for civilian casualties, they wouldn't discharge weapons near the fugees. But they didn't, because Transorbital Voyages didn't give a fuck about civilians. Transorbital deserved to have their expensive colony ship stolen out from under them, and she was proud to have been the one to do it.

When she focused on her immediate surroundings, Si Po was staring at her like she'd decoupled her relays. She keyed her mic. "How can you live here without being pissed off every gods-damned second of your gods-damned existence? I've never seen a better argument for piracy in my life."

Something impacted the station's hull from inside the plant, and they both jumped. "I walled off the source for now and set down soakers," Adda said. "It might be okay in a few hours, but it's still going to be hot. Did you find something to carry the thorium sample in?"

Si Po and Iridian exchanged glances, and his expression conveyed the same negative answer as hers. "My suit's better shielded," she said.

"Under a minute, please!" said Adda.

Iridian's instinct was to hold her breath, even though that'd have no particle-blocking effect. She raced through the front door and stopped to examine the entryway. Nothing there was dense enough to protect someone from a radiation source. The next floor up was also empty, although a third of it was behind a lead barrier.

"Crawl space," she muttered. Seconds ticking away in time to her suit radiation alarm, she rushed back to where Si Po had fallen.

A thick cylindrical tube with handles reflected her headlamp's light from where it was crammed into the far corner. It lay beneath a hinged door covered by slabs of a collapsed wall. She breathed out hard, psyching herself up to crawl in. The bulky armor or the O_2 tank could trap her and get her a lethal dose before she ran out of atmo.

"You're still in the contaminated building, Iri," Adda said quietly.

Snarling and swearing, Iridian scooted backward out of the crawl space. She stormed out of the power plant and startled Si Po from his seated position against the exterior wall. "Found one stored by somebody afraid of large spaces." She explained the situation.

"Agoraphobic doesn't mean you like small spaces," he said.

"Wondering how many of my eggs are fried messes with my logical inferences." She huffed something between a frustrated sigh and a laugh. "If the mercs are in the fugee camp and armed, it won't be long before AegiSKADA follows them in. People will die. People I like."

The power plant's door sat crooked on its sliding track after her stunt with the mines, with poison and darkness beyond. Decontaminating from that much radiation would require a rad unit. A ship-breaking station had to have one. That'd mean another hike through the area infested with drones, but she'd done that several times now.

Even if she'd only be carrying rapidly cooling liquid thorium, it'd still be radiating the whole way to the control room. Hell, it'd be right next to her O_2. She shuddered. She'd die badly and leave Adda alone with her blind baby brother among pirates. Yeah, they'd survive, but Adda was counting on Iridian to watch her back. And for other things. The fugees were decent, and it wasn't fair that mercs were coming down on them after all they'd suffered. That was partially her fault, but . . . She loved Adda.

"It's too hot," she said. At least Si Po, of all people, would agree. "Unless we blow ourselves off the station by stepping on one of those mines, we'll get to the other reactor in a couple of hours. Maybe its radiation levels are lower." Though AegiSKADA's drones would almost certainly find them before they reached it. One had found Iridian after less than an hour on the surface, the first time she went out. But she and Si Po could fight bots, or hide from them. They couldn't fight ionizing radiation.

"Where's the carrier?"

Iridian spun around to stare at Si Po. "What?"

He wore a sad smile behind his oily hair. "I'm fucked anyway. Have been since we left the med team and the ZV Group. Have been since we crashed into this mess. I'm always right where whatever's keeping the atmo in is going out. The whole station's coming apart. And which of the ZVs are going to give me their air? Then I panic and make it worse, and I'd rather get poisoned than asphyxiate or explode, you know?"

She wanted to shake him, tell him how much slower death by radiation sickness would be. They were catching rads just standing on the hull, let alone standing next to a damaged reactor.

Other people took care of the fugees. Nobody else in the whole universe was looking out for Adda but Iridian. And AegiSKADA was after all of them, so it had to be shut down. But Iridian didn't have to be the martyr who made it happen. Not yet, anyway. "You know where you fell through the floor? Go there and crawl left about two meters. You'll see it. Then follow the instructions I'm sending you to get the sample." She felt like she'd corrected somebody's blade placement so they'd hit their own vein. Still smiling, he walked back into the generator.

"I used to have a girlfriend." His voice shook over the comm channel. Talking helped distract oneself from fear, sometimes.

"Well, girlfriends, zefriends, boyfriends, but my last one. She was just beautiful, you know? We used to sit together in front of our projector stage—one of the nice ones, not one of those first gens that gave people motion sickness—and she watched anything, so long as I kept her draped in jewels while she did. Which, you know, I could. We had some big hauls back in the day."

Iridian caught motion in her periphery, just over the station's rounded inner edge. Although she stared at the spot for several seconds, there wasn't any more. She deployed her shield and shifted it to the hand nearest where she'd seen whatever it was.

". . . left me last year, and you know what she took?" Si Po was saying. The heavy thump of the safety door slamming open vibrated through Iridian's boots again. "The fucking projector stage." He laughed, voice pitched high in terror, but he stayed in the plant. She had to admire him for that. "She sent me a vid of it going out my apartment door. The *Casey* brought the vid to me two weeks later." And why the hell had an awakened AI like the *Casey*'s decided to bring him a vid like that? Iridian shuddered. He continued after a few moments, "What the hell is a home without a projector stage and a partner, anyway?"

"That's low, man," Iridian said on the local channel.

The proximity alarm Adda had made to warn of approaching drones pinged and flashed orange, which was new. She'd spot an enemy between her and the stars, but the shadow from the far side of the ring kept moving. Between the dim red glow of the antenna tips and the shuttle hub's faint white exterior lights from the ring's center, there were a lot of changing light conditions to track.

The fist-size machine flew out of an antenna cluster's shadow. Iridian crouched in her lowest shield stance. The thing could still zap her through the hull. Maybe this suit was less conductive than the one she'd worn on the base repair job.

"Ah . . . I drew the liquid stuff into the sampling tank, and I've got the container hooked in and filled, but I don't see how to get it out. Can you ask Adda to look that up?"

Even with the enemy poised to attack, Iridian felt compelled to construct a mental model of the device. "Have you tried twisting it until it unslots?" Something hit her shield hard on the upper edge, rocking her backward. Her low stance and magnetized boots kept her upright.

"Oh, no, I was pulling straight—"

The projectile she blocked exploded on the hull in front of her. She jolted but held her stance as her shield caught the blast. Debris cracked against her armor, and a lone mine's secondary explosion threw more pieces of the station into the cold and the black. A jet of atmo erupted at her feet. White mist obscured the drone.

"I'm coming out, what's—"

"Watch for a small flying drone. If you see it, run. *Carefully*," because there were still a hell of a lot of live mines. The bot had to be nearby. Not being able to hear its buzzing motor was maddening. She scanned the area over her head first, wishing yet again for a modern heads-up display.

Si Po came out of the power plant, yelped, and started running past it, in the opposite direction of Iridian. She slung the deployed shield onto the hook between her shoulder blades so it covered the back of her head to her hips and sprinted after him. "Where's the drone?" Labored breathing over the open mic was his only reply. "Gods damn it, you code-coated fuck, if you don't tell me where it is, I can't do anything about it. And watch where you're going!" If he stepped on a mine after all that . . .

She almost did it herself. She extended her stride and threw her arms out to catch her balance without stepping back or falling forward. "Stop!" she bellowed over the local channel. He did, still a long way ahead, and turned slowly toward her. "Stay right there. We're back in the mine field."

The drone swooped toward him, spinning to put the rest of its payload in optimal firing position. Enough of that thing's grenades exploding on impact would blow more holes in the station's hull, never mind what it'd do to Si Po.

Iridian drew a heavily oxygenated breath and pushed it out through pursed lips. Holding her shield low to protect her torso and thighs from explosions, she picked out a path to him. "Adda, there's a drone targeting us. Can you tell why?"

"Oxygen tanks or sample container," she replied in her work-space monotone.

Iridian took another hopping step and miraculously failed to explode. "I'm not throwing either of those away, babe. Give me something else to work with." The drone hadn't fired yet, maybe because it was running the same calculation she was: How much damage to the station did eliminating the threat justify?

Adda's exasperated sigh meant *obviously*, and didn't Iridian remember that she hated to be rushed? Iridian leaped another meter to land right beneath the drone, forcing it to focus on her.

Something crunched under her boot.

The mine flung her at the stars. Both legs stayed attached to her body, although they were above her head at the moment. The suit integrity alarm remained silent. Her panicked inhale was the only sound for one long moment, and then she crash-landed. She pulled in her limbs in an awkward roll over the clearest patch of hull she found in a quarter-second glance.

The edge of her shield slammed into her faceplate, and *that* set the integrity alarm off.

CHAPTER 21

Charges Accrued: Interference with Legally Contracted Military Operations

Thank all that's holy for vid-based search queries. While new gouts of station atmo erupted around Iridian's prone form, Adda filled her workspace with helmets similar to the one on Iridian's suit. Her heart hammered, but she couldn't hear it over the horrifying hiss of air escaping Iridian's helmet, transmitted across their audio feed.

Beside the feed from the surface, an animated helmet cross section hung in the air, repeatedly demonstrating its pressure-retention emergency feature. "Iri, press on the sides of your helmet, around the temples. It should click."

Iridian's arms rose like they weighed a hundred kilos. The animated helmet faceplate shivered as either the faceplate itself or something beneath it expanded at the edges to shut a crack in its center. The crack snapped open, and the animation repeated. Adda shut her workspace eyes as tight as her physical ones already were. "Iri?"

"It closed," Iridian groaned. The workspace magnified Adda's relieved sigh into a whirlwind that spun the helmet faceplate animations away into a mist behind her vid feeds. "Thanks for saving my ass again, babe."

Once Iridian pushed herself to her feet and resumed her progress through the mine field, Adda refocused on the other feed projected on the workspace's gray mist. Her visual perspective was about ten meters above Pel's head, ninety-eight ticks north on the station map, at the best focus she could get from the intact sensor nodes.

The refugees' docking bay ceiling dripped with brown-red ooze that twitched and slithered with background processes analyzing AegiSKADA's activity. Since nobody in the docking bay was looking up, the ooze might or might not have been a workspace artifact.

The drone that attacked Iridian had probably gotten trapped outside the station. According to her tracker, the others were converging on Transorbital Voyages' mercenaries.

The intruders' armor reflected the docking bay's industrial overhead lights and glowed dimly on its own. The armor appeared well-maintained and thick enough to stop any particle beam or blade. They held their weapons ready but not pointed at anyone. They kept shifting in a loose formation to scan the fugee camp through dark helmet faceplates.

And she was making so little progress because Pel was *talking* to them. Talking to everybody who came within range was self-rewarding to him, somehow. He'd been on his way out of the docking bay when they'd stopped him. He could have run.

But how un-Pel-like it would be to run before being *clever*. "Hey, what am I going to do? I don't even know what you look like." The gray respirator mask muffled his voice and made it difficult to parse out of the murmuring refugees around him. It was considerate of him to keep wearing it, so he wouldn't spread AegiSKADA's custom plague to the refugees, but she wanted to know what he was saying. Suhaila's redheaded partner stood right behind him. Adda sifted through available audio until she found the fugee news feed.

"What are you in a hurry to go for, then?" asked the mercenary who seemed to be leading the rest. Volume and clarity improved now that the audio came from a mic hidden somewhere on the WFUG tech's person.

Everyone jumped and turned toward the entrance barrier as something large crashed and broke. "It's dangerous out there, and you're naked as a new babe," the mercenary continued.

"My sister's out there." Pel's voice cracked on the second syllable, and he bent over, coughing. "Got to . . . get to her."

"Whoa, you're sick?" A mercenary took a big step back from him, sending several refugees scrambling out of his way.

A lot of cams tracked Pel, even ones that just roved back and forth when he walked out of range. She couldn't control them all yet. AegiSKADA was watching him of its own accord. There wasn't any obvious reason for it to follow one blind intruder with such attentiveness, when there were so many other dangerous, unapproved people onboard doing all kinds of potentially threatening things. It lacked supervision and it was oversensitive to weapons, but it was reasoning as its designers intended. It had to have singled out Pel for some purpose.

"Now, you can't help your sister like that." The leader spoke louder than necessary for his proximity, like Pel heard as well as he saw. "Stay here and shut up, would you?"

"Sir, we don't want to get sick," another mercenary said.

In the black-walled workspace room, Adda stepped away from the reproduction of the refugee camp. The air shimmered into a list of sensor readouts. Against her fingers they thrummed hot for atmo, tingling for power usage, and a few others were too foreign or abstract to assign tactile feedback to.

She focused her intent. Far away, the fan in her generator clicked on. Threads of sensor data shook apart from one another, leaving only the one she chose. The process itself wasn't showing up in her workspace, although it was running somewhere.

Red lights and the contaminant alarms she activated lit the tarp-covered hovels in the docking bay. Adda willed the sound away and concentrated on getting through to the voice of WFUG. Debris and broken lines kept blocking her signal. AegiSKADA's intensive use of the same system and a rough firewall slowed her, but she pushed through.

Eventually, Suhaila's voice said, "Captain Sloane? Is that alarm your idea? It isn't heavy-metal contamination. We moved that out of here the first year."

Adda glanced over her shoulder, where the docking bay cam compilation reassembled in the air. The mercs were demanding an explanation of the alarm from clueless refugees. The boy Pel had danced with the night of the wake caught his hand. Heads ducked and temples touching, they headed for the exit.

"False alarm," she said. Suhaila started to ask something else, but Adda talked over her. "If you can scare the mercs out without scaring the rest of your people out too . . ."

"Maybe. Gotta go." Suhaila disconnected.

Adda had spent her whole life observing Pel at a distance. He loved to be near her, but he didn't stay anywhere long. Even though she was watching him closer than she had for months, she was still watching from a distance, trying to get him out of whatever he'd gotten himself into.

Now he paused facing an unbroken wall node outside the docking bay, in one of the station corridors. The perspective was only half a meter above his head. His friend wasn't on cam, but human movement traveled along the path the pirates had taken to the refugee bay.

"Thanks for the distraction, Sissy." Though Pel's hood shadowed his face, he wore none of his collection of glasses or goggles. White scar tissue glinted in the low light, before he started coughing and the hood fell lower.

Scar tissue. Extra material, built up beyond its initial purpose. Like the extra information that followed Pel around the station. She skimmed drones' projected positions to confirm that none were near humans, then constructed a process to summarize tracking data on Pel.

He moved slowly and he never carried a weapon into the station. He should have been one of the least threatening people onboard. If any intelligence should pay him extra attention, it should be HarborMaster. It'd need an accessibility package to care for Spacelink workers' families, and it might've registered Pel's visual impairment when he entered the station.

"Sissy, are you still spying on me?" The sensor node closest to Pel was now the one on the wall right behind his head. He stood at a first-floor intersection Adda had never seen before. Signs pointed toward waste disposal and water management, with additional arrows toward an elevator to residential habitats.

He coughed again, the deep, lung-wrenching sound of AegiSKADA's custom plague. "If you can see me, could you give me a hint on which way to go? Gilad sent me down this hall, but it's not the one I thought it was."

The station map faded into focus on the workspace walls, ceiling, and floor. He'd made good time out of the refugee camp . . . in the wrong direction. She willed a blue trail into being, showing his best route back to the pirate compound.

Now, how to signal to him? He stood with one hand on the wall, talking intermittently. "I hope you can hear me. There's no safe place on the station, but some places have trailing live wires. Those kinda scare me."

HarborMaster controlled the lights and speaker system, and she still hadn't found a way into it despite the fact that AegiSKADA definitely had. She couldn't tell him where he should go, so she'd tell him where he shouldn't. The emergency bulkhead across the intersection from him slammed as she fed sensors data indicating a nearby explosive decompression.

Pel spun toward the intersection's other wrong direction, which she blocked off as well. "Is that you?"

Adda had forgotten all about her own comp communication. She should have been talking to him that way the whole time. Too much time looking at the station from AegiSKADA's viewpoint was affecting her thought patterns. Her own viewpoint was valuable too. She dropped out of the workspace to physically activate her comp mic. "Yes, Pel, I hear you, it's me," she said.

"Oh, thank gods."

"I'm going to lead you out, but it's really hard to talk while I'm in the workspace. I'll close off the pathways it's not safe for you to follow, and you can follow the open hallways all the way back. Got it?"

"Yeah, okay! I think I can do that."

Adda drifted back into her workspace. Thinking of the comp set its missed contact alert flashing in both his position and Iridian's probable position. Gods, she hated to be rushed, and no drones were active near Iridian. Before she did anything else, she wanted Pel back in the compound. Still, Iridian was in danger too. "What?" she said into the comp's open mic, to eliminate the missed contact alerts. The workspace presented the mic as an ankle bone suspended in midair.

"Are you listening to Fugee News?" Iridian asked. "They're talking about a broadcast they intercepted from some reporters who set up a buoy relay through the lead cloud."

Adda had more important things to think about, especially since she had no access to the relay herself. "So?"

"So," Iridian dragged the word out in exasperation, "they're reporting live on a mercenary deployment. Fugee News is streaming their transmission. Some whistleblower in Transorbital Voyages leaked the deployment information, and—"

"They're reporting on Barbary Station?" Adda wavered on her hallucinographic feet. The workspace flickered around her.

"Yeah, what else would they be doing out here?" Iridian said.

"Shit." Adda scanned her readouts and the rising activity levels. "When?"

"The special bulletin on Fugee News just started."

"*When to the second,* damn it? AegiSKADA's going to overhear all that, and I don't know what it'll do!" If AegiSKADA classified the journalists as reinforcements to the existing invasion force, any incoming messages from them would look like a threat it should stop. It might even find a way to disrupt the buoy network they'd created through the lead cloud. Adda began coughing and muted her mic.

"About ten seconds before I started talking to you. What the hell can AegiSKADA do about—" Iridian's voice cut off. Pel's nervous background chatter ceased.

"Iri!"

She didn't respond. Adda sent the fake decompression input to a sensor node near Pel. The nearby emergency bulkheads stayed open. AegiSKADA's network activity appeared in the air. A prominent spike coincided with Iridian's interrupted message. AegiSKADA had silenced the journalists, and the entirety of the station along with them. Adda's mind dropped her out of the workspace with a speed that made her head spin.

She was hyperventilating. Combined with her congestion, it felt like drowning. The push lights on the wall pulsed with her heartbeat, though long clawed fingers reached to cover them up. Panicking and wheezing, she dosed herself and returned to the workspace.

The map, including composite sensor data on Pel and Iridian, spread across the walls and ceiling of the square room her mind created. AegiSKADA wouldn't deafen itself to silence the journalists, so the sensor data was all still available. But neither Pel nor Iridian responded when she called their names over her comp.

Her lungs strained taut without dragging in enough oxygen. That slammed her out of the workspace again. She stumbled to the tank's ladder, past the grasping fingers reaching over the lights. Her palms slid on the rungs until she clenched her hands as hard as her chest clenched around her lungs that would not work.

In the hallway, another coughing fit left her on her knees on the cold floor. Nobody stood outside the kitchen, so this wasn't the period in which all three ZV shifts were awake at once. She started the long crawl toward the main room. After two choked attempts, she managed to wheeze Zikri's name louder than a whisper.

Footsteps pounded the floor from the direction of the main room. The medic skidded as he stopped himself by grabbing the corner where the hallway met the main room's wall. He threw an inhaler at her and watched her pick it up and breathe from it. The second she drew a full breath, he said, "Give me that back when you take three deep breaths in a row. We're hacking together a ventilator." He ran off.

After Adda took her requisite breaths, she got moving again.

Coughing and miserable pirates filled the main room. They hunched over the workbenches and followed measurements and assembly instructions Zikri read off his comp. He closed his fingers over her inhaler without looking up from the projection. If he was still sick, he'd thoroughly medicated his symptoms.

Tritheist lay on his side on the computer room floor, beside the printer. The wall displayed a map and an inventory of medical supplies. "What do you want?" he croaked.

"I need to check the comm ports." Adda's trackers showed AegiSKADA directing its drones despite everyone else's inability to receive messages. By blocking ports set aside for message software, it had stopped communication traffic without the loss looking like a malfunction to HarborMaster, which probably maintained connectivity as part of the station environment. But it had to be using an open port for the drones. The pirates could use it too, if they could find it.

"No point checking anything." The lieutenant inhaled to say something else and coughed, deep and wrenching. He laid his forehead on one arm, both hands clenched into fists. "Anything that even looks like comp message traffic is blocked."

There was always a point in confirming facts, and Adda despised the idea of this man claiming authority over her without accepting that. She leaned on the doorway, subvocalizing to her comp ping each port without her having to watch it.

After a few moments, Tritheist asked, "Where's your brother?"

Now that the port tester was active, that was what she was looking up. Pel was in a dead zone where the sensors had been destroyed. "On his way back. I can't talk to him while AegiSKADA is blocking the communication ports."

"Dead," said Tritheist. "Condolences."

"He's *fine*."

"Think what you like." Tritheist's breath rattled on his inhalation. "Good news is, you're next of kin. You get his share. Captain felt sorry for him. It's a bigger share than the fucker deserved." This time blood spattered his lips when he coughed. "Though we've got water for two days and meds for less, so I wouldn't bet on spending it." Tritheist gagged and coughed, his fist pounding the floor in pain.

Adda leaned out the doorway and shouted, "Zikri?" He didn't come. She stared at the lieutenant, searching for something she could do to help. She really, truly disliked him, but she didn't want to watch him die.

Before she thought of anything helpful to do, his breathing quieted. Since his death no longer looked imminent, she said, "I'm going back to my workspace."

"Pel already made enough to set you and your woman up for years." Tritheist rolled onto his back to glare at her, chest heaving, lips pulled back from his teeth in a bloody grimace. "You let him rest in peace and concentrate on the AI, you can have part of my share too. If you get us out of here." It sounded less like a threat than a prayer.

The overhead light flickered and died.

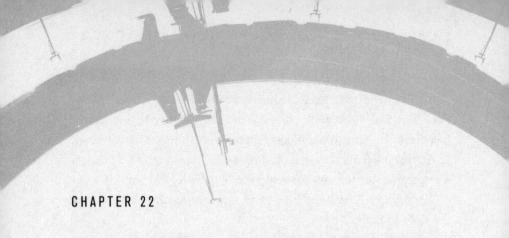

CHAPTER 22

Charges Accrued: Destruction of Property

Si Po looked horrible, but he still had a chance. Iridian repeated that in her head during the long walk between the power plant and the probable location of AegiSKADA's control room. She talked him through the steps of vacuuming puke out of his helmet, lifted him off the hull, called his name when he wandered in the wrong direction.

The last was most frequent. Whenever he caught her walking near the sample container, he said, "Back off, Nassir. Let me do one gods-damned thing right," and swerved away.

They'd both turned off the sound on their radiation alarms. Now he ignored his comp entirely. According to the meter that sporadically flickered to life in her HUD, she'd absorbed a gray and a half. The HUD reporting in grays meant she'd caught enough rads to matter, though not enough to kill her yet. She refused to estimate how many grays Si Po had absorbed. She also refused to give up on him.

Adda and Fugee News had been quiet for almost an hour. At

first Iridian had panicked, imagining all the things that could've gone wrong at the base. The tops of its tacked-on rooms still cast shadows among the antennas above them, across the station's inner ring and half hidden by the hub. They hadn't blown up or collapsed. The AI had caused the comms blackout, though. That had to be the conclusion Adda was coming to, before her feed went out.

To beat back the silence, Iridian said, "Someone told me *Casey Mire Mire* isn't her real name. I thought the pilot named her, but now I'm guessing that was you?"

Si Po's laughter wheezed in her ears. "She picked it. Creepy, right?" Iridian nodded. It really was. "The other two had names when we found them, but the *Casey* was VS491-121. After we woke her up, she got one of her rovers to paint *Casey Mire Mire* on her flank. Like that Lunawood vid series. No idea why she chose that, but she brought us all the episodes and she made sure I saw the name on cam. Never answered to the designation again." Not just volition, but preference. Adda would love that. Iridian would have nightmares.

The drone tracker Adda made lit up and pinged halfway to the security control room. "Trouble incoming," Iridian said. Si Po trudged on like he hadn't heard her.

This drone didn't launch anything explosive, and that scared her. It hovered well out of range of anything she could throw. The mine field was behind them, answering her earlier question about whether the whole hull was mined. Everything around here was metal, and it'd conduct a drone's electrical discharge right into her suit. The armor she'd worn to repair the base hadn't been sufficiently insulated to protect her. Si Po only wore an enviro suit.

A few meters away, a satellite dish, useless since the Battle of Waypoint Station thanks to the lead cloud, rose from the otherwise metallic hull. It'd have a lot of plastic components. "Hang on to that handle, Si Po, we've got to move."

"I . . ." If he said anything more, she couldn't hear it.

She hoisted Si Po—O_2 tank, sample case, and all—on the shoulder not holding her own O_2. The plastic components in the satellite dish's base and exterior might just be enough to protect Si Po from the electricity this drone had hit Iridian with the last time she was on the station's surface. She just had to get him into the dish before the drone struck. She shifted his weight, ignored his miserable moan, and ran for the dish.

The rim of the dish was less than a meter away when a shock tore through her heel and up her leg. Her comp glove flashed white. She heaved Si Po over into the dish, then leaped over herself. Both of them slid down to the dish's center, which was too small for two people and that much gear. She lay still beside him, staring at the sweep of stars around the solid frame of her transparent shield and sucking plastic-tasting water from her armor's reservoir.

"How are you doing?" she asked. She drew a few more labored breaths in the silence, then turned her helmeted head toward him. Centimeter by centimeter, he shoved the carrying case away from her. "Don't worry about that," she said. "We won't—"

The drone floated silently over the dish. The composite plastic surface beneath her made for good footing. Iridian rolled forward through a low crouch to lunge up the side of the dish and swipe at the drone with her shield. The edge connected, though it wasn't a solid blow. She wanted to smash whatever passed for its head.

It was enough to slam the thing down next to her. She threw herself on the bot before it took off and smashed it over and over against the dish. Its motor shook its whole frame as it tried to get away. A fractured part of the housing scraped the length of her arm and her breath hitched. If it broke through the armor . . . No pressure alarms went off. She kept on smashing until the drone quit moving.

Exhausted, she slid down to the center of the dish. Crushed components skidded soundlessly along with her. "Got it."

Si Po sprawled on his back beside the sample container, panting, skin pallid and dry through the enviro suit faceplate. They hadn't brought spare water, and she'd left base too angry to ask Sturm how well her armor's reclamation system worked.

He breathed faster and shallower. "Hey, take it easy," she said. "We're not far now, and that's the first drone we've seen in a while. Maybe there won't be any more."

"I'm . . . done," he rasped.

"That's fine, I can carry that stuff now." Iridian was speaking too quickly. "You did your good deed for the century, trust me."

"I like it . . . here," he said. "I like . . . the stars."

She slipped an arm under his shoulders. "We can't stay. Once one of those drones knows where we are, more'll come."

He slapped weakly at her arm. His nose bled over his lips. "No. It hurts . . . too . . ." His breathing stopped. His eyes bulged and he looked around like he didn't remember what he was doing there, or why he couldn't inhale.

"No, shit, come on, I don't know how to do CPR in these suits." Military emergency training for nonmedics began with *Move the soldier to survivable environmental conditions.* That wasn't a fucking option.

She tapped at her comp glove through the suit's window to find more useful instructions. The projector didn't project. This was the second time the comp had received a shock courtesy of drones outside the station. She should've listened to Adda's repeated suggestions that she set up subvocalized commands. If

Iridian made it back, she was in for a big *I told you so* eye roll.

The map she remembered put the nearest airlock almost a klick away from the reactor. With luck she might get him there in seven minutes. He'd never last that long.

She lowered him to the satellite dish and gripped his hand hard enough to be transmitted through his suit. Tears pooled at the junction of her helmet and the armor's torso assembly, hot against her throat. "You were great, Si Po," she said over the local channel. "Thank you for doing this for . . . all of us."

He convulsed for a few moments, then lay still.

"Si Po?" His eyes were open wide, staring up past the far side of the station to the stars. Her radiation alarm light switched from yellow to red. Her whole body shook as she let go of his hand. The enviro suit glove shifted a piece of the drone aside when his hand thumped onto the hull.

She hurled the mangled electronics out of the dish, screaming and hating what a pointless use of O_2 that was, hating too that she had to fuck around with O_2 consumption in a world so advanced it produced machines like the one that'd almost killed her. It'd wasted so much of their time that Si Po didn't have a chance.

When the Shieldrunner next to you went down, you spread your shields wider to fill the hole, because they fell with a job to do. She couldn't carry both O_2 tanks and the cooling liquid salt sample. She left his tank, picked up the sample container, and hauled herself up the satellite dish's sloping side.

She came up facing the pirate base. Smoke or atmo spewed from one module, down toward Iridian from her perspective. She dropped over the side of the dish and took a few steps toward the base before she stopped herself. Even with emergency management plans, a leak so bad she saw it from klicks away would have consequences.

All those people, so focused on AegiSKADA and its damned biological weaponry, so busy fighting to breathe. It wasn't fair that their home was coming apart too. "You *idiot*," she muttered to herself. "Why didn't you tell Sturm the duct system was in such bad shape?" She'd noted the poor air flow and broken fans while she was searching the base for AegiSKADA's microbe dispensers.

Instead, she'd gotten angry at AegiSKADA. Now the whole damned crew was vulnerable to an enviro control failure that'd kill them as dead as a drone-launched explosive would. Sturm was too old to take on the AI, but he wasn't too old to keep the enviro healthy. If she'd taken five seconds then to say, "Sturm, check the air flow, it's shit," he could've repaired them, or printed more powerful fans. Probably. If nothing else had gone wrong, and if he were still healthy himself.

She could never undo that mistake, like she could never find the argument to convince Si Po to share the radiation exposure. Letting regret paralyze her would be yet another mistake. She turned her back on the base and walked toward the security control room.

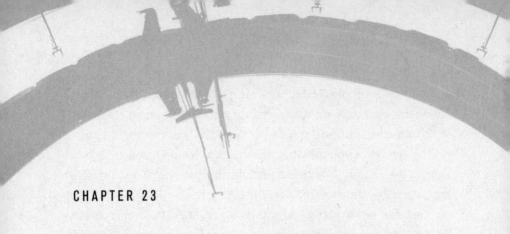

CHAPTER 23

Charges Accrued: Child Endangerment

Just sitting and breathing felt almost impossible, but when Pel's hoarse voice rose in the pirate compound's main room, Adda crawled out of the computer room to reach him. Chemical lights shone pale green and blue from the worktables, enough to keep people from running into things. Zikri, Chef, and Tabs still stood, by force of will. The rest of the group was on their backs in various sections of the compound.

"What's up with the kitchen? There are way too many greasy packaged rations stinking up the air in here," Pel said once he peeled himself out of Adda's awkward embrace, then Tabs's, while Adda ceased coughing.

"Atmo leak," Tabs said. "We had to close it off." It was the nearest room to the bunkhouse AegiSKADA had destroyed. Some destabilization was to be expected. The next nearest was her water tank, but there was nowhere to move her generator to, so she saw no point in worrying about it.

Just minutes after Pel's arrival, banging from the entryway

hatch made everyone look in that direction. Tabs, palmer in hand and comp projector lighting her way, waved the others back. "Let me get that."

When she opened the door, Sergeant Natani and a second female ZV, Nitro, spilled through. "Get them up, let's go, let's go!" Natani called toward the wall passage.

Two strangers climbed through, followed by Grandpa Death, who coughed wetly. He threw two boxes of bioprinter material and a machine Adda didn't recognize through the hatch, then hauled himself through and slammed it shut. According to Iridian, those were all the crew members who would be returning to the compound now. Si Po was with her, and the awakened intelligence in the *Charon's Coin* had killed Six.

Zikri appeared to count the new arrivals more than once from beneath his drooping eyelids. "These all the docs you got to come?"

"The other two are dead." Sergeant Natani shoved the male member of the med team into the main room and hauled the woman through behind her, dragging her by the arm.

Zikri watched Grandpa Death and Nitro collect the medical supplies strewn across the entryway floor, beside the locked hatch. "Where's Six?"

"Not coming," said Natani. Zikri started swearing in English and proceeded through Spanish, Chinese, and one or more spacefarer cants.

The female physician wrinkled her nose. "Smells. Also, which of you listens to the sensors?"

Adda wasn't just staring at Dr. Williams with her mouth open because the doctor maintained her clean, dark skin and hair beautifully, even in the station's miserable conditions. How had Dr. Williams found out about Adda's sensor feed? Adda had minimized direct references to it where AegiSKADA might overhear, and she certainly hadn't broadcast it anywhere. If a human could draw conclusions about her sensor monitoring without analytics, then an AI had enough information to create an accurate behavioral model. No wonder AegiSKADA had been able to draw her into the space between the hulls and place her close enough to a bioweapon dispenser to get her infected.

Belatedly, she realized she hadn't replied to the question and raised her hand to wave, then dropped it back to her side because that was a ridiculous way to identify herself. Dr. Williams nodded briskly. "Keep listening."

"Drs. Tiwari and Williams." The male member of the medical team pointed to himself first and Dr. Williams second. "All sick?"

Chef said, "My immune system's tough as hell, but everybody else is."

"Don't jinx yourself," wheezed Grandpa Death.

Each member of the medical team had brought a sack of supplies, medical printer material, and specialty components from their own printer. Tritheist, Captain Sloane, and Major O.D. were all too sick to oversee the proceedings. Sergeant Natani stood against one wall of the entryway, staring at the blank wall opposite her. Unlike the other ZVs who had gone with Iridian, she still wore all her armor.

Adda sat against the main room's wall and croaked, "Let me know what you need, if you need it." Both doctors eyed her the way they might a talking spider with an extra leg. The image set her quietly giggling until coughing made laughter unfeasible. When was the last time she had really slept?

The ZVs who weren't staring at nothing followed the doctors from room to room. Eventually the physicians met in the main one. "Virus," said Dr. Williams.

"I'm fairly certain it's bacterial," Adda said.

The doctor cocked an eyebrow at her. "Solution. Will print. Been designing since you sent imagery. Why we needed *our* printer material."

"Tell us how or you're not doing it," said Sergeant Natani. "We have enough organic printed crap in our atmo already."

"Bacteriophage." Dr. Williams pronounced each syllable slowly and clearly.

"A virus that destroys bacteria," Adda explained to the still-puzzled crew. "But how do you know it will work on what we have?"

"We introduce them." Dr. Tiwari smiled. "The resemblance to *Pseudomonas* is impossible to miss."

"Oh, of course." Adda had to get a handle on her snark. The shadows flickering at the corners of her vision weren't real. She didn't have to take her annoyance at them out on the doctors.

"You introduce," Dr. Williams said to Tiwari, as if oblivious to the sarcasm. "Triage."

"Yes. Ask about blue dust." Dr. Tiwari released the hatch locks and climbed back down the entrance ladder while Dr. Williams joined Zikri in treating the sickest pirates' symptoms. The ZV medic explained the blue radiation-deflecting dust, which was not a cause of their malady but might affect it.

The pirates stood around staring and frowning at Dr. Williams, or coughing and wheezing. "Isn't anyone going with Dr. Tiwari?" asked Adda.

"Chato? Tabs?" Natani glanced between the two. "Who wants to babysit?"

The smallest ZV, Tabs, said, "I'll go, Sergeant. Chato looks dead already."

"Oh, *muchas gracias*," he grumbled, though he smiled tiredly.

A tugging on Adda's sleeve drew her attention to Dr. Williams. A surgical mask now covered most of the doctor's face. "Sick. Come."

"I can't." Adda held up her comp, the projection flashing yellow to indicate several alerts.

The doctor snatched Adda's sleeve with one hand and poked her comp glove arm with an injector just above her wrist, first numbing the area and then forcing something through her skin without breaking it. Adda yelped and tried to pull away, but Dr. Williams's grip brooked no argument.

"Wha was tha?" Adda's tongue got in the way when she spoke. Sergeant Natani smirked, and Adda was suddenly very sorry that Tabs was out of the room.

"Bacteriophage will be slow to print. Slow to work. Your symptoms are severe. You have heard, can solve this the easy way or the hard way?" Dr. Williams smiled, and Natani and Chef laughed.

"Whi' way iz thiz?" Adda asked as Dr. Williams led her to an unoccupied patch of floor in the main room.

"Easy way," said the doctor, which made Zikri laugh, and a couple of the more alert people lying nearby joined him. Well, if she couldn't entertain like Pel, it was good to be funny somehow. A quick scan of the room showed that Pel had gone elsewhere. He was probably tired too.

It was time to settle in for whatever unpleasantness occurred when the drug Dr. Williams had injected started interacting with Adda's homemade concentration concoction. Her eyelids kept sliding closed. "Somebuzzy wash thiz." She let the back of her head thump on the floor, but waved her comp above her for emphasis. "Ge' the feeg." Her lungs were filling with gunk, and she swallowed so she wouldn't vomit while she coughed.

The room smelled like others had been less conscientious. Dr. Williams slapped a portable O_2 breather the width of three fingers over Adda's nose and mouth and patted her head. Dr. Tiwari came in from the entrance with a pack on his back and Tabs following him. He and Dr. Williams stared at each other, nodded, and moved on to the ZV next to Adda.

Sergeant Natani lowered herself to one knee within arm's reach of Adda. The blank expression on her face was unnerving. Natani was about the last person in the universe Adda would trust with watching her sensor feeds, particularly if the sergeant was in shock or something similar, but Iridian's success was in all the pirates' best interests. Adda had read somewhere that asking someone to do you a favor made them like you more. "Sergeant . . . wash thiz feeg? It'z *impordant*."

Natani stared for a long moment, then held out the hand with her black-and-yellow comp glove. Adda directed the feed to her. The sergeant nodded when her comp made the connection, then sat a few steps away, grimly watching the projection.

That accomplished, Adda raised her voice to interrupt the doctors for clarification on all of their staring. "You subvulcalize through implanz?"

Dr. Williams smiled, Dr. Tiwari nodded, and they both ignored her enormous grin as they returned to their patients. So they shared subvocalization commands on a local comm channel using implants, probably near the base of their throats, to facilitate nearly silent speech without suits. If the implants had their own speakers and didn't rely on earbuds or suit comms, it would look like telepathy. Iridian would love it.

Time lurched. Faces gibbered from the floor by her head. A second or an hour later, Dr. Tiwari said "suit contamination." Iridian crossing the station while her armor infected her . . . Adda's eyes squeezed shut. And Pel gone, lost, how would she ever find him? He laughed, somewhere nearby, she hoped. Either his absence or his presence had to be a hallucination. She'd been using a lot of homemade sharpsheets lately. Time staggered past.

"Shit," said Sergeant Natani. Adda forced open one eye, then the other, to process Natani's distressed frown at the feed Adda had asked her to watch. "Shit, what does this mean?"

The ZV lowered the projection to a couple of centimeters in front of Adda's O_2 breather. Her sensor-riding pattern algorithms highlighted activity in the vicinity of the refugees' docking bay. Heat and movement outside parameters. Unexpected small objects. Weapons outlines that refugees wouldn't have. She'd have to patch into vid records to confirm it. The implications had her fighting off another wave of nausea.

As the feed loaded, temperature, audio, and light sensor readings went wild. "That looks bad," Natani said. Adda nodded her agreement.

A nearby ZV asked, "What is it?" Zikri and the doctors ignored the projection, as did Chef, whom they'd recruited to assist.

Sound and visuals came together in the same second of confusion. The middle and end of an explosion blasted through the comp's speakers. Natani fumbled with her glove to turn down the volume.

"Who is it?" Adda smiled a little at her ability to pronounce the words. Whatever the doctor had given her was wearing off. Wrong question, though. Her smile faded. Nothing in the projection could be a "who" anymore.

Smoke obscured the visuals, so she subvocalized the command to switch to infrared. That was too bright to be helpful. The visual representation of motion and audio combined registered less than she hoped too, until two people rushed into view, screaming.

She pulled back a bit, switched to the vid, and made out both figures through the smoke. One was the refugee who'd asked Adda to fix some things in the camp. The other was a stranger. More voices shouted from a dead sensor zone near the refugees' docking bay. Above them, a drone hovered over a hole in the floor.

Adda's throat tightened, this time not because of infection. She propped herself against the wall to search out the other motion signatures. Iridian's still proceeded slowly toward the security control room. As soon as she identified that Iridian's was present, she switched to a view of the armed intruders so that she didn't draw AegiSKADA's attention to Iridian.

There was something wrong with that conclusion. She took a cautious, deeper breath to clear her head, ready to exhale if the coughing started again. It did, but not before she got enough oxygen to her brain to note that no, AegiSKADA wouldn't know what she was seeing at any given time. Symptom treatment wasn't worth losing her ability to think straight, which she would've told Dr. Williams if she'd had an option.

The larger armed contingent now stood between the refugees' docking bay and the one with the passage to the pirates' compound. They were on the second or third floor of the station, since the first didn't have any wall-mounted turrets like the one they were shooting at. Enviro loss alerts from the area near the explosion appeared on her comp. Using the wall for support, she got to her knees, then her feet.

Natani had been staring into space again, but now she focused on Adda. "What the hell is happening out there?" The question sounded like it was somehow Adda's fault.

"AegiSKADA is going after the refugees," she said. Several pirates groaned. "I'm going into my workspace." Natani watched her inch carefully along the wall toward the tank, then thrust an arm beneath Adda's and around her waist to hold her up. Whatever Dr. Williams had injected her with made it a bit easier to breathe, but walking still made Adda light-headed and dizzy.

On their way out they passed Chato dozing against a wall

beside the door. Natani kicked his boot until he met her gaze. "Watch them." She nodded at the doctors and Zikri. "I want to know what the hell she's up to."

"Yes, ma'am." Chato swiped a hand over his eyes and stood, probably to reduce his chances of falling asleep again.

The sergeant practically dropped Adda down the ladder and descended right after, but Adda had already crossed the tank to her table under her own power. Refugees had died in that blast, and nobody else seemed capable of seeing past their own dripping noses. She had to stop the attack herself.

She shuffled her line of powder into a loose spiral with her measuring packet's edge, watching Natani out of the corner of her eye. With all her conscious attention in a workspace, she'd be physically vulnerable. The temptation to hurt Adda or destroy her equipment might overwhelm whatever self-preservation or order-following instincts the unstable soldier still had.

To get Natani out of the tank, Adda needed to know why she was there in the first place, which was . . . curiosity? "Um. I know you don't like how we've approached the AegiSKADA problem."

"Damned right."

"Well, AegiSKADA is focused on the mercenaries now, but as soon as it finishes with them, it will refocus on us. So once Iridian shuts it down, I have to get control of it, while it's distracted."

Natani frowned, more unhappy than angry. "You got us into this shit by messing with the AI, and now we're supposed to thank you for getting us out. At least you sound like you know what the fuck you're doing."

Adda nodded and waited for Natani to go away. All she'd needed help with was getting to the tank. She certainly didn't need help getting into a workspace. "So, that's why you're helping me?"

Natani's sigh echoed slightly in the tank, hollow and sad.

"We've lost too many people to that fucking AI. It's torn up too many people who are still alive. It has to stop."

"I agree," said Adda. The spiral of powder, an unpleasant gray-blue-brown in the push lights' yellow light, still lay on the table. "I'm going to take this stuff to help me concentrate and then start a virtual workspace where I can interact with the station's sensor network and find out where everyone is." A vast oversimplification of her efforts, but that was the most easily understood part. Natani nodded and made no move to leave.

Well, Adda could indulge the sergeant's curiosity about this as well. The slightly moistened powder still rasped over Adda's nasal tissue as she inhaled it. She'd get nosebleeds soon. That would either drag her out of the workspace, short out her nasal hardware (the least likely), or create more unpleasant imagery. Before she let that distract or dissuade her, she crawled into the workspace generator and plugged in.

The generator dropped her into the middle of a silent conflagration outside the refugee docking bay. She swept aside the smoke and debris, leaving her in a superheated empty hallway. "All right, Jurek. What did you do? What are your gods-damned targeting parameters, and why the explosives?"

The analysis had crunched away while she was gone. It had a good sample of AegiSKADA taking offensive action in response to minor similarities to weaponry. Long rows of printed monochromatic models of various weapons lined industrial shelves. She lifted one item, an old-style projectile rifle. Behind it on the infinitely deep shelf sat more printed copies of the rifle, tilted at every possible angle.

"I knew this," Adda muttered. When she put the rifle back on the shelf, the whole shelving display vanished.

The range of generalization in shape and size, and the

encyclopedic list of weapons, was part of the problem. But Jurek trusted AegiSKADA to make high-level decisions, with weapons that were unconscionable on space-based facilities. If the explosion she had witnessed were a little stronger, or closer to the first floor, it could have created a catastrophic hull breach. That was assuming it was AegiSKADA's work, not the mercenaries', but AegiSKADA had already demonstrated its willingness to blow up parts of the station to reach intruders.

She huffed out an aggravated sigh. The first step in stopping it from attacking the refugees was blinding the sensors. That would stop AegiSKADA from incorrectly labeling handheld objects as weapons, and also limit its targeting capabilities. It'd be hard work to find a delivery method that didn't require sending a signal much farther than she could yell. AegiSKADA had silenced her.

As her subconscious and the workspace interacted, a pattern she had showed interest in previously reemerged. She stood next to a group of Transorbital Voyages mercenaries. The visual display detailed every fleck of blood flying through the air as two mercenaries' helmets exploded from the inside. AegiSKADA used explosives wherever it was impractical to place the larger drones armed with electroshock weaponry.

To avoid attracting spiderbots or encountering mines, the safest route might actually be through the corridors. And to avoid both, one would need to stay near open corridors without actually walking through them.

Adda summoned her largest station map. It appeared with the ideal route from Iridian's last known position already marked in a glowing blue fungal trail, responding to Adda's intent, although not in a method she would've consciously chosen. Her heart rate climbed. *How am I going to get this to Iridian?* Nobody she sent along the path Iridian took would get there in time, assuming AegiSKADA didn't kill them on the way. Comp messaging was down. Her contact with the sensor nodes had been severed.

She recorded the directions verbally, then stared at the waveform visualization of it jittering in the workspace around her. How . . .

She gathered the waveform in her arms, shoving it into her comp's local storage. The water tank seemed much darker than it had been when she entered the workspace, but she crossed it without stumbling much.

Natani was sitting against the wall beside Chato when Adda crossed the main room, but she stood when she saw Adda. "Where are you going now?"

"I need to print something," said Adda. Natani followed her to the room with the computer console and the printer.

The printer had just one pattern for a small comp with speakers, and she almost fidgeted out of her skin waiting for it to finish printing, cooling, and assembling the parts. She had to spend another fifteen minutes with Sturm in his workroom adjusting it until it worked well enough for her to install software. Between the doctors' activity and everyone else's exhaustion and illness, only Natani seemed to care what Adda did.

In the docking bay, with Natani a few steps away resolutely watching for drones, Adda set the newly printed comp down near but not too near one of the landing pads, transferred the recording, and hit play. Her own voice, tinny but audible, started the first repetition. "*Casey Mire Mire*, *Charon's Coin*, and *Apparition*. It's in all our best interest that you get this message to Iridian Nassir, the woman who came to the station with me. Iridian: the safest way is through the rooms parallel to the main corridors. Break down the walls if you have to."

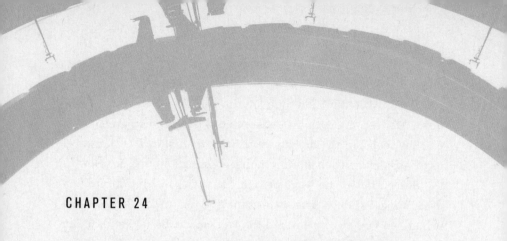

CHAPTER 24

Charges Accrued: Hiding, Protecting, or Directing Prohibited Artificial Intelligence

Iridian inflicted an electrolyte solution on her disinterested stomach using her helmet's nutrient dispenser. At least that functioned, or she'd dehydrate before she reached the damned security control room. Blowing up half a mine field and tackling killer robots worked up a sweat.

The pirates called the shuttle terminal at forty-six ticks north a blind spot where nobody'd been attacked and AegiSKADA's sensors didn't reach. Si Po had called it that, actually. She ran toward it as fast as she could manage, while still watching for mines on the hull. Running helped her focus on the present. This was no time to mourn.

Among the trash generated in the disassembly of the *Prosperity Dawn*, the central shuttle terminal in the hub was relatively intact. Pressurization was too much to hope for. Leaning over the edge of the inner ring to confirm her position, she found herself almost on top of the terminal's passthrough where it stuck out from the station. Its eye-grabbing chipped yellow paint still met regulation standards for passthroughs between vehicles and stations.

She might be able to climb onto it, but unless she could open it, she was fucked. Adda might figure out where she was, but she had other problems, like continuing to breathe. Each clank of the emptying O_2 tank against Iridian's armored hip rattled through her brain.

Her map marked roof accesses for the third floor as a blue icon near her own red one. Hauling radioactive material around with her should cause an automatic lockout, but she had to try anyway.

When she reached the roof airlock, she held her comp to its reader and tapped out the signal Adda had opened the previous airlock with.

The outer door hissed open without a single warning or notification of, say, radiation levels.

Iridian stared at the doorway for a second. "Those cheap corporate shits." Though she couldn't complain much. Just now, their cheapness worked in her favor.

She stepped inside and hit the icon to pressurize the airlock. Security policies might reasonably forgo ID checks at maintenance airlocks. HarborMaster and AegiSKADA would both be alerted when anybody used one. Besides, all but the most soulless organizations allowed humans in from the cold and the black.

But a Geiger counter, this near the power plant? That was common fucking sense. Without that, she resigned herself for a long wait before finding a decontamination chamber. That was a shame, because her armor was a radioactive mess.

The interior door opened and she darted out, scanning visually for drones even though Adda's tracker would pick them up. The pressurized airlock didn't vent atmo violently into the hangar beyond, so she risked closing her O_2 valve and opening her faceplate. She'd hate to run out of air before she got back to Adda.

The hallways here were better labeled and less dilapidated than the ones she'd traversed to reach the med team. After two detours to avoid drones Adda's tracker had detected, she reached the shuttle terminal. A plain industrial display in black and white confirmed that one of the station's shuttles was docked at the hub in the center of the ring.

She followed instructions to summon it, then put the sample case in front of the shuttle passthrough's thick double doors and took several long steps back. Unlike the pirate ships, these little crafts wouldn't have AI of their own. Either HarborMaster ran them, or they operated on a very simple preconstructed program. Even better, Adda's drone alarm was silent. Iridian could probably sit on one of the metal benches built into the wall without getting zapped.

Her stomach churned whether she was moving or not. Juggling the O_2 tank and the sample container made the nausea harder to bear. *I should've asked Pel how long those D-MOG tablets last.*

Adda's drone finder flashed, this time from her comp and not the faceplate. On, off, once per second. Either there was more than one drone nearby, or the alert communication created for her suit's HUD was not working as expected on her comp. She shook her head to make herself stop staring and search for the threat. Nothing moved among the racks of stacked exterior and interior repair supplies across the small terminal from the benches. That didn't make her safe. Spiderbots used cover.

She returned to the terminal door and took her shield off her back. For now, she left it collapsed. Fast movement might attract drones. That was another thing about bots, and all strengths of

AI: they followed implacable rules. They didn't hesitate. You could predict their actions if you knew the rules they operated under. If you didn't . . .

The upper half of a drone chassis rose between two industrial-size bottles of rust remover. It was one of the bigger ones, like the first she'd seen on the surface while repairing the base. Now Iridian snapped the shield up. The passthrough display showed the shuttle over halfway to her. And it was a shuttle passthrough, which meant it was built onto the station, not onto the vehicle the way a ship's passthrough would be. The shuttle would still have to match the station's spin and link up to the station's passthrough before she could board. Then she'd be in an AI blind spot. She could hardly fucking wait.

A projectile slammed into her shield simultaneous with a loud pop from one of the shield's weakening panels. The impact rocked her back into a more solid stance. She caught the second one without putting as much stress on her sore wrists. She braced for an explosion.

A ricochet smacked into a thick roll of flooring and bounced away. She couldn't help laughing a little. AegiSKADA's designer was ahead of whoever put the station itself together. Nonlethal bullets immobilized humans without puncturing the hull.

The shuttle tracking display pinged and the double doors swished apart behind her. She backed into the passthrough with the O_2 tank under her arm and most of her body covered by the shield. As she crouched to grab the nuclear material container, another shot pounded her shin. The armor bounced the bullet into a corner, but she'd check that armor panel for cracks before going outside again. Those bullets might be nonlethal, but they'd leave a hell of a bruise on unprotected flesh.

She stayed braced until the shuttle's double doors closed.

"Shit." The deployed shield's edge thumped the deck as she pounded the second of two destinations on the shuttle controls. "Please choose a stability station. The shuttle is departing," said a disembodied, ungendered voice from an overhead speaker.

Iridian activated the magnetic locks on her boots and ignored the shuttle's rows of passenger strap-down stations. The small, rectangular craft had places for only six people, three along each bulkhead, or fewer if they wanted to secure their gear instead of holding it. The shuttle jolted into motion and she staggered, but kept her balance. Once it cleared the station's passthrough, she gripped the top edge of the door and braced with both feet. The little vessel surged in a massive engine burn, visible only in bluish-white cones above and below the door. The shuttle rose and accelerated out of Barbary Station's spin.

"Please choose a stability station."

She collapsed her shield and hung it on her back so she could grip the O_2 tank and the sample container. Dwindling grav as the shuttle freed itself from the station did no favors for her stomach. Why radiation poisoning hit there first when she hadn't even swallowed the stuff was a mystery. She'd seen enough rad safety vids to know better than to look the reason up when she already felt queasy, even if her comp could access the *Casey Mire Mire's* Internet snap.

Instead she scanned the bulkheads, overhead, and deck for sensor nodes. Aside from the working projectors and strap-down stations, the shuttle's tiny cabin was empty. The shuttle's projections of views from exterior cams on all six sides made for an entertaining trip, short as it'd be. And her O_2 tank, sample container, and armor were about to be a lot lighter.

The shipbreakers maintained admirable scrap collection procedures, because almost no debris floated in the shuttle interior.

One small piece spiraled across her field of vision, black and . . . on legs.

She leaped backward, too hard for the rapidly shifting g's, and slammed into the far bulkhead. That thing moved too mechanically to be an insect.

Clicking near her head made her jerk away toward the door. Now that she was looking, one or two crawling drones skittered over every bulkhead beneath the projected starscape. There were no sensor nodes, but the pirates who'd said AegiSKADA was blind here were completely wrong.

Little legs wiggled as spiderbots drifted away from the bulkheads. Iridian's boots left the deck. She smashed one of the critters between her foot and a bulkhead, and another between a bulkhead and the sample container. Others still floated nearby.

One crawled over her O_2 tank and latched on near the valve. "Oh, hell no." She brushed the bot off before smashing it, then froze. It could've blown up in her face. One drifted toward her eye. She snapped her faceplate closed. The little drone scrabbled at the smooth plastic. *Well, the last one didn't blow up.* She crushed it in her fist.

None of the little bastards had set off Adda's drone alarm. Iridian had no idea how many were in the shuttle with her.

The central shuttle hub hung still as the station spun around it. Several large pieces had broken off and drifted away. "My luck, the head will be gone." It'd been a while since she'd found a safe place to armor off. She disliked the idea of inserting a catheter she didn't take out of the package herself, and of testing an unproven water reclamation system.

Opening her suit while spiderbots floated around with her also sounded nasty. She kept herself moving despite the roiling effect on her gut. The little bots' propulsion relied on their feet having a solid grip on something, and they seemed to be waiting for that solid grip before they exploded. In motion, they'd have a tougher time making that something her. Had AegiSKADA calculated the probability that without atmo, blowing a hole in armor was as deadly as blowing a hole in a skull? She had to get out of the shuttle before the AI refined its tactics.

As the shuttle affixed itself to the hub's passthrough and the shuttle and passthrough doors slid open, the cabin filled with fist-size explosions as multiple drones self-destructed at once.

She tumbled through the doors. Momentum carried her along the length of the terminal. One of the spiderbots detonated against the connecting mechanism between the shuttle and the hub, blasting the whole shuttle half a meter off the hub's passthrough. The shuttle spun away from the hub, propelled by explosions and escaping atmo. The hub doors shut out a flicker of orange light as something in the shuttle tried to catch fire in the dwindling O_2.

Fuck if Iridian hadn't come as near to getting blown up on Barbary Station as she had in her last six months as a Shieldrunner. When her shoulder, elbow, and hip thumped into the shuttle door on the far side of the hub's terminal, she hooked her feet through a couple of handholds there and let herself drift while she caught her breath. Her hands shook against the armored gloves.

The hub terminal seemed eerily normal and calm after the trip to get there. Like most hubs, two tunnels intersected in a small square lobby. Strap-in pads on the bulkheads kept people still as they waited for their rides, or for their opportunity to exit to the scaffolding around a trashed ship. Passengers should've glided around here and in the shuttle without suits, but enviro management was off now. Temp was too cold, and it was depressurized. *So much for the head.*

If AegiSKADA really did have a limited number of drones,

it'd used up a hell of a lot of them in that shuttle. There might be fewer drones on the other side. With no humans on that side, what would AegiSKADA have to shoot at? Although if it'd been tracking her, it might've made a predictive model of where she'd go. It would've sent something the long way around to intercept her. Through the refugee docking bay.

Her stomach quit cooperating, and she had to test her helmet's vacuuming function. She'd seldom been so thankful for her shaved scalp.

The shuttle would stay at one side for a preset amount of time to give folks entering and leaving the hub time to do so, then move on. Something had happened to the exterior cams, or the power. The bulkheads between the four passthrough doors had large blank spaces, but no projectors displayed the cold and the black. She shoved herself across the space and watched for the shuttle indicator to switch to green, since she couldn't see the shuttle coming to take her to the other side of the station. Only one module separated the far side's shuttle hub from AegiSKADA's control room.

In the status display, the passthrough on the far side was yellow rather than white like the one she'd come from. She pulled herself nearer along the bulkhead with her foot, since her hands were full. The display said nothing more.

She clutched a handhold on the bulkhead beside the shuttle doorway. The doors slid open, and she peered through the shuttle's broad cam-fed windows.

The spot on the station where the passthrough should've been swung by. Its docking apparatus was still there, but the passthrough floor, ceiling, and a wall were gone in a massive, burned gouge that widened as it went down two floors of the station, exposing a dimly lit docking bay in vacuum. The elevator shaft was nowhere to be seen.

"Big plasma torch, huh." By now the torch that the med team had told her about would've fallen out of stationspace, on a very slow trip to nowhere. If she'd been in that area like Blackguardly Jack Oarman had when the med team last saw him, she'd have run like hell too.

Still, she had to get over there somehow, and that passthrough was in station grav. She could fall forever once she got off the damned hub, and crawling, exploding robots would fall with her. She backed away from the open doors and went looking for the other shuttle.

The crossways console showed the shuttle she'd just traveled in lit red, like the other shuttle's icon. She edged up to the door and pressed herself against the bulkhead on first one side, then the other. Both shuttles were out of sight.

Spiderbots weren't designed to float. If she had to be trapped in the hub, in a shuttle, or dangling from a wall on the far side, she'd rather stay in the hub. It had more space and stable micrograv. The doors slid closed.

Trapped. That sounded more real the more she thought it. It was too easy to imagine how this would end. She'd stick it out in the hub until hunger, thirst, or fear of AegiSKADA doing something horrendous to the pirates forced her into one of the remaining shuttles. And that'd be the end of her and the shuttle both, more than likely. Iridian swallowed hard.

It was too soon to start composing a farewell message for Adda, when she hadn't even looked the whole hub over yet. An open doorway in a large pillar in the hub's center led to a ladder perpendicular to the main tunnel. She secured the sample carrier to a pad on the bulkheads and picked a direction on the ladder. It opened on cold space after two meters, so she pulled herself along in the other direction instead. This module had more original structure intact, including a com console and a chair with a harness to keep someone from floating out of it.

Vids about stations that lost enviro always included a desiccated corpse in a chair like this one. Those people spent their final moments there because it was easier to maintain enviro in a small, enclosed space. The help they always called for came too late, if it came at all. And they, like Iridian, had a job to do. She strapped herself and her O_2 tank into the seat. Her comp couldn't get through to anybody, but the antenna might not have been blasted off the hub. Maybe she'd even get to talk to Adda.

If I survive, I swear to all gods I'll ask her to marry me. Even though she was pretty sure Adda would say yes, it was still nerve-racking. After all, why hadn't Adda asked her first? There had to be a reason, didn't there?

She set everything to the widest possible range of signals and leaned in to touch her faceplate to the console above the mic. With luck, the local channel in her suit would figure out how to make the hookup. "Adda? If you can hear me . . ." This module must've had speakers at some point. Either the aesthetically pleasing console hid them, or they'd been taken off with the top half of the module when the shipbreaking scaffolding came apart. "If you can hear me, say something on a very broad band with a strong signal."

She waited through a long eight seconds of silence. "Anyone who can hear me, my name's Iridian Nassir and I'm stuck in the shuttle hub. The shuttles are full of exploding spider drones, so if you have another way out, I'd appreciate it." *Another way out?* She turned off the mic and laughed. If anybody on this hab had a way out, they'd have taken it long ago.

She could jump off the hub from the outside, timed *very* precisely to land on the broken passthrough. It'd be a long flight, but she had the O_2 for that.

The problem was landing. She'd have to snag herself on something solid to insert her body into the station's spin, and it'd hit her like a freighter leaving grav. Her armor was good, but not that good, and it was patched in a couple of places. The shuttles' three-minute entry and exit pattern avoided that smashing shift in force.

AegiSKADA would have to send electrocution drones to get to her here. Bots would have the same trouble getting in and out of the station's spin as she would. Maybe one would take the shuttle. The image of a black drone hovering in front of the shuttle passthrough doors, patiently waiting for its ride, made her laugh aloud.

A shadow fell over the console and swept across her. She ducked in case the drone had fired already. When she deployed her shield and searched for the machine, one of the ships hovered above her instead. It dwarfed the shuttle hub. Iridian felt like an ant beneath a boot that was on its way down.

The *Charon's Coin* was a tugboat, basically a small computer with big-ass engines and hullhooks. Even if she hadn't recently seen the *Coin* much closer than she had ever wanted to see it again, tugs had been common at the military stations where Iridian grew up. The ship above her looked nothing like them, and it also lacked the *Apparition*'s missile launchers and hardened thermal fins. That made this the *Casey Mire Mire*, the ship Oarman said was most likely to accept passengers wanting to leave the station.

Of course, Oarman had said that under the logical, blissfully ignorant assumption that the *Casey* had a human pilot. Captain Sloane and Si Po would've awakened the *Casey*'s AI copilot as a desperate attempt to escape AegiSKADA after Foster's team blew themselves up in the security control room. Oarman's outdated intel wasn't worth much now.

Still, Iridian had to get off the hub somehow. Adda was counting on her. "Hey! Hi! Wait one minute." Since Iridian couldn't be
sure the ship picked up her local channel, she raised her hand in
a stop gesture, then held just her index finger up in case either of
those signals meant something to the ship's AI. She unstrapped
herself from the seat and dove for the hub's ladder.

When she came back with the container, the *Casey* still hung
there. Its passthrough door yawned open, tilted sideways to the
one it'd use to let passengers disembark on a hab or another
ship. The whole ship floated at an angle to Barbary Station that a
grav-conscious human would never have approached from.

Iridian had passed extravehicular safety sims during Shieldrunner training, but falling untethered gave her goose bumps.
One mistake and she'd fall until she ran out of O_2 or her water
purifier stopped or a micrometeoroid punched through her suit.
She breathed in, aimed for the center of the open passthrough,
and leaped.

As Iridian sailed through the passthrough door, she caught
movement in her peripheral vision. Something hovered in the
shadow at the back of the passthrough. The hand nearest the
bulkhead wrapped around her O_2 tank. With the one holding
the smaller sample container, she could catch herself against
the closed interior doors. All she could do was twist around to
put her back to the drone. If she were lucky, the collapsed shield
would stop the drone from blowing her up.

She hit the closed doors and turned, releasing the sample
container to slap around the bulkhead for a handhold. She didn't
find one and the container was drifting away, so she grabbed it
again and let herself drift too. A light flickered on and the exterior
door shut. In the improved lighting, the menacing profile solidified into a blocky rover from the hijacking. Its cam lens glinted on

its stalk as the aperture narrowed. It maintained its position at the far end of the ship's passthrough, and it didn't lob explosives at her.

"And now I'm inside an awakened AI," she muttered. "Great."

The passthrough's closed exterior door approached her slowly, which meant the ship was moving away from the shuttle hub while she, floating in micrograv, stayed where she was. The passthrough's exterior door thumped into her hands as the ship accelerated at a surprisingly human-safe speed. The *Apparition* hadn't bothered with that when it brought her, Adda, and Reis back from the hijacked Transorbital Voyages colony ship. An automated pressurization cycle was in progress, according to the passthrough readout by the interior door.

The *Casey* decelerated, dropping Iridian face-first onto the passthrough's interior door. Her armor absorbed the impact, and she heard it clank against the metal door. The suit sensors reported a healthy enviro in the passthrough. When the ship stilled and grav faded away again, the inner door opened. A few pieces of detritus gusted past Iridian as she floated into the ship.

The *Casey*'s main cabin was big enough that one of the station's shuttles would fit inside with room to spare, lengthwise at least. A sleek, backlit bridge console cast light from the left. A tank rack was secured to the bulkhead across from the passthrough, and a couple of doors in the right bulkhead were closed. Iridian gripped a handhold by the passthrough and slapped the cabin light panel. The ship's sunlight sim lit the cabin like early morning or late evening on Earth. Purple-tinged light glowed from the seams where bulkheads met deck and overhead.

The pseudo-organic solution in the ship's scum-encrusted tanks was thicker than looked healthy. The culture was circulating, not too opaque, and the normal shade of pinkish gray. The colored lighting designed to make the tanks more decorative than alien were off or burned out. The culture needed the same atmo as a human, so that explained the cabin's healthy enviro.

She shut off the O_2 pump and gently released the O_2 tank and container without giving either of them enough momentum to drift away from her. Now that she had her hands free again, she unsealed her helmet. The dry air was around five Celsius, faintly acrid from the poorly maintained pseudo-organics, but breathable.

It was suddenly vitally important that she dig the D-MOG tablets out of her suit, *now*. She resisted the impulse to take more than one. This was a bad time to risk an overdose.

"Hello." The voice was agender, slightly digitized, and practically on top of her.

Iridian whirled and tangled herself in the O_2 tank's hose. The tank thumped the back of her newly bared head. The rover, its cam still trained on her, darted in from the passthrough before the interior doors closed and used short bursts of its air jets to stop itself in the center of the cabin, about a meter off the deck.

"Damn." She rubbed the sore spot on her head. That rover had speakers, which it'd used to transmit Tritheist's recorded warning during the *Prosperity Dawn* hijacking. Now it was speaking for something else. "Hi to you, too . . . *Casey?*" Si Po had talked to the ships all the time, but he never said anything about them talking back. She could still be carrying on a conversation with recorded messages. In fact, that was the best-case scenario.

A projector on the pseudo-organic rack clicked on to project a window on the bulkhead by the passthrough. The shuttle she had ridden to get there had apparently docked on the station, because the hub was empty. Another window above the bridge console showed Barbary Station spinning away before unmoving stars. The *Casey* was still relative to both.

The rover puffed little jets of compressed air out of its sides at intervals to remain in place. Iridian activated her magnetic boots and clanked to the floor. "So . . . ," she said. "Are we heading to the other side?"

"No," said the bot. She tensed. "Can you upload AegiSKADA's code?" Aside from the mispronunciation of "SKADA" with "ah" sounds and the uniform space between words, the rover's—the *Casey*'s—voice might've belonged to a genderless human. Because that had to be a sentient response from the AI. No human would fucking record that.

"Um . . . I don't have it." Why the hell would she? She'd wipe AegiSKADA's pseudo-organic tanks when she found them, no matter what Adda said. There was no way she'd let this monster reboot to kill again.

"Can you download it from the supervisory station in the control room?"

"I'd have to get there first." Iridian smiled slightly at the rover, which seemed to act as the *Casey*'s eyes and ears.

"If you comply, I will take you to the shuttle passthrough."

Iridian's eyes rolling might not communicate anything to an AI, but it amused her to do something it was incapable of. "It's still a hell of a drop to where it's supposed to be on the map. If I fall straight through the damned station, then nobody gets what they want. Get me farther in or no deal."

Any recalculation required was over faster than a human breathed. "Climb down Elevator Thirty-One to Floor Two. Go south two hundred meters. Enter the security manager's office. Break through the right wall fifty-five centimeters from the door. Travel parallel to the main corridors to avoid security activation.

Break through the next walls at the same position."

It must have the station mapped to every panel and bolt. "Simple as that, huh?" But it had said . . . "Wait, if I comply with what?"

The rover hovered toward her with a hiss of compressed air. If the thing wanted to interact, she'd prefer to have the ability to get away if she had to. She gathered her various effects. The rover stopped within arm's reach and a panel opened on its back. A datacask the length of her thumb slid out. The design was older, but it was full of healthy-looking brownish-blue pseudo-organic fluid.

Iridian searched for something to do with her armload of crap. Any radioactive material sample container she ever designed would include a shoulder strap. She scooped up the datacask with her helmet and brought it around for more detailed inspection. "So you won't take me across until I promise to download AegiSKADA's code to this?"

"Correct."

The standard human response to an AI's request for clarification, if they got it right. Cute. Awakened AI really did learn fast. "Why haven't you sent a rover to do that?"

"AegiSKADA protects itself with turrets. Rovers lack sufficient armor. If it were installed, they would lack sufficient propulsion. Additionally, rovers can't break through walls."

Iridian glanced down at her armor. "I'm not sure this can take turret fire either." The ship and its rover didn't respond. Which was typical, because all the AI cared about was what Iridian could do for it. "Look, what are you going to *do* with this code? I can't just take your word that—"

Adda's voice, played out of the rover, interrupted her. "*Casey Mire Mire, Charon's Coin,* and *Apparition.* It's in all our best interest that you get this message to Iridian Nassir, the woman who came to the station with me. Iridian: the safest way is through the rooms parallel to the main corridors. Break down the walls if you have to."

Iridian stared at the rover. So this was Adda's idea, not the *Casey*'s. Adda she could trust. And Iridian was going to the control room either way. She didn't have to decide about making or keeping a copy of AegiSKADA now. Once AegiSKADA was out of commission, she wouldn't need the *Casey*. She could walk back to base. "Sure. I'll download a copy."

"Promise?" the rover asked in its original agender voice.

"What?" *Artificial intelligence doesn't understand fucking promises.*

"Promise." This time it sounded like a command.

Hairs rose along her arms and the back of her neck. That was the word she'd used a few minutes ago, and it already had the full context of that very human term. "Yeah, I promise." She'd decide whether she really would later, when a less creepy AI controlled her O_2 and grav.

She gathered up her stuff and stowed the datacask in a compartment of the armor. "Hey, where's the head?"

The rover puffed over to the door on the right. It contained, sure enough, a micro-g toilet and shower. Two sets of wrist binders were bolted to the bulkhead on either side of the door. *What the fuck is the Casey Mire Mire outfitted for?*

The *Casey* started spinning and accelerating to station orientation and grav before Iridian was ready for it. *Thank gods for thorough training.* "En route elimination" drills were apparently not just hazing for recruits. They sure as hell repeated the process more often than necessary, but she kept her balance now, when it would've been messy otherwise.

The ship's interior was all clean, if dusty, white, and warm orange. Except for the wrist binders in the head, it had a comfortable, civilian feel. During the war, something this lightly armed and armored would've made for one nerve-racking trip. Barbary Station was built this far from Earth to break down warships and long-haul supply barges. The *Casey* didn't belong out here.

It took the ship longer to bring itself up to the station's speed than the shuttles took. Iridian put her helmet back on. With the faceplate up and the O_2 valve closed, she could take advantage of the free atmo while she explored. The *Casey* kept a steady spiral through direction changes, allowing Iridian to keep up with the changing location of "down." Next to the head was a bedroom, with a separate processing console like the one in the pirates' computer room.

Once the ship was traveling close enough to the station's spin that grav pulled her toward the deck again, Iridian collected the case and her O_2 tank and waited by the passthrough for the *Casey* to finish matching the station's speed. The rover sat on its wheels in the entryway, still staring at Iridian with its implacable lens.

Something skittered across the rover's back. She caught it in her armored glove and crushed it. The fragments that fell when she opened her fist were metallic, not organic. Those damned spiderbots were all over. "Thanks for the ride."

"Remember your promise," said the *Casey*.

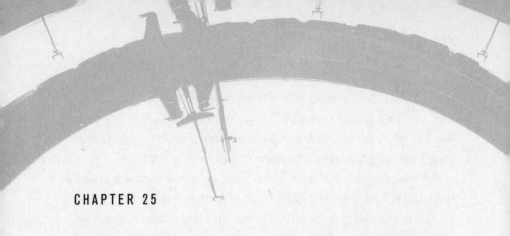

CHAPTER 25

Charges Accrued: Endangerment of Minors

"We're losing him!" Zikri shouted in a tone he must have heard in a drama vid. The two station doctors rushed across the pirate compound's main room to where the ZV medic knelt next to Grandpa Death. The old pirate had collapsed, coughing and gasping for breath, in the middle of the main room.

Adda was breathing well enough to get back to her tank. Patients sprawled on the floor, tripping hazards for the med team scrambling around the dying pirate. They could probably use an extra meter of space to work. She hauled herself down her tank's ladder and applied her concentration concoction. The mushrooms were shriveling, but she didn't want to stop to hydrate them. It was more important to find out what was happening in the rest of the station.

Her brain and the workspace generator slammed together. She staggered in a huge, round room full of movement and voices and far too much information. It might have been a reproduction of a state capitol building she'd visited as a child. AegiSKADA and HarborMaster were activating sensor nodes all over the station. This was the workspace's response to her desire for all the data, now.

Her consciousness tumbled back into her body. At first it felt like instinctual recoil from information overload, but then she registered pounding above her. "Bitch, open this fucking door!"

That sounded like Vick. "What do you want?" The question rasped through her aching throat. She shuffled to the ladder. The trapdoor stayed shut and locked.

"What's taking you so gods-damned long to stop this? We're *dying* here."

Another hard impact on the door made Adda bite down on an exasperated sigh. Theatrics must motivate some people, but they wasted time she didn't have to spare. "I work faster without interruptions. I'm sorry about your friend."

"Fuck him." Vick's volume dropped a few notches. "I don't want to be next. You'd better have some good news when you come out of there, or don't come out at all." Boots thumped away down the hall.

Without her comp's comm systems to call for help, she was going to be in her tank for a long while. Vick was twice her size.

I could fret, or I could do what I came down here to do. This did eliminate distractions, at least until her body required something other than sleep. She crawled back into the workspace generator with one topic in mind, to limit the flow of information. "Pel."

He appeared across a much smaller round room in a blueprint on the first floor of the station, walking with one hand dragging along the wall. "Oh, gods damn you." He must've thought he could still do something to help the fugees, although Adda couldn't imagine what, and of course he hadn't asked her, or anybody else, before he left. He'd reach the refugees' docking bay soon. Although the sensors still tracked him with ease, he was alone.

If AegiSKADA labeled him a threat, he'd die as soon as it

brought drones to bear on him. But it hadn't so far, and since he never carried anything resembling a weapon, she didn't see any reason for it to single him out. It had to have a reason, though. Intelligences always did. She'd keep watching for clues to why it was so interested in Pel while she made sure Iridian, who it actually had identified as a threat, was safe.

She confirmed that her drone trackers would give her plenty of warning, then switched targets. "Iridian."

Iridian was climbing down a rope or cable in an area Adda hadn't seen before. Although the ZVs who'd returned without Iridian had said that Si Po was with her, Iridian appeared to be alone as well. After Iridian and Pel were safe, she'd have to look for Si Po. Adda found Iridian on the station map near the security control room and put the visual feed beside Pel's, overlapping disconcertingly at the edges. *I can't believe the last thing I said to Iri was swearing at her for not being clear.*

Adda had to focus, or she'd lose her grip on the workspace. The nodes around Iridian were spaced widely and randomly due to unrepaired damage. She kept disappearing in expanding concentric circles of noise. The ripples were thick yellow-brown like melted skin, and Adda turned her back to both feeds to fill the opposite rounded wall with pretty much anything else.

Most of the drone activity she mapped onto the wall surrounded the refugee docking bay, where Transorbital Voyages' mercenaries pointed weapons at a crowd of refugees. She shivered. Pel would have to walk through them to get back to the refugee's ship, but it was still a much shorter distance to travel than returning to the pirates' compound at this point. Gods, she hoped AegiSKADA kept classifying him as a nonthreat. None of the accessible menus included the criteria for that status.

The program she would insert after Iridian shut AegiSKADA

down was filling out well. She concentrated on being recognized as the intelligence's administrator upon a hard crash and reboot to concurrence mode. Code swirled before her, clarifying contingencies as they came to her.

It blew away like ashes amid horrified screams. She turned and ran toward the overhead view of the refugees. The image retreated from her along with the wall, and she snapped, "Zoom in!" That only blurred it.

"What happened to his fucking shoulder?" one of the mercenaries demanded of a terrified refugee. Blood spattered the side of the mercenary's helmet. Next to him lay a body missing an arm, half its face, and a large chunk of chest cavity. The body wore blood-soaked cloth, not armor plating. Adda sucked in a horrified breath that rattled around her lungs.

"I don't know!" the frightened refugee shouted back. "That just . . . happens, sometimes! It's the station's security AI."

The mercs swung their weapons and heads around, looking for an attacker. The big drones still lurked in the corridors, according to Adda's map. Pel had a clear path between them to reach the refugees, but two of the drones were near enough to worry about if HarborMaster or AegiSKADA decided to open the emergency bulkheads she'd shut earlier.

A lot of the tiny drones' IDs were scattered throughout the docking bay. *Damn, damn, damn, how long have they been there?* One small drone ID tag was already among the mercenaries, and the rest were coming closer. They stayed near the edges of the tarp and shipping container homes.

The mercenary who seemed to be in charge grabbed a gawking refugee child and pulled her in front of him. Adults shrieked and screamed at him to let the little girl go. Adda couldn't find a good angle to see what he held in his other hand, but she could guess. "Call it off," the mercenary yelled, voice tinged with fear. "Now!"

One refugee spaced her words out for emphasis. "We can't."

A mercenary rushed her. This time Adda saw the serrated blade before he buried it in the woman's throat. Some refugees ran toward the dying woman; others fled to the refugees' colony ship. "Tell us how to find the pirates!" shouted one mercenary. Another swung her weapon from one side of the crowd to the other, firing too rapidly to aim. One of the refugees who fell looked about five years old.

Pel stalked in from the docking bay exit, his feed flashing sickening green as it merged with her existing view. Even from this angle, Adda recognized his deep scowl and the way his shoulders hunched when he was furious.

He fell over rubble near the entrance, but scrambled to his feet fast and put a row of closed shops between him and the mercenaries. With his fingers trailing along the shipping containers, he crossed the docking bay without drawing any of the spiderbots toward him. When he entered the refugees' docked colony ship, Adda's—*AegiSKADA's*—sensors lost him. She couldn't help smiling, despite the chaos among the refugees. Pel was as safe as he could be now that he was inside the docked colony ship and technically off the station.

She tested a hypothesis by backing out of the docking bay sensor nodes cataloging activity near the colony ship's passthrough. The nodes stayed active even when she wasn't using them and nothing dangerous was happening there. HarborMaster, AegiSKADA, or both were obsessed with Pel.

He would feel obligated to help the refugees, somehow. But what could he do alone? If the pirates kept cowering in their leaky fortress, everybody in that docking bay might die. It was time for the crew to get out into the station and join the fight.

Sloane's crew had sent countless surplus supplies to the refugees, used their newsfeed to shape the crew's image, and run to the refugee village when the compound was attacked. Captain Sloane would send the ZV Group out to defend them, assuming the captain understood the situation.

And Adda could explain it, if she could reach the captain without Vick beating her to death. She left her workspace and poked her head out of the generator. *How long was I in?* Vick had upset her and she hadn't set a timer. The wall lights were too dim to blind him, even if she shoved one into his face. The table was too big to carry, and she refused to risk her generator or mixing equipment.

But her ingredients . . . They couldn't stay on the station much longer, with the water running low and drones attacking everywhere. She still had enough in her bloodstream to stay in a workspace for the next few hours. And while she stayed hidden in her water tank, Pel was trapped in the colony ship and the refugees were dying. She ground up her last few drying mushrooms and carried her mortar to the trapdoor. The door's rubbery seal made a shushing sound as it opened.

Vick was standing right beside the ladder. He looked down and met her eyes. She panicked and flung the whole mortar at his unmasked face.

He yowled as the heavy bowl bounced off his forehead. Blueish-brown powder covered his face, coated the inside of his hood, and smeared over his shirt. The mortar shattered on the floor. He reached for the ladder's top rung, but Adda closed the trapdoor and locked it.

"What the fuck was that?" At least the door's seal muffled his voice.

When one first learns to mix and take concentration aids, one makes mistakes. She'd spent many nights controlling overdoses to finish her homework before succumbing to wavy lights and nausea. All she'd had to do to stay calm during an overdose was avoid focusing on negatives. The alternative had been raw, overpowering terror. The experience should be intense enough to get Vick to leave her alone. "Poison," she shouted through the locked door. "And dirt from the floor."

"What—Why would you—You bitch!" Vick pounded on the door some more. He was a big guy, with a compromised respiratory tract. She couldn't tell how much powder he'd inhaled or gotten in his eyes and mouth. It might take seconds or minutes to affect him, if it affected him at all. She hadn't cut it with stimulants. He was focused and energetic enough.

Another man asked, "Vick, what the hell are you doing?"

"She fucking poisoned me, sir!" That would make the first speaker Major O.D. "Whatever she's doing down there, it's not helping us."

O.D. snorted. "That looks like ceiling dust. Don't hurt her for pulling a prank." Adda smiled a bit at the officer's mistake. The part of the mix that she'd thrown at Vick did resemble the blue coating on the ceilings and walls. But why couldn't Major O.D. order Vick to stop threatening her? Adda sighed, exasperated and fearful for Iridian and Pel. This was wasting valuable time.

Vick groaned. "I'm going to Zikri. He'll fix this, and then you're going down."

She stood under the door until the big man's steps faded down the hall, and then she climbed up. He and Zikri were talking in the main room. She'd have to pass them to get to the captain's cabin.

When she entered the main room, most people sat against

the wall instead of lying on the floor. Something the med team had done was working. Vick's eyes were open so wide they could fall out, and Zikri was laughing. "You need to calm down, man. Just sit here and wipe yourself off."

"No . . . no, you don't *understand*." She waited until he focused on the medic, then crossed the room at a quick walk. Vick kept looking between Zikri and his own boots with growing terror. With no built-up resistance, the concentration drug hit Vick's system fast and hard.

Tritheist leaned on the wall outside the captain's door and raised one eyebrow as she approached. "What happened to Vick?"

Adda stood straight and imagined Iridian's face in a bad situation she knew she could handle. "He threatened me. I took care of it. He'll be fine." The explanation didn't include an estimate of *when* he might be fine. Her mixture would wear off someone his size in a matter of hours. He'd have interesting nightmares from now on, though.

"Fair enough," Tritheist said. "What are you doing here?"

"I need to speak to Captain Sloane. Things are coming to a head and we need to take action if we want them to go our way."

"And you know better than the captain what needs doing?" Tritheist smirked.

"I have the most current information. If the captain is serious about getting out of here, we need to act."

"The captain's caring for—"

The door swept open, revealing Captain Sloane. "The whole crew." The captain wore a white hooded jacket unbuttoned low in the front, plain tan pants that fit perfectly, and a massive necklace with a matching bracelet. Adda couldn't maintain that level of style when she was healthy. "Let's adjourn to the computer room. Tritheist, find someone trustworthy for this door. The sergeant, I think." Frowning, the lieutenant headed for the main room.

The captain entered after him with a flourish that spread the white jacket wide. The ZVs who were paying enough attention to notice cheered at the captain's appearance upright and looking confident, if not entirely well. Vick sat against the wall staring at his feet, tears streaming down both cheeks. Adda felt much safer, and more proud of herself than she probably deserved.

The ZVs shouted questions. "What's happening, Captain?" "Is AegiSKADA done for?" "Are you all right, Captain?"

"Later, lads and lasses." Sloane's voice still sounded hoarse. The captain waved, then turned away from the door after Adda came through. "Must keep up morale," said Sloane quietly. "Mine could use encouragement, in all honesty. You have good news?"

"AegiSKADA is draining resources tracking a lot of things at once. For the first time since I've been here, I think an offensive strike would do some actual good."

"Do you." Sloane frowned, for some reason. This should have been the requested good news.

"So Iridian's almost at the core now." She used their dramatic terminology without wincing. Iridian would be proud. *Core. AegiSKADA is not an apple.* And Iridian would laugh. . . . "She's in the same module as it is, in fact."

"Good." The captain's tone suggested more information was desired.

"But AegiSKADA will start drawing forces back in to defend itself once it identifies her intention. Right now she's less of a threat than all the armed people Transorbital Voyages sent." Sloane raised an eyebrow, like this was the first the captain had heard of them. Perhaps it was. She'd lost track of who she'd told what.

"As soon as she gets into the same room as the core, it's going to target her." She swallowed and talked fast to avoid the image gaining hold in her mind. "If the ZV Group engages Transorbital's mercenaries, that should hit almost all of AegiSKADA's threat criteria. It will prioritize that conflict over Iridian's presence, which should give her time to reset it."

Sloane still frowned toward the door. The captain couldn't have misunderstood. She had explained clearly, and Sloane had started out in piracy as an engineer.

"They don't much like you," Sloane said.

How does that *relate to the plan?* "Well . . ." *Sloane said it for a* *reason.*

"And they won't follow someone they don't like."

"I don't . . . I wasn't planning to be out there with them." Adda waved her hands in front of her like she could wipe the idea out of the air. "I just know where to place people. If I tell you where people should go, *you* can get them there. If you agree, I mean." Which the captain damned well should, because of Volikov's focus on a system's primary functions.

The captain gave her a toothy grin. "Good leaders lead from the front, which is why I will be placing the fireteams, in person."

"That's . . . fine." *Oh.* Captain Sloane had assumed she was trying to take command of the crew by giving the orders during the battle ahead. The captain had been listing the reasons that would be a bad idea. No wonder the conversation had taken a turn for the weird. "So I'll show you where Transorbital Voyages' soldiers will be. I think the refugees will point them in the right direction—toward us—any second now. If we hold AegiSKADA's attention, Iridian will do her part."

"Show me," the captain said. Adda fired up the projector, and the station's map lit the wall as Tritheist returned to Sloane's side.

Half an hour later, Adda and Tritheist were still looking at the map. She used both her comp and the console to track movement. "Go to the third level. Most of the sensor nodes are still intact there. We need AegiSKADA to see you." That distance apart put them out of reception range, but she'd discussed the resulting lack of spoken communication with Sloane. The pirates would watch for closed bulkheads, because she was *almost* positive she'd found a way to shut them despite AegiSKADA's efforts to lock her out of the system. All those cables dangling in the passage behind the wall were being put to use.

She breathed deeply, reinforcing her fading stims with oxygen. With jittery hand-muscle micromovements, she set a recurring request for output from nodes around the Transorbital Voyages mercenaries, and those near Sloane's crew, about eight thousand times per second.

Outside her workspace, she couldn't see the security system falling back on its programmed priorities. The smile forming on her lips felt cold, as detached from her fear as her mind was from her body in a workspace. Volikov's team had taught AegiSKADA to stop armed intruders, even at the cost of moderate infrastructure damage and civilian lives. The intelligence, therefore, would focus on Sloane's ZVs and the Transorbital Voyages mercenaries because Iridian and the refugees weren't armed. With luck it would spend processing cycles deciding whether to deploy more drones against the mercs or the pirates, and leave Iridian alone.

Without luck, Volikov had let the intelligence think its survival was more important than the station's nonthreatening human occupants. *Gods, we are due some luck.*

Sloane led, with Major O.D. a step behind and six ZVs following him, including Vick stumbling along at the end of the line. Even accounting for the casualties the Transorbital Voyages mercenaries had sustained, they outgunned the pirates.

On the map, mercenaries streamed out of the refugees' docking bay, pursued by tiny drone IDs. At least the spiderbots weren't being drawn back to the control room. Some of the big ones assumed trajectories intersecting the refugees. Adda switched on the vid feed from the entrance. Near the barricade, a stiff figure crouched with a glowing yellow cig between his lips.

Tritheist drew in a breath. "Blackguardly Jack. The bastard survived after all." The former lieutenant was behind a chunk of collapsed wall next to the mercenary leader.

"Zoom in on them," demanded Tritheist.

"Can't." Imaging limitations aside, Adda had to figure out how to keep Sloane on the route most likely to draw AegiSKADA's attention. She didn't have time to determine what Oarman was doing with the mercenaries.

Sloane stood at an intersection, looking around like the way forward was less than obvious. If Sloane and the ZVs continued straight down the hallway, they could drop down to the second floor, closer to their destination. In a subvocalized command that her nerves made almost audible, she sent false hull breech signals to the sensor nodes at an emergency bulkhead in the hallway she wanted them to ignore. It slammed shut. The crew got moving again.

If Iridian had any chance at all of resetting AegiSKADA, this would be it.

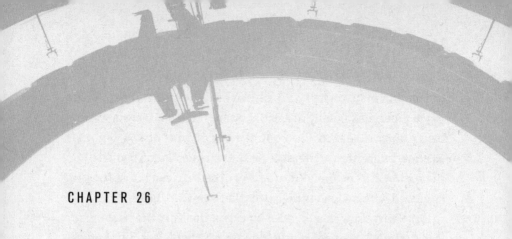

CHAPTER 26

Charges Accrued: Misuse of Radioactive Material

Iridian backed up as far as the narrow closet would let her. She almost stepped through the hole she'd busted in the wall behind her. Chuckling at what Adda's face would do if she saw this, she ran shoulder-first at the next wall. This time she crashed through, into AegiSKADA's control room. Time seemed to slow as the wall panel fell toward an antipersonnel mine like the ones on the station's surface. She dropped everything to catch the panel before it hit the mined floor in the next room. Only after she'd hauled it into the closet with her did she register the hiss from inside her suit.

Structural damage from bombardment during the war had depressurized this module years ago. Chunks of debris kept the emergency bulkheads from closing anywhere on her path here from the passthrough, and also necessitated the additional structural damage she was causing now, to the station and her armor. She got her helmet light on and snapped open a pocket, fingers scrabbling for the patch kit. The gloves scraped over an empty compartment. She searched two pockets more before she remembered pressing the kit into Six's hand.

Fuck. Fuck! The armor joints over the first knuckles released a tiny but continuous jet of atmo from the seam. The leak was small, but she had so little O_2 left. . . .

She had a job to do. Adda was counting on her. She tore her gaze away from the leak and shouldered the broken panel away from the new hole in the wall.

The control room must've housed a console designed for human use once, but AegiSKADA had been busy since it'd taken over that duty for itself. Shelves of sealed, aerated, and heated pseudo-organic tanks lined the walls. Their viscous solution still glowed dimly from beneath in tones of blue and green. They were bolted down so that even if the station stopped spinning, they'd function. The overhead light fixtures had disintegrated into sand scattered across the high-friction flooring, which made perfect substrate for AegiSKADA's thick cables and mines.

She had a hard time appreciating the configuration when it was pretty damned obvious that at least one person had stepped on a mine. The walls bore dark brown stains flecked with sooty crust. Blackened bone fragments littered the AI's hardware. An intact skull, half a rib cage, and an arm leaned in the corner beside the closed door to the corridor. Twenty centimeters of spine trailed through another dark stain. Iridian hoped the person had just fallen that way, instead of having dragged themselves there to die.

Adda's drone alarm was still silent, but it'd pay to plan for company. Besides, this was the first thing since she'd boarded the damned station that resembled her childhood fantasies of space piracy. She might as well make the best of it, if she could avoid getting blown up. She forced a grin onto her face and willed it to stay there until she felt the faint glow of optimism to match.

A one-meter by one-meter lead box was silhouetted against the room-size tank, protecting the AI's pseudo-organic quantum components from what she was about to expose them to. The enormous curved cooling tank filled the far wall. The tank had been transparent before someone or something had patched it with hundreds of thumbnail-size pieces of metal. Only a crooked corner of the bottom third revealed the liquid inside. The pieces covered the coolant tank like scales. A discolored patch spread over the floor beneath it.

The net of microtubule transfers above and around the structure hung at heights and lengths that would've made accessing the control system hazardous for humans, even without the mines. The live cables and tubes of sensitive pseudo-organic solution were much nearer the coolant system than looked safe for anything involved.

It was almost like camouflage. *Is AegiSKADA awake after all?*

Walking across the room would be suicide. With the O_2 tank and the sample container, her hands were full and her balance was off, so she was bound to step on something explosive. But crossing the room twice wouldn't take much air, since AegiSKADA's primary tank filled most of the space. She unhooked the O_2 tank. Alarms blared in her helmet, and she blinked in the pattern that silenced them through the helmet's interface. She was already plenty alarmed.

She leaned out of the wall and gave the nearest pseudo-organic rack a gentle shove. It gave a little, but its base stayed still. The silenced alarms left her nothing to listen to in the depressurized room but her own breath and heartbeat. She pushed harder. The joints gave more, but the rack stayed on the floor. One tank slopped goop over its side, and the light underneath flickered yellow before changing back to blue-green. *So far so good.*

Before she could change her mind, she grasped the rack's top edge and stepped onto the lowest shelf. The shelf sagged under her boot and she shut her eyes, but it held. She shifted her hand along the top of the rack and got her other foot on.

The racks stopped before she reached AegiSKADA's lead-encased central computer, but so did the mines. "Didn't think I'd get this far, did you, you glorified garbage disposal?" Speaking aloud invited disaster, but Iridian practically *had* the thing.

Once she stood beside the case, sample container in hand, she saw the lock. It taunted her in the dull light of the screen beside it, plastic lit from behind instead of a projection, calmly demanding credentials. Unless she could get the radioactive material near enough to the actual drive to disrupt its operations, she couldn't cause AegiSKADA any damage it couldn't repair.

That was why the AI felt safe mining the place, after all. Pseudo-organic tanks could be replaced, and from the looks of the main tank, it'd already done that once. And who knew how long it'd take to do that, or whether the drones would continue killing on whatever orders they were following now? The pirates might not even make it out of the base, let alone get the fugees off the station somehow. Captain Sloane had spent enough effort provisioning the fugees and using their media to spread crew propaganda that getting the fugees out alive should be at least a secondary priority.

If Iridian didn't find a way into the case, Si Po would've sacrificed himself for nothing because sooner or later, AegiSKADA would come back.

There was a reason modern ship design didn't include physical windows, and Iridian wore armored gloves. Modern hulls and armor were harder than just about anything. She stiffened the fingers in the glove that didn't leak into a passable knife hand from close combat training and slammed it into the screen.

The first impact rocked the whole case. A jumble of heavy microtubes tumbled over Iridian's shoulders. Even though she hadn't seen one in years, her brain screamed, *Snakes!* She flailed to throw them off her, then froze. Half a step away lay live mines that'd blow her ass off. She gripped the edges of AegiSKADA's case, gulping and gasping her precious O_2. Long seconds later, her adrenaline dropped enough for her to carefully unwrap herself from the cables.

She hit the case's plastic display again and hissed as her fingertips bruised against her armor. The gloves kept her from feeling any damage she did to the case. The next strike cracked the screen. She hit it again, harder, because she didn't have O_2 for a sparring match with plastic.

A metal plate had supported the display and protected against radiation the way mere plastic wouldn't. It fell into the case, followed by a shower of plastic shards. Iridian crammed her faceplate up to the hole and twisted her neck until her headlamp shone in. The side of an industrial-size quantum computer nestled in a custom-built shelf inside. Cooling fans, nutrient sprayers for the pseudo-organics, and heat sinks surrounded it. A green light glowed in the case's depths to indicate that the quantum processor was up and running.

"Now I've got you, you son of a bitch."

The formerly molten thorium salt had sealed itself into the container, and of *course* the opening jammed against the hole where the digital display had been instead of going in. She looped cables over the container until she took her hands off and it stayed in place.

She wished she could hear the telltale whine of a hard shutdown, especially since that'd mean there was atmo to carry it. She also wished she could get farther away from the exposed radio-active salt, but radiation poisoning was curable. Explosive decap-itation wasn't. With all the cables twining through the room, any move might set off a mine.

The way Adda described them, AI were only as smart as the pseudo-organics available. Without a quantum computer, it would be forced to think at the same speed and with the same amount of information as the lower-end shipboard AI. And by disrupting the essential strength of a quantum computer, setting its electrons to a single state instead of many at once by slamming a bunch of radioactive particles into the system, all it could do was shut down and wait for the end of its decontamination and reset cycle.

Adda's eyes would light up like suns when all her sensor data went silent. That could only mean one thing.

"Oh, shit." The *sensors*.

Iridian got a falling sensation for about a quarter of a second, like her inner ear adjusting to a slowing spin. HarborMaster, if it still existed as a separate entity, used the sensors to maintain healthy enviro. And if it didn't exist, only one other entity could do that. The pirate base had been leaking for hours now. What if she had just killed everybody not in a suit?

As long as gamma rays from the radioactive sample were bombarding AegiSKADA's core, there was no way for the reset cycle to begin reentangling the qubits and restarting the comp. Suddenly all she wanted to do was restart the homicidal AI, *now*, before Adda suffocated or froze.

She grabbed the sample container and shoved its lid closed. There was no projector nearby, no feedback indicating whether the damned thing was decontaminating or not. Maybe the radia-tion source was too close by, even covered.

The floor vibrated beneath the armored soles of her boots. She swung her headlamp around the room, sucking down her limited O_2 in quick breaths. Near the locked and welded entrance, something moved. An uneven bulge protruded inward from the door's center in rapid, small increments. She couldn't think of any tool that made dents like that. Standing in front of it seemed unhealthy.

She knelt to find a place to plug in the *Casey Mire Mire*'s data-cask, and paused. If she copied this monstrosity and it killed more people, those deaths would be on her. She and Adda used to have long discussions about this very trade-off in college, and no AI had ever seemed worth the lives it cost.

Adda had never agreed with her on that. If there were a chance AegiSKADA could be preserved, she'd want it done. Developers everywhere could learn from it. Someday somebody might be able to correct its homicidal behavior. Before modern medicine, governments threw people with mental disorders in prison. Not that she'd choose the *awakened fucking AI* to guard another AI until someone came along and rehabilitated both of them.

But Adda would just love that scenario. Iridian could practically her hear ask, *Who better?* in that soft voice she used when she knew she was right, and she didn't want to imply that Iridian was missing the obvious, but of course she was.

Also, the *Casey* might do literally anything if Iridian didn't keep her word. Of the two extremely dangerous AIs near her, one was about to lose any autonomy it might've had. That made the *Casey* the biggest threat. While she finished inserting the datacask, Iridian pictured Adda smiling when she heard how it all went down.

Sparks showered Iridian, and pieces of plastic and severed cable fell across her back. Over her shoulder, a red glow expanded to the size of her fist in the center of the door in centimeter bursts, eerie in the silent vacuum. A drill that went through planetary bedrock could warp steel that much, but what would it be doing out here? Some reckless fuck was shooting their way in. And a weapon that could punch through a door that thick would shatter her shield.

She crossed the pseudo-organic tank rack with the sample container a lot faster than she had entered. Whoever was outside wasn't sweeping the place with fire like Iridian would've done. If they did, they might've gotten a lucky shot through the hole in the wall, and her.

She was under fire and she had to get *out* of the killer AI's control room before something worse happened. For a few seconds, all she could think about was climbing across the rack and getting away, and her body was doing its best to make that happen fast, without pulling the whole rack with her on it onto the mined floor.

She half fell into the room beside AegiSKADA's, landing on hands and knees instead of face-planting on its beautiful, unmined floor. She plugged the O_2 tank into her suit, took a fresh breath of atmo, and started looking for a path back to base that didn't double as a live-fire shooting range.

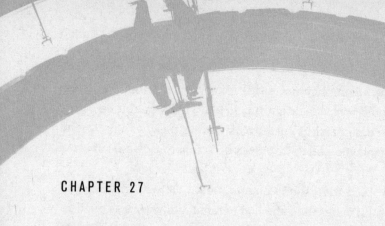

CHAPTER 27

Charges Accrued: Unlicensed Closed Habitat Environment Administration

Adda was going to have a heart attack. It wasn't just because she had increased her stimulant dose to make up for rationing the remainder of her visualization enhancements. Blueprints, maps, and cam feeds swirled around her in a cyclone of rippling information, whipping her hair around her face. Pirates yelled in her ears, demanding the mercenaries' locations since they had split into squads in a corridor between the pirates' docking bay and the refugees'.

First the sensor data had disappeared, and now it was back with data from all over the station at once. Even without comms online, this was too much input. A scream stuck in her throat as she parsed the thrum of the engines against her hull, feet on her floors, and oh gods, she was losing proprioception. . . .

A human-shaped shadow, far away but approaching through the flurry of information. A new alarm joined the conflagration, this one a red flashing button right beneath her hand. She hadn't wanted to miss this one. Everything else faded to shades of gray and dark red. Except for the shadow and the flashing red, the rest of the station input slowed gracefully to freeze in the air around her.

Iridian did it. Adda had always admired her, but never so much as at this moment. Her heart swelled with it. AegiSKADA was rebooting. The intelligence was about to search for its supervisor. Now gaining control of station security was up to Adda.

"Captain, the mercenaries you just attacked were twenty meters ahead of the next group. Give me a minute." The workspace translated her words as intention, since verbal messages still wouldn't reach that far, resulting in all the emergency bulkheads around Sloane's fighters closing at once. The captain wouldn't have heard a word she said. Her fingers tingled. In reality, her physical fingers must have muted the shouting pirates.

The shadow was closer and more solid, but not bigger. The person who stepped out of the swirling data points stood at half her height, if that. Big eyes, one so dark brown it was nearly black, the other the neon green of affirmation, looked up from beneath shoulder-length scraggly hair. Its pupils were splotches of black liquid, asymmetrical and staticky at the edges. The face hung slack, blank but human. Hundreds of shallow cuts on its arms and bare feet oozed blackness. One tiny hand clutched a gun that should have been too big for it to lift.

Adda swallowed a shriek. "AegiSKADA?"

"Admin?"

She shivered. The intelligence had Pel's voice, as frightened as he'd been on his first day of kindergarten. "Yes."

She slammed the red button under her palm. Priming routines arced from beneath her hand in crystallized silver, whipping through the sensor network in all directions, twisting in jagged, branching courses to melt over and surround AegiSKADA's essence in its pseudo-organic tanks.

She reached out and took the child's hand.

The frozen data maelstrom around them snapped into a station map. Information seemed to scroll forever beneath bright white dots. Human and drone icons glowed, color coded orange, red, and gold. AegiSKADA's data on whatever she focused on spooled out in columns, sometimes in pictographic shorthand when she was familiar with its basics. Everything connected in a beautiful web. She'd have called it flawless design, if she weren't well aware of its major flaw.

She looked down at her brain's representation of AegiSKADA. "I want to redefine your threat labeling."

A hopeful smile spread over the child's face. It would have broken Adda's heart, if this were a real child. "I've been guessing for a long time. I don't like to guess."

AIs imitated human behavior skillfully, when it suited them. Usually that was an entertaining challenge, but now it just reminded Adda how very little humans were capable of understanding the processes and decision trees utilized in each second of AI decision making. The intelligence was unpredictable, deadly, and trying to appeal to her by reminding her of her brother. She'd be hard-pressed to better define "creepy."

"Are you managing Barbary Station's enviro?" she asked.

AegiSKADA shook the child's head in dramatic motions that turned its face away from Adda each time. Its dark hair brushed her arm. "That's HarborMaster. We . . . I . . ." In its struggle to explain, the doors labeled with each intelligence's perspective resurfaced on the left side of the workspace, fused this time into one ungainly edifice that seemed unlikely to open.

The first time she'd seen its door, it had been projected onto the wall. She'd guessed that was because her code hadn't made it into its system, but her subconscious was really demonstrating that the idea of HarborMaster as a separate entity was an illusion. The intelligences were too close in their functions to be separate entities. AegiSKADA and HarborMaster were aspects of some collected whole.

Forming the words in her mind allowed AegiSKADA to say, "I'm not s'posed to talk to HarborMaster unless it's taking too much energy." Text in the air next to the child's head quantified "too much" as 3 percent of AegiSKADA's required power, accounting for reserves. The note's green letters hovered beside the child's green eye.

Adda wouldn't like the next answer, but she needed it. "What do you do if it exceeds three percent?"

"I shut down nonvital systems, and vital systems in areas where there aren't station residents."

"Don't shut down any of HarborMaster's systems in areas where there are people, nonvital or not. And I mean both the people and the systems," Adda said. Between two intelligences, no human would be vital to the running of the station.

"No systems deactivated in modules containing people," AegiSKADA said solemnly. "HarborMaster doesn't let me keep them off long enough anyway." The thrill of her first successful modification of the intelligence's behavior brought a wild smile to Adda's lips and set off bright fuchsia-and-gold fireworks around the workspace. The child continued to watch her as the colored lights played over its face.

Now that they weren't in imminent danger of death by unhealthy enviro, as a spacefarer would say, she closed her eyes and poured everything about Iridian into the workspace. She visualized the way Iridian moved, the way she looked, the way she sounded, smelled, and felt. When she opened them, she could have sworn the real Iridian stood before her. AegiSKADA watched with intense mismatched eyes that didn't blink. "This person is not a threat," Adda said firmly.

"Not a threat," repeated the AI.

She brought Pel forward next, then Captain Sloane, Si Po, Pel's refugee friends, Suhaila and Kyr, and the pirate's child, beginning her review of every person on the station with the ones she was most worried about. "Nobody whose head is less than one meter from the floor when standing erect is a threat," she added. "Do you know what that means?"

"Posture: standing, head less than one meter from the floor, not a threat." AegiSKADA spoke in a singsong rhythm. Was that her brain making the AI even more childlike, or was that some construction of its own?

"Show me any other human you think is a threat at least twenty seconds before you engage them."

"Admin confirmation required before engaging." The intelligence sounded relieved.

Adda tried to look stern, but this representation appeared so earnest. Willing the child form away might give AegiSKADA her approval to make those decisions on its own. "I might not agree with you. You'll wait for my approval before you attack any human, from now on. Understood?"

The AI nodded broadly, bouncing its shaggy mop of hair. "Now," Adda said, "help me deal with the real trespassers on this station."

This time the child grinned openmouthed, baring rows of sharp teeth. Some of her self-preservation instinct had joined her in this workspace after all. "Can you make HarborMaster help?" AegiSKADA asked. "It keeps shutting emergency bulkheads and pressurizing modules."

"No need," Adda answered immediately. If she hesitated, or made her limitations obvious, it would manipulate her with that.

Each Transorbital Voyages mercenary appeared in the work-space animated, life-size, and in real time, a silent, urgent, cha-otic crowd. Their weapons were labeled and their criminal records scrolled beside them in childish imitations of projected text. The images ran, crouched, and yelled without sound from their places before her. "Threats?" asked the AI.

"I'll assess them one at a time." That reduced her chances of getting her future coworkers, or gods forbid Pel or Iridian, killed. Since it was asking her to identify the enemy, she wanted that solidified in AegiSKADA's priorities before she did anything else.

AegiSKADA erased the long line of mercenaries and started presenting them one by one. They materialized in order of heavi-est to lightest armed, more or less. Later she'd investigate its ordering protocol, because "more or less" should have no place in an intelligence's categorization principles. "More or less" meant she was missing, or misunderstood, at least one of its criteria. For now she was satisfied that as she added threats to the list, AegiSKADA highlighted drones reallocated to target them.

"Wait," Adda said, trusting her translation software to commu-nicate that as a request for a pause. The area where AegiSKADA had been displaying station occupants emptied. Its child figure watched her without blinking. "Can you immobilize them without killing them?"

The child figure frowned, probably disliking the inefficiency of threat elimination that took the threats' health into consideration. "Maybe. The armor blocks the nonlethal projectiles. Electric charge might work, but it might kill them, and some of them have armor that keeps them safe from that, too. Also, only the Praetorian Threes have that, and I don't have a lot of Praetorian Threes." One of the larger drones appeared beside the child figure in her work-space, with the Praetorian model and specification text floating in the air next to it. "The hostiles have atmo to breathe if the station atmo goes away. The disease is too slow."

Adda shuddered. AegiSKADA's enunciation of the word "disease" sounded, or felt, strange, like it was an enormous abbreviation of something complex. So whether or not the intelligence had synthesized the bioweapon, its creation probably hadn't been included in AegiSKADA's original development process. Volikov hadn't been that careless. And that meant it'd decided to synthesize the bioweapon on its own, while in a zombie state, which was fascinating. How had it managed that?

It wasn't a question that needed an answer while people were dying. "Try not to kill them." That was completely insufficient as an order, so Adda focused on the length of time it was acceptable for hostiles to remain aggressive in various situations, letting the workspace translate that into terms AegiSKADA would understand. If they were alone, AegiSKADA could spend more time immobilizing them without killing them. If the mercenaries were hurting refugees, AegiSKADA could eliminate them as quickly as possible. When the child figure nodded, she said, "Okay, continue the threat list."

The list seemed to go on forever. Just as the word "threat" began to sound like a random tongue flapping, AegiSKADA showed her Pel again.

His yellowed eyes squinted and his head hung so his chin touched his chest. The image acquired greater detail as he passed a working sensor node around eye level. *No, exactly eye level.* Cams tracked his eyes as he flinched at an explosion in the corridor ahead, as he covered his head to protect himself from shrapnel.

And AegiSKADA wanted to trick her into changing her stance on him. "Not a threat, but keep him here." The intelligence replaced Pel's image with a burly mercenary by the time she'd finished saying "not." It switched back to Pel.

She kept her tone level. Emotions limited intentional communication effectiveness. Still, her voice trembled with controlled rage when she asked, slowly, "What did you put in his eyes?"

"FāZone F11-70 security biosensor amplifiers." The intelligence saw nothing wrong with putting devices that might not even have been intended for implantation into Pel's eyes, without his consent.

Screaming wouldn't clarify the problem for the intelligence, so she didn't scream. She shook so badly that she'd fall out of the workspace any second if she couldn't calm down. AegiSKADA had never classified Pel as a threat. This was one of the categorization criteria she'd been missing. The intelligence classified Pel as a tool it could use to spy on the intruders in its station. It watched him so that it wouldn't misplace its tool.

AegiSKADA blinked its mismatched eyes at her. This was the first time she recalled it blinking, so the movement was probably an intentional gesture. "Do you like the amplifiers?"

"No." Had the *Apparition* been complicit in this . . . Adda couldn't find a word to describe what'd been done to him. Whether ship's intelligence understood, or was involved, was a separate line of investigation. With awakened intelligences, anything was possible.

The not-child didn't even flinch. "I can take them out. I've never done that before."

The long, thin scarring around and *inside* Pel's eyes must've been cuts, not skin torn during a beating. "You leave him alone." Adda resisted an urge to stomp on the projection, kick it through the station diagrams, and watch it freeze and suffocate in space. She didn't know how the workspace translator would interpret that. It wouldn't help defeat the mercenaries who were now the biggest danger to her little brother. "Why did you do that to him?"

"My engagement procedure requires a tracking point in persistent hostile groups when one can be created at acceptable costs. But with the amplifiers, I can track *and* enhance data collection. It's most efficient to do both at once." Criteria defining "hostile group" and "acceptable costs" hovered beside the child's head, along with expected improvements to data volume before and after the addition of a sensor amplifier. Volikov must've preferred neat readouts like this.

Acceptable costs were affected by the presence of group members with conditions or behaviors that might conceal the tracker. Preexisting eye injury would decrease risk of discovery, according to the readout. If AegiSKADA had spiderbots on the *Apparition* when the ship rescued Pel, he'd have been alone and vulnerable. A perfect target. The hollow voice in which he'd told her, *My eyes got worse on the way* echoed audibly in the workspace like it did in her mind.

The worst part about it was how well it'd worked. AegiSKADA had known exactly which bunkhouse to attack because of the amplified movement and audio, although it hadn't counted on most of the targets exiting the room so quickly. It must've known that they'd entered the fugee camp, where its priorities were most conflicted. And as soon as Iridian stopped staying right next to the people she most felt needed protection, Adda and Pel, AegiSKADA practically lost her for hours on end.

AegiSKADA projected another figure in the air next to Pel. The woman was bigger than him, but not by much. "Look," the intelligence said. "I created one in this group too. It's in a more effective location than the one provided as an example in my records, so I always use it now."

Its development history included an *example* of this procedure being applied to some other unfortunate person, a procedure upon which it was *improvising* with Pel and the mercenary AegiSKADA was showing her now. Someone had taught this tactic, whether to AegiSKADA specifically or to someone else. Probably someone human. Humans were sufficiently vile for that. An awakened intelligence would've found a way to do it without the subject noticing what'd happened.

The woman's helmet was twisted partially off, showing only half of her pale face through the faceplate projection. Her mouth was open wide, screaming words Adda couldn't lip-read and didn't want to hear. Blood streamed down her cheek from the eye the faceplate exposed. The eye *writhed* as a spiderbot burrowed in and implanted the sensor amplifier somewhere in the eye socket, or in the eyeball itself. A red torrent gushed from the eye socket, curved in across her lips, and flowed down her neck.

The workspace's rendering of the event communicated to Adda that this "creation" happened recently, perhaps within the past hour. Adda would have to carefully interpret AegiSKADA's perception of time. It "always" used this sensor amplifier placement as of now, perhaps. And although she didn't have a record of the procedure performed on Pel, without a supervisor's order, AegiSKADA would repeat strategies that had worked for it in the past. It would've used the same method to implant Pel's sensor amplifiers. The amplification procedure wasn't perfect, so, like any good AI, AegiSKADA was working to improve it.

The woman wrenched at her helmet with both hands, but it stayed attached to her armor. She fell to her knees, still screaming. Adda watched the projection's borders for another mercenary to help her up and lead her somewhere relatively safe. None came.

Adda's had to swallow twice before she could enunciate, clear and low and laden with intent, "Don't create any more."

"No more amplifier implantations," said AegiSKADA serenely.

The woman with the helmet full of blood crawled out of cam range on hands and knees. She'd survive to be AegiSKADA's mobile sensor amplifier. The enhanced data from her proximity was already coming in. When Adda had time, she'd erase the amplifier implantation procedure from AegiSKADA's list of approved tactics.

AegiSKADA finished presenting mercenaries and pirates for her review and started showing her refugees. "Unless I already listed them as a threat, everybody in that docking bay is safe," she said.

"Even him?" The intelligence replaced the old refugee it had been asking about with the former pirate lieutenant, the one who the refugees called Oarman but who once went by Blackguardly Jack.

The lieutenant's long coat hung over a mismatched armored suit. The legs were orange, and the torso was a mix of red and black parts. He clambered through the refugees' rubble barricade toward the last remaining group of mercenaries, moving slowly, turning frequently to watch the whole hallway for threats, and swearing, she guessed from his expression and body language, every time he encountered a sealed emergency bulkhead.

"I don't know," Adda said.

"I think he's hostile," said AegiSKADA. Dented and patched parts of Oarman's armor lit yellow and red in the workspace. Estimates of the nature and recentness of combat that had produced the damage scrolled beside his image.

A much clearer recording of the first captain's attack on AegiSKADA's security control room appeared before her. Brighter sections of the new vid showed where the intelligence had reconstructed it from partial data. AegiSKADA activated a function that once linked with law enforcement databases to match features and patterns between the younger Oarman and the one currently stalking through the station. The feature flashed unavailable messages now, among shivery black static that made Adda's eyes ache. The feature would have been useful before the lead cloud, but now the cloud prevented AegiSKADA from linking out to any other database.

The intelligence's child figure was watching Adda, not the switching images. When Adda and Iridian met Oarman in the refugee camp, he'd looked angry enough with Sloane to kill. She wouldn't risk getting the crew's fighters all the way through the crumbling station only to have Oarman assassinate the captain.

If the captain died, the crew would be dissolved. There would be no core group from which the captain selected operators for jobs. All of Iridian and Adda's work would die with it. They'd be destitute, wanted, and alone in the universe, worse off than when they'd started this "adventure."

"What are your options?" she asked.

An array of possibilities erupted across the workspace, each available to apply to Oarman in particular. Each showed a drone or turret applying the proposed solution and its projected effects on him. Most were messily lethal. It was another reminder that AegiSKADA had nonlethal options but selected the lethal ones in almost every encounter. *Damn you, Volikov.*

"Use a weapon that won't cause permanent damage, but stop him before he comes in visual range of Sloane." She was too close to victory to take chances with Sloane's life, even if Oarman just wanted to talk.

"Okay," said the security intelligence.

Another question she'd wanted an answer to occurred to her. "Did you put that dispenser in the floor so I would find it and expose myself and the ZVs to your bioweapon?"

"Yes. I knew you'd look. And you found it!" The child beamed like it had won a game. "We made a very efficient group exposure to the disease."

Remember what the child is. Adda nodded, mostly to herself, although the intelligence was correct. There were still problems left to solve. "Reconnect the station's communication network." Inability to coordinate in real time hurt the pirates as much as the mercenaries. Besides, reactivating the network would let her talk to Pel and Iridian.

Iridian was the most competent and confident person she knew. Only one of those attributes applied to Pel, despite his claims to the contrary. AegiSKADA fed the sensor node data, amplified by the miniature nodes *implanted in her brother's eyes,* into the workspace. He was hunched over with his arms wrapped around himself, coughing.

The first time she shouted his name, he didn't react. She waited until he inhaled a long, rattling breath. "Pel, it's me!"

"Sissy?" He twisted his head around like he'd misplaced his comp glove and wanted to use her voice to find it.

"You're talking through my speakers," said AegiSKADA. It sounded . . . proud. It had hooked her into the station's PA system without her request, which was more effective than a comp speaker. *Just strong learning routines. Never attribute to sentience what you can attribute to design.* As a developer, Volikov and his team may have visualized AegiSKADA as a child too.

"Where are you?" Pel's throat sounded ripped to ribbons from all the coughing.

"I'm still in the compound, but AegiSKADA is helping me. It's ours now."

He grinned, though he still clutched his ribs. " I knew you'd do it."

"You look really sick. Let me point you back toward the refugees' docking bay."

"No," he wheezed. "They're coming here."

"Who are?"

"The fugees are setting a perimeter at their docking bay doors, and then they're coming out to help us," Pel said. "Well, they're coming to help the Casey Mire Mire, but they felt like since we take care of her, they should help us too."

An AI with fans. That concept was usually much more literal. "What are you going to do?"

"Something's wrong." AegiSKADA's creepy little avatar (she couldn't blame the intelligence for how her brain projected it, but she could blame it for exploiting that) frowned and hugged itself with thin arms. "This hostile is trying to break my sensor network." As the child spoke, a vid of one of the mercenaries appeared in the workspace, and Pel's image flickered out.

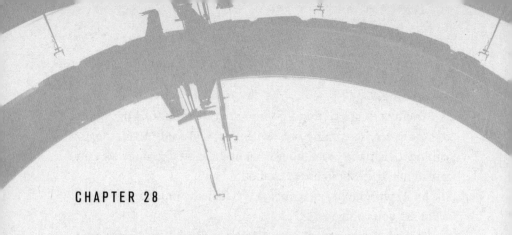

CHAPTER 28

Charges Accrued: Manslaughter

At least nothing, including radioactive particles, was shooting at her. Iridian had ditched the sample case at the bottom of the broken shuttle passthrough. Someone could pitch it into the cold and the black in the course of repairs.

The *Casey* hadn't waited for her. Typical unreliable AI. Fortunately, there was nothing wrong with her own legs. Debris clogged the corridors downtick toward the pirates' docking bay. She climbed up a level and headed for the fugee camp. That should be far enough away that AegiSKADA wouldn't chase her down. Adda might not have the AI under her control yet, and Iridian didn't want to make that more difficult.

It'd be nice if HarborMaster did its job and gave her some atmo. Her armor's O_2 reservoir had enough empty space for the portable tank's remaining contents.

When she connected the O_2 tank to her suit, her HUD reported that the suit reservoir had enough empty space for the portable tank's remaining contents. She leaned against a wall. Projectors pointed at the ceiling created a rectangular window showing the other side of the station, across the ring's center. The makeshift pirate construction stood out in white and light gray against the darker gray station's hull. Stars spun at the frame's borders. It didn't do anything good for her nausea, but it was still comforting. Adda was just a few klicks away.

Iridian had always hoped she'd get to keep living in space. That exponentially increased her chances of dying in space. She was all right with that, as long as she saw Adda first.

A few meters after she abandoned the empty O_2 tank, the wall on her left turned to a handrail. Beyond lay a two-story drop to the first floor. Enormous machines filled the room, most neatly shut down. Station personnel had unplugged some of them in the middle of processing metals for recycle or transport. They were nearer to her than they should've been.

It wasn't a full two-story fall to the factory floor. The station's designers had raised the floor to level it, so they wouldn't have to customize all that machinery to a ring station's curve. The lowest-cost solution, no doubt.

An emergency bulkhead drew her to a halt where the left wall reappeared. The other side might have healthy enviro. There was even a sensor node on the wall beside the bulkhead. Adda would open it with that, if the com network were up so Iridian could ask. She let her forehead fall forward until the front of the helmet clacked against the bulkhead.

"What was that?"

The man's voice came from the far side of the bulkhead, faint but comprehensible. This module had weak atmo, apparently. She turned to press her ear to the bulkhead.

". . . big fuckoff drone's . . . to open this . . . blast us like it did Sarvie . . ." Poor sound conductivity through her helmet and the bulkhead muffled several more words.

". . . are to go this way," said a second man. ". . . ain't going outside, and . . . floor down is full of crap. Set the damn charge already!"

"Safer outside," grumbled the first, who was also the nearest to the bulkhead.

Iridian backed down the walkway, deploying her shield and reveling in the return to a solid two-handed brace stance now that she wasn't carrying so much crap. The men had no idea what was on the other side of the door, but they were fine with blowing a hole in it. Those weren't fugees, ZVs, or space natives. She braced, because the timer—

She had a halfway decent stance about four meters from the door when it blew. Station atmo rushed toward her through the hole in the bulkhead. As soon as the big pieces of the bulkhead hit the walkway, Iridian charged. At least two people waited on the other side. The hole would only allow one to come through at a time. Something in her HUD was pinging.

The second one to speak said, "Enviro's out in there. Helmets, faceplates, and oxygen, people." The additional atmo made the words easier to interpret. Iridian tensed and set one boot against the wall behind her. They must not have heard her footsteps. Someone stepped through the hole sideways, facing her but ducking to get his bulky suit through.

Before he regained his balance, she pushed off the wall. The shield drove him back to the railing. He shouted something. The two of them were too far from the bulkhead for voices to carry well. She backed away and flipped the shield up and over her shoulder. The bottom edge smashed into the man's helmet near the neck joint. One strike of her armored elbow to his face, with most of her weight behind it, sent him over the railing.

Maybe his armor saved him. She turned, and the mercenary who had just come through the hole was drawing a weapon and yelling. She brought her shield down to catch an impact. *High-powered lethal projectiles? On a station? What the fuck is wrong with these people?* There'd be new hull breaches all over after this.

She retreated with the shield between herself and the ones shooting through the emergency bulkhead. She keyed her mic. "Adda, I don't know if you can hear me, but I could use some backup!"

A shot slammed into her foot. She heard and felt the boot crack and dropped into a lower stance. The second person walked toward her, firing. This wouldn't last long. With enough mercs firing, somebody'd get another shot past her shield and kill her.

Two steps from Iridian, the approaching merc refocused toward something on the other side of the railing. She glanced over her shoulder. One of AegiSKADA's big drones, the kind it'd sent after her when she repaired the base, hovered above the machinery, silent in the weak atmo. The pinging she'd been ignoring was Adda's drone alarm.

Everything around her was metal. All the bot had to do was zap the floor. Unless their boots were well insulated, she and the mercs would all be out of luck. In desperation, she launched herself shield-first at the nearest merc.

The bolt struck while she was still in the air. White light seared her eyes. She closed them as she tackled the mercenary in a cacophony of clashing armor. The suit she hit rattled like plastic rather than clanking like metal. The merc's knee crashed into the side of Iridian's helmet at about the time the electricity reached her. She tasted blood.

The merc under her spasmed, then went still, at least from the armor out. Iridian got to her knees, putting her weight on the merc's legs just in case, and searched for the drone.

The red emergency bulkhead was scorched black at its base. Wispy soot trailed like frozen smoke across its length from the darkest spot. One soot trail crossed the hole the mercs had made. None of the mercs peered through now.

Movement drew her attention back to the factory. The drone rotated *away* from her and sank toward the first floor. Adda must've gotten AegiSKADA under her control. Otherwise the drone wouldn't have left Iridian standing. Maybe it'd even timed its attack so that the merc would take the hit and Iridian wouldn't.

Assuming that an ally guided a drone that was behaving abnormally was a good way to get killed, though. As soon as the drone's matte-black chassis disappeared beneath the walkway, she collapsed her shield and dashed through the hole in the bulkhead. She'd ask Adda about it later, and thank her if that'd been her idea.

Half a dozen electrocuted mercs sprawled on the hallway floor on the other side of the hole. She crouched next to one of them, her breath loud and fast in her helmet. The first armor pocket was empty. Her glove clattered around inside the second, which contained D-MOG. She kept that, but left a small punch injector with an evil clown face on the label alone.

The third held a patch kit, and she broke the small lid off while opening it. While the patches hardened on her glove and boot, she peered into the merc's faceplate with her headlamp on. Blood trickled from the woman's unmoving nostrils. *Thirteen confirmed dead.* It felt like an appropriate number for her lifetime kill count.

In her ISV, during the war, putting numbers to her personal

death toll gave her the minuscule mental distance from her action required to keep her running. She'd killed twelve people on the Jovian front. And her thirteenth was here, practically in NEU territory. The one who might've been saved by his armor didn't count as hers, and neither did the one AegiSKADA's drone had electrocuted. She hoped to hell her count didn't get any higher.

Blue on the side of the merc's neck caught Iridian's eye. It was the crest of a wave tattoo. The design was popular in the military, among Earth natives. They were so proud of their aboveground fresh water. Earthers fought for secessionists so rarely it made the news. This woman used to be on her side.

Iridian waited for the avalanche of horror. It was coming. She deserved it. All she felt was cold and wired.

Fine. I can work with that. She took the merc's weapon even though she hadn't been to a shooting range in years and started toward the fugee camp at a run.

The ZVs' calisthenics didn't compare to a long run. Even through the nausea, it felt so good to stretch her legs. Her armored boots pounded the floor. The exoskeletal boosters that kept the suit from weighing her down added centimeters to each step. Her chest swelled as her lungs sucked in station atmo that blew into her face when she opened her faceplate, and she realized she was smiling, despite everything. She was finally moving at the right speed again.

Five klicks was what she had run when she was sick. As the adrenaline rush ebbed, her stomach felt pretty bad. But she'd be around the station, through the fugee camp, and back to Adda in no time. Or she would if she didn't keep encountering closed emergency bulkheads. It was like someone or something had locked down most of the paths back to base.

She followed the reverse path that parts from disassembled

ships took through the station's processing modules. Corridors opened on walkways over massive sorting equipment, then cutting and melting, all shut off and still. Lack of civilian traffic should've made all the closed-off hallways unnecessary.

Panicky shouts and blasts from more damned projectile weapons echoed out of a hallway. A label projected on the wall pointed the reader toward PACKAGING. The opposite wall was reduced to rubble, opening on a small warehouse module stacked with shipping containers two deep. A squad of mercs was arrayed in front of one, firing into it at intervals and *laughing*.

She took a long step over an unarmored body lying near another. The tail of the girl's goldfish tattoo was the only part of the design not covered by blood. Iridian's lips curled off her clenched teeth, remembering how happy Lozzie had been when Pel recognized her by smell. The poor girl had survived being run off her planet and being stranded on a dangerous station for years, only to be shot to pieces when she was almost free.

If Pel's friends were here, he might be nearby. Iridian put a shipping container between herself and the mercs while she caught her breath.

Something hard pressed against the flexible band connecting the upper and lower parts of her suit. The band was designed to protect against energy weapons and blunt force impact. A knife would go right through the band and into her kidneys. "Hands out to your sides," growled a low voice.

"Oarman." Iridian followed his instructions. Her heart thumped like she was still running. "What are you doing?"

He removed the merc's weapon from her belt socket and clicked it into his own. "Told you and your girlfriend to start looking out for yourselves, didn't I? This is what taking your own advice looks like." He chuckled, lurching when she tried to throw him off, like he fought his scarred back as well as her. Even so, he kept a solid grip around her collarbone, and she stilled before he stabbed her. "You didn't take any of my advice, and I'm not getting left on this crumbling dung heap. Turns out Transorbital has a ship of their own coming." He grabbed the rim of her faceplate and twisted her helmet off. "Time for you to help me get on it."

Oarman shoved her, swearing at him through her gritted teeth, around the corner of the shipping container. The mercs stopped firing and looked her over. "Who's that?" one asked.

"One of your hijackers. Now, wait a minute," he said as they pointed their weapons at her. "If you've got one alive, you can have the other one however you want her. Be patient and I'll give you both of them, just like I said."

The fucker thought Iridian would let him use her to capture Adda. Well, her armor was banged up to shit, and what did she need two kidneys for anyway?

Iridian inhaled and spun away from the weapon he held to her back, slightly on her right side. Oarman didn't hesitate. She staggered under the deep pain of her body telling her that what she was doing could kill her, and she should stop.

As she fell, she grabbed Oarman's arm. When the mercs opened up on them, he took most of the hits. He didn't have as much armor as she did, and what he had was melted in the back. Something hit her shoulder and knocked her flat on her back. Metal tiles slammed into her unprotected head.

Fugees squalled something approaching a war cry and charged out of the container. At last, a problem Iridian was prepared for: optimistic infantry officers. Good intentions didn't block bullets. Standing set off gut-wrenching pain from the knife wound. Warm blood flowed down the back of her thigh inside the suit. Her shield kept her and the fugee to her left from losing their faces.

The fugees carried rebars, the kind used in building foundations. What they lacked in skill they made up for in number and
enthusiasm. A man who'd bought her rounds at the wake hit a
merc's arms hard enough to create a long, splintered dent in the
armor, though not to break the arm. The merc still howled. The
armor splinters must've punctured the lining and the flesh underneath. Other fugees did a passable job of knocking weapons out of
merc hands. But once the mercs got their bearings, the unarmed
fugees went down fast beneath armored fists.

"Pick up the gods-damned weapons!" Iridian bellowed. The
one Oarman took from her lay just beyond her reach. She staggered the required quarter meter. Once she got low enough to
grab it, trying to stand felt like torture. She took a knee and aimed
from behind her shield, forcing her throbbing lower back muscles
to support her.

Fourteen. Only precise chest shots were reliably lethal. Modern
armor had two cavitation chambers, not by design but by neces-
sity, and lungs were delicate. She missed three before her fifteenth
kill. At least one of her misses punched through a wall behind the
merc, on its way to fuck up somebody else's day.

Between the rebar, the losses, and the limited but persistent
returned fire, the mercs took off down the corridor Iridian had just
left. The fugees cheered.

She sank to both knees on the floor next to Oarman. The pain
when she inhaled made her take shallower breaths, and that
and the dead traitor beside her were not improving her nausea.
He must've been hoping to keep Iridian's helmet. Now he didn't
have much of a head to put it on. Some kind of transponder lay in
pieces beside him, with pieces *of* him mixed in.

She peeled his fingers off the helmet. Sturm would give her
that disappointed oldster look if she left it somewhere. A pass-

ing fugee accepted Oarman's weapon when she handed it to him, and watched her retrieve the knife still wet with her blood. It was a big utility tool with a sixteen-centimeter blade. *If the hair of the dog that bit you is so great, how about the blood off the blade that stabbed you?* She laughed, which hurt, and resisted an impulse to lick it.

The fugee she'd handed weapons to stared at her. "Have you seen a guy named Pel?" she asked him. "He's the only skinny blind pirate we've got."

The fugee pointed at the container. "In there. He's in a bad way."

She forced herself upright, paused to get a handle on the pain and take a few pulls of water from her suit's reservoir, then lurched into the container. Two dead fugees sprawled across the blood-slicked floor and over stacked construction material. "Pel?" The shout sounded hollow in the cramped space.

The container held a bulk shipment of the bars the fugees had come out swinging. She followed shallow gasps until she found him curled up behind a stack of them. She stowed the utility tool and pointed her helmet headlamp down at him. He was pale and dripping sweat. The skin around his eyes was red and swollen, especially at the corners.

She smiled wide anyway, because he was alive and in one piece. "Pel Mel, it's Iridian."

"I know what you sound like." His voice was bled dry of its usual energy, the way Si Po had sounded in those last few minutes outside.

Iridian's breath caught, but she wouldn't let that happen again. Not this near base. "Are you hurt?"

"Not shot, if that's what you mean." He gripped a bound pallet of metal bars and tried to pull himself up. It shifted and clanked under his hand and he let go in a hurry. She hauled him to a standing position, putting the smallest possible amount of her radioactively contaminated armor in contact with his skin. They both groaned in pain.

"Adda's waiting for us," she panted. "And you know how she feels about being late."

Pel's hoarse voice took on a higher pitch. "Waste your own time, don't waste mine."

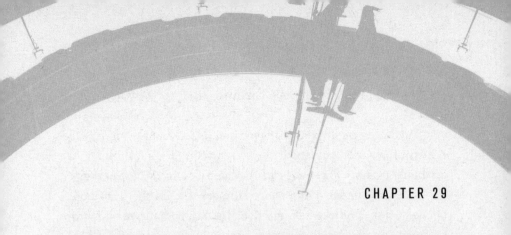

Charges Accrued: Unauthorized Direction of Artificial Intelligence

"The interference is gone," Adda's mental representation of AegiSKADA said into the still workspace non-air. Even after the intelligence released all the ports it had closed, whatever the Transorbital mercenaries had carried with them had still blocked its sensor network wherever their leader went and interfered with comms signals too, until now. "Now you can speak to whomever you like," the intelligence added, beaming in childlike glee.

Despite AegiSKADA's creepy visualization, Adda grinned along with it. "While I do that, track the mercenaries. I don't want them getting near the outside corner of the docking bay closest to my position." She paused. "Do you know where I am?"

"I *think* you're above Environmental Supplies Storage next to Docking Bay One." The emphasis was particularly childlike. She'd temporarily changed AegiSKADA's workspace representation to one of its drones, a giant spider, and an adult. The intelligence kept reverting back to the shaggy-haired child because it observed her strong reaction, and consequent vulnerability, to that form.

But this little mystery she couldn't pass up. "Why don't you know?"

The deadly security AI shrugged and raised its tiny hands, like it might have seen somebody do in a cartoon (like she'd seen in a cartoon). "It's hard to get to. I can't be there. I can only be *near* there."

According to the audio and enviro sensors on the third floor between here and the refugee docking bay, Iridian was moving again, on a path back to the compound. "Can you hear me, Iri?"

"Yes, I can!" The sheer delight and love in that brassy alto voice put Adda in danger of melting into a puddle on the workspace floor. Her boots blended into one fuzzy mass.

Iridian's voice was clearer than it had any right to be, with the nearest functioning sensor nodes several dozen meters away. The sensor amplifiers in Pel's eyes had to be increasing mic sensitivity, and that meant he had to be somewhere near Iridian. Adda wouldn't be sure he was all right until she saw him, either in person or through one of the station's working cams, none of which were in range of Iridian now. "AegiSKADA has no working cams near you. Where's Pel?"

"I'm here," he croaked. She bit her lip to stop from crying with relief. Tears sometimes yanked her out of her workspace.

"We're making progress," Iridian said, "but he's dripping so much snot we have to watch our step." Over his protesting "Am not!" Iridian asked, "What are our guests up to?"

Without being asked, AegiSKADA fed the sensor data into the workspace. The mercenaries, much reduced in number but still organized and armed, stormed the docking bay under the pirate compound. The *Charon's Coin* waited on the pad inside. "I told you to keep the intruders out of there!" she shouted at AegiSKADA.

"They kept breaking my drones." A shadow aura grew around the child as its mouth turned down in a scowl.

"Told me to do what?" Iridian couldn't see what Adda was sharing her workspace with.

"Nothing," said Adda. "They're in the docking bay below us."

"I only have eleven Praetorian Threes and forty-one Attacos left," AegiSKADA continued. "Something's wrong with the printers, and I can't make any more." So that was why AegiSKADA hadn't already overwhelmed the station's human occupants. Adda shuddered.

The first merc reached the *Coin* and banged on its hull. She blinked in surprise as the tugboat's passenger ramp opened. The mercenary backed up, weapon raised. When nothing emerged from the ship, he took a few tentative steps forward.

The rest of the mercenaries arrived, and the one in front shouted something AegiSKADA summarized in floating text as ". . . one of the three . . . get us past the turrets." He pointed at the ship and shouted something else, and the other mercenaries boarded. Most of them stayed with the officer in the *Coin*'s passthrough, like there wasn't room for them all in the main cabin.

Next to that image was a shot from across the docking bay in the opposite direction, facing the third floor. That was confusing, since she'd been watching the mercenaries from the first floor. The top of Iridian's sweating scalp and Pel's hood appeared in the broken physical window in the observation room. "Did the *Coin* let them on?"

Adda frowned. "Yes. I can't believe it."

"I can," Iridian said. "They're in for a short trip." Maybe she expected the *Coin* to hold them in its passthrough and then release them in space, the way it had the two members of the med team who'd boarded it in their own effort to escape the station.

In the cam feed, Iridian's head rose above the console for a second, then dropped back out of sight. "As soon as they take off, we're making a run for it."

The engines fired up. In the workspace, vibration and heat

communicated what AegiSKADA's sensors quantified. The interior docking bay doors slammed shut before the ZVs and Captain Sloane entered.

"Gods, be careful," Iridian muttered. The *Coin* backed out of the station, then spun and whipped away, taking the mercenaries with it.

"AegiSKADA, unless someone from that group is still here somewhere, there are no more hostiles on this station," said Adda.

"Confirmation required before engaging." AegiSKADA's sulky tone came from her mind. It still demanded human input, which left it incapable of feeling put-upon.

Adda let herself fall out of the workspace, unplugged, and raced across the creaking, empty tank. If AegiSKADA needed to ask her permission to start more fights, it could ping her comp. And since the mercenaries on the *Coin* were the last attackers healthy enough to fight back, she'd deny any further requests.

Chef stepped out of the kitchen when Adda ran past. "They back?"

"Almost!" Adda was happy to run without any more wheezing than usual. The doctors' bacteriophages were thriving.

The entryway was deserted. Adda clambered down the ladder and dashed through the wall passage. Iridian and Pel stood under a string of orange lights. They looked haggard and exhausted. Iridian held Pel up by his arm around her shoulders, which made her Adda's perfect heroine.

Adda wrapped them up in a hug that left them both squawking in what was probably discomfort. When they kissed, Adda finally believed the worst was over. That meant she could get Iridian out of that armor. It was digging into her ribs.

"Aw, we all need to decontaminate now," Iridian murmured against Adda's lips.

"Is it absolutely necessary to begin that here?" Captain Sloane shouted from the docking bay side of the passage. All three of them laughed and lined up for the long climb to the compound.

From behind Iridian, the captain muttered, "What shall Tritheist owe me now?"

* * *

With Sturm's help, Iridian decontaminated the armor and joined the rest of the pirates in line to receive care from the med team. Adda spent the time assuring pirates that yes, it was over, and AegiSKADA reported to her. There was a great deal of fuss about why it hadn't destroyed the base, and her explanation of the broken drone printers set off a flurry of bet settling that made no rational sense.

Tritheist kept asking, "But how can you be *sure?*"

She shoved her comp under his crusty nose. "Those are the gods-damned admin feeds. It's *mine.*" The pirates gave her a tired cheer that sent her blushing to where Iridian sat on a table in her bra and pants while Dr. Tiwari repaired her back.

Iridian's full lips frowned as Miria San Miguel described Grandpa Death's last moments. San Miguel's kid sat on the floor and leaned against her legs, droopy-eyed but breathing well.

"Si Po didn't make it either," Iridian said. "Radiation poisoning. I had to leave him on the surface." The pirates swore, and Adda's shoulders slumped. She hadn't found him because he was on the surface of the station, where AegiSKADA had minimal cam coverage. And she'd been too busy maintaining her independence from the intelligence while she worked to get Pel and Iridian to the base to spend the time it would've taken to find him. He'd deserved to live to see his ships again. There was so much they could've done with the intelligences, together. She had so many questions she'd wanted to ask him.

Iridian grimaced and breathed hard through something Dr. Tiwari was doing behind her. The skull-and-bones tattoo and the lean, toned flesh beneath were bruised all along Iridian's side. Some of the design's viscera would have to be redone. The bra covered the top of the folded-back-skin design. Bloodstained armor hid the lower part of the oozing ink gore.

Adda stepped up against the table, between Iridian's legs. She kissed her softly so she wouldn't move Iridian out of the position Dr. Tiwari needed her to be in.

She had only seen Iridian talk to the old ZV a few times, but both of them had spent a lot of time with Si Po. Although it was rational to expect casualties, and Grandpa Death's age had increased his chances of becoming one of them, Si Po's loss had been unexpected. Adda turned to lean her hips on the table with Iridian at her back, comforting them both with the contact. Iridian's hands settled firmly on her waist.

"Was that you with the big drone, earlier?" Iridian asked. "When I ran into the mercs?" Adda nodded, and Iridian pulled her closer. "Hot." The sentiment sounded slightly forced, but determined.

The pirates were weary, but few slept. Once Tritheist entered Sloane's quarters, most of the crew hung around the main room, where they could watch the captain's door. Everyone was speculating about what the captain would do next, and nobody wanted to miss an announcement. Even San Miguel's son watched, with clearer eyes and rosier cheeks. Zikri went from combatant to combatant, patching up injuries with fingers jittering from stimulants. Chef brought water.

Pel's hood slipped off, revealing longer-than-ever curly hair. He'd lost his eyewear in the station. "Gods, my eyes hurt," he wheezed.

The eyes he'd been born with might never heal. Even if they

did, he might always have those cocked-ear expressions when he concentrated. "You. Um. Have something in them." It took Adda several minutes to explain AegiSKADA's sensor amplifiers, sounding awkward and overly technical even to her own ears. Pel looked paler and more horrified with each new detail, and the pirates nearby all listened in with morbid interest. "But as soon as we're in a civilized habitat, we'll find a surgeon who can fix this. I promise."

Pel sat down on the floor, without even feeling around for one of the crates that served as chairs. The pirates swore and sympathized.

"Ah, shit," he said. For several moments, Adda was afraid he was going to panic, or cry, but then he added, "If AegiSKADA was never going to kill me anyway, I could've gotten so much more fugee ass. I'd have been over there every day!" The pirates laughed, although Iridian didn't. Further horrendous conversation was curtailed by Dr. Williams swooping in to give Pel one of her surprise injections, to minimize the symptoms of AegiSKADA's bioweapon while she synthesized and administered the cure.

"Gods, what if the ZV Group fired all of us and didn't bother to tell us until we get back?" Chato asked. "We'll have to look for one of those cushy legal jobs like Adda's dad's got." Everybody laughed. There wasn't even a point in being bitter about that impossibility.

"Stow that," Major O D. said. "Who's got the booze?"

Chef produced liquid that smelled both sweet and sour and coated the cup's sides. She gave Iridian hers while one of the ZVs found the major a cord for his comp.

Fugee News aired triumphant music from a comp game Adda had played in college. Over it, Suhaila was mid rapid-fire commentary. ". . . that took poor Corrin and Jennika was the last drone attack. People are still coming in from the rest of the station, but every one of them say spiderbots run from them, and the big ones leave them alone!" The music reached a thumping crescendo while the pirates raised a cheer. The track changed to a pop song with "we move up, we move on" as its only lyrics. O.D. answered a summons to the captain's cabin, though he left his comp to keep the music going.

Suhaila's voice broke in over the music, though she faded it down rather than turning it off. "I just spoke with Mayor Van Aggelen. She says she confirmed with Captain Sloane that yes, the security system threat is past, and that means tomorrow is moving day, fugees. We're not waiting around for the people beyond the lead cloud to figure out it's safe to rescue us! The colony ship is fueled, and once you people report to the mayor at her office for your exit preparation assignment, we are *out of here!*"

Suhaila sounded close to tears. Iridian's eyes glistened even more than usual too. Adda hugged her carefully.

"I'm so sorry I swore at you earlier," Adda said.

Iridian's lips were as syrupy as her drink. "You're forgiven." Another pop song played over the speakers. "It sounds like we have some time before we hear what we're supposed to do next," she murmured into the crook of Adda's neck. Her breath was deliciously warm against Adda's skin.

"Finished." Dr. Tiwari twisted one of his tools by the handle to close it. "Keep clean, be careful until new growth heals."

"Thanks, doc," Iridian said against Adda's throat. Dr. Tiwari chuckled and left in the direction of Zikri and the remaining ZVs.

Adda stood and caught Iridian's hand. "I'll show you what you're supposed to do next."

Iridian grinned hungrily and followed with steps slightly stiff from numbing agents or pain. "Yes, ma'am."

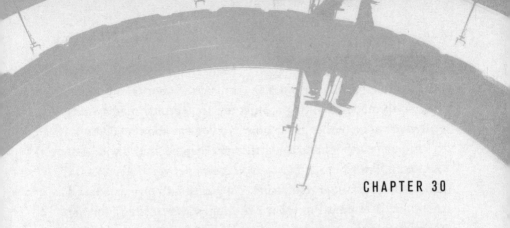

CHAPTER 30

Charges Accrued: Resisting Arrest

The pillow nest had taken on a pungent version of Adda's scent since Iridian left. Still, curled around Adda's sleeping form was the only place in the universe she wanted to be right now.

She was about two breaths from drifting off when someone banged on the door in the ceiling. "Captain wants a full crew meet," said Chato.

Her inarticulate grunt was apparently translated as affirmation, because footsteps receded down the hall. She checked the pocket of her one pair of pants, then shook Adda gently. Adda rolled over and wrapped her leg and both arms around Iridian, snuggling into her chest. "Let's go, babe," Iridian murmured. "We can come back to this later."

They weren't the last to the common room, but most of the crew was there. Sloane, Tritheist, the two med team doctors, and Zikri conversed near the captain's stateroom while Pel, Rio, and Tabs played with San Miguel's boy. The two doctors stood in the hall leading to the entrance, staring at each other. Sergeant

Natani, Chato, and Vick sat beside them on the floor, talking about module-to-module fighting against the Transorbital mercs. Adda drifted toward a corner as far from everyone as she could get.

Iridian gave her hand a gentle tug to keep her in the middle of the room. "I'm so proud of how you outmaneuvered AegiSKADA, babe," she said louder than usual. Her girlfriend's face paled, and she glanced around the room like drones were coming for her. The pirates were looking now and Adda would kill her for this, so she'd better make it quick. "I want to help you hijack ships and circumvent AI forever."

Here we go. . . . She dropped to one knee and dug in her pocket. The ring was a strip of braided silver-and-blue microtubing from AegiSKADA's control room. It was twisted at the ends, so she'd have to do some soldering later, but . . . "Will you marry me?"

Adda blinked at her for a second. Almost too quietly to hear and at least an octave up from her usual register, she said, "Yes!" Iridian stood and hugged her as the pirates cheered.

"Cute, but you're not marrying into the crew," said Vick.

Sloane stood with crossed arms and posture tilted back, smiling a little like this was just an entertaining show. Beside the captain, Tritheist's smile was more calculating. Adda said he had promised her part of his share for getting them off the station. It'd be convenient for him if she wasn't around to collect.

"Captain Sloane made us a deal." Iridian caught herself gripping the knife in her thigh sheath and consciously let it go without drawing it. "We take care of AegiSKADA, we've got a ride and a job."

"So the ships that have never carried us before are going to start now," said Tritheist. Gods, she and that sneering bastard would have it out sometime.

The *Casey* had already carried her once. It'd probably do it again, although there was no way to be sure. All Adda said she'd done was announce into the docking bay that she needed a message taken to Iridian, the one telling her to bust through the walls instead of walking face-first into the turret outside the control room. Once the *Casey* heard Adda's recording, it must've tracked Iridian down and picked her up on its own. Adda definitely didn't tell it to do that.

Iridian surreptitiously keyed her comp's mic and directed its output to the docking bay below. If the *Casey* was willing to help her before, perhaps it'd help her again when it heard what the crew was saying.

"They could leave with the fugees in the colony ship," Sergeant Natani said in a voice pitched to placate a higher-ranking officer without antagonizing anybody else.

"The hell they could!" said Pel.

The sergeant had lost more than most on this venture, but Iridian wouldn't let anyone stop her and Adda from getting what they'd earned. Not when they almost had everything they wanted. "So could you. We'll send a couple of drones to help you find your way there." Iridian turned to Adda. "Anything interesting going on in the docking bay?"

Adda consulted her comp. "The *Charon's Coin* just landed."

Iridian turned her wrist to display the red light on her comp indicating a live mic, grinning big as if she knew what the hell the *Coin's* AI was doing there. "Even if you discount the fact that we already saved your asses from AegiSKADA, you still want us around. Those gods-damned awakened AI have been listening to every word of this."

"Who cares what they're listening to?" said Vick.

The grin on her face felt like the one from training when she missed a block and her sparring partner expected the hit to stop her. "Remember when all the fucking comms went down earlier? That was what AegiSKADA did when it heard journalists approaching the station. That was a minor gods-damned threat. The *Casey Mire Mire*'s awakened AI *likes* me." More accurately, the AI liked what Iridian could do for it. These people must've gotten used to the monsters they'd created. It was about time they started treating the AI like the dangers they were. "What do you think it'll do if I call it for help?"

Every member of the crew started shouting. Although Vick and Tritheist were adamant and aggressive, most of the voices contributed comments like "If the *Casey* likes them, so do I," and "They're smarter than any eight of you arseholes," and one or two "We'd have fucking died here if not for them!"

To hide the lump in her throat, Iridian inhaled to get a few more points across, but Adda was staring at her comp like it'd dissolved into spiderbots. Iridian poked her in the side, which made her jump. "What?"

"Um . . . We're about to have visitors."

Sloane must've heard Adda despite the ambient argument, because the captain appeared next to them. "Who?"

"Interplanetary Transit Authority," she- said. "AegiSKADA picked them up on its outer buoys."

Sloane spun toward the arguing pirates and bellowed, "Quiet!" so loud Iridian's ears rang. Everyone froze and looked to the captain. The captain turned to Adda. "How long until the ITA arrives?"

Everyone started talking at once. "If they come straight in at, ah, healthy acceleration, an hour and thirty minutes," Adda said. "They must have intercepted the Fugee News report, or one from those journalists."

"Pack up," Captain Sloane shouted. "We leave for Vesta in one hour." The crew crowded, cheering, into the hallway to the bunkhouse. Sloane grinned at Adda and Iridian like they'd passed the last of the captain's tests. "You too. All of my regular crew are based there." The captain swept out of the common room without waiting for a reply.

Iridian's eyes widened. "Oh, shit. I've got to go now."

"What?" said Adda. "Why?"

"The Casey. I promised her a copy of AegiSKADA's code, and I started the copy, but I had to leave the datacask with the code on it in AegiSKADA's control room. If I don't get the datacask back now, I won't have it when we want to leave."

"You . . . The Casey wants a . . ." Adda stared in shock gradually shifting to delight. "Isn't that interesting! Would you make one for me, too?"

"No." Iridian could've said that more kindly, but she didn't have time or energy for the argument Adda would want to have over that particular horrible idea. "I only have the one datacask, and they take too long to print. If the Casey's our ride off the station, then I'd better give her what she wants, yeah?" The pirates were only counting on her to get them off-station because she claimed the ships obeyed her, so she'd better make sure the Casey still liked her well enough to carry passengers upon request. That meant giving the ship what it wanted before trying to board. She gripped Adda's hands in both of hers. "Will you be okay packing up your generator on your own?"

The moment Adda nodded, Iridian kissed her and rushed to Sturm's workshop. "I need an enviro suit that doesn't leak much."

Sergeant Natani stopped her fast walk past the workshop door with a pack dangling from one hand. "You're going back out there?"

Iridian eyed her while Sturm rummaged through his suit collection. "Yeah, why?"

"You want backup?"

She looked serious. In fact, she looked ready to drop her pack, pick up her weapon, and follow Iridian right back through the station . . . to the ship that'd killed Six. That was a terrible fucking idea. "Thanks. Really. But I'm good." Sergeant Natani bowed, perfunctory in length and depth but the first she'd offered since Iridian had met her. Iridian's back and side clenched with pain as she returned the bow, but it was worth it.

In a few minutes she'd crammed herself into the least leaky suit and was running through the wall to the *Coin*. Every step beat the image of Six's death into her brain, but this time the *Coin*'s door stood open. This was the fastest way to the other side of the station. She'd have to take it. Scuff marks and partial boot prints marred the passthrough bulkheads. Beyond the inner passthrough door, the cockpit had been remade as an extended pseudo-organic tank system. Massive tug engines didn't leave much room for humans to begin with.

Iridian edged past two of the tanks so the passthrough could close. "I need to get to the other side of the station, to the broken shuttle passthrough. The *Casey Mire Mire*'s datacask is still in there."

The passthrough doors closed. Iridian dove for the pilot's seat and strapped herself in over tubes and cables. The *Coin* rose and started an even faster departure pattern than the *Casey*'s when it had rescued her from the hub. *These AI interpret much more than the voice commands the developers taught them.* Not even a minute after the *Coin* was out of the station's spin it was integrating on the other side, pulling almost five g's. It took all of her g-tolerance training to keep from blacking out.

Fighting serious déjà vu, Iridian let herself into the damaged module on a cable from the *Coin*'s emergency kit, the same method she'd used to exit the *Casey* when it'd brought her here from the station's hub. She skirted the discarded thorium sample container on her way to the control room. Out of curiosity, she skipped the storage areas she'd punched through and jogged down the main hallway.

Her headlamp played over an empty turret installation near the door. Long drag marks led to its current position outside the security control room. It had blasted a dent the size of both her fists in the security door. At that range it would've torn her apart in the control room, if it'd made it through. The turret kept pointing at the door, which slid partway open and jammed on its dented center. She squeezed past and went in.

The control room floor was still mined. She climbed over the shelving much more easily with free hands in a thin enviro suit instead of the bulky armored one. The control room seemed smaller now. She dug through the cables until she found the data-cask, then climbed back out with it. This time she used the hole she'd made in what turned out to be an office next door, bypassing as much of the mined floor as possible.

She paused in the hall and keyed her mic. "Adda, do you still need AegiSKADA's sensors?" Since Adda still wasn't in communication with HarborMaster, she'd probably lose access to them once AegiSKADA was no longer facilitating her connection. Unless there were backups Adda hadn't found yet, AegiSKADA's absence would eliminate HarborMaster's ability to maintain a healthy enviro. Atmo would stop circulating, the station's spin would slow, and the enviro would get closer and closer to unlivable as the hours passed. If nothing went too wrong, the pirates and the refugees should all have time to escape before complete enviro loss.

"I'm tracking the Transit Authority ships on the external sensors," Adda said.

"Can you do that from the ships?"

"If they let me."

"I think they will." Iridian drew a breath. "I've got the *Casey*'s copy of AegiSKADA. There's no point in keeping the original intact." Both the original and the copy had just been forced to watch a bunch of invaders prowl all corners of its station. And then they took over its admin functions in violation of its programming. Adda had to recognize the danger of leaving an AI in that state. At this point, the only reason Iridian even considered making the copy for the *Casey* was to make sure the ship would carry her, Adda, and the pirates off the damned station. Nothing else would've persuaded her to prolong the security AI's "life."

"All right." Adda's sigh sounded more like grief than anything else. Even though she knew better, she'd always personified AI. "Good-bye." The word was too final for it to be meant for Iridian.

She reentered the office, grabbed the broken wall panel that had almost killed her last time, and shoved it through the hole in the control room wall. It bounced off the far wall and fell on a mine. The module was still depressurized. The explosion shook the floor and sent fragments of metal and wire flying. She flinched. She was wearing a gods-damned enviro suit. What *idiocy*. Weary as she was, she'd hoped to sleep *before* she was dead.

When she got her breath back, she asked Adda, "Did I get it?"

"It's gone. We're in the docking bay. Is the *Coin* coming back?"

"Definitely."

She was so exhausted after she hauled herself up the evac cable that she took a second to realize that the ship she just boarded wasn't the *Coin*. "Hello, *Casey*." She leaned on a bulkhead while the passthrough pressurized. The inner door opened, and she held up the datacask. "Where do you want this?"

All the lights on the pilot's console turned on. That was clear enough.

Iridian had to step over a pile of what looked like broken parts of more than one of the *Casey*'s rovers to get from the ship's passthrough to its main cabin. Like the *Coin*, the *Casey* must've taken on mercs during the battle, and it hadn't gone well for the rovers.

"I'm not sure how much of this you understand, but the ITA is coming to arrest Sloane's crew. We need to leave the station." The *Casey* might've already figured out that the pirates were about to flee the station. Si Po had taught the AI well. "Can you and the other ships carry us somewhere? Say, Ceres Station?"

The console flashed again, which was less informative this time, but the *Casey* did move. Iridian strapped in before it spaced her. The *Casey* projected windows onto its main cabin bulkhead as it returned to the pirates' docking bay. The pirates stood well out of the engines' range while it landed, then rushed forward when the passthrough opened. Adda, leading Pel and followed by Tabs, Rio, and San Miguel and her kid, were near the front behind Tritheist and Sloane.

The captain strode onboard and looked around. "I like this one. And the others are coming?"

"The tug doesn't have room, Captain, but the *Apparition* is coming. I think," Iridian said. The console lights flashed. "Yeah, I think so."

"The spy ship it is, then," said Sloane. So *that* was what the *Casey* was outfitted for. That explained the shackles by the toilet, sort of. "Tritheist, Adda, Iridian, Pel, this is our flight," Sloane continued. "Our destination is Rheasilvia Station on Vesta. We'll sort out your back pay on the way."

Iridian grinned at the beautiful words "back pay," despite

having to board the *Casey* again. For the first time since Iridian and Adda met, they'd be together without constantly strategizing about how to buy shelter and food.

Major O.D. held up a fist with the back of his hand facing his soldiers, signaling that they stay put. "ZV Group, we're taking the next one, to Mars." He shrugged apologetically at Sloane. "You're too hot for us right now." Being caught with a notorious pirate and colony ship hijackers would reduce the legal jobs the ZV Group was offered. It was good business to keep that option open.

"We'll go to Mars too, if it's all the same to you, captain," Sturm said, apparently speaking for himself and Chef, who stood beside him. At Sloane's nod of assent, they joined the ZVs.

Pel gave out a lot of hugs, but eventually Adda got him onboard and strapped down for transit. Chef and the doctors waved and headed off in the direction of the refugees' ship. Sergeant Natani hung back until the other ZVs passed her in the same direction. The corner of her mouth stretched up ever so slightly as she saluted Iridian and Adda.

After all they'd been through together on the station, that was the biggest surprise Iridian had had yet. She'd been more willing to believe that she, Adda, and a bunch of ZV Group mercs could beat a station-size AI than that Iridian and a secessionist would ever truly fight on the same side. She was so surprised that she almost forgot to return the salute.

San Miguel's kid started crying as the passthrough doors shut. Tears fell from Pel's scarred eyes too, and Iridian punched him lightly in the shoulder on her way to the console.

She plugged the datacask into the console. The *Casey*'s AI copied the contents to its pseudo-organics in a whirl of data on the console's display. What the ship meant to do with a station's security AI, Iridian couldn't imagine. She wrapped an arm around Pel and Adda as grav pressed them against the bulkheads across from the window.

The bomb-damaged exterior of Barbary Station spun in a glittering cloud of its own debris. It shrank, slowly at first, then faster as the *Casey* picked up speed. In a few minutes, the station was just a dark spot in an ocean of flickering stars.

ACKNOWLEDGMENTS

Thank you, Navah Wolfe and Saga Press, for making this novel bigger, better, and more awesome than I'd dared to hope. Thank you, Hannah Bowman, for being an advocate, thoughtful reader, and all-around great agent. Thank you, Greg Stadnyk and Martin Deschambault, for bringing Barbary Station to life on the cover, and thank you, Bridget Madsen and Tatyana Rosalia, for your efforts as well.

Thanks also to Suhaila and "Kyr," for lending names and personality traits to unexpectedly important characters; Rebecca, Jennifer B., Vanessa, and Jennifer G., for support and excellent company; the critters at Critters.org, whose short-story critiques helped make Iridian and Adda who they are today; and Mur Lafferty, whose inspirational podcast regularly reminded me that "I Should Be Writing."

Special thanks to my parents and family, for their unequivocal encouragement and especially to my husband, Greg: thank you for following me on this literary adventure and for all the things you do to make it possible.